Christmas on the
Home Front

Clarke's roots are dug deep into the North East. She
inspiration from her mother, who was born in a
Durham pit village during the First World War,
nt on to become a military nurse during World War
nie and her husband now live a stone's throw from
illage where her mother was born. She has written
y about the North East in novels which she hopes
er love and respect for the region's lost mining
ities.

e has four adult children and four granddaughters,
her and her husband's days with laughter, end-
ding these two elders astray.

Also by Annie Clarke

Girls on the Home Front
Heroes on the Home Front
Wedding Bells on the Home Front

ANNIE CLARKE

Christmas on the Home Front

arrow books

1 3 5 7 9 10 8 6 4 2

Arrow Books
20 Vauxhall Bridge Road
London SW1V 2SA

Arrow Books is part of the Penguin Random House group
of companies whose addresses can be found at
global.penguinrandomhouse.com.

Penguin
Random House
UK

First published in Great Britain by Arrow Books in 2020

www.penguin.co.uk

A CIP catalogue record for this book is available
from the British Library

ISBN 9781787462601

Typeset in 10.75/13.5 pt Palatino by Jouve (UK), Milton Keynes
Printed and bound in Great Britain by Clays Ltd, Elcograf S.p.A.

For Jason Hopper – a shining star
in loving memory

Chapter One

Mid-October 1942, Massingham Pit Village

Fran stood in the kitchen of her family home, 14 Leadenhall Terrace, with her friends Beth and Sarah, though none of them wanted to be here at this precise moment. Fran in particular baulked at the knitting needles and wool her mam, Annie Hall, was passing out to each of them.

'Oh Mam, must we?' Fran grumbled. It was mid-morning, on a Monday, and unfortunately for the girls it was another full hour and three quarters before they would be heading for the aft-shift munitions bus. Each pair of needles had been stabbed into a ball of pale yellow wool that Annie had pulled out from three tattered baby coats she'd found at a jumble sale.

Mrs Hall wagged her finger, which meant yes, they must. 'We mams warned you yesterday that I'd be up and at you today, for it's more than time you started these master-pieces for Sophia Massingham's babe. Especially as she and Reginald are the salt of the earth and run their pit as though the pitmen are their own kin.'

Uh-oh, thought Fran, we're on to emotional blackmail. But it was true, of course – the whole village loved the Massinghams.

'You'd better pay attention, Fran, for knit them you will or . . .' Annie raised her eyebrows and looked at each of them in turn '. . . the bairn'll be walking before you three

1

cack-handed lasses get round to producing anything. Which means you have to . . . ?'

'Knit, knit and knit again,' the girls chanted in unison, trying not to laugh.

'Why?'

'Because now we're in a race against nature.' Fran pointed at Sarah, who grinned and took over.

'And deep winter will soon be upon us—'

'And we still haven't knitted the woollies we promised,' interrupted Beth.

Fran, Beth and Sarah sighed together, because although their spirits were willing, the needles seemed to have lives of their own whenever they were shown a ball of wool.

While her friends explained this to her mam yet again, Fran thought of Davey laughing on the telephone last night when she'd grumbled about her mam's plans for this morning, and the lecture she'd given them. Her husband of six months had said, 'Knitting for the babe at last, eh? Well, you've put it off for so long on the pretext of no time or too much work, I'm not surprised the mams have put their combined feet down. I mean, *work*? What work?'

'I reckon when we next meet, you'll pay for that remark, young man,' Fran had laughed. 'You, who sit throughout your shift fiddling about as though you're playing around with crosswords.'

Now, though, in the kitchen, she felt such a longing for him that it hurt, and she remembered moaning, 'Oh Davey, I just wish I was knitting for our own bairn, lad. I need something of you, for I miss you so much.'

'We'll have one, precious lass, just you wait and see.'

Silence had fallen between them while she dug around for something to lift their mood. 'Oh, yes, Eva's come up with an idea, the little madam.'

Davey had sighed, though she could almost see his smile.

'Oh Lord, not another scheme from that incorrigible bairn. Tell me – make me laugh.'

So she had, explaining that Eva's best friend, Melanie, another orphaned evacuee, had been adopted by an aunt and was off to live in Wales just before Christmas and that, though heartbroken, Eva wanted to organise a farewell party before she left Massingham Hall. 'Typically, our Eva has planned for everyone else to do the work, starting with Stan, Sid and Norm, who have been ordered to find a Christmas tree to her liking when the time comes.'

'Oh, and then there'll be the Proggy Rug Co-op led by your mam, who'll be instructed to provide the eats from everyone's rations,' Davey had said, laughing. 'Luckily for Sophia, she'll be busy with the new babe, so not too involved. But The Factory Girls group will have to be the entertaine—'

'Are you a mind-reader?' Fran interrupted.

At that point, the call-box door had opened and Sarah had yelled to her brother, 'Talk quickly, Davey, it's too cold for me and Beth standing out here, waiting on her ladyship. It's fine for you down in the south.' Whereupon she and Beth had crowded in while Fran repeated what he'd said.

'Spot on, our Davey,' shouted Beth. 'Eva's made a list of all that's to happen, ticking it off when I swear she hasn't actually *asked* anyone—'

Sarah had snatched the receiver from Fran, sharing it with Beth. 'I reckon the co-op's been giving her lessons on being bossy.'

Now, in the warmth of the kitchen, Sarah was waving her knitting needles and wool. 'These put me in mind of Davey's phone call yesterday,' she said, 'and us telling him about Eva doling out jobs without a by your leave. Just look at what's happening right here and—'

3

Beth interrupted as the girls sniggered. 'But the difference is, we *did* actually agree to knit these cardigans, 'tisn't just your mam making it up. So, I reckon we should get on with it because we have to catch the bus at midday.'

'Oh, who's sucking up?' Fran chanted. 'Well, let's do it, then, for Mam's at least shown thought getting yellow to match our Factory skin.'

The three of them burst out laughing as Annie whispered, 'Don't remind me of those dreadful explosives you work with, please. You know we mams spend our time doing our best to forget.'

Sarah stopped and tugged the needles from her ball of wool, deep in thought as the clock ticked and the range firebox glowed, throwing out heat. 'With us talking of your mam not making things up, I found myself thinking about that Daisy who made such a habit of fibbing. Has Davey heard any more after she ran off from the mother-and-baby home? Didn't he say she might have been seen in Scotland last month? It's the babe that worries me. I can't imagine how the silly girl will be coping with the bairn all alone.'

'No, there's been nothing more seen or heard,' Fran answered, not wanting to think about Daisy in any way, shape or form after she'd been such a horror at Bletchley Park, where Davey worked as a decoder. Daisy had accused not only Davey but his marrer Daniel of forcing themselves on her. The lads couldn't understand why until it became apparent she'd wanted someone to share the responsibility of the baby she was expecting. A baby whose father was, in fact, her dead RAF boyfriend.

Of course, Davey, kind as he was, and Daniel too, had asked Daniel's vicar father to try and find a place for her in a home for unmarried mothers, as apparently her own parents weren't interested. It was from this home that she had disappeared months ago, taking the baby with her.

Annie was knocking on the kitchen table, which brought the girls to order. 'Attention, please. We haven't all day, so sit down and watch closely, for I'm sick of showing you how to do this. It isn't as though you know nothing about knitting, for you learned at school. It's such a simple thing, but to make it even easier I'll show you how to cast on using your thumb.'

Fran smiled as her mam took her place at the head of the table, nodding at them to sit. It was like being back at school, watching her mam wind a strand of wool around her thumb before looking at each of them in turn, just as their teacher had done.

'Watch close, because while you do, I have to tell you that we *must* help Eva and obey the ticks on the list, for it's her farewell to her marrer. Mind, I have an inkling all our chores will start growing, a bit like Topsy. That wee lass doesn't think small, oh no, not at all.'

The girls groaned and waited, knowing more was to come. Mrs Hall smiled. 'Eva now wants an even bigger group of singers around the Christmas tree at Massingham Hall, which she insists is to be set up in the sitting room. So you girls need to recruit four or five others to join in with The Factory Girls, though it doesn't matter whether they can sing, for the bairns'll no doubt drown you all out. Now, the festive season will be on us before we know where we are, so best you start sorting it, in your minds at least, eh? Knitting's good for that, gives you time to think. Watch carefully now.' Annie Hall shook her head, causing a strand of her grey hair to come loose from her bun.

The girls copied Mrs Hall, first making a slip stitch onto a needle, then winding the wool around their thumbs, while Sarah muttered, 'But that's all very well, Mrs Hall, for though Eva's got us down as certainties, we still haven't agree—'

Mrs Hall continued to cast on and rode over her. 'Agreement's nowt to do with owt, our Sarah, and it'll be good for you all to be involved in a party. And you know you want to send Melanie off nicely, for we'll all miss her. They came as a pack, those bairns.'

'And hunt as one,' Sarah laughed.

Mrs Hall nodded. 'That's about right, little devils, but really it will be good for you all. For a start, it'll take Fran's mind off Davey, and calm Beth's rage when she gets to thinking about her Bob and that divorce he wants. And let's not miss you out, Sarah, still swooning over our Stan, though you've been married, what, over seven months? If he's busy at the Hall after his shift, sorting the tree or whatever else the bairn decrees, then you'll be there, so might as well give you something to do.'

Fran raised an eyebrow. 'So it's Eva doing *us* the favour, then?'

'Concentrate, Fran. Dig that needle into the wool round your thumb, now you've finally made your slip knot. By, look at that pig's ear – never seen such a do over a bitty cast-on stitch.'

'Rest easy, Mrs Hall,' Sarah said, admiring her own slip knot. 'You know very well we'll do as we're told, for you'll be sure to strangle us with the wool otherwise.'

'But Mrs Hall knows we have to make a bit of a fight of it,' Beth laughed quietly, already on her second stitch, 'or it's no fun.'

Annie Hall looked up from her casting-on to check theirs, before nodding. 'Listening to you, it makes me realise hunting in a pack's not a new thing. Now, keep going, and while I think of it, there's a piano in the Massingham Hall ballroom. I'd forgotten about it – and the ballroom, come to that. Perhaps we can bring it through to the sitting room in time for Christmas, then Iris Walters can

6

accompany you, for Viola will be singing, not playing the saxophone. Even if it's a bit out of tune, it'll be better than the organ with all the puffing and wheezing. Just one squeak from her tubes and it'd set everyone sniggering.'

Struggling to push the needle through the wool, which she'd wound too tightly around her thumb, Fran said, 'It's the organ's tubes, Mam.'

'Well, that's as maybe, but that's splitting hairs,' Mrs Hall replied, grinning. 'I'll talk to Sophia about the piano, and then maybe suggest it to Eva. As long as she has a labour force that does the work, she reckons anything is possible. Makes me frightened to think of what she'll be like when she's eleven. She's bad enough at ten. You know what, I reckon any day now she'll gather her evacuees together to warn them off forming a union. I can see her telling them there's no point, for she'll not have her orders questioned.'

'Wonder who she reminds me of, our Fran?' Sarah muttered, making another stitch and nodding towards Mrs Hall. 'Such a poor wee lass you are, Franny, having to live with a sergeant major.'

Fran was battling the wool and sighed. 'It's why I'm such a nervous wreck.'

Annie took no notice. 'I reckon the co-op can bake a few tarts from the apples stored by Old Ted up at the Massinghams', but our Eva will have sorted what she wants already, so why am I bothering?'

The laughter was quiet as they continued casting on. Fran created a sixth stitch, then a seventh, and was feeling that at last she was on her way when her mam spoke again. 'The pattern says thirty five stitches, so keep at it. This will be the back.'

The girls turned as one to look at the clock above the range, but no, it wasn't nearly time to leave. They grimaced and worked on until each had thirty five on their needle.

'That's grand,' Annie Hall said, nodding. 'Now we will work with a knitting needle in each hand . . . No need for that face, our Beth. It's easy as pie – well, until you come to the armholes, that is, then you might wish for death.'

The girls sighed.

'So, we will now knit one, pearl one for the rib, and you'll see how easy it is to welcome the wee mite,' Mrs Hall continued. 'A few cardigans isn't too much to ask in the grand scheme of things, is it? If you're reasonably good souls, anyway.'

The girls sighed again and did as they were told, for this last comment was just another example of the co-op's blackmail technique.

Annie, however, appeared to be musing, and Fran sighed as she recognised the signs.

'You could take the knitting on the bus, girls, and work on it to and from the Factory. Why not take it into work as well, and work on it after your meal?'

'Oh aye.' Fran waved her knitting at them all. 'Just think of the guards at the entrance finding these metal needles when they search us. They'll have them off us quick as a wink, and give us a tongue-lashing into the bargain. So best we leave them at home.'

'I'll be down there, frisking them and taking the needles back just as quick, let me tell you, but maybe you're right,' Mrs Hall replied. 'Now, I'll remind you that there were rips in the knitted coats I bought, so the wool, though it's wound into a ball, is broken. You'll have to join it together, but no knotting, mind. You knit it with the two ends side by side, just for two stitches, and when it's finished, use your big-eyed sewing needle to weave in the ends.'

She smiled at them, as though all the problems of the world had just been solved. Fran pressed her lips together against a retort, which would have died a death anyway, because her mam was roaring on. 'Wait, I've an idea. I reckon Bert'll keep the knitting in the cab of his bus, so you *can* take it. Then knit it up on your way, and during your return. Good, that's everything sorted.'

All four continued to knit and Fran found her shoulders relaxing. She could feel the wool, the cool of the needles, and hear the clicks. The repetition was soothing, which was what her mam had always said, and it pushed the absence of Davey into the background. Just as it did for so many other wives who'd had one night with their husbands, and then nothing. At least she had the phone calls, so best to stop being such a misery guts.

Beside her, Sarah dropped a stitch. 'Oh no – look.'

She held up her knitting as Annie Hall came round the table. 'Watch, everyone,' she said.

They did as commanded and learned how to recapture the stitch, and it was Beth who said, 'Poor wretch, it thought it had escaped, but let's face it, if it wasn't Mrs Hall spoiling the poor wee thing's break for freedom, it'd be my own mam, or yours, Sarah – talk about a hunting pack.'

Mrs Hall gave Beth one of her looks as she returned the knitting to Sarah, but after a beat, as they knew she would, she laughed. 'Two more rows, girls, then a cuppa, and how about "good girl" honey scones?' She returned to her own seat, taking up her knitting with a satisfied look.

Fran raised her eyebrows. 'You were that certain we'd fall in line you've baked them already, you wicked woman?'

'Well, you're good lasses, and will make the extra effort for the evacuees, poor wee bairns. Eva will miss Melanie sorely, and I wish Wales was next door, but it is what it is, so Massingham must make it better for her and make it the best farewell Christmas party ever.'

Mrs Hall ended a row, then pierced the ball of wool with her needles before heading for the kettle boiling on the range. She poured water over the used tea leaves already in the pot, then hurried into the scullery, collecting the scones and placing the plate in the middle of the table. They were already split and thinly spread with butter and honey.

Beth completed her row, just a step behind Fran, but Sarah dropped another stitch. 'I reckon this wool's got a life of its own.'

She couldn't pick up the stitch, and dropped another into the bargain. Mrs Hall brought over the teapot, poured them each a cup, then went to Sarah. 'Oh, lass, you're making a right dog's dinner of it. Give it to me a minute, and for the love of Mike, watch.'

She caught the stitches, checking that Sarah *was* watching, and handed it back just as Fran set hers aside and sipped her tea, looking over at Beth.

'So, Beth, you'll be sick of the question you're asked too often: nothing more from Bob about the divorce?'

'Nothing, and if I do get a letter from him and not his solicitor, I'll send it back to Grimsby, "Return to Sender", much as he did to me, his wife.'

'How do you really feel, pet, now it's some months further on?' Mrs Hall asked as she busied herself wiping down the range. It was the question Fran had wanted to ask, because her friend still hadn't regained the weight she had lost after Bob left.

Beth concentrated on finishing another row, then reached for a scone. Taking a bite, she chewed, swallowed and only then looked up. 'I'm a bit scared sometimes, for as you know, he was right horrid by the end. I'm with my mam, though, and you marrers, and in Massingham, and that's what's important.' She smiled at them all.

'You are, and will always be, pet.' Fran squeezed her arm.

'It's strange, really,' Beth said. 'For though I feel better about it, I'll be going along, doing ordinary things, and suddenly I remember something we did together in the past.' Beth's voice sounded far away. 'Or I see his face in a shop window and think he's behind me, angry because I won't help him pay for the divorce. But as I send my wife's allotment from his pay to him and Heather for the babe, the divorce is his business to pursue.'

She looked around at them, the scone forgotten, only one bite taken. 'But you know what, I can kick him out of my head easier now, just like a football – wham, bang. What's more, I make sure I miss the goal and he goes blasting away for miles. You see, I'm still so angry, as well as being out of kilter.' She grinned and attacked her scone, as though feeling better, and then they all licked their fingers. Mrs Hall tutted, but smiled as she fetched a damp flannel from the scullery.

'I'm starting to wonder if I ever really knew Bob,' Beth mused, 'for he was off to war so quick, and then at sea . . . But I really mean it when I say I don't want any more of his nonsense.'

She started another row; knit one, pearl one. 'Besides, as you said, Mrs Hall, it is what it is. Our Fran says that too – drives us all mad, it does.'

Sarah burst out laughing while Fran pulled a face, loving this girl for her courage.

'If the wind changes, our Franny, you'll stay like it,' said Beth.

'Talking of wind,' Annie called from the scullery, 'check the back door's shut, would you, Franny. Seems to me it's rattling.'

Fran did, but it was closed properly. She returned. Sarah was head down, knitting, Beth too, so she set about hers while her mam pottered about. The only sounds were the gurgling of the range and the ticking of the hot plate. It was all so normal, when out there in the world, Fran thought, the war was raging. El Alamein might turn things in their favour, if the Allies could keep fighting. Nearer to home, some husbands were cheating on their wives and some wives were probably doing the same; others were just filled with love and yearning, as she was, longing for the lad she had grown up with and knew like the back of her hand.

Fran found herself wondering if Bob was away escorting convoys, the first of which had apparently just got through to Russia. Well, she damn well hoped he was, for it was time the man concentrated on his job and did some good, or Santa wouldn't bring such a miserable human being anything for Christmas. She half smiled, but without humour, for her rage towards him almost equalled Beth's.

They knitted on, rewarding themselves with sips of tea at the end of each row, but a sudden banging on the front door made Fran spin round, confused. Then, as her mind raced, she froze, for the front door was only for the police, or telegrams, or – Telegrams?

'Oh no.' Fran threw down her knitting; the ball of wool rolled across the table. She rose, her chair scraping on the flagstones, and rushed to open the door into the hall.

As she wrenched it open, she heard the girls pushing back their own chairs and her mam calling, 'No, Franny. Let me.' Fran didn't slow as she rushed down the hall, but still her mam reached the sneck ahead of her, pulling the front door open, her arm out to stop Fran and the girls, but . . . there was no one there. Fran eased past her mam and stepped into the chill of Leadenhall Terrace, looking up and down the cobbled street, the wind snatching at her hair.

The others clustered around her. 'Massingham bairns, I reckon, for they're not in school in the mornings – that's the evacuees' time,' Mrs Hall muttered, slapping her hands together as though she wished it was their backsides.

Fran was almost crying, her throat thick. 'I thought . . .'

Sarah hugged her. 'We know. We all thought, lass.'

Her mam slammed the door behind them. As they entered the kitchen, Fran stared. The coals were burning brightly in the range's firebox, flames licking at them. 'What . . . ?' She felt a draught, then saw the back door ajar.

Her mam pushed past, shouting, 'By, the bairns must have got us to the front and come in . . .' She stopped by the table. 'But not Massingham bairns, no.'

They looked around, checking, but what was there to steal?

Mrs Hall stared at the girls, confused. 'What on earth is going on? Oh, hang on – it'll be Madge taking her boots off on the yard step. She sometimes comes early to work on her proggy rug before we go to Massingham Hall to help with the bairns.'

'But who was at the front?'

'Oh, I don't know. Perhaps someone who got the wrong house and went on his way?' her mam said, raising her voice. 'Come away in, Madge, you're heating the yard, lass.' She collected up Fran's discarded ball of wool, pushing her needles into it before handing it back. 'Madge?' There was no answer, just an odd mewling noise.

'A cat?' queried Beth.

At that, Mrs Hall glared as the door swung further open. 'Chase it away, Madge.'

Again there was no answer. The flames surged. Still there was the mewling. 'If it's that bliddy tom of Mrs Pritchard's after me cock and hens again, I'll have its guts for garters. He's nothing but a nuisance, like his owner. Yowls and gets them in a tizz so they stop laying, and I'm not having it.' She grabbed the broom from the scullery and marched to the back door while the three girls stood back, laughing.

'Oh, Mam,' called Fran, 'they'll peck him to death if he ever gets in, daft old puss. Madge, just see him off, eh?'

Beth pulled at Sarah's arm, suddenly sounding alarmed. 'Madge hasn't answered. I wonder . . . D'you reckon it's been Bob all along, knocking at the front, then coming round the back, waiting to pounce? But why come here and not me own home?'

Mrs Hall looked over her shoulder at Beth, then snatched at the door, and Fran heard her gasp as she almost threw the broom back into the room. Fran moved forwards while Beth called, 'Is it Bob, Mrs Hall?'

Fran had almost reached the door when her mam seemed to tip over, collapsing out of sight. 'Bob,' Fran yelled, snatching up the broom, 'get away from Mam, you hear.' She flung the door so wide it crashed back against the kitchen wall and began to shout. 'Go . . .'

She stopped when she realised what was happening. Her mam hadn't collapsed, but was bending low over something. But what? It was then that she saw . . . 'Oh, what? What . . . ?' Her voice sounded far away, even to her own ears. 'No, Beth,' she said, 'it's not Bob. Quick. Look. Both of you.'

Her mother was reaching for the bundle on the step, saying, 'Oh, I don't believe it. Oh, who'd do . . . Holy Mother of God.' Her mam's voice was a mere whisper as she straightened up, carrying the bundle of blankets and looking helplessly at Fran.

Sarah and Beth had gathered behind Fran. 'What? Whose? Why?'

Fran dropped the broom and reached for her mam, who nodded. Fran felt the chill of the blankets as she pulled them down. Yes, it was true, it was a bairn. Pale and quiet, but very much moving and breathing.

*

14

Beth stared as Sarah helped Fran guide Annie to the table, and all the while her anger towards Bob was building. Not just towards him, but this bairn too, for she feared it was Bob and Heather's babe. Well, who else's? She stirred then, running out and across the backyard in her bare feet, checking up and down the back lane. 'Hello, hello,' she called. How dare he? Surely, he wouldn't? But would Heather?

There was no reply, no Bob. There was nothing but the usual Massingham noise: the singing of the wind in the pithead winding gear, the banging and crashing of the tubs bringing coal to the surface screens, the grinding of gears as lorries took the coal to the station, bairns laughing. Then she heard different sounds: a car revving and a door slamming, a woman shouting 'Drive.' It was brief, unrecognisable and came from Main Street.

Beth was already flying along the back lane, heedless of the freezing cold cobbles, seeing the car, dirty and mud-covered, roar past the head of the lane before she was halfway to Main Street. 'Heather? Bob?' Her voice wasn't working, and instead of a shout, she heard little more than a whisper. She kept on running, her breath heaving in her chest, her feet slipping until she reached the road, looking to the right, shading her eyes against the low glare of the winter sun. The car was in the far distance, taking the Newcastle fork.

'What? What on earth? Bob doesn't have a car.' Her voice was still a whisper. She turned and ran back to the house, slamming the gate behind her and passing the hens. She was about to enter, but noticed a bag to the right of the door, perched on the seat of the old chair beneath which young Ben placed his boots after school. She picked it up; it was heavy. Still panting, she carried it into the kitchen where the girls were talking together while Mrs Hall sat at the

15

end of the table, crooning to the bairn, the knitting abandoned, the teapot and cups too.

Beth laid the bag near Mrs Hall, not wanting to look at the bairn, or hear it. Why bring it here? Why not Beth's own home? Were they watching her? Wasn't it enough that they had the salary allotment? Surely they didn't want her to take responsibility for the child as well?

She shook her head and turned to shut the door, but the broom was in the way and she hadn't the energy to move it. Helplessly, she made her way to the small group at the table. Find some calm, she told herself, taking a deep breath, fixing her eyes on the babe. The blankets had been pulled down, and there . . . Oh heavens. She felt faint with relief, because this bairn was too big, too old, seven months, maybe eight months, and Bob and Heather's would be younger.

She sat at the table, drenched with relief, but only for a moment, for the babe was so wan and thin, too cold and too quiet. Besides, if not Bob's, then whose? She heard herself say, 'Who'd do this? Why choose you?'

She heard the sneck on the yard gate lift. Fran half rose. Beth waved her down. 'Don't leave your mam.' She rushed to the door, pulling it wide.

It was only Madge, with Beth's own mam, Audrey, who called, 'We've come to chivvy along our Annie, pet. I know we were to work on the rugs here for a bit, but we met Madge and decided it was best we take the rugs to the Hall. It'll help our Viola, for Sophia's so laden with the bairn she's almost past walking. I don't care what Dr Dunster says, it's either a whopper or it's due sooner than mid-November. Maud is waiting for us down the road.'

Beth stood gaping at them.

Madge pointed to the broom. 'What's amiss? Why are you looking so gormless, our Beth?'

Still Beth couldn't speak.

Alarmed, Madge and Audrey stepped over the broom and pushed past her. 'Is it our Annie?'

Beth saw that Fran was standing at the table, moving the knitting to one side, carefully unpacking the bag, laying out its contents: baby bottles, clothes, nappies. Finally, there was a letter. Fran held it up. Beth's mam stepped forward and snatched it from her while Madge squatted by Annie's chair, staring at the bairn. Beth picked up the broom, leaned it against the wall and shut the door.

'By, this babe isn't thriving,' muttered Madge. 'I know it's cold outside, but even so, look, the little soul needs warmth, food, a doctor.'

Annie nodded and moved nearer the range while Madge kept pace, rubbing the bairn's hands, blowing her warm breath onto them.

Audrey Smith stood next to Fran. 'It's addressed to you, Fran.'

'I saw that before you ripped it from me hand.' Fran smiled briefly, then took it back. She unfolded the sheet of paper and scanned it.

Beth saw Fran begin to tremble. The babe was mewling again, and aye, it did sound like Mrs Pritchard's tomcat.

Audrey snapped, 'For the love of God, lass, read it out.'

Fran had to read it twice to herself, because she couldn't understand it the first time, or believe it the second. She looked up, staring across at her mam, who was rocking the bairn as she walked to and from the range. Fran let the letter drop to the table, saying, and meaning it, 'I'll strangle her, so I will.'

'Who?' shouted Beth and Sarah.

'Daisy.'

The baby's wail was suddenly louder. Annie hushed the

17

girls, soothing and cradling the bairn until she settled. Madge, who was wearing a green eyepatch, picked up the letter and read it. Mrs Smith peered over her shoulder and Annie muttered, 'If someone doesn't read it out, I'll be shaking the lot of you. Who did you say, Fran?'

'You know, Daisy from Bletchley, and after that from the mother-and-baby home, until she did a bunk.'

'The one who caused all that trouble with our Davey and Daniel? Oh, for the love of Mike—'

'We need to boil water,' Madge interrupted quietly, 'to sterilise these bottles and get something warm into the wee thing, quick as we can.'

'Of course, you're right, Madge. Pan on the shelf in the scullery, Beth,' Annie said. 'Sterilise the bottles and teats once the water's boiled. From the size of it, surely the bairn'll be old enough to drink it merely warmed.'

The door opened, and in came Maud Bedley. 'I've given up waiting for you. The wind on the corner of Main Street got right up my drawers.'

'There's more than wind up our drawers here, Mam,' said Sarah. 'Come over, but shut the door behind you. We're trying to keep the room warm.'

Annie had become quite still and was staring at her daughter.

'Mam?'

'If it's really Daisy's, when is she coming back for the bairn?' Annie stopped. 'But we mustn't trouble with that. It's the bairn we need to sort. Read the letter, pet.'

Fran nodded as Beth placed the pan on the hot plate, which Madge had perked up by opening the vents on the firebox. Beth scuttled on more coal. 'Hush, Beth, quietly, eh,' Fran called softly. She read out the letter, equally quietly, but grimly.

' "Fran, I know that you are a good person, for Davey has

talked a lot about you. I didn't want to have my baby adopted and because you are good, I know you will keep her till I am able to have her back. It will be good for your mother, Fran, as I know her own Betty died, and guess what, my baby is called Betty too, to make it easier for you and your mother to be good to her. Don't try and find me. But please tell Davey's friend Daniel to let his father know. The old boy was kind and found me the mother-and-baby home, but I suppose that's what vicars do. I will come for her, one day. Davey gave me your address for I meant to write to say I am sorry for upsetting you. I never wrote, and I am sorry and I ask for your help.

'"Gratefully, Daisy."'

'Davey said she was devious, and I reckon he were only part-way right,' Sarah said. 'It's a girl, and how *very* devious naming the bairn Betty. Do you think that's actually her name? I remember Daniel telling us at the beck after your wedding tea, Fran, that the bairn was about three weeks. That would make this little one—'

'Seven and a half months, or thereabouts,' Beth interrupted.

'I bet she's called something else really,' Sarah muttered. 'As though that makes any difference as to whether you'll keep the lass. For I know you will, though you don't have to, you know. This is blackmail. Not co-op blackmail, proper blackmail, and the bairn's the hostage.'

Chapter Two

Massingham Hall, the same morning

Viola set off down the basement stairs, heading for the kitchen, her arms full of the evacuees' clothes. It used to be that only Monday was laundry day, but with eleven bairns, six of them footie-playing boys, and four adults, one a temporary pitman, you could kiss goodbye to that. There'd be more by Wednesday. What's more, soon there'd be nappies, baby clothes and bedding too. But when? Poor Sophia looked about to pop, but Dr Dunster still insisted there was a month to go, so she'd become a mite bigger yet.

The clothes almost slipped from her grasp. She paused, leaning on the bannister, clutching them to her before setting off again, wincing at the memory of Reginald telling Sophia yesterday that Ralph had weighed ten pounds when he was born. Sophia had paled, and Ralph had frowned at his father. Later, over cocoa, Ralph had told Reginald that if he'd had the sense he was born with, he'd have kept such a fact to himself.

Reginald had blushed, for he adored his second wife more than life itself, but the cat was out of the bag and it had clearly preyed on Sophia's mind overnight. Well, thought Viola, taking another step, it would prey on hers if she and Ralph ever had children.

'Ten pounds is more than a big bag of spuds from Mrs Adams' corner shop,' she muttered aloud. She looked ahead, thankful the door to the kitchen was shut or she'd be just as bad as Mr Reginald, as the bairns had taken to calling him.

She continued down the stairs, thinking of Ralph as a father, but then stopped again, because although they were 'walking out', he hadn't asked her to marry him, and why would he? He was the heir, an Oxford University undergraduate and had become a pitman, and once the war was finished he'd be out of it and into a more suitable position. Would a better sort of lass come with it, leaving her to do . . . Well, what, apart from nurse a broken heart?

Well, maybe she'd work in an office, for that's what her marrers, Fran, Beth and Sarah, could do when their munitions work ended. Or maybe she could stay here, as the help – but no, not if Ralph loved someone else. She shook her head, the movement dislodging Eva's cardigan and Ralph's knitted pullover, which fell onto the next step down. 'Damn.'

Balancing, Viola stooped and reclaimed them in one easy movement, tossing them on top of her pile, holding them in place with her chin, wondering how much longer the school cardigan would fit Duchess Eva, as she often thought of that extraordinary child.

She carried on down, rubbing her face on his pullover – *his*, Ralph's. The co-op had knitted it for her brown-haired lad who had finally learned to leave his boots in the boot hall, and tiptoe across the kitchen in his filthy socks, trying to leave as little muck as possible. On the way he'd blow her a kiss before disappearing into the former butler's quarters, where there was a bath. He even cleaned the black rim when he finished, though that had involved a bit more of a tussle.

'Mark you,' she murmured aloud, 'there aren't many in his shoes who would stoop to being a bath cleaner, let alone a pitman.' She smiled to herself. 'Talking to myself is the first sign of madness.'

She didn't bother to even think of an answer, for hadn't

the whole bliddy world gone mad? Her mam certainly used to talk to herself when she'd stirred the washing in the copper, her face streaming with sweat. Viola spoke again as she felt for the next step, whispering this time, 'Oh, Mam. Oh, Da. Bliddy bombs, eh? Oh Donald, bliddy Dunkirk, eh?'

It was a mad world, right enough. One that had taken her parents and her brother.

She realised she had stopped again and was staring at nothing, her mind on pitmen, sons of gentry and baths, suddenly piercingly envious of Sarah washing the coal from the back of her hewer husband, Stan. How wonderful must that be? At least Sarah had grown up with Stan, married him and knew her future. But then, how stupid: no pitman knew his future; the job was so dangerous. And what would happen to everyone's future even if they survived the war? Would they still be British, or under the Nazis? Would Ralph . . . ?

'Enough,' she whispered. But she thought about how, as they walked together in the gardens on clement evenings, Ralph would say, 'I am so in love with you.' Sometimes he would add, 'Viola, I am trying to make amends for the brat I was as a boy, and as a younger man.'

'Fran said you were a pain in the backside, but you've grown up at last,' she'd often whisper back, and they'd laugh.

Silently, she asked the question that rose up in the early hours and which she had never dared voice. Did he see an ex-munitions girl from the back streets of Newcastle, brought in to help Sophia with the bairns, as his penance, with her remaining one and a half hands and one and a half ears?

Viola felt the clothes shift again. She really should carry them down in a couple of trips. She dug deeper with her chin. 'You stay put, you beggars.'

Hurrying down the remaining steps, she was so glad that at least they didn't have to be wrung, for there was, thanks be to heaven, a mangle. Somehow it always nipped her fingers, just as it had Sophia's before the co-op had insisted on light duties for her. The very thought of that order, and the fierceness with which it had been given, still made Viola and Sophia laugh.

The clock on the wall above the telephone table said it had just gone eleven thirty. The co-op would be arriving between one and two o'clock for lunch, by which time the bairns would have been brought home from school by Farmer Thompkins in the tractor trailer. Would he hear the Christmas carols they were practising for Melanie's goodbye?

'By, what colour eyepatch will Madge will be wearing today?' She realised she was muttering aloud – again.

The telephone rang as Viola reached the bottom. She sighed as she crossed the passage and called to Sophia Massingham through the half-glazed kitchen door, 'Don't you dare get up to answer it, Sophia. Reginald will pick it up in the study any minute now. Remember your blood pressure, and besides, we need the carrots chopped for the bairns' dinner. Where does the morning go, eh?'

The telephone continued to ring. Viola willed it to stop. She saw Mrs Phillips standing on a chair, reaching for a copper pan hanging amongst others above the kitchen table.

The Massingham Hall cook looked over her shoulder at Viola and shouted, 'Aye, Viola, I'll bonk her on the noddle if she makes even a flicker of a move. Best you answer it if it doesn't stop, because himself's likely hiding in the netty, like most men when they're needed. Taken the newspaper in too, I 'spect, giving advice in his mind to the Government. Most men do a lot of that too.'

Sophia was laughing, her face plumped up with pregnancy, strands of hair escaping from her French pleat. Still the telephone went on ringing. Viola sighed, then dumped the washing on the floor before picking up the receiver, looking through at the other two and calling, her hand over the mouthpiece, 'I'll tell Mr Reginald what you've said, you see if I don't, Mrs Phillips.'

Sitting on one of the high stools set at the end of the huge pine table, Sophia wagged a carrot at the cook, who snapped, 'Don't shake it, cut it . . .' She paused. 'Boss.'

Laughing, Viola said into the receiver, 'The Massingham residence.'

'Is that you, our Viola? It's Madge—'

'Ah, I hope you're phoning to say you're coming early? We could do with some help. We're just sorting out some washing, and making a stew. We've planned enough for us all as usual, and then the wee girls want to finish their proggy rugs so they can get paid by Briddlestone's before Christmas. It's footie with Alfie for the boys, though, as he's not driving Regin—'

'Stop your blather, lass. Yes, we're coming early, but not with the proggies, so the bairns'll have to draw pictures, or all go to the field. We're cycling up instead, with . . . Well, the only way to say it is: I'll be pulling the cart and in the cart'll be a wee bairn. We need Mr Reginald's know-how, you see.'

'What? Sorry . . .' Viola shook her head. 'I didn't hear that right. Start again.'

Mrs Phillips was clambering down, the pan still on its hook. Sophia had stopped chopping the carrot and was watching Viola.

Madge continued speaking. 'Oh, it's complicated. Remember that Daisy who went missing – you know, the one who gave Davey and Daniel a bit of a time down south and upset Fran . . . ?' She waited.

Viola did. 'Yes, but—'

'The lass's only gone and dumped her bairn on Annie and Fran's back step. Poor wee thing, all wan and puny. We thought to come up, as Mr Massingham's home today, isn't he?'

'Aye, but—'

'For he'll know who to talk to at – well, you know, where the authorities have their burrow.' Seemingly without drawing breath, Madge stormed on. 'The girls have gone to the Factory and of course we can't leave the bairn alone in the house. We'll tuck her up tight and warm . . . We need to sort it right now or we'll burst with the stress. Dig Reginald out of his study, for he needs to attend to more serious matters than war production. We can't have any snooty pants in a suit, tie and starched collar strutting into fourteen Leadenhall Terrace wearing a homburg, picking the bitty thing up and taking her off to an orphanage.'

'But—'

'I can see it now, can't you? Rows of cots and a load of busy people wearing uniforms and tired scowls, meaning well, but how can they love so many bairns? Course they can't, not like Annie would, or Fran or the co-op or the whole of Massingham, who'll make sure the bairn'll be happy. Who knows, too, if Daisy'll come back for her, so we'll have to make sure the bairn doesn't forget her. But we know nothing about how to—'

'Slow down, Madge, take a breath,' Viola shouted, trying to keep up with the stream of words.

It was then that Sophia waddled out from the kitchen, supporting her huge belly with both hands while Mrs Phillips tutted and flapped her apron close behind.

'Dear Mrs Phillips,' said Sophia, 'I am sure this scurry from the table to the phone won't hurt my blood pressure or my baby, but thank you for caring.' Her voice was soft but her actions firm as she took the receiver from Viola. 'Madge, dear Madge, it's Sophia. Now, Viola is quite right, draw breath and tell me slowly what is wrong.'

Viola exchanged a smile with Mrs Phillips. Oh yes, the two of them and everyone else might call Mrs Massingham 'Sophia', but there was no question who was the boss. As Madge started talking again, Viola and Mrs Phillips pressed closer to listen and at last they understood. Viola's fury started to build. How dare the silly girl run off from the home with the babe, and then make a pig's ear of it and drop her on a stranger's doorstep, especially in this cold? How did she know where Fran lived, anyway? What if they hadn't been in? 'But . . .' she almost shouted.

Sophia held up her hand, just as though she was another Annie Hall. Viola fell silent.

'You will not cycle up, Madge,' Sophia was insisting. 'Alfie will come down in the Rolls to collect you all.' Sophia's voice was calm and measured, though her hand, which she still held up, trembled. Viola reached out to grip it. Sophia squeezed hard and smiled at her.

'I'll fetch a chair,' Mrs Phillips insisted, but Sophia shook her head, released her hand and instead supported her belly. 'No, dear Madge, listen to me, for splendid though your cart is, I wonder if the journey will be unnecessarily taxing for a little one who has probably had quite a day already. We have the Rolls and Alfie available so it makes sense to use him. After all, Alfie pops down and picks up the co-op and their frames if the weather is inclement, so such a thing is not unusual.'

Viola and Mrs Phillips heard Madge agreeing before Sophia carried on. 'Of course you're right to bring her, and to try to curtail any gossip. After all, a strange baby landing at number fourteen, where Stan and Davey can call home, might well lead people to make two and two equal sixty-one. So, we really need to sort things out before she becomes the talk—'

Madge said something the other two couldn't catch.

'I agree, not to the house, but he will meet you at the top of the back lane, on Main Street. So, dear Madge, perhaps position someone to watch for Alfie. The little one could then be carried to the car in a bundle of blankets, which may well look like material for rug-making. Someone else could carry a few frames for the children's activities. Meanwhile, Reginald will find out who to contact within the authorities and do so. I will call Dr Dunster and beg, if necessary, that he come immediately to examine the little mite.'

Viola was grimacing in tandem with Mrs Phillips, for only now were they beginning to see all the ins and outs of a mysterious baby's arrival – the first of which was her health. Everything else was secondary. Sophia powered on. 'Thankfully, the children are not due back from school for quite a while, so there's time to set things in motion before chaos descends. Does all this sound sensible?'

'Aye, pet, it's an avalanche of sense. I'll go and tell the others.' Madge was sounding more like herself.

'Good. Alfie will hurry down now and be waiting for you.' Sophia stopped, put her hand over the mouthpiece and looked at Viola and Mrs Phillips. 'What have I forgotten?'

'Nowt,' Mrs Phillips and Viola said together.

'Very well, we will see you soon, Madge, and we'll have milk for the babe, if you bring some bottles we can sterilise. Even if you have already done it, perhaps they should be done again after the car ride here? Most of all, try not to worry. We're all in this together.'

Sophia replaced the receiver and turned towards the stairs. 'Now for Reginald, who surely is back at his desk.'

'I'll go,' Viola decreed, holding her back. 'You chop those

27

carrots, eh? We have your feet to put up, as Dr Dunster ordered, and evacuees to feed. But, Sophia, you were grand.'

Sophia put a hand to her forehead. 'How absurd, I feel quite done in, but first we must call the doctor.'

Viola picked up the receiver. 'I will do that. If I need reinforcements, Mrs Phillips will drag you out.' As the telephone rang at Dr Dunster's surgery, which was also his home, she watched Lily Phillips lead Sophia to the tattered old armchair by the range, then pull across the footstool.

'Feet on there, head back, close those eyes, just for a minute. I'll bring water.'

Mrs Dunster answered. Viola explained, and the doctor's wife said, 'Yes, he'll be there once he's finished his lunch. Rather early but he's was out well before dawn on a call. It's a nice bit of lamb's liver, but I don't let him have onions, for obvious reasons. Can't have him bending over a patient's bed and letting himself down, can I? He's there to cure people, not make them relapse.'

Viola managed not to laugh, but instead said solemnly, 'Indeed, you can't. So when may we expect him?'

There was a pause. 'Twenty minutes, on the dot which brings us to midday.'

'We need to keep this between us and the co-op, Mrs Dunster.'

'My dear young lady, I didn't come down in the last shower, and perhaps you're forgetting there is such a thing as the Hippocratic oath which a doctor's wife should also abide by, or so I think. How is your hand from the munitions explosion, by the way? Healing nicely now? And your ear? Matches Ralph's, doesn't it, after he lost half his in the motor-car accident? Don't worry, we'll all see this babe is sorted.'

'Do you know any officials who might help?'

'Tell Reginald to get on the telephone to Billy Tointon,'

Mrs Dunster said. 'He's a frightful old fusser who feels he is a bundle of importance and indispensable at the office where they sort out these things. I was at school with him. You might tell Reginald to mention my name. Beware, though, Bunter Tointon, as we called him for he likes his food, always had a drip on the end of his nose as a child. We became adept at dodging it – and Bunter himself, since he's a terrible bore. Let's hope nowadays he makes use of a handkerchief.'

There was a click and she was gone.

Viola poked her head round the door and brought them up to date, but said nothing about the drip. Sophia levered herself onto her feet. 'These carrots wait for no man.'

Mrs Phillips took Sophia's arm, helping her to the table and hoisting her up onto a stool. 'I reckon we'll need a crane any day now. You look about to burst.'

Suddenly they were all laughing, more loudly than the remark warranted, but it did them good. It was then that Sophia turned to Viola. 'Oh, dearest girl, I'm so pleased that you are here and not at the Factory, though I know Fran, Sarah and Beth miss you mightily. We bless the day you arrived, don't we, Lily?'

Viola felt her shoulders relax and it was only then she realised they had been up by her ears with the stress of the morning. 'Well, I'm just as pleased.' There was a moment's pause and she wanted to ask, 'But what about Ralph? Do you mind? Am I too common?' Instead, she said, 'Now I need to see our high-and-mighty lord in his privy chamber.'

She heard them carry on laughing as she hurried up the stairs, all thoughts of washing abandoned.

Reginald Massingham was working at his desk, his scarf around his neck. It had been knitted by the redoubtable Annie Hall, and as he pulled it tighter he was exceedingly grateful. She had purloined an old sweater of his that she had declared was past its best. However, she had then suggested that *he* sit at the kitchen table and pull out the wool, then roll it into balls for reknitting. Of course, he hadn't dared demur, for Annie Hall's suggestions were orders, but also because it had been a glorious moment of normality.

It seemed a lifetime ago that his work revolved only around the running of his factories and Massingham coal mine – Auld Hilda, as the locals called it. Though why, no one knew. Perhaps his father would have known? Reginald leaned back in his chair, looking out of the window at the front lawn. The trees down by the ha-ha were shedding their leaves, just as young Ralph had shed his support of the Fascists, though that had been a while ago.

Thank God that part of Ralph's life had been put to good use and here he was courageously working undercover, not only to thwart and destroy the local Fascist cell run by Tim Swinton, but, perhaps more importantly, to discover the identity of the top man, the ultimate traitor. God only knew how many cells were under *his* authority.

To keep Tim Swinton sweet, Ralph passed on harmless news from Reginald's friend Professor Smythe and his intelligence team, about happenings in the area.

Reginald reached for a cigar and rolled it between his fingers. Ah, a little dry, but they'd been obtained before the start of the war. He sighed and placed it back in its wooden box, leaving the treat for later, and stared at his half-written report for Smythe's eyes only, concerning a person he had come to suspect at one of his factories. But it was no good, he couldn't concentrate.

Leaning back in his chair again, he longed for the war to be over, for everything to be done and dusted, for the Allies to win and secure democracy and freedom, so they could rebuild and go forward.

Then there was the baby, and darling Sophia's blood pressure, and the evacuees . . . Would Sophia be all right, and the baby? How would Eva cope without Melanie? Would Viola still love Ralph at the end of the war? Lord, he hoped so, for the boy loved her with all his heart. Would the co-op still find time to come and help with the children – all of them, including his and Sophia's child? Would Massingham Hall, and Massingham itself, still be one big family? Well, it was up to him to make sure it was.

But if they lost the war, what then? How could he keep them all safe? For there were Communists and trade-union stewards in his workforce, and they'd be picked off by the Germans. Well, he and Ralph had worked out an escape route that might work, by sorting a way to alter papers, courtesy of Smythe. These men could continue in the pit, for Massingham would protect them, of this he was certain – or almost, because inadvertently things might be said.

Reginald steered his thoughts round again to sitting in the kitchen, pulling wool, his mind free of worry. Was that what Mrs Hall had realised? That just a few minutes doing something relentlessly repetitive with friends and family could be a lifesaver?

He laughed out loud now, picking up his fountain pen, hearing again her tuts as he fumbled and fiddled until he got the hang of rolling the wool into balls while they all listened to the chat of the evacuees.

Increasingly aware of the chill, he rubbed his hands together, blowing on them, then adjusted his scarf again, pulling it over his head and ears, as Davey had once said that he had to do in his decoding hut. He glanced at the unlit fire, pleased that he and Smythe had helped Davey get into Bletchley Park. But enough meandering – what was important now was to keep warm. Should he light the fire? No, there was always the kitchen to warm him, in more ways than one, so he'd take a break shortly. He was about to set to work again when he heard a tap at his door.

'Come in, darling.'

The door opened. 'It's me, actually, Reginald.' Viola entered, blushing.

He grinned. 'Well, I happen to know you're someone's darling.'

Her blush deepened, but then he saw her brace her shoulders and lift her chin. Uh-oh, he thought, what's happened?

'That's as maybe, Reginald, but we have a crisis, and Sophia—'

Reginald was already on his feet. 'Is it her blood pressure, or the baby?'

Viola held up her hand as he rushed round the desk. Her voice was sharp. 'No, but then again, yes, Reginald, though not *your* baby. Follow me, please. Sophia will explain. It's really quite complicated.'

Viola swept off and he followed, not understanding, but thinking, good Lord, she's been recruited into the co-op sergeant-major class. Just look at that hand held high. He felt quite outflanked, because there was no hope for a mere male amongst these women.

Viola was showing him a clean pair of heels, leaving him to catch up, and all the while he hoped his son didn't bugger up this burgeoning love affair. Somehow he felt he would not, and who knew if Christmas would bring good news? Somehow the joy of it often made magical things happen.

He finally caught up with Viola as they crossed the tiled hallway.

'Whose baby, then?'

Chapter Three

The evacuees arrived back at Massingham Hall at one o'clock as usual, rushing from the Thompkins' trailor, across the garage yard, down the steps and into the kitchen. They were led by Eva, as befitted her status as leader of the pack, and hurled themselves at the co-op, who stood in front of Sophia and Reginald, acting as a buffer.

'Hello, hello.' The co-op and Viola held out their arms.

'Have a good morning?' Viola asked each bairn as she hugged them in turn.

Abe looked up at them all, grinning. 'Bit parky out there, but well enough for footie.'

The women stepped aside and, more gently now, the bairns moved closer to Sophia and Reginald, faces upturned for a kiss, then each in turn patted Sophia's bulge before dispersing.

'How do, wee bairn,' Abe murmured. 'Bet it's grand and warm in there.' He moved closer to Reginald. 'How do, big old daddy of the baby?'

'Less of the old, and I am doing very well indeed, Abe.' Reginald cuffed him gently and smiled, tweaking his ear. 'I hope you are too, and that much was taught and just as much learned. Tell me all about it over the most startlingly tasty stew Mrs Phillips and the ladies have produced. But first go and warm up, dear boy.'

Annie was watching as Reginald laid his hand on the orphan's shoulder, and she hoped the special bond between those two survived the advent of the Massingham family's new arrival.

At that thought, she imagined Daisy's bairn being taken to an impersonal orphanage by the authorities and felt panic rise. Pull yourself together, Annie Hall, find some bliddy gumption. She only realised she had said the last two words aloud when Maud Bedley nudged her.

'Doing a Tilly Oborne impression, canny lass? Well, I hope she's giving our Bert hell on the Factory bus, which'll mean the world is going on as normal, even if ours has gone a bit haywire.'

Annie leaned against her for a moment. 'Oh, Maud, I'll need a pile of gumption to keep the bairn with us. After all, a pit house isn't Buckingham Palace, so I'm not sure what I've got to fight with.'

'Maybe it's not a palace, but number fourteen is full of good people, just like the rest of Massingham. Was the bairn still asleep when you checked upstairs?'

'Oy,' Stephen objected, as Abe elbowed him to one side of the range.

'Mrs Hall, Stephen's had his turn,' complained Abe. 'Look at his face – red with heat, it is.'

Annie wagged a finger at Stephen, which was quite enough for him to give ground and join the others milling about the table, talking nineteen to the dozen about the new teacher, Mr Moran, who had arrived at the school with an eyepatch.

'Not like yours, Madge,' Eva called from her prime position next to Abe at the range, peering round at Madge's green one.

Madge sat up straight on the stool where she was writing out a mixture of times-tables lines for the children to work on later in the day, and grinned. She reached out and steadied Sophia, who was heaving herself onto the stool next to her. 'Settle yourself, Sophia, then write out a few of these, eh? But I reckon we'll surely need that hoist Lily talks about.'

Viola peered over Madge's shoulder, pointing to eleven times eleven. 'You've written in the answer.'

Madge stared, then rubbed it out. 'Sorry, I was too busy thinking about what Doctor Dunster said before he left.'

'Hush,' whispered Viola. Then against Madge's ear: 'Remember, the bairns aren't to know about the babe until Annie can keep her. Imagine what they'd feel if she was taken away, for their sense of security and belonging would go with her.'

'Oh aye, I wasn't thinking,' whispered Madge, but it was too late.

'Doctor? I didn't know he was coming?' It was Melanie, who looked alarmed as she nudged Eva aside in order to share the warmth. Their noses were still red from the cold.

Abe sat on the footstool in front of the armchair, looking preoccupied. As if he was coming awake, he said, 'You see, Mr Moran's patch were black, which I told him were for mourning, and what's more—'

'What's more,' Marty called through from the boot hall, 'Abe said he should marry Madge and they could wear the same cheerful ones, and everyone would know they were Mr and Mrs Moran, with two good eyes between 'em. Get yer boots off and your slippers on, you lot, or we'll all have our backsides tanned, won't we, Mrs Bedley? I reckon your Sarah must have had hers skelped a few times when she were a bairn?'

As the children traipsed out, the adults, including Reginald, who was standing behind his wife, were determined not to laugh, even when Maud Bedley called, 'Oh, she certainly did, and you certainly will – and I bagsy *your* backside, Eva.'

They returned with their slippers on and Eva ignored

Mrs Bedley, for they knew no one was ever smacked at Massingham Hall unless they had done the unforgivable, but no one knew what that was, because no one had done it yet. Eva, along with the others, moved ever closer to the range, all of them chilled from the boot hall. Abe had again managed to bagsy the footstool. Tommy took the arm of the tatty armchair, crowding Enid, who was safely ensconced. She moved a few inches away, pressing up nearer the fire.

'Abe said Mr Moran should come to the Christmas party Eva's organising for Melanie,' Tommy said, pulling Enid's plaits before being pinched by her.

Abe said, 'Tommy said it were Mr Moran's duty as a new teacher, for we need a bass,' said Abe. 'He also told him that he'd best try on your eyepatch, Madge, or maybe you'd bring him one of his very own he could wear in school.'

It was only when the laughter subsided that Enid shook her head. 'Nothing funny about that because Mr Moran said yes.'

'Of course. He wouldn't dare not,' muttered Reginald, squeezing Sophia's shoulders.

Madge winked at Annie, who suspected what was coming. Sure enough, Madge put her hands on her hips and looked at Tommy, then Abe. 'Do you mean to tell me, you two, that when he said yes, you meant yes to marrying me just for me eyepatches? By, I'll have to go and have a talk with that wee man and if I like him, I'll set a date.'

'No, we didn't mean that. I . . . well . . . we meant he'd . . .' Tommy stood up, looking horrified. 'We didn't, did we, Abe?'

Eva, shaking her head, muttered loud enough for Sophia and Annie Hall to hear, 'Our Tommy's ten – he should know when he's having his leg pulled. Boys are right daft, got no sense.'

Mrs Phillips came from the scullery with a pile of plates for the table and organised the children. 'Lay 'em out nicely, and the cutlery too. Do *not* touch the blades of the knives, or the prongs of the forks, because no one wants your germs. The stew is ready and Viola will dish it. Oh, wait a minute – you have washed your hands, haven't you?'

The children tore into the scullery to do so, and taking her chance, Annie slipped into the hallway and nipped up the stairs into Sophia and Reginald's bedroom, where they had made the bairn comfortable.

Annie settled the blanket over the little one as she nestled in a drawer. 'Lisa . . .' There, she'd said the name she had decided upon. It wouldn't be Betty, as she'd explained to Maud Bedley, and Audrey Smith, and then Madge as they'd travelled to Massingham Hall, adding, 'For as you know, I have a Betty. She might have died, but she's still alive in my family's heart.'

Yet she had found herself unable to actually call her that till this minute. Why? She didn't know, but it suddenly seemed as if 'Betty' had never been mentioned. Yes, *Lisa* had consumed mashed carrots, and then a little stewed apple mixed with a tiny drop of honey, before guzzling eight ounces of milk. 'Let's see what the little bairn makes of that,' Mrs Phillips had cooed. 'If it's too much of a change, we'll know soon enough.'

Reginald had taken the sock drawer from the bottom of his wardrobe and Annie had folded a blanket for a mattress, then tucked in a cut-down sheet over that, and a similarly cut-down sheet and blanket for covers. Now she touched Lisa's blonde hair lightly.

'Well, little *Lisa*, when Dr Dunster came he thought you had the makings of a fine wee soul,' she whispered. 'You're just in need of sleep, security, warmth and food, so we'll do our best for you. That's if this Mr Tointon . . . But no, it was a Mr Smithson that Reginald finally spoke to. It is he who will decide if Fran and I can be your guardians.'

She looked towards the window, shaking her head, for it had taken an age for Mr Massingham to get through to Mr Tointon, but he had finally made contact with his secretary as Annie stood pressed close to him in the kitchen corridor. 'He's unavailable,' she'd heard the secretary say to Reginald. 'In case you hadn't noticed, it *is* lunchtime.'

'Well, how silly of me, for of course he will be busy living up to his Bunter nickname,' Mr Massingham had muttered.

'Mr Tointon will return your call when he gets back, *if* he is not too busy,' had come the stiff reply.

Even the women sitting around the kitchen table had heard the slam of the receiver as Reginald showed just what he thought of that and stormed back into the kitchen, muttering, 'Jumped-up harpy. I'm beggared if I'll wait for Bunter's non-existent reply. I'll put in a call this minute to Smythe. He knows everyone, or knows how to find them, anyway.'

Reginald had indeed done that, and had then tried again, using Smythe's contact details for an Albert Smithson, the boss who breathed rarefied air. As before, Annie had listened while Smithson's secretary also explained that her boss was unavailable, but if Mr Massingham cared to leave a message with her, she would ensure it reached him.

Reginald informed her of the issue in detail, and added Professor Smythe's name for good measure. Smithson's secretary repeated that she would ensure that he made contact the moment his meeting had finished.

'One must assume that this is the meeting between a nice piece of off-ration venison and his chomping jaws,' Reginald had said to the woman, ice in every word. He shut his eyes, knowing it was not her fault, and thanked her, hoping that she would also find time to eat.

'Yes, indeed,' she had replied, 'but mine will be spam sandwiches.'

They had both laughed at this and she had reiterated that she had written down all the details – names, addresses and the urgency of the situation – and she was sure contact would be made. When pressed, she had said it would almost probably be after two fifteen, though Mr Smithson might decide to visit, not telephone, as he occasionally did. As Reginald replaced the receiver, Annie had thanked him and asked him to pass on her gratitude to Professor Smythe.

'Ah, I think it is of no consequence,' Reginald murmured, 'for the Professor's words were, "What are we fighting a war for, if not for the well-being of every last child in the land?"'

Annie fretted now, turning from the window to Lisa, for Smithson must not make contact, or perhaps arrive before the children had gone to the field with Alfie. What did almost probably mean? Well, whatever it was, they would have to manage.

Tucked in a corner of the crib was a letter, hastily written by Dr Dunster, addressed to 'Whom it May Concern', giving his diagnosis of the health of the child and her needs, which amounted to, he had told them, 'Let the child remain in a loving family and beggar off back to busying yourselves elsewhere. Or words to that effect.' When he saw Annie's look of alarm, he had grinned. 'Dear Annie, I dripped with insincere respect and the milk of human kindness, trust me.'

As well as Dr Dunster's letter, there was Daisy's, passing the child into the Halls' care.

Dr Dunster had taken Sophia's blood pressure before leaving, so that if questioned by the bairns they need not lie. He was glad he had done so, for within five days her blood pressure had risen – not a lot, but enough for a ticking-off. He had pointed to her feet. 'Get that big tum off those poor little things. Can't you hear them begging for mercy? Give 'em a break, woman, and rest.'

He'd clicked shut his Gladstone bag, then patted Sophia and Annie on the shoulder and disappeared up the back steps in his usual flurry.

Annie looked down at the child. Ah well, little Lisa, we'll do our best, but honestly, that . . . She stopped herself, because she must waste no energy on fury for a mam who had left a bairn on a doorstep with strangers, for that is what they were.

There was a light tap on the door and Reginald asked, in a voice just above a whisper, 'May I?'

Annie waved him in.

He tutted when he saw the pile of socks he had tipped out onto the bed. 'Oh Lord, I need to tidy those away, after which I must remember where I've shoved the wretched things.'

They shared a smile. He leaned over, staring down at the baby. 'One forgets how small they are, but also how surprisingly heavy.' For it was he who had carried Lisa up the stairs and then laid her in the makeshift cot.

'Your babe will be much smaller than this, for Lisa is between seven and eight months, if the girls remembered correctly,' Annie said.

He turned and grimaced at her. 'I was thoughtless enough to mention—'

'Indeed, we heard that Ralph was a porker.'

'Ah, my stupidity goes before me. But truth to tell, so was his mother, whereas our Sophia is a slip of a thing.'

'A fact of which you had the presence of mind not to remind her, I hope?'

'Ah, I clearly I have no presence of mind, dear Annie.' As Annie chuckled, he leaned down further. 'There you are, sweet child,' he whispered. 'You carry on resting, because after fresh air and a full belly, everyone needs a bit of shut-eye.' He pulled up the blanket a fraction, then straightened. 'She doesn't deserve to be moved again when she has found the right home.' He tapped Annie's arm. 'I can't think of any better guardians than you and Fran.'

'We just have to remember she belongs to Daisy, so she is merely loaned to us. Which brings me to your evacuees, Reginald.' They stepped away from the bed, but still spoke in whispers. 'With Melanie leaving, the other three orphans need some certainty about their own security. The evacuees with parents will be returning to them at war's end, but what about the gaping hole in the orphans' lives? You still have Eva, Marty and Abe, now that Melanie has been claimed by her aunt and is off to Wales. Of course, they all know that your door is open for the rest of their lives, but those three need to belong permanently to someone, and surely that someone is you?'

Reginald led her towards the door. 'Just for once, Annie my dear, the Massingham family is a step ahead of you, pushed by Ralph, would you believe. I have asked my solicitor to try and trace any living relatives of those three. If there is no one, then we will be speaking to someone like Mr Smithson with a view to official guardianship prior to adoption, since that takes time. But you're right, their security is essential. All this depends on whether the children are agreeable, of course.'

'Of course they'll be agreeable, and it doesn't in the least surprise me that Ralph was the initiator.' She smiled. 'He lost his way for a while, but is back on track. So all in all, you best make a friend of our Mr Smithson when he finally replies. I wonder if he would care for a pheasant, or even a brace? Not as a bribe, of course, but perhaps as a gesture of goodwill.'

They shut the door quietly, dawdling past the prints of Massingham Hall along the landing as Reginald laughed softly. 'Sophia's thought exactly, my dear Annie. We have some hanging in the game pantry.'

His raised an eyebrow and winked, which was as good as a contract, and Annie knew, if she didn't already, that all the pressure that could be applied without it appearing to be pressure, would be. They headed downstairs and were crossing the hall as the telephone rang. It was one thirty. They quickened their stride and Reginald led the way into the study, hurrying to his desk and snatching up the receiver. He listened, then said, 'Ah yes, Mr Tointon, how good of you to return my call. In fact, I have made contact—'

Standing next to Reginald, Annie heard Bunter Tointon interrupt: 'Yes, yes, I have been informed by my secretary that a child has been deposited at a terraced house in Massingham, in which no blood relatives live. I must advise you that the child should be delivered immediately to Addington Orphanage, whereupon, and after due process, a decision will—'

It was Reginald's turn to interrupt. 'Now look here, this *is* a child, not a sack of coal to be deliver—'

Annie snatched the receiver and held it against her breast. 'Reginald, may I urge you not to upset the apple—' She drew a breath. 'We need everyone on our side.'

Reginald's colour was alarmingly high as he stared at her, then took back the receiver. 'Right you are, Toin—I mean, Mr Tointon. But may I get back to you in short order? I am expecting a call from a Mr Smithson. Perhaps the name rings a bell? Your superior, I believe, but I thank you most sincerely for your call. Once he and I have spoken, I will update you. Incidentally, I hope that your luncheon was adequate?'

There was utter silence, not even a squawk from Tointon. At last, Annie heard Tointon's voice and she pressed closer to the receiver. 'Ah, Mr Smithson. Indeed, yes, yes, Mr Massingham. Quite. Well, no need to return my call, for I'm sure I will be included in any decision-making. Good day to you.' There was a click. They looked at one another before Reginald replaced the receiver.

'Bloody little arse,' he muttered. 'Mark you, I expect that's a misnomer, it's probably a fairly hefty one. Oh dear, I do beg your pardon, Annie, but, in all conscience, one has to speak the truth, for I bet it *is* a whacking one after "luncheon". Shall we advance on what little is left of the stew?'

He wiped a bead of sweat from his forehead as Annie burst out laughing.

They found everyone still sitting around the table, chattering, though some of the children had finished.

'Did you answer the telephone in the study, darling?' Sophia asked, poking her stew about her plate, but looking anxiously up at him.

'Don't play with the stew, eat it all up,' urged Maud. 'There's rabbit in there too, and though you might not like it, young Sophia, the babe will.'

'I did answer it, darling.' Reginald took his place beside her as Eva perked up.

'Someone nice, Mr Reginald?'

Reginald brought Sophia up to date in a rushed whisper while Viola diverted Eva's attention.

'You finish yours too, young lady, and while you do, think about this farewell Christmas party you are planning. It might only be October, but time passes so quickly and the send-off must be special and full of Christmas cheer. We have Mr Moran coming for certain, it seems, but start listing the carols that we, and whoever else you manage to corral, will have to learn. We also need to fix a date once we know when Melanie actually departs.'

'Plus,' Madge added, 'we have rugs to make when we've washed the dishes, unless the lot of you would rather go down to Long Meadow to kick a ball about while the day is still fine? We can catch up on the rugs tomorrow, and the good news is that some of the co-op and Alfie will make up an opposing team, or so we've decided.'

As Annie raised her eyebrows, the evacuees' hands shot up into the air. 'Footie, please,' they yelled in unison.

'We'll beat you hollow, see if we don't,' yelled Marty.

'You and whose army?' Audrey taunted. 'Hurry up, Eva, then you all do your chores quick as you can, and we can get off.'

Annie helped herself to some stew, blessing these wonderful women, for the absence of the bairns would leave a clear field for Smithson's call. Opposite her, Eva was picking out bits of parsnips and edging her plate with them because they were one of the two things the child couldn't abide. The other was the skin on custard, as she had informed them on her arrival.

The clock ticked on. Mrs Phillips shrugged into her mac, hat and scarf and headed home. The children began to wash the dishes.

Annie slipped upstairs to find Lisa still asleep. She checked again that all was ready and Dr Dunster's and Daisy's letters were lined up on the bed. She was back downstairs as one forty-five loomed. Reginald patted the stool next to him, and there they both perched, at the head of the table, while Madge sat on the arm of Sophia's chair and checked her knitting, for the mistress of the house was like the co-op's daughters: a beginner.

Keeping his eyes on the children in the scullery, Reginald whispered to Annie, 'I am worried Smithson will jump the gun and telephone, or appear, any minute.'

'Shall we move them out in case he comes?' Sophia whispered back.

'Aye, why not, and forget the chores, just this once,' Maud agreed.

'I'll fetch Alfie and he'll take them off,' whispered Madge, and she was gone, running up the steps to the yard. Within a couple of minutes, Alfie burst in, with Madge behind.

'I need my teams right now. Quick.'

Abe appeared in the scullery doorway. 'What's your hurry? We always have to finish our chores.'

At that same moment there was a loud clatter of feet in the yard and the sound of Ralph, Sid, Norm and Stan shouting and laughing.

'Howay, anyone for footie?' called Ralph from the steps.

'Thought we'd come up with Ralph and get you all to the meadow since it's a nice day and you're a bunch of layabouts,' Stan said from the yard.

'Who's for a roasting, eh?' called Sid and Norm together.

Ralph led the way in, black with coal dust, the others following. He rustled Alfie's hair as they passed, but Alfie waved him away. Viola cut them off before they reached the table, standing firm, arms akimbo. 'Stop right there, you four.' Pointing at Alfie, she instructed, 'Take the bairns to the meadow now to warm up. The lads'll be down after they've showered – quickly, mind – which is when the co-op'll come down too. Off you go.'

Alfie tugged his forelock. 'Aye aye, Captain.' He galvanised the troops and left with the bairns, who whooped and yelled as they roared across the yard, while all the adults breathed a sigh of relief.

Viola looked at the pitmen. 'I hope you've brought clothes, lads, or you'll be getting a mite frozen, for you'll be wearing your birthday suits on the meadow. But at least you'll be clean. Boots, then bath, *now*.'

Chapter Four

The four pitmen tramped to the boot hall without a word. There they removed their boots, leaving them outside the back door, then tiptoed into the kitchen, passing Viola, who was waving them onwards. As Ralph reached Viola, he touched her arm. 'Sweet girl,' he whispered, thinking no one else could hear, but of course they could, and smiled. Viola longed for his kiss. He moved closer. Their eyes met. 'This evening,' he whispered and followed the others.

Stan paused by Annie, his teeth white against the black of his face. She smiled back. 'You playing an' all, Mam?' He didn't wait for an answer, his smile fading. 'Mam, something's wrong, I can tell. Not our Fran, is it? Or Ben?'

Annie forced a laugh. 'Howay, lad, just reeling from the bairns' excitement. Off you go, take your turn in the bath. You'll be last at this rate, so best you hurry.'

Stan leaned across her, engaging with Reginald, who was trying to look busy. 'What's amiss, Reginald? There's summat up.'

Wild-eyed, Reginald looked at Sophia, who called, 'Off to the bath, Viola said.'

'Get in here lad,' Sid yelled from the bathroom. 'Stop dropping your dust everywhere, or your ma-in-law'll be after you with her broom.'

'That's right.' It was Norm, about to take his life in his hands by the sound of his smothered laughter. 'It's the one she rides around the sky when there's a full moon.'

Maud, Sarah's mam and therefore Stan's mother-in-law,

46

roared with laughter but was it only Annie who heard that it was false? Just go, she wanted to scream, because it wouldn't do to have them here, asking questions, causing a scene if Smithson arrived.

Stan set off for the bath, but turned and looked hard at his mam. Annie knew she'd have to tell him about the arrival of Lisa, but not yet, for she didn't want a gaggle hanging back and haranguing Smithson. Reginald checked his watch, and then the clock: coming up for two fifteen. He made his way to the door, whispering, 'I'll go to my study and answer the telephone from there, but if we've heard nothing by three, I'll contact him again.'

They all nodded in agreement as Audrey removed the sterilised bottle from the pan before they followed Reginald up the stairs, then carried on up to the bedroom. Lisa was still asleep and Audrey whispered, 'Thank the Lord she's resting, and with a wee bit of colour. I were right worried when I first saw her.'

'I hope Smithson is reasonable,' Madge muttered, adjusting her eyepatch, a sure sign that the worry was getting to her.

Lisa stirred. They backed away. She settled. 'Let's leave her,' Annie whispered. She was aware she was wringing her hands.

As they began to leave the room, Maud whispered, 'I just hope he's sensible when he does—' She stopped, for there, on the landing, were all four pitmen, their hair wet, wearing clean clothes.

Annie pushed the women out and followed, attempting to close the door behind her, but Stan moved past and entered, the other pitmen behind him. The mams watched from the doorway as Stan, the only one to actually approach the crib, stared down at Lisa. He picked up the two letters from the bed and read them, carrying them out as he

47

shooed the others before him and shut the door. The women leaned back on the bannister, waiting.

'Sophia told us, Mam. She thought it best to stop me fretting down at the meadow, in front of the bairns.' Stan's voice was so soft, the women strained to hear him.

Sid took the letters from him, checking with Annie, who nodded, for there was no point in keeping it from them now, and of course, Sophia was right. The other two crowded round and read over his shoulder. Norm muttered, 'Bliddy hell, fine kettle of fish. And so far no call, not on the dot of two fifteen, anyway?'

The women nodded.

'Righto,' whispered Stan. 'Sophia said that the telephone won't ring any sooner if you're sitting looking at it, so we've been told to make sure you come out to play.' He smiled, but it didn't reach his eyes. 'It helps us lads, it does, fresh air, a run around, a bit of yelling. By, when were the last time you did that? So, Sophia will stay here with Reginald to look after her blood pressure and the bairn – Betty, is it? Which is a bliddy cheek, and who's to say it's true?'

Annie said quietly, 'No, there's only one Betty, so this little mite is Lisa, close to Elisabeth. And it's you who must head for the meadow right now, and say nothing to the bairns. We don't want their sense of security being shaken by this visit from the authorities, for if it goes badly, they'll likely fear for themselves.'

Stan merely shook his head. 'No, you'll come too, the co-op needs to whack the footie to get rid of whatever will be roaring through you all. Viola's to come too, Sophia says. Reginald'll rush down when the bloke telephones.'

The pitmen led the way to Long Meadow, skirting the vegetable patch, with the women just behind, the mams worrying about their girls at the Factory. Annie said as they strode along, 'I pray they are concentrating and letting us deal with this.'

Audrey nodded. 'I know, but on the bright side, it'll give my Beth something other than Bob to fill her thoughts.'

Ralph sighed. 'The trouble is, Beth is stuck in limbo, and now you and Fran are, Annie, until the authorities make a decision. But you couldn't do anything other than contact them, for word would travel, one way or another. Tell you what, we lads will meet the girls off the bus. What is it, eleven?'

'Midnight. The aft shift finishes at ten – there's a war—'

'—on,' everyone shouted.

Sid elbowed Ralph. 'You stay tucked up in your cot, lad. If it's anyone, it'll be one of us, for it's just a hop and skip to the bus stop.'

'Race you,' Norm yelled, as they walked alongside the walled garden. 'Last one's in goal. That includes you, ladies, so get your running feet on.'

Madge lifted her skirts. 'Up and at 'em, lasses.' She tore ahead, down the track, her hair falling from her bun, running neck and neck with Norm, but now Annie, Maud and Audrey gave chase. After keeping pace with them for a while, the lads tore ahead, with only Madge managing to keep up.

The women still ran, but at more of a jog, while Sid called to his marrers to make it a proper race. He bet a bob he'd win. That did it, and with their caps pulled down, their strides lengthening, they sped off. Madge let them draw ahead. Panting, bending over with hands on knees, she waited for the others to catch up, laughing fit to burst. 'By, I enjoyed that,' she gasped. 'I was a good runner in me day.'

All five walked for a little, then Viola muttered, 'Come on, let's not lag behind. Let's show them what little girls are made of, eh?'

Laughing, they picked up speed, tearing along, and Annie realised she was enjoying covering the ground fast. What's more, it did indeed feel as though the worry was being blown to one side. On and on they ran, skirting the compost heaps and the saplings. Now they were all in a rhythm and catching up on the lads, though, as Madge panted, 'They've manners, and are letting us all arrive together.'

Long Meadow was in sight and as the lads slowed down, the pitmen almost tripped over their own feet. Annie and Audrey shared a look and burst out laughing, for the bairns had stopped their game and were gathered in a group, with Alfie behind them, cheering. The girls shouted, 'Come on, the co-op,' while the boys cupped their hands around their mouths and yelled, 'Up the pitmen.'

'Get some gumption, lads, you can win,' yelled Abe.

'Come on, come on, the hewers,' called Marty.

The women were in a line with Stan and the lads by now, and it was Ralph who called, 'Let's show them a burst of speed.' In a row, they all dug deep and ran and ran. Together, they reached the meadow, where they dragged in deep breaths, with Sid muttering, 'It's these bliddy fags that do it.'

Madge panted and coughed next to him, spluttering, 'Nowt to do with the coal dust, then?'

Stan shook his head. 'Time's a-wasting and we've these toerags to roast. Up and at 'em, team.'

The bairns were leaping about, calling and laughing, and it was Melanie who shouted, 'It's us who'll be roasting you good an' proper, you wait and see.'

Everyone was laughing, and it was something Annie had thought she'd not be doing today, or for a while yet. She took her position in defence, obeying Madge's pointed finger.

'That's right, Annie. Let's put the hewers in as forwards and I'll go in goal, eh, for I can't see people coming in from the side.'

Alfie blew his whistle with a flourish and Eva beat Stan to the ball, passing to Abe while the shouts and thwack of boot on leather mingled in the afternoon air. On they played. The women ran, kicked, missed, fell, laughed, and it was only when Alfie blew and blew his whistle, waving his hands, that they stopped, exhausted.

It was then they heard Reginald's frantic call.

'Ladies of the co-op, quick, back to the house. Leave the brats of all ages to enjoy themselves. Remember, we have Melanie's party to discuss, and our Viola's birthday too. But nonetheless, you come too, Viola. We'll send you from the room when we have moved on from the Christmas farewell.'

The evacuees began jumping with excitement as the women left the meadow. Stan murmured to Sid, who was bouncing the ball, 'Bliddy hell, what'll that bloke say? That's what worries me, because we know damn well what damage Mrs Pritchard can do with her forked tongue.'

Stan looked confused, and it was Ralph who spelled it out. 'She'll say there's no smoke without fire, and why would the babe be left on the Halls' step unless it's yours? Or Davey's? On and on she'll go about who knows what. Trouble is, it does make you wonder, after Bob, and with Davey being away too . . .' He stopped, shook his head. 'But no, anyone but Davey. He's as straight as a die.'

Norm and Sid nodded, looking worried. Alfie blew the whistle and brought them back into the game, though not Stan, who stood there watching but seeing nothing, for his mind was at Bletchley with Davey, so far away, such a different world – a bit like Bob in Grimsby.

But no. Stan shook his head. That was nonsense. Besides,

the letter didn't say that Davey was the father. It *was* the RAF bloke, surely? He felt the sting of the football as Tommy yelled, 'Kick it, man, don't just dream. We've got to beat you fair and square.'

There was no talk of parties, or anything else, as the women followed Reginald at a run, trying to keep up, but in the end, as the gap widened between them, Annie called for him to slow down, and he did.

'Let's be clear, it's nothing to do with arranging parties, is it?' Annie panted when they drew alongside. 'Smithson's called or is here, isn't he? Me with me hair all flyaway and me boots muddy.'

They were bunched up, elbows pumping as well as legs. 'Bloody idiot's not here, but at Leadenhall Terrace.' Reginald's voice jerked as he ran. 'He telephoned from the call box. He thought you were there. Oh bloody hell, it's so infuriating. Anyway, that's the top and bottom of it, and he's been waiting since two fifteen. He was irritated with me, I'll have you know, because he said of course he would want to check the suitability of you as guardian in your own abode, so why would he think we were anywhere but there, and why waste a phone call? Pompous ass.'

'You didn't cause a scene?'

'That's exactly what Sophia asked, Annie, and no, I was charm itself, muttering profuse apologies, which hurt, very much. Bloody idiot. Him, not me.'

The co-op exchanged looks and couldn't help grinning. Reginald roared on, speeding up and shouting, 'Apparently, after receiving a cup of tea from, as he put it, "an informative neighbour", Mrs Pritchard, he found his way to the telephone box on Main Street.'

The women groaned.

'Never mind that,' Reginald called back. 'I will be there

with you, and who knows, the milk of human kindness might just have seeped into the old witch, for the Vicar's been attempting to smooth her sharp edges these last few months. Smithson says he can wait another thirty minutes only, for then he has more pressing matters to deal with back at the office, hence our running fit to burst. I'll show him what pressing matters are, you see if—'

'You mustn't, Reginald, for heaven's sake,' roared Madge.

Reginald was panting. 'You're right, and I won't, of course. Fortunately, Lisa woke a few minutes ago and I brought her down to Sophia, who changed and fed her. She'll bundle her up in a blanket. If I could have driven over the ha-ha to fetch you, I would have done, but I will instead take you all, and Lisa, at speed into the village, and stay during the interview. Must get a move on . . . get the car ready . . . and then we can dash off. Viola, come with me to help Sophia, eh? I've no more breath, ladies. See you . . . back in the yard . . .'

They were all running faster now, but still Reginald and Viola drew away, with Reginald calling over his shoulder yet again, 'When you reach the yard, ladies, hop straight into the car. You can fiddle with your hair on the drive down, for Sophia will find . . .' They could hear no more as the pair seemed to streak towards the edge of the vegetable garden.

'By, once there was a time we could do that after a game of rounders or the like . . .' wheezed Audrey.

'Bliddy long time ago,' Maud groaned, her breath coming in small bursts.

'You stop,' called Annie. 'I'll go on.'

Madge and Audrey were both running alongside her, with Maud just behind. 'What, and miss the chance of setting Smithson right, because that canny witch will have set it out all wrong,' Maud panted. They roared along the footbridge over the ha-ha, then jogged on, panic and worry coursing through Annie, who regretted coming up to the Hall today, regretted Davey ever starting at Bletchley and meeting this wretched girl, regretted . . .

She thought about Daisy, Bletchley, Davey, and again. Oh no, was that why . . . ? Surely the bairn wasn't *his*? On she ran, her mind awry because now the thought was there . . .

They had gained a second wind by the time they swung into the yard to see Viola with a brush and hairpins in one hand and a brace of pheasants hanging from two fingers of the other, while Sophia held Lisa. The Rolls-Royce was ready, the exhaust spluttering. Sophia pointed to the open car door.

'The back seat will take you all. The frames are in the kitchen. We'll get the bairns to do some proggy rugs so they can fulfil Briddlestone's expectations.'

Annie stood back to allow the others in, then turned. Sophia handed over Lisa.

'Madge, grab the brush, quick now,' said Viola. 'Reginald, here's the bribe.' She moved round the Rolls to Reginald's open window. He snatched the pheasants.

Viola waved, then shouted, 'Wait, wait.' She ran down into the kitchen cold store, returning with just one bird. 'Offer this to the old witch as a thank you for giving Smithson a cup of tea.'

Sophia nodded. 'Oh, good idea, though of course she might already have dripped her poison. If so, perhaps she'll choke on the bones.'

Reginald muttered to himself, putting the additional pheasant alongside the brace on the front seat. 'Good grief, you're frightening when you are pregnant.'

'Do stop rambling, Reginald,' snapped Madge, sitting beside Annie. 'Come on, get us down there, quick as you can.'

Reginald blew his wife a kiss. 'You look after her, Viola. She's precious.'

Viola slammed the rear door shut. Reginald put his foot down and off they tore, crunching across the gravel drive as the co-op tried to smarten up. They brushed one another's hair and straightened their collars. Madge tucked Annie's strands into a French pleat, pinned them using the hairpins, then leaned back and checked. 'Right, lass, you'll do.'

As Reginald swept down towards the village, they tried not to think of Smithson having tea with Mrs Pritchard, who lived at number 18 and whose tomcat was as big a nuisance as his owner.

They were passing between drystone walls, the sheep huddling into the top corner against the rising wind. No one spoke and Lisa fell asleep once more. 'What a day she's had,' Madge breathed. 'She must be fair exhausted, for who knows how far they travelled to bring her to Massingham.'

Lisa stirred, her arms reaching out. One hand seemed to be feeling for someone, perhaps her mam? Annie placed her finger in the little hand; Lisa gripped it. On, Reginald drove, while Annie silently begged Smithson to wait, and hoped and prayed Mrs Pritchard hadn't ruined this babe's life, for an orphanage so easily could.

As they entered the village, the slag heap was smouldering, the wind snatching the smoke. If they opened the windows, the sound of the pit village would give her strength and courage, Annie thought, for I am almost home. As though reading her friend's mind, Maud opened the window and there were the sounds of children playing, women talking, the clip-clop of the drayman's horse pulling the rattling beer barrels.

She waited, and there too was the wind in the winding

gear and the smell of sulphur all around. In the distance she heard a train taking the coal hewed at Auld Hilda's coalface to where it was needed. Aye, Auld Hilda was the pit that had given her man a job and taken his life, but never mind that, for the pit village had enclosed her, loved her, kept her going.

They left Main Street to turn into Leadenhall Terrace. A black Austin saloon was parked outside number 14. All along the street, women stood on their doorsteps, waving as they passed. Standing outside number 18 was Mrs Pritchard, with a man. She nodded to them, her arms crossed over her flat chest, her pinny fluttering in the breeze.

Reginald pulled up behind Smithson's car and Annie's heart beat fit to burst. She looked down at the babe, her tiny hand still gripping her finger. Annie searched Lisa's face, worried, for Maud was quite right, the poor wee thing had not only been left on the doorstep just this morning, but had then travelled to Massingham Hall, been given food she was probably not used to, had then been hidden away upstairs, and was now here again.

Was there to be another journey? If . . . if Mr Smithson took her, how would he manage in the car? Well, she'd have to give him the drawer waiting for them in the kitchen. Lisa could travel in that on the back seat.

Reginald stopped, pulled on the handbrake and switched off the engine outside Annie's house. No one spoke. Annie looked down at the babe, who was smiling at her now, two white teeth on the bottom, and the top gum showing the hint of another. 'Well, sweet babe, they'll come out one day, when you're at school, and we'll put them under your pillow for the tooth fairy to take, and leave you a farthing each time, eh?'

'You be careful now, our Annie,' Maud said quietly. 'She

might be back with her mam by then and we're not about to let you have your heart broken, not again.'

'If Smithson lets her stay at all, that is,' added Audrey. 'So you hold yourself back, eh?'

Annie kept her smile, for the babe was still watching. 'That's as maybe. But she's a bairn, and while she's in my house she'll be loved,' she insisted, 'and when she goes, that's my problem, not hers. Until then, we'll talk of her mam, or what Davey can tell us anyway, and that she was called Betty, so 'twill be easy for her to respond to that name when she waves us all goodbye.'

The answer from the others was raised eyebrows. Reginald called from the driver's seat: 'Yes, that's the way it has to be. No holding back, but always be aware they might one day . . .'

They? thought Annie, feeling that Reginald must be thinking of the orphaned evacuees. Oh Lord, she sighed. So much unconditional love needing to be given, no matter that it might be only a loan.

Chapter Five

Mr Smithson met them at the front step. He and Reginald tipped their homburgs at one another and shook hands, while Madge reached for the sneck and opened the front door. Smithson raised his eyebrows. 'Security is not high on the agenda, then?'

For a moment everyone paused, not one of the co-op understanding. Reginald merely smiled. 'Doors are not locked in Massingham, Mr Smithson. There is no need.' He turned and called up the terrace to those still watching from their doorsteps, including Mrs Pritchard. 'Is that not so, ladies?'

Mrs Pritchard was the first to nod and call back, 'Oh aye, for we know one another like the backs of our hands. It's altogether safe. I hope I gave you no reason to think otherwise, Mr Smithson, over our cup of tea. Fresh tea leaves they were an' all, once I heard you were from the authorities.' She looked up the street, pursing her lips, wanting approval, and the neighbours all nodded, though with eyes only for Lisa.

Mr Smithson merely nodded. 'Very nice cup of tea, too, Mrs Pritchard. I thank you.'

With Lisa in her arms, Annie led the way inside, walking through the hall to the kitchen, where lightness and warmth filled the back room. The drawer rested on the linen box, but the babe was awake and restless, so Annie held her out to Mr Smithson, who, startled, had to let his briefcase drop to the floor before taking her. Annie pulled out a chair, absolutely determined this man should understand that it was here that the bairn should be, for as long as she needed them.

For this, he must understand that Lisa was not a bag of coal, as Reginald had pointed out to Mr Tointon. Therefore, he must feel the weight and warmth of her, see the shine of her silky hair, the perfection of her face, the dimples on the backs of her hands, and accept that she was a living being, not a tick in a box.

'Tea?' she asked, gesturing to the chair. 'We also have fresh tea leaves. Sit yourself down, and you too, Reginald. She's a dear little babe, is she not? We will take her while you try to drink your tea. Can't have her scalded, eh?'

Mr Smithson sat with a bump as Lisa wriggled and reached out for his face. After a moment, he held out his finger for her to grip and said, looking intently at the child, 'My son did this. Apparently, the moment they're born their grip is so strong they can take their own weight. Of course, one would not try, so how they know . . .' He trailed off, looking down at Lisa, who was giving him a gummy smile.

No one dared to speak as Mr Smithson smiled back, as a father, not an official. But then Lisa fretted, let go of his finger, thrashed about, trying to sit. Maud said, 'We think she's about seven and a half to eight months. She was born early March, or so Daniel told us back in April.'

Smithson was clearly not listening as he tried unsuccessfully to pacify the babe. Madge took Lisa from him and walked up and down. Reginald moved Smithson's briefcase to the side of the man's chair before settling himself at the end of the table. Smithson straightened his tie. 'Perhaps no tea. I am somewhat awash with it, and with conversation, though it's all kindly meant.'

Everyone looked at him, but Lisa grizzled, so Madge

bumped her onto her shoulder, patting. Lisa reared back, pulling Madge's hair. Madge grimaced as she disentangled herself, saying, 'At least it's not my eyepatch. Reckon she'd like the sparkly ones a bit too much.'

Annie watched and listened to the chatter as her mind raced. 'Conversation?' she finally queried.

The range ticked, much like a clock. The firebox smouldered like the slag heap. Still Mr Smithson did not reply. Reginald spoke into the silence. 'That reminds me, I happen to have a brace of pheasant, which perhaps you might find useful, Mr Smithson? They need to hang a little longer, but it makes a break from the monotony of daily rationing.'

Maud and Audrey had settled themselves opposite Mr Smithson whilst Annie still stood. He looked around at them all, then again, scanning Madge and Lisa, then Reginald. 'Pheasants? Could such an offer be construed as a bribe?'

Reginald flushed. 'Indeed not. It's simply that I have some to spare.'

Thankfully, Lisa chose that moment to really bawl. Annie rose and found a wooden spoon in the scullery, handing it to her to hold. The bairn hit Madge with it, so Annie took her. 'Hey, hey, the spoon's for chewing, so have a go as you've a tooth coming at the top, sure as eggs are eggs. Let's tell lovely bashed and bruised Madge to sit down, eh, while Mr Smithson comes upstairs with me, for he'll want to see where you're to sleep, or so we hope, till things are sorted properly.'

Lisa chewed the spoon as Annie nodded to Madge. 'Take Mr Smithson's seat, for I know he's in a hurry, with other matters awaiting his attention, and it's good of him to come so prompt. But I reckon you realise, Mr Smithson, the importance of a quick, even if temporary, settlement into a loving home, eh? So while you're having a look around at where Lisa will sleep, I will also show you the letter that was left with her.'

'Don't forget Dr Dunster's letter,' piped up Audrey. Smithson spun round to see who was speaking. 'He were very obliging, Mr Smithson, for he was telephoned from Massingham Hall and came within half an hour to check the babe's well-being.'

'Quickly now, Mr Smithson, for like our Annie said,' Maud began as Mr Smithson looked and found her, 'we don't want to hold up an important man like you.'

Annie felt they were rather over-egging the pudding, but then Reginald leapt to his feet and held open the door. Looking harassed, and after checking the clock, Mr Smithson followed, his briefcase in one hand, his hat in the other. As she led the way down the hall, Annie heard Reginald say, 'Well, after entertaining the evacuees to a game of footie, I expect you ladies are more than ready for a cuppa? What say I practise my tea-making skills? I am happy with used tea leaves, of course, but Mr Smithson deserves fresh.' She winced. Now that really was a bit too much.

The door shut on the chatter. Quietness fell as Annie led the way upstairs, Lisa safe in her arms, not crying, but making soft noises. They entered her bedroom. 'We have a cot in the attic. It was Ben's, my youngest – thirteen years old and at school for a few years yet. He will fetch it down.'

She was aware her heart was beating hard and fast again, for Smithson had walked to the window and was looking out onto the street. He was so close to the glass his breath fugged it. It seemed too quiet, as though the world had paused. Well, in a way it had. She kissed the bairn's head, promising Lisa silently that she and Franny would bring roses back to her cheeks, and be her family until her real one came for her. When or if? She sighed.

But first there was Mr Smithson, who was now running his fingers along the window sill. Was he looking for dust? Yes, for he examined his fingertips. Still he stood, staring out again, until finally he turned back to her. 'Mrs Pritchard told me of the Proggy-Rug Co-operative?'

Oh, thought Annie, is that good or bad? 'We are widows who earn our living making rugs and selling them to Briddlestone's. We teach the evacuees schoolwork at Massingham Hall, and craft skills, including proggies. We are working on their times tables at the moment.'

Mr Smithson walked over and sat on her single bed, undoing the leather straps of his briefcase and taking out a notebook. He removed his pen from his breast pocket. 'Football being on the curriculum, perhaps?'

Annie rocked Lisa, but smoothed her hair with her other hand. 'Well, Alfie, the chauffeur, does that, and Ralph, the Massinghams' son, with my eldest son, Stan, and his mar— Well, his friends—'

'Marrers will do, Mrs Hall. I am familiar with this world. Continue.'

'Today, for instance, they arrived to play footie with the evacuees, all eleven of them. We also joined in.'

'And Lisa? Who had care of the child?'

Mr Smithson was removing the top from his fountain pen and began to write as Annie answered, 'Mrs Massingham, Reginald's wife, who is pregnant herself. This is one of the reasons why she needs us, but with eleven children we were going up there before ... well, before she was expecting a baby. We are glad to help.'

He looked up. 'You are paid?'

'A little – the Massinghams insist. But we weren't keen. Bairns are bairns, after all, and several were orphaned in the bomb—' She stopped, horrified at herself. Should she have alerted him to the orphans? Would he now take them to an orphanage? Surely, though, the woman in charge of the evacuee programme had already done the paperwork, so it would be written down somewhere? She relaxed a little.

'What would happen to the child if you continue such work?'

It isn't work, thought Annie, it is caring, helping. To her horror, she realised she had indeed said those words out loud. Mr Smithson merely wrote them down.

'Letters?' He held out his hand, still holding the pen. He read Dr Dunster's first, then Daisy's.

When he had finished, he said, 'The child is called Betty, but you have taken it upon yourself to change her name.' It wasn't a question, but an accusation. The room seemed to darken. Annie came to stand before him. He had to look up at her.

'My own bairn was born, lived a bare few minutes,' Annie explained. 'Her name was Betty. As a father, you will understand that for me and my family, Betty still lives. As Lisa is also short for Elisabeth, I decided that Lisa is what I will name her. That way Lisa can be loved for herself. If we are allowed to keep her within our family, and this community, we will explain to her that she has a mam and that her mam called her Betty.'

He wrote this down, saying nothing. When he had finished, he asked, without looking at her, 'And this Daisy, what is the connection? Who is Davey? And what about Daniel and his father?'

Annie drew in a deep breath and explained about the— No. She stopped, for best not to be specific. She started again, saying Fran's husband worked in a centre doing war work with many others, including Daniel and Daisy. Daisy had discovered she was pregnant but then her RAF boyfriend had died, and apparently her parents weren't interested. 'So, Davey and Daniel, also a war worker, helped by contacting

Daniel's father, who is a vicar, asking if he could arrange for a mother-and-baby home. But before adoption could be arranged, Daisy fled with the child, because she refused to give her to strangers. I suppose that's why she decided to do what she did – leave her with the wife of a friend who had helped earlier.'

Yes, thought Annie, said like that it made sense. Davey was a friend, and Fran was his wife – how could she have feared there was another reason?

There was a long pause. Mr Smithson rose and again stared out of the window. Then, without looking at her, he asked, 'Is Betty your son-in-law's child?'

'Certainly not, there is no sounder man than Davey Bedley.' Annie's mouth was dry. 'Besides, Lisa bears no resemblance to him whatsoever.'

'Ah, so you have checked. Not that sure, then?' Mr Smithson turned and smiled, but it didn't reach his eyes.

At that moment there was a rat-a-tat on the front door. Mr Smithson replaced the top of the fountain pen and returned it to his breast pocket and the notebook in his briefcase. 'May we?' He pointed to the stairs.

As they descended, they saw Mrs Pritchard and Maud in the hall. They looked up at Annie, who still carried Lisa, now asleep. Maud herded Mrs Pritchard through to the kitchen as Annie and Mr Smithson followed. Audrey brandished the teapot. 'Are you sure you won't have one, Mr Smithson?'

Reginald took Lisa from Annie. 'Do sit, Annie, you'll have a long night ahead of you. I need practice, anyway.'

Mrs Pritchard looked at him askance. He smiled at her. 'My dear Mrs Pritchard, I'm sure you will have heard that we are expecting a brother or sister for Ralph. All so exciting. A younger friend for Lisa, hopefully.' He looked at Mr Smithson.

Mrs Pritchard said, 'Mr Smithson was asking me why a babe would have been left on your doorstep, Annie,' said Mrs Pritchard. 'I explained that probably the reputation—'

Annie stiffened. 'Reputation?' She knew she sounded wary.

Mrs Pritchard smiled. 'Your family's open-heartedness must have spread as far as Davey's workplace, wherever that might be. Oh aye, as the Reverend Walters and I were saying just the other day, if there is help needed, you will be the first to hold out a hand – you and your family. Sometimes we forget that, particularly those of us who have things on our minds. You know, perhaps, that my Cathy lost *her* babe? They live down south, and I couldn't help her. It put me in a right state, quite lost my way for a year or so. Daft, as the Reverend says. I should just have come to you for solace, but how could I trouble you, when you had lost your Betty?' She sat in the seat that Madge had vacated.

Everyone was staring. Annie came to her, still carrying Lisa. Mrs Pritchard held out her arms. 'May I?'

Annie passed over the bairn. Mrs Pritchard looked down at the child, who grasped Mrs Pritchard's finger, as she had done with most of them. 'Mr Smithson were on about the family, weren't you, sir?' Mrs Pritchard asked. 'He thought maybe your Stan, or Franny's Davey, were the father. As I said, that would be impossible, for them boys are as straight as anyone can be. And just look at that little face – it's no way she's like either one of them.'

Maud came to stand next to Mrs Pritchard and smoothed Lisa's hair, saying, 'I hope her dead father is looking down and protecting her, for if her mam can't cope at the moment, she left her with a family who can.'

'Aye,' muttered Mrs Pritchard, 'and the Proggy Rug Co-operative will be there to help, just like I said, Mr Smithson. The community too, of course.'

For a moment Mr Smithson stared around, and then came the sound of running across the backyard.

'Mam, Mam, I'm back.'

Reginald looked at their guest. 'Ah, that's Ben. Have you seen and heard enough, Mr Smithson? Because he doesn't yet know. Best to break the situation to him in private, don't you think?'

Mr Smithson picked up his homburg and nodded at the women, his gaze lingering on Lisa for a moment before he made his way into the hall with Reginald and Annie in his wake. The two exchanged looks, both stunned by Daphne Pritchard's behaviour and words.

Stepping into the street, Mr Smithson waited, looking up and down the terrace. The women were no longer standing on their doorsteps. Reginald collected the brace of pheasant from the Rolls.

'If you don't care for pheasant, I will try and persuade one of the co-op to take them home.'

Smithson smiled his wintry smile, still as bleak as the wind. He shook Reginald's hand and gestured him to one side, away from Annie. Though his voice was low, she heard him ask, 'You vouch for this family?'

'Oh yes, of course. I am more indebted to Annie Hall than I can ever explain. Lisa will be a lucky girl to be in the care of such a mother and daughter. Fran is as remarkable as her mother. She works—' He stopped. 'Well, at a nearby factory. What's more, Lisa will be returned to her own mother whenever that is required.'

Smithson merely nodded, hesitated, then took the pheasants. 'Thank you. Mrs Smithson and my son will think Christmas is upon us early.' He returned to Annie. 'I can't promise anything, for I have enquiries to make of Daniel's father regarding the mother of the child, and I also need to obtain from him the addresses of the mother-and-baby home and of the grandparents of the child. They might prefer for guardianship to remain within the family.'

'I understand,' said Annie.

'I felt sure you would, having met you. Perhaps, Mr Massingham, I should contact our mutual friend, Professor Smythe, for I somehow doubt the veracity of the information that Daisy provided for any of these good people. Was there really an RAF pilot? What really is her parents' address?'

He smiled sadly. 'I have to tell you, Auberon also vouched wholeheartedly for Mrs Hall, and her daughter. I do, however, still have to dot the i's and cross the t's, or I'm not doing my job. I do hope you both realise that it is not personal. In the meantime, play footie, Mrs Hall, with your delightful friends and community. Sleep when you can, build up this child, for she appears to have been somewhat neglected. From my words you will see that I am allowing you temporary guardianship. Temporary, mind – a form of probation. Things have to go through their proper channels.'

He turned to Reginald. 'I believe we have concluded this matter?'

Reginald hesitated. 'I do wonder if Auberon managed to mention . . . ?'

Mr Smithson was putting on his hat, pulling it down firmly against the wind. 'Ah yes, thank you for reminding me.' He indicated Annie. 'Should we talk in front of . . . ?'

'Oh yes, indeed you should,' Reginald laughed, 'for Annie will have my guts for garters if I don't pursue the security of these orphans.'

Annie held her breath: the orphans. She smiled widely and nodded. Mr Smithson continued.

'Guardianship would be a given, as you have already been allowed to accept evacuees. Soon – once I have contacted all, or indeed any, relatives – in co-operation with your lawyer, my department will be able to make a decision as to adoption and put this matter to the court. This, of course, Mrs Hall, I cannot consider in your case, for the mother, though missing, still lives. Good day to you both.'

This time his smile was broad. It changed his face.

They watched him drive away as Annie said, 'Thank heavens, and thank you, Reginald.'

'Enough,' replied Reginald. 'Your actions speak for you, but quite frankly, the Wicked Witch of the North East swung it. I think perhaps we'll have to rethink our feelings towards her. Though it's hardly surprising we have them, for she has been dreadfully unkind in the past. But the Reverend has done what vicars should and worked some magic.'

'When the rest of us didn't,' Annie muttered as they returned inside.

Reginald pulled her back and whispered, 'I'm not having that. We're not mind-readers. And now we wait, you and me, for the investigations to slowly wind their way to a conclusion. We are moving forward, though, and I must not forget to hand over the pheasant to Mrs Pritchard, and you must explain to Ben – but let's finish our cuppas first, eh?'

As they walked back to the kitchen, Annie felt she hadn't had such a tiring day for a very long time. She also hoped Daphne Pritchard was right about Lisa bearing no likeness to Davey, for was Annie the only one who had noticed how the colour of Lisa's hair exactly matched Davey's?

Chapter Six

That evening, Fran arrived back from the aft shift ready to drop, but as she slipped into the low light of the kitchen, the first thing she saw was her mam soothing Lisa while trying to pour milk into a pan.

'Oh, Mam, it's after midnight, ' Fran whispered. 'Let me wash and change into my nightie, then I'll take her. Can't be getting the yellow on her.'

She rushed into the scullery, strip-washed, making sure she had shaken any powder from her hair, and then put her clothes in a bundle for dadding tomorrow. Slinging on her nightgown, old cardigan and a pair of socks, she came back into the warmth and took the babe.

'Howay, pet,' Annie said, a tired smile on her face. 'That'll get your Davey's heart a-racing.' Fran tried to smile back. 'Anything wrong?' her mam asked as she poured the milk and put it on the hot plate, just for a minute, literally.

As she paced the kitchen with Lisa, Fran shook her head. 'No, just weary. I prefer the fore shift.'

Now that the milk was warm, Annie poured it into Lisa's bottle and Fran sat in her da's armchair by the range, looking at those dimpled hands trying to hold the bottle. She did not look at Lisa's fair hair, for children were often blonde, it meant nothing, or so Fran had been telling herself since she'd had time to absorb the bairn's arrival. The problem was, she didn't know if she believed it.

While Lisa snuffled and sucked, Fran listened to her mam tell of her day, of Mr Smithson's visit, and of Daphne

Pritchard. 'So, we have the bairn for now?' was all she asked, feeling the weight of the child, and though she knew nothing was this wee being's fault, she resented everything about her.

At half-past twelve, she insisted her mam sleep in the front room, which was where Fran herself slept, with Davey when he was home. Annie protested, but Fran was adamant as she changed and winded Lisa, pacing with her, a gauze square on her shoulder. Was pacing all one was destined to do with a baby?

'No, we take this in shifts.' Fran's voice was almost a chant, because Mrs Oborne had said that rhythm helped settle babes. 'I will sleep in your bed and Lisa will go in her cot. It is down from the attic?' Annie nodded and Fran continued, 'Good. I am on the aft shift this week, so I can lie in. You will be up with the lark, to get Ben to school and deal with the babe. So best you do as you're told and go to bed.'

Her mam nodded and did just that. Fran took the bairn up to the front bedroom, realising that she needed changing, *again*. She winded her, *again*, and laid her in the old cot Ben had put together and wiped clean. She carried the nappy down, sorted it, left it in the bucket with the others, all of which had been kindly donated by the village, her mam had said. They would be boiled up in the morning. Fran returned to the hall, walking past the front room where she did not want to lie, not now, because . . . Well, because.

She kept her cardigan on and crept upstairs into the cold bed, listening to Lisa snuffling, moving and then sleeping. Eventually, she managed to do the same, though at two Lisa's crying woke her. Drunk with tiredness, Fran stumbled from her bed and stood over the cot.

'Hush,' she whispered. 'Hush, little one.' She reached

over the bars and rubbed Lisa's tummy, but she was having none of it and struggled to sit, then fell back. Fran crooned 'Cheek to Cheek', for little Eva had sung that at her and Davey's wedding tea, but then her voice faded. 'Are you Davey's bairn, with your hair so blonde?' she whispered. 'Is my Davey like Bob? Has the other world changed him? Is that really why you were placed on our doorstep?'

She'd have sworn not, for she and Davey were two halves of a whole, but why would Daisy bring this child here, to Fran and her mam? Why?

She heard a tap on the door, so light it was more like a scratch. 'Go to bed, Mam, it's my shift. You'll wake our Ben, and he needs his kip,' she called quietly.

The door opened, and it was the lad himself.

'I'm not a bairn, Franny,' whispered Ben. 'I could be in the pit next year.'

'But you won't be, you have your education,' she replied.

He came to stand beside her. 'She's a poor wee thing, Franny. Whoever's she is.'

Did he, too, think she was Davey's? Fran stared at him.

Ben leaned into her. 'She needs looking after, so best you pick her up, eh? It's what our da would have wanted.'

Fran reached down and picked up Lisa, then wrapped her in the blanket made of knitted squares that the women of Leadenhall Terrace had produced just that afternoon, in a matter of hours. She handed her to Ben, and he paced back and forth as Lisa nestled in his arms.

'I know she has blonde hair, Franny, and I reckon it vexes you, but it means nowt. I were thinking, you see. William's sister has blonde hair and so did he, in the photo they have. His is dark now. Don't be tricked, our Fran. Davey isn't Bob.'

'But—' she murmured.

71

'No buts, buts are bad, that's what our da would have said. He'd have taken her in, not minding whose she was. So brace up. There's no fault in this wee bairn.'

Fran found herself laughing, wondering when this lad had become so wise. Together they nursed Lisa until she slept. Only then did they separate, he back to his room, and Fran tucking herself into her mam's bed, where she slept without waking till morning, though her dreams were not of acceptance but doubt.

When Fran did come to, at ten, Lisa was gone from the cot and the room was still dark from the blackout. She pulled it aside to find the sky was blue. She dressed and hurried down to take over her shift and pace with Lisa, only to find her mam had tucked the babe into the cart, fashioning a harness to contain her and a pillow to prop her up, and had wheeled her to the hens. Fran went out to Lisa as her mam returned to the scullery. Lisa was asleep, her face in the shade. Fran studied her: the shape of her eyes, which she knew were a grey-blue, her nose, her chin. Why are you here? she thought.

Hurrying to the corn container, Fran lifted the lid and scattered the seed through the chicken wire. 'There, ladies and gentlemen.' She lifted her face to the sun. 'Ah well, Da, a right kettle of fish, eh, but you've done a good job with our Ben. He has more common sense in his little finger than I have in my whole hand, and he has a brain too. Look at how he's almost as good as Davey at setting a crossword – earning money from it, too.'

She rested her head against the wire, for it was Davey who had brought on Ben, Davey who had contacted his own editor and helped set up the young people's column in the crossword magazine. 'Davey's a good man, Da,' she whispered, 'but I'm so bliddy angry. Is it at him? Or *her*? Or the bliddy situation? It's not the bairn's fault, but I can't . . .

Well, I can't ... I don't know what I mean, but she has blonde hair, Da, and she were left on *our* doorstep.'

Her mam called her in for tea and toast and left her to eat while she boiled the nappies in the scullery copper. Fran listened to her mam's shouts as she talked of the party Sophia was intent upon to celebrate Viola's twentieth on 14 November, with the assistance of the evacuees.

'Aye, it's definitely to take place in the ballroom, or so Alfie said Sophia would like, when he called in first thing to bring more milk from Farmer Thompkins. Seems that, though the bairns keep changing their minds about what to do for Melanie's farewell, what is certain is that they liked the sound of having whatever it is in the ballroom. It seems it is just neglected, and all it needs is a coat of paint, and a clean.'

'Really? Oh Lord. So these bairns – tell me, is it all of them, or one in particular?'

'I don't need to answer that,' her mam laughed. 'No doubt we'll be hearing Madame Eva's further thoughts as they come to her, and it'll be no use hiding below the parapets, for she'll hunt us down. There's also a really big tree on madam's list for the Christmas farewell, and apparently something a mite more Christmassy than just a few carols, though what I dare not think. Some sort of a show was being talked about. I daresay the minute Eva returns from school she'll be peeking in there and giving it the once-over. Alfie says it *could* be a mite grand, with some elbow grease.'

'And somehow we'll all have volunteered.' Fran dusted her hands free of crumbs and delivered her plate to the scullery.

She was about to wash it when her mam said, 'I'd rather you took the bairn out and about in her cart, like I used to take you three. Might as well get the public bit over and done with.'

Fran really didn't want to, but nodded. 'Aye, it's a nice enough day. I'll be back for the bus.'

When she returned to the cart, Lisa was awake and though she'd slipped down a little, she was gurgling at the hens. 'Howay, little one, let's go and meet the world, eh, and the gossip.'

She walked the bairn up the back lane, but only after her mam had brought out a white bonnet she'd knitted while Fran was asleep. 'It'll keep her warm, for that wind has a bitter edge, even though the sun is out. Don't forget, you must get on with Sophia's knitting on the bus. I'll put it in your bag, and make sure Bert keeps it safe in his cab. Can't let all else go while we sort things here, lass. Who knows, our Madame Eva might request knitted decorations for the Christmas tree.'

Fran groaned, then headed towards Main Street, the bairn laughing as they bumped over the cobbles. Fran talked to her about Auld Hilda, then alongside the back of Mrs Pritchard's she picked up the wooden spoon the babe had dropped on her blanket. She held it out to her and Lisa grabbed it. The bowl was nearest her mouth. She bit on it. 'You keep doing that. It will help with that top tooth.'

They continued over the cobbles, Lisa giggling away, and it was a good sound. There was some colour in her cheeks, which were still too hollow.

'Ah well, Lisa,' Fran said softly. 'Here we are, you and I. Do you know, me da made a cart like this one, which could be pushed or hooked on a bike for when Mam took one of us with her to the shops. This one should have proggy frames in it. What are those, you ask? Well, you stretch your hessian across the frame and cut strips of material to prod through, and you end up with your own proggy rug. But there's time enough for you to learn more about them. So that's what should be in this cart – not a bouncing bairn like you.'

She peered over the handles, but Lisa's hair was hidden by the bonnet, and she couldn't see her grey blue eyes. Eyes that were paler than Davey's rich blue, even if her hair was a match.

'Stan, Sid and Norm built it from Da's design to help the co-op. Our Madge attaches it to straps on her bike and toils with it to Massingham Hall. Maybe Stan will build another, so they can take you as well as the rugs. Maybe.' For who knew if Lisa would be staying? Who knew bliddy anything?

She reached Main Street, turned left and carried on, for this walk was to bring anything out into the open that the community might feel needed saying and it was right that they said it to her. Aye, this was her kettle of fish, for after all Lisa was here because Daisy was someone Davey knew, and Fran wasn't having her mam facing any repercussions.

Beatrice Adams, Maisie's mam, stopped her bike on her way to a customer. Fran could see the spuds and even a marrow in her basket. Ah, that must be for old Mr Norton, whose wife had died and whose rheumatics were too bad for him to work his allotment any more. He was right partial to a bit of marrow.

Beatrice leaned her bike against the wall, grinning at Fran. 'Heard so much about her – let's have a peek. Heard about Daphne Pritchard too. Makes me feel right bad for thinking the worst of her. But . . .'

Fran shrugged. 'Well, she *was* a right pain, but it seems that it only needed Reverend Walters to work a miracle.'

Mrs Adams let Lisa play with her finger. 'Ah well, miracles help, but best if we all remember that we need to sort out the facts, eh, before letting summat dark build to a bliddy great wave, our Franny?'

Fran straightened, not able to meet the shopkeeper's eyes. Beatrice wasn't finished, though. 'Best, our Fran, that no one thinks too much around a tot turning up on the doorstep or they'll end up going down the plughole. I expect your lad'll be phoning today, as you go to the bus. He'll need to know about Lisa because he won't have heard, unless he's got lugs like a bat. But I'd better get on. Old Norton likes a chat just as much as he likes a marrow.'

She pushed her bike back onto the road and pedalled off. Fran pushed Lisa on, knowing she could expect the women to be standing on their doorsteps, and they were. One, Mrs Young, waved a wooden teething ring. Fran stopped.

'By, can't have you bashing Madge again, eh?' said Mrs Young. 'This was our Sandra's, and for her bairn if she has one, but Andy's gone off to war, and they weren't a good pair anyway, first boyfriends aren't. Though your Davey worked out like a dream – joined at the hip, you were, from the minute you arrived into the world, our Franny. Nice to know your lad so well, eh? Don't forget that you really do.'

Fran nodded, not wanting to hear about how well she knew Davey. 'Sandra's all right in the sewing workshop, is she, Mrs Young?'

Mrs Young shook her head as the other women of Leadenhall Terrace listened and more joined them, including Daphne Pritchard. 'She's not really got enough vision. Her good eye looks like a fried egg by the end of the day. She needs different work, so if you hear of any, let me know, eh?'

'What about the Massingham family?' called Mrs Pritchard. 'Mrs Massingham's to have a bairn, and she and Viola can't cope with eleven bairns and a wee one, even with the co-op.'

Fran left them to it, for the talk at the Hall was indeed of Sandra being asked, but that was up to Sophia to organise, or Viola. She hurried now, because time was drawing on and she had a few more streets to walk along. Would Davey phone? Would she answer? If she did, she must be calm.

Beatrice said she must realise the truth and not be drowned in a dark wave. Mrs Young had said Fran really knew Davey. Could the two women read minds?

She knew the answer as she walked on and others came to their doors, handing over a gauze nappy, or a baby's bottle, or a cardigan. They were placed around Lisa's feet, as though in homage, and Fran was patted on the arm, and told what a grand lad Davey was. As she arrived back home, Fran dragged the cart up the front step and into the hall. No, Beatrice Adams and Mrs Young weren't witches, they were members of Massingham village, so no more needed to be said.

By the time her mam had propped Lisa up in a high chair lent by a neighbour and was feeding her mashed carrots with a bit of egg yolk to see how she fared with it, Fran was on her way to the bus. Sarah waited at the end of her terrace, Beth at the end of the next, and all three of them walked together. Their bottles of water made their bags heavy, as usual, but today their knitting was jammed between these and their gas masks. They slowed as they approached the call box, and at five to twelve on the dot, the telephone began to ring.

Fran hung back. Sarah yanked at her arm. 'On you go, lass. Look at Bert sitting behind the wheel making that face of his, holding up five fingers because he wants to go at midday.'

Fran pulled open the heavy call-box door and let it ease shut behind her. She lifted the receiver. 'Hello, Davey.'

'Fran. Fran, it's good to hear your voice. I haven't long, and I tell you, lass, I'll be right pleased when you're back on the fore shift, for I have to beg our Norah to let me out for me dinner a few minutes early so I can catch you.'

'How are you, Davey?'

77

'Bliddy perplexed. I overheard Norah telling Daniel to get to the office ten minutes ago. He's not back but something's amiss, I reckon. I miss you, Franny, and the beggar of it is that this war's going on a while yet – but if you repeat that, I'll have to kill you.' He laughed; she tried. 'Fran, what is it?' he asked.

Bert hooted as she said at last, 'Daisy left her bairn on our doorstep yesterday, with a letter saying she'd be back, but until then she knew me and Mam'd look after the little scrap.'

The receiver felt heavy and cold in her hand; the strap of her linen bag dug into her shoulder. Bert hooted again, and Sarah and Beth were outside the door, gesturing for her to hurry up. The silence continued until Davey whispered, 'How bliddy dare she? How did she even know our addre—' He stopped. 'Oh no, she asked for it, to write and apologise to you for the lies she told about me and her . . . Well, you know – I told you. So how's the bairn? Is she all right?'

'Oh, so you know the bairn is a she? Do you know that she has fair hair? Pretty bitty thing, called Betty.' Fran could hear the coldness in her voice and she didn't bliddy care, for Daniel hadn't said whether it were a boy or lass when he came home for their wedding.

Davey paused again, and when he replied he sounded strange. 'What do you mean? I know because Daniel's da told him, of course, and he told me because we work together, and are marrers. What's wrong, Fran? Are you ill? Oh no, of course, you're tired. You and your mam must have been up with the lass, when you've both enough to do. Oh God, I'm right sorry, Franny. It's all my fault, I shouldn't—'

The girls were pulling at the door. 'He says he's going,' Beth yelled.

'I reckon he means it,' Sarah added, waving to Bert like a madwoman. 'We're coming. Wait. Wait.'

'Shouldn't what, Davey?' Fran shouted into the receiver. 'What? But I have to go. Bert's in a hurry.' She snatched a look at her watch. 'Oh, bliddy hell.'

'I'll phone tomorrow, see how you are, how things are, an' all, and—'

She slammed the receiver down because she felt as though she never wanted to speak to him again and couldn't think straight.

Chapter Seven

Davey replaced the receiver, suddenly aware of the noise of Bletchley Park reception hall, and almost stumbled out of the booth, glancing around for Daniel, but there was no sign. He hurried across the hall and down the steps. The wind was sharp, but it didn't clear his head. Fran? Oh Fran, it's not my fault, so don't be like that.

He crunched along the gravel to the canteen hut. Daniel must be digging into spam, or whatever culinary heights the ladies had achieved today.

A breeze rippled the surface of the lake. He found his steps faltering, for his wife was off to work in a munitions factory, so no wonder she was edgy. After all, the work was hard, tiring and dangerous enough without having to cope with a babe descending out of the ether. A babe who would need feeding, changing and soothing throughout the night as well as during the day, and Fran and her mam had enough to do and Daisy damn well wasn't their problem. Or his, come to that.

His head was whirling with the news and he stood, his hands deep in his pockets, staring at nothing, feeling rage and worse – guilt. Damn it, why the hell had he given Daisy Fran's address? Why had he and Daniel helped her at all? Well, for the sake of the dead pilot, was why. If there ever was a pilot?

Suddenly nothing stood firm. Nothing. Had they been duped, or rather, had they caused Fran to be duped? Damn Daisy to hell. What had she been thinking? Well, what she always had – what was best for her. Yes, that was it. Whoever the father was, Daisy was making waves, which was what she always did.

This time it was Franny paying the price. God in heaven, she would be worn to a thread, for she'd be trying to take as much weight off her mam as she could. Would Mrs Hall get too attached and grieve all over again if or when the damned girl came back to pick up the babe? Ben would help, though. Yes, and Stan. Of course they would, and the other girls, not to mention the village. But not him, not down here. He quickened his pace. 'Damn it,' he cursed. 'Damn and bliddy damn.'

He stared from the canteen hut to the lake. He needed to walk round it, find some peace, but Daniel might have collected spam fritters for him and they'd be congealing. The thought of them made him feel sick, but if he didn't eat he'd never last till teatime, or at least his stomach wouldn't; it would rumble away and drive everyone mad. He laughed, though it was a bitter sound, because he was being ridiculous; a rumble wouldn't be heard above the clatter of the Typex decoding machines as they bashed at their keys.

He set off again, not even cheered by the promise of scones for tea at Mrs Siddely's because he felt very alone and all he wanted was to be with Franny, to beg forgiveness for causing her problems and making her angry. But had it been anger? It could just have been tiredness.

He pushed open the canteen door and the muggy smell of overcooked cabbage was the same as ever, even though his world seemed to have shifted. He slowed, picturing his da's allotment, the rows of cabbages, leeks and sprouts, and how the gang would sit in Simon Parrot's shed, the Canary Club, and sift the birdseed, drinking home-made beer while the girls tried the elderberry wine. Finally, they might do a bit of digging or picking, talking quietly. Home. Together. Auld Hilda's slag heap smouldering.

He should have asked Fran if she'd pulled any cabbages when she was round there. He shook his head. Don't be so bliddy daft. She'd probably have slammed the phone down, for of what importance was cabbage when she and her mam had just become mothers to a stranger's babe?

Mothers? At that moment the real consequences of Daisy's actions began to take root: his wife and his mother-in-law were being asked by Daisy to be just that to her child – mothers.

Over to the left he saw his fellow lodgers, Colin and Martin, and between them two spaces. He spun round to the serving hatch, scanning the queue. No Daniel. He hadn't been by the phones, so where the hell was he, and why had he been called to the office?

He made his way through to the decoders' table, tapping Colin on the shoulder. 'Howay, where's our lad?'

Colin looked round at him. 'I have no idea. He went to the office, didn't he? Been a naughty boy, eh? I thought you'd bump into him after talking to the beloved Fran.'

Davey shook his head, setting off to the door, then calling back over the clatter of cutlery, plates and chatter, 'I'll linger about and find out what's going on.'

Martin cupped his ear, frowning, and shook his head. Davey pointed to the queue and then to his watch, holding up his hand, fingers spread. Colin gave him a nod. Aye, Davey thought, five minutes should do it.

He ran back, skidding to a stop when he saw Daniel leap down the steps, his striped scarf streaming behind, and set off at a trot towards Davey, who waved him down.

'You've been a while?'

Daniel shook his head. 'I had to get hold of Dad, to get him to pass on the details of Daisy's mother-and-baby

82

home to someone and the office let me use their phone to pass on the bloke's contact details.'

'Hang on . . . Daisy?' Davey muttered. 'Lord, I'm beginning to hate that bliddy girl. She's only gone and literally dumped her bairn on Fran's back step with a note, for heaven's sake, saying she knew Fran and her mam would look after Betty. Which happens to be the name of Fran's wee sister who died soon after birth. Heaven knows if that's the baby's name in reality. So this bloke . . . Daisy is . . .' He was unable to find the words.

'So that's why this fellow from some local authority wanted that information and "more" but "couldn't explain",' Daniel sighed, pulling Davey along. 'Come on, we have a date with spam, and we'll talk as we eat. No doubt Colin and Martin will add a dollop of advice, wanted or not.' They shared a look, trying but failing to laugh.

As they neared the door, Daniel said, 'It was a Mr Smithson, who Doris said was rather posh who left the message, which might well be why she let me touch the precious desk telephone. What's more, she pretended to type throughout the brief chat with my dad, but I could feel the draught from her wagging ears. Dad said he'd call Smithson from the home, which is where he was off to, that minute. Then I had to call Smithson back to let him know, and Doris was right, he *is* posh. When I pressed, asking if they'd found Daisy, as I assumed that's why he wanted to know these things, he merely said, "Not quite."'

Daniel opened the canteen door, saying over his shoulder, 'So your news explains the whole damn thing.'

Davey entered into the cabbage fug again, hot on Daniel's heels, and made for the serving hatch. There was hardly any queue but why would there be, because their shift was already seated. They didn't even look at their plates, but thanked the women serving behind the counter and turned back towards their table, skirting around the others until they reached their groups. They squashed themselves onto the bench between Colin and Martin. Davey nodded at those sitting on the opposite side of the table, but they were all too busy discussing the answer to a crossword.

Colin waited for Davey to finish his spam fritters, then asked quietly, 'What's up? Seems to be a bit of bustling about with you two?'

Daniel had finished too, leaving the batter on the side of his plate as always, just like Eva and her parsnips. But Davey couldn't bear to remember details of his Massingham world because what he wanted was to *be* there, with Fran, helping her. He turned away, too, from Fran's tone, because it was all so confusing and then suddenly he wondered if Daisy was perhaps being kind? Had she in a clumsy way been trying to replace Annie's dead babe? He shook his head.

Martin leaned forward and called across Daniel. 'Come on, out into the fresh air. We can't talk here.'

They left their plates on the trolley and headed out, passing a table of Wrens. 'No pud today, boys?'

Martin shook his head. 'Sweet enough, but you might like two, eh?'

'Ouch,' muttered Daniel.

Once they were outside, Martin shrugged. 'That one has a tongue like a razor, pitches in to one and all from a position of nil strength. There's talk she's going. Let's hope so.'

Davey thought of Mrs Pritchard. 'We've one of them in Leadenhall Terrace, but there's no talk of *her* going.'

They stopped to look down at the lake, where ripples still played. Colin and Martin lit their pipes, sucking fit to burst, while Daniel and Davey turned their backs to the wind and lit up their Woodbines. It was then that Davey filled them all in, concluding with Fran's strangeness as the phone conversation drew on, her fury, or was it tiredness? Her silences, his silences . . . 'That damn girl just goes on causing trouble, unless she was trying to be kind and replace the lost babe?' he muttered. 'It isn't my fault, though it feels like it is.'

At this Colin shook his head, stabbing at him with his pipe, his university scarf hanging down. 'Don't be so bloody daft, man. Of course Daisy's not being kind – she's her usual selfish self. No wonder Fran's strange and angry, and can't you see why that might be, for God's sake?'

Davey didn't understand. 'I've just told you – that damned Daisy left her bairn on the back step, that's why. How would anyone feel if—'

Martin dug his hands in his pockets, keeping his eyes on the lake. 'What most would feel is – why *my* back step?'

Still Davey didn't understand and he in turn stared at the lake, where three geese were landing. They were so beautiful in the air, but such a flurry of ungainliness and panic on landing, much like a trainee pilot. That image brought Daisy's RAF boyfriend to mind, and Davey realised he didn't even know his name. Then he thought about Daisy's accusation against him, Davey Bedley, who had supped too much beer and been led back to her room, but was too drunk to do anything even if he'd wanted to, which he hadn't. He'd only been capable of collapsing on the girl's bed, on top of the covers, not under them.

He blessed again the broken elastic that had caused him to sew up his drawers, thereby disproving her accusation, because the thread would have had to be broken to remove them. Her lie had been firmly laid to rest after she had done the same to Daniel, just because she'd wanted someone to believe they shared responsibility for the care of her child. Who on earth else had she tried to implicate?

'What are you thinking about?' Daniel asked him.

Davey's cigarette was burning down quickly in the wind. He drew on it, coughing. 'Daisy's lad dying so young, leaving a bun in the oven, a bun that you and I, Daniel, were almost conned into believing could have been ours. Were we fools to help her in the end? Is that why she left the lass with Fran? Thinking we'd just go on being there? No wonder Fran's—'

'Oh, Holy Mother,' Colin almost shouted. 'Fran's what?' He sounded almost belligerent as he stabbed at Davey with his pipe, his chin thrust forward.

'Fed up, tired, furious . . . Oh, I don't know, just strange, cold, angry, not like her at all, but then we were cut off.'

Martin chimed in. 'Or have you considered that she just put the receiver down?'

'What?' Daniel stared at Martin. 'Why would she do that to Davey?'

Martin shook his head at the pair of them. 'Call yourselves bright sparks, able to break codes, even recognise the signature of a Nazi signals operator so you can place the origin of a message and therefore track troop movements? Oh, Lord save us.'

Davey was looking from Colin to Martin, then Daniel. Finally he shouted, 'What the hell are you talking about? Aye, she was bliddy strange, and cross, but that wasn't my fault. How could it be? I said I were sorry, what more—'

Even as he was saying it, he was running through their conversation in his mind and stumbled when he came to – now, what was it? Oh, that was right: 'I said, "I'm right sorry, Franny. It's all my fault, I shouldn't—"' His anger sharpened, his confusion was gone. 'She said, "Shouldn't what, Davey? What?" That's what she said. Then the line went dead.'

He stared at his marrers, his *Bletchley* marrers, realising at last that Fran, who he had loved all his life, known all his life, didn't trust him and thought the bairn was his. He stormed blindly off, ignoring the lake and the geese now busying themselves on the far bank. Instead, he strode towards the decoders' hut, hearing rapid heavy footsteps crunching the gravel as the three of them ran after him. He quickened his stride, but they gained on him and now Daniel swung him round. He tried to pull free, yelling, 'She thinks . . . me wife thinks I'm lying. How could she? How dare she when I love her, live for her, breathe her? How could she, just because the babe has fair hair? Yes, that's what she said. Well, the bairn's da probably had that colour—'

Colin and Martin caught them up. 'Shut up,' Colin roared, pushing Daniel to one side and grabbing Davey's lapels, shoving his face so close that Davey reeled from the smell of tobacco on his breath. 'Shut up – grow up. What the hell do you expect? A bairn turns up on your wife's doorstep, the daughter of Daisy *and* . . . ? Eh? Of course she'll wonder about that, anyone would, so you button down and sort this bloody mess out. It's not Fran's fault, it's that damn Daisy's – and yours, for not seeing what's under your nose when Fran rang, so don't go getting on your high horse or you'll fall and break your neck, or your heart, you daft fool.'

Davey tried to pull away. 'That's rubb—'

'It damn well isn't.' Martin, standing beside Colin, took over, though Colin still gripped Davey's lapels. Martin's voice was a mere whisper. 'Think about it. There's that Beth you talk of ditched by a husband posted away – ditched for his more interesting tart, and now he's got a baby. So . . . so . . . Mr David Bedley, decipher that, for heaven's sake.' Martin put up his hand. 'I know, I know, the letter didn't say it was yours, but bloody hell, that's what it looks like.'

Daniel stood silently by, listening to Martin. 'I never thought . . . Oh, that little bitch.'

Davey swung round, at last loosening Colin's grip. 'She's not a bitch, Daniel, but I want to call her that, for I'm so bliddy angry that she can doubt me. How?'

This time it was Martin who pulled Davey round as Daniel hesitated, trying to find the words to reply, but then he found some, and they came in a torrent. 'You are a bloody fool, Davey Bedley. Have you lost your mind? Fran's the last person in the world I'd ever call that awful word. How could you even think I meant her? It's Daisy who is. Well, I'm going right back to the office to call my dad again, he might be back, or I can get Mum to phone him at the home. I want proof of this pilot's existence. I want to know who he was, what he looked like, who knows, maybe the staff saw a photo?'

Davey's hands were clenched, he felt buffeted by the shouting. Others were staring as they passed. Daniel wasn't finished.

'And I don't want to hear even a tiny bit more nonsense from you, so shove off and feel martyred somewhere else. Tell you what, you said you jump in the beck summer or winter, so there's the damned lake – take a run at it, it'll cool you down. How can you not see that anyone would wonder why *Davey's* wife? Why? It's so bliddy obvious why the poor girl'd think that.'

Davey stomped off into the clatter of the decoding hut, hating the world, Daisy, even Fran, because none of this was fair. He shrugged out of his mac and draped it over the back of his chair, keeping his scarf on. Norah looked up from her desk. 'Where's Daniel?' she called above the noise of the clacking machines. 'You're usually together.'

Davey merely scowled at her, but heard Martin tell her that the lad was finding out something to do with the earlier message she'd passed him. Norah snorted, the smoke from her cigarette resting in the ashtray, streaming straight up. 'You'll not to get into heaven, Davey lad. St Peter doesn't like scowls, or tantrums.'

Colin stopped by her desk. 'He's a lost cause, Norah, destined for a warmer place. He has the most dreadful habits, the picking of the nose, the—'

Norah roared with laughter and waved him on. 'One day, when I feel stronger, you can tell me all, but I haven't had my lunch yet.' She took note of the time. 'And high time I was recharging the fuel pit, too.' She rose, nodding towards Davey. 'He's usually sunshine and light, which we need in this dim, dark place.'

Davey heard as he checked the settings on his machine, even though he knew nothing would have changed since he had adjusted them this morning. 'Well, it's your fault,' he snapped, 'for it's your grade that insists the blinds are on blackout duty virtually all the time, so no wonder it's . . .' He stopped, staring at the machine.

Norah pulled a face at Colin and Martin. 'Oops, love's young dream's not such a happy bunny. Bit of a barney with the wife, eh?'

'Something like that,' Martin nodded. 'Must get on, there's a war to win and every minute I'm away from my machine the defeat of the monsters is in doubt, such is my brilliance.'

Norah blew a raspberry, slipped into her huge knitted cardigan and tightened her scarf, which she, like everyone else, wore almost all year round as protection against the draughts from the ill-fitting windows. 'I sincerely hope you left some spam, pig's ear though it is.'

She waited for Davey's usual retort, but Colin quickly filled the silence. 'It's not the ear, oh senior lady.'

This time she directed her usual reply to Colin rather

than Davey as she headed out of the door. 'Well, they could still slip in a pig's ear, so stop being a smarty-pants.'

Davey heard this and the laughter, but today it meant nothing. He began work, decoding the messages that had been piled high beside his machine while he was on his meal break. Even as the fury raged he still marvelled at the brilliant minds behind the creation of the huge Bombe machine that whirred and rumbled every night to unscramble the new Nazi code setting, which changed every twenty-four hours at midnight. The new setting was carried to their hut the moment it was cracked and was useful only until the following midnight. All such a race against time.

But, he thought, I bet those brainboxes didn't have wives who had virtually accused them of being unfaithful, when he had long ago confessed his ridiculous drunken escapade and been laughed at for his incorruptible drawers. He punched in another and then another intercepted message forwarded from listening stations all over the country.

Davey felt Daniel brush past his chair, stopping to tap the top of his head. Davey ignored him, relentlessly punching, clack-clack.

Daniel settled himself down at the next table before saying, 'Mum's going to contact Dad, and get him to write to me if he uncovers anything. If they find a description of him, you can tell Fran, and that will put paid to your mammoth sulk. Anyway, there's time between now and then to grow up. Stranger things have happened.'

Davey ignored him, pressing an A key and producing a D, and so on and on, until eventually the original message appeared in German. Davey knew enough of the language to make it out . . . He stretched.

Yes, this was what was clever and important, not Fran's doubts. Not his marrers shouting. After all, he shouldn't have to prove himself – that's what none of them would admit. Fran and he had known one another for a lifetime, and she should therefore trust him.

An hour later, a Wren brought more intercepted cyphers and took away those he had completed. He sat back, pulled his scarf tighter and began on the new pile.

At the end of his shift he took the bus home, travelling with the other three, but not talking. He couldn't. His throat felt tight, his mouth was dry, his mind strange and empty. The four of them walked through the village in silence.

Mrs Siddely had made scones because it was almost the end of the week and it was a reward to the men for helping the children with their homework. They ate their sandwiches first, then their scones, but still Davey couldn't join in the chat. He went up to his room after refusing a cup of tea and lay on his bed, wanting to be with Fran, but also to stop loving her; but all the time not knowing how he could live his life without her, because she was his life.

Daniel entered without knocking, a half-full bottle of Mrs Siddely's sherry in one hand and a glass in the other. He waggled the bottle at Davey. 'From our landlady. She says don't be such a daft fool, but knows you'll take no notice, so her orders are to finish the sherry, go to sleep and cope with your headache in the morning.'

He placed the bottle on the side table after pouring a glass full almost to the brim, closing the door quietly on his way out. Davey sat up, reaching for the glass but careful to spill none of its precious contents. He drank it down in one, coughing at the sweet, rough passage of the sherry. He had another, then another because he didn't know what to do with his mind, which was usually full of the joy of Fran. But Fran was angry, and thought the worst of him. He kept drinking, and slowly he grew tired and his eyes felt heavy.

Chapter Eight

The next day, Fran, Sarah and Beth met up as usual and headed for the bus. 'Any sleep last night, pet?' Beth asked.

Fran shook her head. 'Not a lot, but some. Lisa didn't want to settle. Ben was good, he took his share, singing a lullaby as she had woken up. It didn't send her to sleep, but it did me.' They laughed. 'Mam did her share during the day, bless her, and is getting back into the wee-bairn routine.'

They slowed at the call box, though Fran didn't know if she wanted to speak to Davey. The five minutes they waited passed slowly; there was no call. Finally, the clock above the dairy chimed midday. The bus idled. The workers were all on board except for the three of them and another two. Mrs Oborne was talking earnestly to Sandra Young.

'Is she pointing the girl towards Massingham Hall?' Sarah wondered, switching her bag from one shoulder to the other. 'By, this bottle of water gets heavier by the minute.' All the time, her eyes were on Fran until finally she nodded at Beth.

Beth gripped Fran's hand. 'We'd best go, and don't give Davey a thought. He'll be in a sulk because you were "off", nowt more. That's what men do when they've upset you, so don't you be thinking that he's the father. No, this is our Davey I'm talking about, well, *your* Davey – not Bob.'

'That's right. He's me brother, and he'll be spinning about. I could strangle him. It's time he grew up.' Sarah took Fran's arm and kept her walking.

Fran felt inexpressibly sad as they approached the bus, and then a sheet of newspaper caught her eye. It was being blown along the road, helpless in the power of the wind. She pulled away and picked it up, then smoothed it out, folding it neatly and dropping it into her bag. There, she thought, have some shelter, for she could do with a bit too.

She looked at Sarah and Beth; her heart was breaking, for this was so much bigger than a sulk. This was a lack of trust and she hated herself, but worse, she hated him, her Davey.

The three of them clambered up the bus steps. Bert shouted, 'Got your knitting tucked away with your water, I 'ope, for I remembered to bring me own bag today. We'll keep it in there, eh, once we arrive? Then it's clean and ready for you to get cracking again on our way home. By, it's taking a long time, girls, so best get a wriggle on, for I were thinking a few knitted Christmas decorations'd be a grand idea – sheep, a manger, a babe, robins. You can hang them on the Massingham Hall tree when you have the Christmas sing-song.'

'You drive, and keep your suggestions to yourself, or you'll be tied up in the wool and looking a mite like a lemon,' Mrs Oborne called. 'Let's get the cardigans done first, eh?'

Looking in his rear-view mirror, Bert cackled. 'Enough from you, you old besom.'

The girls walked down the aisle to the seat at the back. As Bert drove off, for Fran it was as it had always been, but at the same time nothing like it. She gripped Beth's hand when they sat down and whispered, 'I thought I understood about you and Bob, but I didn't, not until this bairn arrived. I'm sorry, really, truly I am.'

Beth squeezed back. 'The bairn is called Lisa, dear Fran. You need to start using her name, since she's to stay until a decision is made. Whatever's gone on, it's not her fault. Time to be a grown-up.'

Sarah took hold of Fran's other hand. 'Beth's right. She's a sweet wee thing, and Daisy is just taking advantage. It's me brother's fault for knowing her, but that's as far as it goes. You know that, you really do, and that she's not his, I'm sure.'

But she didn't sound sure, because who could be? Fran wanted to sink her head into her hands, because she couldn't get the blonde silky hair out of her thoughts, and that huge question: why *our* doorstep?

Bert changed gear and soon they were leaving Massingham behind. Out came the knitting, and talk around them drifted to Sophia's babe, and to the evacuees' Christmas party, which was now definitely to be held in the ballroom, and then on to Viola's twentieth as well.

Fran listened, because Christmas was a lifeline at the moment: the carols, the scent of pine, the decorations, the paper chains, the mince pies, the presents, the love . . . She finished a pearl row, turned the needles and started on a plain one. She didn't want to think of love. Instead, she said, 'You see, for the bairns the Christmas farewell has to be special so Melanie can remember the last time they were together. It'll not be on Christmas Day, but as near as makes no difference, or so Sophia told Mam.'

Sarah smiled. 'My mam says the bairns want to invite their school friends, and the villagers, young and old, to thank them properly for being kind.'

'My mam said if it seems to be growing every second,' Beth laughed, 'that's because it is. But the bairns still don't know exactly what they want.'

Nearby, Mrs Oborne laughed as Maisie added, 'But they'll surely tell us when they *do* know, and every idea in between.'

'Aye,' called Mrs Oborne, 'but the co-op reckon it'll even come to bit of a show with singing and dancing, like the Factory Girls, but with carols thrown in, of course. They fear they'll be asked for Christmas-fairy costumes because our Eva said as much, but Abe said he'll not be a fairy, and an elf was out too.'

Fran found herself laughing. How strange. She seemed to be operating on two levels.

Tilly Oborne added, 'Have they pinned your feet to the floor until you agree to do a spot too, you girls? I bet they want Ralph and the lads to sing, an' all, for they make a good sound, or so I gather Eva thinks. So, best you girls get involved and make sure that somehow you can make it a silk purse, not a sow's ear, eh?'

'You girls knitting as well as chatting?' Bert called. They grimaced and carried on. As always, they dropped almost more than they knitted, but progress was being made and that's what they had to remember.

They dropped their knitting into Bert's bag as they left the bus and he muttered, 'Well, no doubt she'll be touched, but I pity the poor pet who has to wear them, that's all I can say.'

Mrs Oborne, the last to leave, stopped on the steps. 'Well, you always say a sight too much, our Bert, so put a sock in it.'

He winked at the girls. They laughed their way towards the guards and as they reached Barry, Fran felt better, for this was work and she welcomed the need to concentrate, for it was most likely to be detonators, as it had been all week.

'By, our Fran,' murmured Barry, glancing at her pass and looking down into her bag, checking for metallic contraband, 'it's surprising you haven't brought beer instead of water, or maybe a bit of brandy, since it's said you're looking after a friend's bairn. Poor lass, you'll have found out for yourself that such a wee thing doesn't know the meaning of sleeping through the night. Or our lad Pete didn't, anyway.'

'You've heard?'

Sarah was waiting with her as the other terrible twin, Harry, checked Beth's pass and bag. Barry just guffawed. 'Daft question, you know how news travels – it got to us this morning. Your mam'll likely welcome the little soul, after her sadness.'

'Stop your yacking, our Barry,' bellowed Mrs Oborne. 'We've jobs to get to. Just pass us through, or frisk us if you feel so inclined, but I warn you, me Steve won't care for that and will take you behind the bike sheds.'

Barry was laughing so much as he waved Fran and Sarah through that he started coughing and had to take a break. Mrs Oborne tutted. 'Now, this is a right pantomime. Come to think of it, I can see you as the back of a cow, and yon Harry as the front. 'Twould be an improvement on your looks anyway, our Harry. And Barry, I reckon being a cow's bum is what you're made for.'

Harry passed her through, laughing fit to burst. The group walked together into the Factory site, with its one-storey, flat-roofed buildings stretching far into the distance. One day, Fran thought, she'd walk right to the end of the straight road along which others were now heading on their way to their various sections. To the left were the heavy-shell-filling sections, dug into the ground to protect against accidents and the resulting massive blasts. They reminded her of the Anderson shelter that Dr Dunster had in his back garden, covered in earth for growing marigolds and lettuce in the summer.

On they walked, and Fran said to Sarah and Beth, 'Detonators are a damned sight easier than a babe that doesn't sleep. I can't wait to get to work on something that's only likely to blow me up, not drive me to distraction.' They smiled at each other as she carried on, 'Barry's words didn't gladden my heart, let me tell you. I thought things would improve quickly—'

Mrs Oborne sailed alongside like a galleon, linking an arm with Fran. 'Things will. It were Barry's missus who got up, anyway, and sleep is sometimes a trouble when a babe is teething, so of course when she has a full set of gnashers she'll sleep. Anyway, think how you would feel being carted about, dropped in a stranger's house and left to get on with it. You'd have a bit of a tantrum, wouldn't you, and a damned good cry.'

They turned left towards their section and as the path narrowed they were forced to go two by two. 'Like going into Noah's ark,' called Maisie, Beatrice Adams' daughter, who was ahead of them.

They entered through the double doors and hurried now into the whitewashed changing room, where the senior security officer for the section, Miss Cynthia Ellington, waited. Alongside was her fellow security officer, Mrs Raydon. Fran whispered as she passed, 'Glad to hear you and Simon Parrot have set the date, Cyn.'

'I'll rip out your Stan's gullet for him,' Cyn whispered back, 'for I swore the lads to secrecy until I had my thoughts in order. We just felt Christmas seemed as good a time as any, especially as I hear the evacuees are having a big party for Melanie. We thought we'd slip to the registry office earlier on the same day, have a quiet drink and then come and listen to the carols, or whatever they're cooking up, which is as fine a way to celebrate as any. There might even be snow, which would make me happy, for a Christmas without it is a bit flat.'

'Did you say a quiet drink?' queried Valerie. 'Well, best

you do come to the knees-up at Massingham Hall, for anything else is no way to kick off married life. I reckon you were even thinking of having that *quiet* drink at the Canary Club shed on the allotment, with the four reprobates, Stan, Sid, Norm and Ralph?'

Cyn flushed. 'Well, why not?'

As everyone changed their shoes, tucked their hair into turbans and removed all contraband, Sarah shouted over the hubbub, 'Because, dear senior security officer, the evacuees have plans for those four, and for anyone else who is showing any signs of life, or so we fear. And I reckon that's the very reason you chose that date – so you had a good excuse to say, "Sorry, evacuees, neither of us can help, we're getting married," as though that would stop the little devils. They'd drag you out of the registry office and bung you into Father Christmas outfits, soon as look at you.'

The group laughed as they continued to divest themselves of any hairgrips and jewellery. A couple of girls were winding their headscarves around their hair to keep out the explosive chemical powder they were working with. Sarah, Fran, Beth and Mrs Oborne replaced their own shoes with the mandatory detonator anti-spark felt ones.

As she checked her side of the room, Mrs Raydon asked, 'Any silk or nylon?'

Everyone waited for Maisie to say, 'Chance would be a fine thing.' The laughter was familiar and comfortable. Mr Swinton, the section supervisor, swept in at that moment, dressed in his green overalls. Maisie whispered, 'Hello, Daddy.'

Only Fran heard, and smirked. 'Will there be a wedding between him and your mam any day soon? At this rate, Simon could hire out the Canary Club as a celebration venue. Bet he'd sell his home-made beer and elderberry wine too.'

Maisie winked. 'That's a thought. As for a wedding, no idea, but as long as they both have a spring in their step, nothing else matters.'

'Afternoon, ladies. I'll quickly run through the rules, which of course you know by heart, but best to remind everyone. It seems to have worked so far.' He began ticking them off on his fingers while the women chanted them silently in their heads, much as they had done with their times tables when bairns.

'Any coughing, step away from the bench. Felt shoes for the detonator section. No singing there, no talking. No metal, no silk or nylon anywhere. Concentration, absolute obedience. No loose talk outside the Factory, or inside, because one section does not need to know what another does. No wandering about the Factory without an escort . . .' On he went, and again it was familiar, and comforting, to Fran.

Once the women had been double-checked for missed items they were ready, and followed either Miss Ellington or Mrs Raydon to their respective workshops.

As they walked down the corridor, Beth no longer tapped the war posters: Dig for Victory, Be like Dad, Keep Mum, We Can Do It. 'I don't tap because there's no reason to keep Bob safe any more. It's Heather's job.'

'Oh, Beth,' Fran said softly.

Fran wouldn't think of Davey in the decoder hut today. But she knew she would still tap the posters to keep him safe from a possible bomber. For a moment, she saw him. But she made herself go to the hatch, queue behind the others on the aft shift and pick up the small pot of fulminate of mercury she would use to fill the tiny copper detonator cups; mercury that could break down and seep into her skin or be inhaled. While she did that, the fore shift left.

99

As they moved into their places behind the steel screens with the Perspex windows and picked up the masks left by the fore-shift workers, Beth whispered, 'Tell me if I go mad like the hatters, eh? You'll know when you find me swinging from the lights, cackling.'

They all laughed quietly.

'No more talking, not even whispering,' Swinton said from behind them. 'Remember, it has been outlawed in detonators since the accident back in the spring.'

They apologised and he moved on. Fran loathed the masks they had to wear; the cotton-wool wadding grew hot and itched, made claggy by someone else's breath. It was a bit like a pitman's bath, with the father of the family using the water first, when it was nice and clean, but by the time it reached the youngest son, it was black as pitch.

Swinton walked back and whispered, 'On you go, lasses, be safe.'

It was the pitman's prayer, and quite right too, for Swinton had been a pitman until he had injured his back.

The girls adjusted their masks while the conveyor belt brought along the first tray of copper caps and Fran sprinkled in the mercury, using the spoon thingy, as they called it. As usual, Fran's head soon began to ache and her skin itched, especially around her mouth, but today she barely noticed. Next to her, Sarah worked silently, and on the other side Beth too. Fran was comforted; she was one of three, and when Viola was with them, one of four. Fran stopped, holding the spoon above the detonator caps, the copper glinting, her breath uneven, for she could hear the incomprehension in Davey's voice again. She could feel his arms around her on their wedding night, the love that was always in his eyes – for her. She thought of his drawers, sewn up. Or so he had told her. But had he told a lie? Her Davey?

'Fran,' whispered Beth, 'don't stop, we've targets.'

She nodded and worked on, in spite of the mask and the powder they all felt still seeped through into their lungs, then to the rest of their organs. She'd itch tonight as usual, but as long as she didn't make a mistake, as long as there wasn't an explosion, she'd be alive enough to scratch. As she placed the copper cap in its stand, she decided she must grow up, as Beth said, so she would go to the call box at twelve tomorrow and she and Davey would talk, and if he didn't call, she would go the next day, and the next. But . . . But . . . Why *had* Daisy left the bairn with her? So perhaps she wouldn't listen for his call. Perhaps Davey was like Bob, away in a different world, and it had changed him?

Work. Concentrate.

The hours passed. Fran sprinkled more powder on more copper caps, returning each completed tray to the hatch. She finished another and another, taking a ninth from the belt as it trundled along. What are you doing, Davey? Were you too angry to ring? Too guilty? Be quiet. Concentrate. She sprinkled the powder. Was her headache improving? She felt a cough coming. She lay down the spoon and stepped back, coughing. Sarah worked on, as did Beth, and Mrs Oborne, who turned briefly to check on them all. Dear Mrs Oborne. Dear Cyn Ellington. Did their security officer really think they'd let her get away with a couple of celebratory wedding drinks in the shed?

What would happen to Daisy's bairn when it was the Christmas 'do'? Would she be put to bed in the Massingham Hall nursery with the new baby? When would Sophia's babe arrive? Would they have the cardigans finished? Why not knit Christmas puddings to hang on the tree?

What would eventually be decided for Melanie's Christmas farewell? Would the evacuees really wear fairy and elf costumes, or perhaps Eva would decide on angel outfits?

She smiled at the thought of Eva as an angel. Would the lads and the Factory Girls be ordered to look like Christmas trees? Well, she wouldn't put it past that young madam, who'd probably deck them with paper chains. There'd have to be food for the villagers who would be trekking up in the cold, and there should be drinks. Perhaps they could order some elderberry wine from the Rising Sun, because surely the Massinghams would pay for it, or Ralph, and not just for Melanie's do, but for Viola's party as well? Oh, yes, Ralph'd want to make that special, but how special? Would he propose?

While Fran was thinking, she was also concentrating, filling the copper caps, placing them on the stand, and another, and another.

Should they invite the parents of the evacuees, except for the orphans, of course. But when was it to be? Very close to Christmas, but when? A Saturday, of course. If invited, where would the parents sleep? The girls could help Viola make up bedrooms at the Hall, or perhaps they could go back to Newcastle that evening by train? There'd have to be food for Viola's party too, so where would they get enough food for two parties? Could they run to mince pies? She drew close to Sarah. 'Perhaps we need to do some real thinking about Viola's party, as it's soonest?'

Sarah started to cough and stepped back from the bench. Fran moved with her. They stood together. 'Never sure if it's me imagination making me cough,' Sarah muttered, 'or all this powder around the place. And aye, we do need to get our heads around it. Mid-November isn't far away, and what about a gift? But forget the gift for now – it's the food that's one of the problems. Maybe everyone will bring some? That's best, but it's more the drink. Best I ask my mam, for I'm not going to trouble myself if the co-op and Sophia have already sorted that side of it. This business with Lisa has taken them off the boil, I reckon, but now the bairn's here until she isn't, they'd better get themselves back bubbling again, eh?'

Fran found herself giggling as Mrs Oborne sidled up to them, coughing. 'Damned powder, it gets in your throat and loses us time when we have to stand back like this. But we don't want to cough and drop the spoon, create a spark and Bob's your uncle. Remember them pantomimes where the old hag is standing there, then there's a puff of smoke and she's a lovely princess? Would suit me to be that hag, it would.'

Fran wasn't really listening. Instead, she was mulling over Sarah's words about the co-op getting back to bubbling again, because of course she needed to as well. After all, she and Davey had always said they would be able to deal with anything if they had one another, and the anger was hers, not his. The trust was up to her, too. She stepped forward to the bench and began work again.

Just before Mrs Oborne returned to her place, she stood behind Fran and whispered, 'I reckon the evacuees'll need more than a few carols and a bit of a dance. They need a fairy to wave a wand and magic something, for it's Christmas and . . .' She stopped. 'But what do I know? Perhaps the bairns could act out a carol, like a play, and bring in a song and dance, or we could get Alfred from Sledgeford to play the spoons, like a variety show?'

Beth, back in her place, swung round, frowning. 'Anything but Alfred and his perishing spoons.'

'Hush now,' Miss Ellington said as she walked past their bench. 'I know you four are expert enough to whisper and work safely, but we're nearly at the meal break, so leave it until then, eh?'

They collected more mercury from the hatch, filled more copper caps, working to a rhythm. Fran thought of her knitting and how dropped stitches interfered with her rhythm, but her mam said that by the time she was knitting for her own bairn, she'd be a dab hand. Her own bairn? No, she'd not go there, not this minute.

Their meal was some sort of vegetable stew, with what could be a bit of cheese. They weren't sure, but it was warm and they were hungry, and somehow food cleared 'their tubes', as Valerie said.

Mrs Oborne, all elbows and munching jaws, powered through it, and then her rice pudding. She rose to clear away her plate and bowl, which looked so clean they might have been licked, then collected the cups of tea. As she returned, a couple of women from the sewing workshop called out, 'You going to let us know when Harry and Barry need that cow costume you threatened them with, Tilly?'

Tilly's laugh was raucous. 'Aye, I'll leave that to hang over their heads as a threat when they start getting too big for their boots, eh?' She placed the tray in the centre of the table. 'Help yourselves, ladies.'

They did, sipping their tea, discussing their favourite carols, offering to bring something from their rations for the food at Melanie's Christmas 'do', which seemed the safest thing to call it at this stage. Susie from Minton village said she'd sound out Mildred and Stevie of the Rising Sun about his supplies of wine and beer. 'The pub could surely spare some,' she said.

Miss Ellington came and perched on the corner of the table. 'Don't forget, your mams will have had some ideas, but contribute what you have and they'll no doubt use a few of them.'

Before anyone could answer, a voice cut through their thoughts.

'Well, Fran Bedley, I hear that Davey's by-blow has been dumped on your doorstep, meaning you've been left carrying the baby, eh?'

Was it Fran's imagination or had the whole canteen fallen silent? She looked up at Amelia Cartwright. Amelia who delighted in causing trouble, who had spilled the beans in the Rising Sun about the Factory fence coming down in the snowstorm, which had been closely followed by a thwarted break-in. Amelia who had pinched the Factory Girls' booking at the Rising Sun on New Year's Eve when their shift had run late. Amelia who Miss Ellington told them had been warned for her loose talk. Amelia who had sent an anonymous note to Davey, telling him Fran and Ralph . . .

Fran felt hot with rage. She leapt to her feet. Miss Ellington grabbed the table to save herself as Fran pushed past.

Amelia stepped back, startled, but it was too late, Fran was already grabbing her shoulders and shaking the girl. Amelia shrieked. Fran was glad and shook her harder. Amelia's head bobbed in time, her shrieks louder still, but Fran had had more than enough of the whole bliddy world and her voice was hoarse as she roared, 'You're a bliddy bitch and know nothing. How dare you mention my husband? How dare you bad-mouth him? There's no one finer than Davey Bedley—'

She felt hands pulling at her as Amelia struggled. Still they pulled, until Fran was dragged away, leaving Miss ruddy Cartwright flushed and panting, but only for a moment, for then she swung round and screeched to Miss Ellington, who had helped grab Fran, 'You saw. You all saw Fran attack me.'

But the whole of the canteen, including the serving ladies, were magically talking or working, and no one had noticed a thing. Instead, Mrs Oborne forced Fran to sit, while Sarah and Beth and the rest of the rescue party straightened their clothes and sat too.

Miss Ellington responded. 'What I witnessed was you, Amelia, taunting Fran, as you often do to so many people, and for which you have received an official warning, as recommended in Mr Gaines's report. Remember him, here on behalf of Head Office to produce a post-accident investigative report?'

'I'm going to Mr Bolton, he'll sack the cow,' Amelia screamed.

'There's that word cow again. Is someone trying to tell us summat? Do I really need to get Harry into an outfit?' asked Mrs Oborne.

Those sitting at tables nearby laughed and someone called across to the sewing workshop, 'I reckon we need a costume, lasses. One that'll fit Harry and Barry.'

Amelia, looking as though she would burst with fury at the guffaws, pushed past Miss Ellington, only to be baulked by Mr Swinton, who had appeared from nowhere to stand in her way, his grey hair perfectly parted, his green overalls still pristine. He rose on his toes, a sure sign he was displeased.

'Yes, we will indeed go to Mr Bolton. Come along, Miss Cartwright. Fran, you carry on with your duties once the break is over. If I need you, I will collect you from your workshop.'

His voice was ice-cold, his face pale with fury. Fran wondered if she was for the sack, or Amelia, or perhaps they both were? Oh Lord, what a fool, for she must keep her job now there was Lisa to provide for . . . She paused – she had used the bairn's name.

She started to rise, for she must go with Amelia to Mr Bolton, to apologise and beg, but Miss Ellington pressed her back down onto the chair. 'Sit still, be quiet. This girl must be dealt with. And you, keep your hands to yourself from now on, and your mouth shut. Let Mr Swinton and me sort it out.'

'We'll keep an eye on her, Cyn,' called Mrs Oborne.

Miss Ellington hurried to catch up with Mr Swinton and Amelia, hoping that this time the wretched girl really would be sacked, because if she wasn't swanning about in high heels playing at being important in administration, she was pushing her own singing group or shooting her mouth off.

Cyn found herself touching the posters along the corridor as Beth used to do. Was it in the hope of finally getting rid of this girl? Why *did* Amelia feel so entitled? Was it because she had once gone out with Ralph Massingham? Whatever it was, it was no coincidence that after she had been shouting the odds in the Rising Sun about the Factory fence, there had been an attempted break-in. By whom, they had never discovered.

Finally, Cyn caught up with Mr Swinton and his charge. No one spoke as they reached Bolton's office. In silence, they waited while Mr Swinton rat-a-tatted on the door.

'Enter.'

Mr Swinton led the way, with Cyn behind Amelia. Mr Bolton, recently promoted from Deputy, to Section Manager, was writing in a ledger. He looked up, his middle parting somewhat crooked, his white collar worn and his tie spotted with food. The problem was that they were all working such long hours one's appearance became trivial.

Mr Bolton screwed on his fountain-pen top. 'Yes? A deputation?'

Before Mr Swinton could speak, Amelia thrust her way to Bolton's desk, leaning over it as though she was going to grab him. Alarmed, Mr Bolton sat back, looking from Amelia to Mr Swinton. 'What the—'

Amelia launched into a tirade of complaints. 'It's that Fran Bedley – she grabbed me, she did, shook me, attacked me, damnable factory girl. All I did was joke. She must be sacked—'

Mr Bolton stood, threw down his pen and roared, 'Silence.' He glared from Amelia to Mr Swinton, and then at Cyn. He put up his hand to Amelia. 'Sit down this minute, and do not dare to speak to your superior in this manner.'

Amelia sat in the chair to one side of the desk, shocked, her mouth hanging open.

'Would you, Mr Swinton, do me the honour of explaining this interruption?' Mr Bolton's voice was ominously quiet.

'Delighted, sir. This young woman taunted Fran Bedley, who as you know is one of my finest workers and, along with her Massingham colleagues, unfailingly reliable, though not without her tragedies. There was the death of her father in a pit-roof fall, following on from the death of her newborn sister . . .'

Mr Bolton looked weary and waved Cyn and Mr Swinton to the two other chairs ranged in front of his desk, then sat back down. 'Yes, I know all this, and that she was badly hurt in an explosion when temporarily transferred to Scotland with Sarah Bedley, and I have every sympathy, but what has that to do with today?'

Everything, Cyn wanted to say to him, because Amelia was the girl who had made it her life's work to destroy the leader of the Factory Girls, hating her – and the others – because they were more successful, more admired. Instead, she kept control and calmly explained about Amelia's arrival at Fran's table, how she had been clearly intent on goading her. Cyn was balling her hands so tightly that her nails dug into her palms.

'Goading?' Mr Bolton queried, looking at Cyn, his hand held up to Amelia, who had blurted out, again, 'It was a joke.'

Cyn continued to explain what had been said, and then Fran's response. Mr Bolton yet again held up his hand to Amelia, who nonetheless shouted, 'That's a lie.'

Silence fell. Finally, Mr Bolton raised his eyebrows at Mr Swinton. 'Is what Miss Ellington just said, any of it, a lie?'

Mr Swinton shook his head. 'That is what happened, Mr Bolton, and I can't have my girls upset. It's a dangerous enough job as it is, and to have a constant irritation is too much. I refer you to—'

Mr Bolton nodded. 'No need. I recollect clearly issuing the warning to Miss Cartwright and it seems that no heed has been taken. Thank you for your attention to this matter, Miss Ellington, and you, Mr Swinton. Perhaps you would leave us now.'

They rose. Amelia paled, but Cyn had no pity left for her. Her girls, her workers, who beavered throughout their shifts, putting their lives at risk, should not have to put up with these barbs. They left, and Cyn walked down the corridor until she realised she was alone. She turned to see Mr Swinton outside Mr Bolton's door, listening. Cyn hurried back on tiptoes and did the same.

They heard Mr Bolton explaining that he would not have his workforce upset when the work *they* did was skilled, irreplaceable and brave, unlike that of a typist in administration. One who, moreover, had already transgressed by discussing the work of the Factory and a temporary weakness in its security.

'I will therefore be terminating your employment with us, Miss Cartwright. Of course, your resignation might suit us both, and allow a reference to accompany you on your journey south. This is something only you can—'

'I will complain to Head Office,' Amelia replied, her voice tremulous. 'I will explain that I was attacked. You're a rude, ignorant man. I will—'

Cyn and Mr Swinton heard the tap of her high heels across the floor, and they fled down the corridor as quietly as they could, hearing Mr Bolton's roar as Amelia opened his office door.

'Miss Cartwright, that is more than enough. Go to your locker and pack up your things. I will immediately inform the new administrative officer, Mr Andrews, of my decision. He will escort you to the gates. You may not return, *ever*. There should be a bus down by the crossroads. Best put on more sensible shoes, which I presume you wore to work.'

'I will be back,' Amelia shouted. 'I will, because my father knows people in Head Office, and . . . and . . .' She burst into tears and stormed along the corridor as Cyn and Mr Swinton ducked into a broom cupboard just in time, standing quite still in the dark.

'Why did I ever think she'd go quietly?' Cyn murmured. Mr Swinton stood, his hand on the sneck, listening. They heard her heels slamming on the tiles.

Fran was back in the detonator workshop when Mr Swinton entered. He came to her, coughing to warn her, then tapped her on the shoulder. 'Perhaps you'd like to accompany me to Mr Bolton's office?' he whispered.

Fran wouldn't like it, but did, following her supervisor out and along the corridor, her mask hanging down around her chin. She didn't ask Mr Swinton why, because she was already trying to work out how she could find another job. Perhaps she could be Sophia's nanny and take Lisa with her, for she'd have to move in. But what would her mam think? And how could she look after two babies? It wouldn't work. Perhaps Mrs Adams needed help in the shop? But no, because she had help. If Davey ever telephoned again . . . She shrugged. Normally she would talk to him, they'd find an answer. What had she done? She should have trusted him. Was she mad?

It felt like miles to Mr Bolton's office. They stopped outside his door. She knocked, looking sideways at Mr Swinton, who patted her arm. 'Be not afraid. Enter.'

She did, thinking that though Mr Swinton sounded like an Old Testament prophet, his words steadied her. Mr Bolton was at his desk, Cyn standing behind him, both looking at a letter. He waved Fran to a seat. He let the letter fall to the desk. 'I have written out a letter of termination of employment.'

Fran nodded. 'I expected it, and I shouldn't have shaken her, but I were so angry. But I need me job, Mr Bolton, I really do, for we have the bairn now and Davey doesn't earn much and—'

'It is a letter of termination for Miss Amelia Cartwright. It has to be signed off by the Factory manager, and then by Head Office. With Miss Ellington's and Mr Swinton's help, I have enumerated all the instances she has failed to comply with the standards required of our employees. Miss Cartwright might well try and appeal my decision, but to no avail, for it is supported by Mr Gaines's report. However – and this is an important point – she claims you attacked her, and that it was unprovoked. I have been able to ascertain that there was in fact intense provocation, as has happened habitually since she arrived here. I need your confirmation that this will not happen ever again.'

Fran wasn't sure she understood. Was she being sacked, or warned? Her thought must have shown, for Cyn said, 'No need to worry. We have various witness statements from the catering staff to the sewing workshop that make this event understandable, if not acceptable.'

'So I can keep my job?' She couldn't believe it.

Mr Bolton came round and sat on the corner of his desk, frowning. 'Well, that is where I have a proposal. I know that you were injured in Scotland, I know that you have commitments at home, so perhaps a nine-to-five position in the administrative office, under Mr Andrews, might be more conducive to you now? I know from your file that you have office experience, and your diligence goes before you.'

Nine to five, thought Fran. Typing, shorthand, feeling clean, no itching, no yellow, safe – but without my marrers, without the danger money which Mam and I need even more now.

Was it an order? Was it take it, or leave? Was it a richly deserved punishment?

Fran looked down at her yellowed skin, felt the itch of her mask as it hung down around her chin. She would have to, if it was that or nothing. 'I need the danger money, Mr Bolton. It's right grand of you to offer it, but you see . . .' She petered out.

Mr Bolton merely nodded, smiling round at them all. 'As I feared, but I had to offer you the chance of safety for I hear you have much on your plate.'

Fran swung round to look at Mr Swinton.

'Don't you worry, Fran,' Mr Bolton said. 'Someone else will bite my hand off to work in the office. We just have to hope that Miss Cartwright doesn't appear back after her appeal. But that's my problem. Back to work now, chop-chop, targets to be met.'

Fran left the office with Cyn, leaving Mr Swinton to talk with Mr Bolton.

'Even if the wretched girl does wangle it,' said Cyn, 'she'll be on another warning. You're off the hook, Mrs Davey Bedley. So best you two make it up, eh. Life's too damned short, Fran, to ditch a good man, for he is, you know.'

That evening at Massingham Hall, Ralph received a telephone call from Tim Swinton, the Fascist son of that salt of the earth, Mr Swinton.

'Good evening, Ralphy boy. Any information for me?'

'Sadly not.' Ralph had been advised by Professor Smythe, his counter-espionage handler, to keep his replies short so that Tim would have to do the talking, and perhaps make mistakes.

'Not doing too well, then, are you, for I know that the conveniently loose-mouthed Amelia Cartwright has been given her marching orders by the section starched collar, but the girl's father has been straight on to someone at He—' He stopped. 'Well, never mind where. Anyway, she will be returning. So, time to get back into the girl's good books, for she's the one that let drop in the pub that the fence was down. That girl is plain stupid, it seems to me, which is helpful. So, get to it when she returns.'

Ralph protested. 'But—'

'But nothing. I know you have a bit of a thing going on with the half-a-hand, half-an-ear wench, but Viola Ross can help you with nowt about owt in the Factory. You've a job to do as our reconnaissance man. Don't forget for a single minute that we need to slow production. Any news of seams opening in the pit? I have other eyes there, so will know if you aren't keeping up.'

There it was, Ralph thought, an actual admission that Tim had other eyes at Auld Hilda. Did he also have someone in the Factory's Head Office? Was that what 'H—' had meant? Yes, it must be. *And* Tim'd named Amelia. Ralph felt a surge of triumph, even though it was through Tim's errors, not the great Ralph Massingham's own cleverness.

'Pull your finger out when Amelia comes back, eh? Pig and Whistle will make a change from the Rising Sun, where she mentioned the fence. New territory is best, eh?' said Tim.

He rang off.

A couple of minutes later, the telephone rang again, just as Ralph expected. It was Smythe, and why not? The line was tapped by the Professor's team.

'My word, he's getting tired, panicky or slack, but who cares which?' Smythe said. 'Well, "He" is Head Office in all probability, and someone in the pit? Just as we thought. So play it sensibly, Ralph. Keep an eye on Eddie Corbitt, as I've said before. Could be he's the eyes and ears, and the doer of bad deeds, or not. As for Amelia, we are almost sure she's just a nasty, stupid girl but . . .

'The pair were in Oxford at the same time. She a temporary typist, Tim working for an import-export business. Perhaps he put her on to the Factory, claiming it was everyone's duty to do war work. He clearly knew her well enough to expect her to blab, just as he expected you to do as you were told and leave university like the good little Fascist he thinks you still are. As you're aware, we need to identify the cell's top man. Urgently. Keep at it.'

Three days later, Daniel and Davey scrambled out of their beds in the room they shared, snatching a look at the alarm, which hadn't gone off.

'It was your turn to set it,' snorted Daniel.

Davey shook his head. 'Not so. We tossed, and you lost.' He threw his sock at Daniel, who sat on his single bed, scratching his head, as Davey dashed to the door. 'Beat you to the bathroom.'

They tore along the landing in their pyjamas and queued behind Colin, resplendent in scarlet pyjamas sewn by his grandmother. Colin banged on the door. 'Get a move on, for heaven's sake, Mart. What are you doing, putting on your make-up?'

Martin's reply was as languid as always. 'Now I've smudged my lippy, so I'll have to start again.' Davey, Daniel and Colin were laughing so hard that when the door opened, Colin, who had been leaning against it, fell in, only to be caught by Martin. 'I know you're pleased to see me, Colin, but this is ridiculous.'

Colin slammed the door behind him just as Davey heard Matty, Mrs Siddely's eight-year-old son, call from the bottom of the stairs, 'Mum says if you don't come down for breakfast, she'll come up there and wallop you all, since you're behaving like children.'

'Did you hear that?' Daniel called through the door. 'You're about to get walloped.'

Davey walked barefoot to the top of the stairs. 'We'll be down in a minute, Matty.' He saw that the lad was halfway up, and already wearing his Cub Scouts uniform. 'By, you're up and about early for a Saturday. It's only just gone seven, lad.'

'The Scouts, Brownies and Guides are looking for jam jars in the rubbish tips for the WI's jam-making. The Government says they'll give them extra sugar.' Matty leapt down the stairs, calling to his sister, Dawn, 'No, you can't come. You're too young.'

Dawn, who could mither for England, was doing just that as Colin came out of the bathroom, only for Daniel to leap in, calling, 'There, Davey, Dawn sounds just like you. It's high time to telephone that wife of yours.'

Davey waited his turn, knowing he should contact Fran, but he was so ashamed, so embarrassed and still so damn angry, with Daisy as well as himself. The thing was, he hadn't dared phone as usual, for what if there was no answer?

Colin and Martin were dressed and racing down the stairs into the dining room. 'The good clean boys are ready for brekkie, Mrs Siddely, while the bad ones are not, so we'll have all four.'

By eight, the four lads were running along the road for the bus, with Colin and Martin well in the lead and Daniel calling, 'Promise Glenys a kiss, Colin, if she makes Ted wait. We know she's sweet on you, but only because you've always got the right change.'

'Save your breath and run like the devil,' Davey panted, knowing he was out of shape and needed to toughen up for the pit, for one day the war would be over. He couldn't bear to think of Fran not being there for him, so he might have to go to another colliery. There'd be no crossword magazine to bring out every month either. What was the point without her? Young Ben could help and earn enough to get himself through university, but Ben wouldn't be there for him without Fran. What had he done?

They reached the bus and clambered on board, slapping Ted on the shoulder.

'You're four layabouts,' Ted yelled at them. 'Sit your arses down and be quiet – and for Pete's sake, get here on time.'

As he plonked himself down next to Daniel, Davey yelled back, 'Though you say you haven't a brother called Bert, I reckon you're lying, our Ted.'

'I'm not your anything, Davey Bedley,' Ted roared as he swung the bus round the bend and Glenys fell onto Colin's lap, to roars of approval from the passengers.

As she scrambled up, blushing furiously, Colin said, 'Now, now, Glenys, don't be forward when I'm yours for the asking.'

All Davey could hear were groans as Ted headed for Bletchley Park and all he could feel was his torn heart.

They arrived in good time, piling off the bus, showing their passes and hurrying up the concrete drive to get out of the wind, then along the gravel path to their hut. Norah met them at the door, shrugging into her cardigan, a cigarette in the corner of her mouth. 'Shove over, I'm off to the little girls' room. You're early. The night shift's not finished. Martin and Colin can nip to the common room, but you two reprobates, Daniel and Davey – to the office.'

Norah was easing past them. 'Doris is holding something sent in the post. It's marked urgent,' she muttered, the ash on her cigarette falling to the ground. 'She's had to open it for security reasons, but I'm sure you'll be interested in the contents.'

Daniel gripped Davey's arm, but Davey was ahead of him. 'From your da?'

'Let's hope so.'

They turned and headed to the main house, leaping up the steps, flashing their passes at the guard, who sighed and called them back. 'I need a proper look, young gentlemen.'

It was their turn to sigh. 'They've already been checked at the gate.'

'But not by me. Bit of an exercise on today.' The guard checked them both. 'Something's waiting for you, Mr Peters. It's in the office. Doris is interested.'

'I know she is, in me, but I am waiting for my princess.'

The guard gestured. They laughed, and hurried to the office. Doris was there and at their entrance pointed to the cardboard box. 'I didn't look properly, but had to check, you know how it is.'

'Of course,' Daniel agreed. He picked it up and showed it to Davey, who opened the flaps and saw, on the top, a scrawled note.

Dearest Daniel (and Davey),

This was in the keeping of one of Daisy's friends. Daisy didn't take it with her because she was worried she'd lose it, whereas Sally was going to live with her parents and promised to make sure it was kept in a safe place. The home contacted her. She lives locally now, in service, and the baby is still with her parents. She brought the box to me on her afternoon off. It says nothing of Daisy's whereabouts, but might well be of use. And yes, the babe was called Elizabeth though never Betty, and born on 3rd March making her a bit over seven and a half months. Hope it helps, Dad

Davey sighed deeply. By God, Daisy was cunning.

Daniel said, 'And we now know so much more, not least when the baby was born.'

Doris pointed at the door. 'You have a common room – have a look at it all there, not here.'

Daniel tugged his forelock. 'Right you are, missus.'

Doris merely raised her eyebrows and returned to work while the two men hurried back to their hut and straight through to the common room at the end. The night shift had another fifteen minutes to go, time enough to examine the contents.

Colin and Martin joined them around a low table as Davey emptied out the box. They sorted through the photographs and gradually grew quiet.

'He's a nice-looking lad. It says his name is Peter Renfrew.' Colin was scanning one of the letters. 'Listen,' he said. ' "Dearest Daisy, how lucky I am to have met you. I love you so much, and you are everything to me. Really, truly, you are my family, for I have no other. Together we will create our own little world, when this bloody mess is over." '

While he listened, Davey was looking at a photograph of

Daisy and Peter together, young and happy, with Peter so blond – or so the black and white photograph indicated – and handsome in his uniform. Both seemed so full of love. Silently, they shared the letters, the photographs. When they had finished, Davey said into the silence, 'I feel bad. I reckon she went off her head with grief, but I couldn't see it.'

'None of us could,' Martin agreed. 'Why the hell didn't she tell us how in love they were, how awful the loss?'

Davey shrugged. 'Lord knows. I reckon these belong with that baby, but who knows if Daisy will ever reclaim her, poor girl. Listen, Peter says here, "We will marry, of course, and have this child, and we will be a family."'

The telegram denoting his death was there too, because Peter Renfrew was never to marry, never to meet his child.

Davey just stared at the letters and photographs. He must go back to Massingham. He must show his beautiful Fran, his marrers and their families, that Daisy had been in love, and was loved in return, and that her child should be too. That was what he must do, but first he must tell Fran he was so sorry, so stupid, so hurtful, and he would rather die than do that again, for she was the love of his life. He gathered everything up, putting it all back into the box.

'What's to do?' murmured Daniel.

'I'm going home and I'm taking these, Daniel, if that's all right, for I need to put things right with Fran. She and her mam deserve to see all this, and then the others as well. It's only right for them, Daisy, the babe and me. For I've behaved like a complete fool.'

Colin leaned forward, putting the top back on the box. 'And if Bletchley doesn't let you?'

'I'll go anyway.' They were alone in the common room, but could hear the scraping of chairs as the night shift left. They should be in there now, starting their shift.

Martin shook his head. 'You'll not get what you need if you rush and barge about the place. We need a plan. Norah must be onside, and she will take our case to whoever needs to approve it. So, think – why should they let you go?'

They all sat as though they were dummies until Daniel said, 'Hang on, I've had ten days' leave, what about the rest of you?'

Colin and Martin nodded. 'Yes, that's right, one way and another,' Colin muttered. 'A week, and then three days for my cousin's funeral.'

Martin nodded. 'I've had at least that.'

'What about you, Davey?' Daniel asked.

'Six days, said Davey slowly, counting in his head. 'Three for Stan's wedding, and three for mine, by the time I got there and back. Oh, no, that's wrong. Five. I took the overnight train back both times and crawled in, more dead than alive and half an hour late. Don't you remember Norah giving me a kick up the arse?' They all nodded.

Martin picked up the box. 'Right, let's nobble our Norah before the shift really gets started. We have five minutes.'

'I'll do the talking, and maybe the rest of the incoming shift will get behind us, for I'm pretty sure they've got more leave under their belt than you, Davey,' Daniel said, shaking his head. 'What's the matter, love it here too much, do you?'

Davey followed them, knowing he'd been too immersed in his work to even notice, and that those were days he could have been with Fran. Oh God, he'd done so many things wrong.

It took the whole room to clamour for Davey's release 'from this toerag prison', as Roger from London called it. He insisted on wearing two scarves, one wool, one silk, for the silk against his skin reminded him of better times, as he told whoever would listen.

In the end, Norah looked up, her hands over her ears. 'Enough,' she roared. 'You should have started work five minutes ago. Give me that box, and I trust I have your permission to share it with those who have probably forgotten what grief and love is. This will remind them.'

She stood, her cardigan falling around her. 'You, Davey Bedley, get your head down and make progress on the intercepts, and I will tell them you just get in the way anyway, so best you are gone from here until you catch up your days.'

Half an hour later, Davey was in a taxi, complete with the box, heading for Mrs Siddely's. Once there, he asked it to wait, rushed upstairs and packed his pyjamas, toothbrush and basics, knowing he had clothes at Fran's. Mrs Siddely was waiting at the foot of the stairs as he came down with his small case.

'Doing a runner, Davey?'

'Are you coming back, Davey, for I need your help with my homework?' Dawn asked, round-eyed.

Davey grinned. 'Oh yes, but I have my wife to see. The other three will help, like they always do. We're a gang.'

He kissed Mrs Siddely. She laughed. 'Ah, then you've found out something that'll help your Fran accept the babe, eh?'

He stepped back. 'Must be something to do with the sherry.'

She smiled. 'Good luck, be sensible and don't sulk, it's not a nice look for a grown man.'

Davey knew he deserved that, and kissed her again. 'Say goodbye to Matty for me. We'll set another crossword puzzle on my return, in six days. They gave me one extra. Imagine that, Mrs Siddely – I'll be with my Fran for five whole days, if she'll have me, for I've been so stupid.'

Mrs Siddely smiled. 'Oh, she'll have you. A bond like

yours can't be severed that easy, though it might take a while, so you'll have to pay your pound of flesh and grovel a little.'

He gripped her hand, then squatted. 'Bye, little Dawn. You keep going with your times tables, eh? How far have you got?'

'Five times,' she said. 'It's an easy one, but I don't know why it is.'

Davey was already half out of the door, but looked back at her, smiling. 'I always found that too. It seems to fit somehow, doesn't it?'

Dawn was nodding as he ran back down the path. He liked these two children and felt sorry that they had no father, who had been killed at Dunkirk. He threw his case onto the back seat and leapt in after it. 'Drive like the wind, if you would, kind sir. I have the ten o'clock to catch, with a travel warrant, an' all.'

'Somewhere nice, lad?' the taxi driver asked as he drove away, bashing through the gears.

'Oh aye, off to see me beautiful wife,' Davey replied, because he hoped and prayed that for Fran it would be nice. Please, please, she must still love him, in spite of the fact that he was the biggest fool out, for how else could he go on? He thought he knew how Daisy must have felt, and was ashamed.

Chapter Nine

That same Saturday morning, Ralph eased himself out of bed, aching, but when didn't a pitman who'd been hewing coal all week? He stood and stretched, rotating his neck, groaning at the stiffness, but time was moving on. It was almost four and the fore shift, which now started at five, waited for no man. Ten minutes later, he was creeping to the top of the stairs, hoping to hear Viola calming a child after a nightmare, or even telling one of them to go to sleep, it wasn't morning, but no. He sighed, because just hearing her soft voice sent him off to work in a better mood. He tiptoed down the stairs in his socks. Ralph knew Stan didn't wear any, he couldn't see the point, because they only filled with coal dust, but the other marrers, including Ralph himself, disagreed. The boots rubbed their bare feet more than the coal-dusted sock.

He grinned as he reached the hall and padded across the tiles, wondering not for the first time why the four of them spent so much time arguing the toss about socks as they fell out of the cage and headed up the main seam. Perhaps it was more than a habit, and was in fact a talisman?

Maybe today he'd stay quiet and see if anything amiss happened on shift, but as he opened the green baize door behind which more stairs led to the basement kitchen, he found himself shaking his head. What if it *was* good luck, and he broke it? He hurried down, stopping when he heard a crash from the kitchen, listening, but no, nothing. He took the stairs two at a time, slowing as he neared the bottom, straining to hear. Nothing. Had it been it an intruder? Or maybe the wind?

He passed the dresser, pressing himself against the wall, inching along now, and peering through the glass of the door. No one there. But he wasn't imagining it. Perhaps it was Sophia? Was something wrong? But no, a crash was more likely to be a burglar, after the food in the pantry, perhaps the pheasant – ah, a black marketeer? Not that bloody Norris Suffolk?

There were sounds from the scullery, and then out came Viola with a plate of toast. He grinned. Viola, his love, Viola, alone, no bairns, much as he also loved them. Viola up so early. He tapped on the glass, she looked up, saw him, blushed, waved the plate at him, and the love was there in her eyes. He entered, walked round the table, pulling her close. Loving every single thing about her. 'I thought it was a burglar or Norris bloody Suffolk. I was going to belt him, so might as well—'

He stopped as she put a finger to his mouth. 'You will certainly not belt me instead.'

They laughed as he pressed closer, removing the plate from her poor hand and placing it on the table. 'Ah, I'd best rethink . . .' he breathed, so very close to her. 'Perhaps the solution is to kiss you.'

'That could be the answer, bonny lad,' was her whispered reply.

He did, and her lips were soft and yielding and he just wanted to stay like this for ever, her arms around him, his around her, but she was already drawing away.

'Enough. I thought to get you your favourite, soldiers and a drippy egg, to start your shift.'

He kissed her again. 'I love you so much, Viola.'

He leaned his forehead on hers, wanting to propose, wanting them to grow old together, but that question must

wait until her birthday party, so they could announce . . .
He stopped, feeling anxiety course through him – what if she said no?

Viola smiled, and pulled away. 'I have to time the egg, or it'll be rock hard. So cut up your toast, and there's bread and dripping to get ready for your bait. You, lad, pour some tea into your flask, but save a cup for now.'

He did as she ordered, sitting at the table, loving the sound of her busyness, the precious peace and normality of her and of his life at this moment – well, as much as life could be normal in wartime.

'Howay, lad, it's ready,' she said, bringing over his egg, and one for her.

'Am I expected to share my drippy egg soldiers, with you, Miss Ross?' he asked.

'It's best, if you want to live another minute,' Viola grinned, 'but time is passing, so best get on, eh. Who knows, any minute the herd might sense we're both up and stampede through the door.'

Ten minutes later, he was kissing her goodbye, attaching his bait tin and flask to his belt and leaving her, feeling the wrench like a physical pain. As he climbed the steps into the yard, he heard her call from the doorway, 'Be safe, my dearest boy.'

He rushed back and hugged her, kissing her. 'I love you, Viola Ross.'

She smiled against his mouth. He ran up the steps to the yard again, waving without turning because otherwise he'd only go back. He tore towards the garage, his boots clattering on the cobbles, finding his way by the moonlight of a pre-dawn October morning.

'Get those legs pumping,' Viola called softly. 'It's four thirty, lad.'

He dragged out his bike and pedalled away, though he

125

had to look back once more, he just had to, and in the darkness he imagined her waving. 'I love you,' he called, trying not to wake everyone, and heard her laugh as he thrust down on the pedals. He left the yard, cycling along the front of the house, the gravel flying from beneath his wheels. It was down to Sid that he had a better bike. The lad had heard of two at the back of a motor mechanic's garage and Ralph had bought them both. They were nearly new, with saddles more like sofas. He had given the second to Alfie, as recompense for all those months he had hired the lad's old one, shaking it into an early grave.

He grinned as he remembered how the two of them had decided to keep the old one as a spare, though Viola had thought it belonged in a museum. He freewheeled down the slope of the driveway, whistling, because he was feeling the happiness he basked in, now she was in his life and loved him; and said it as often as he did. He'd taken his mother's ring to be reset and then altered to fit, and would need to collect it from Newcastle when it was finally done. Wrights, the jeweller's, had promised it would be ready by her birthday. Well, it must be.

Riding no hands towards the main road, he thought he'd have a drink or two of Stevie's Rising Sun special homemade beer, which he had ordered for her party, before asking her to join him out in the orangery. There he'd propose, down on one knee, doing it properly, then they would return to the ballroom and announce it to all and sundry. He grinned at the mere thought, and made himself refuse to entertain the possibility of Viola refusing him.

The wind was harsh, the morning as dark as ever. He lowered his head, his cap keeping him warm, his bait tin swinging on his belt. Sheep were dotted around the fields to the north of the road, grazing. Over to the right, Auld Hilda's slag heap smouldered. He started to sing 'Cheek to

Cheek', his mind on Viola. Well, when wasn't it? Old Will the milkman rattled along Main Street, pulled by his new horse, Frankie.

'Best you hush yer caterwauling, Mr Ralph,' Old Will yelled, 'or you'll scare the horse and set the dogs to barking.'

'Right you are, Will.' Ralph laughed, touched his cap in salute and turned right to head through Massingham to the pit just as the hooter began to soar over the village. He got up a head of speed, bending low as he puffed up the incline towards the pit yard, keeping an eye out for the lads amongst those on foot or on bikes, but they must be ahead of him. So he joined the rest of the shift winding its way through the opposing force of the night shift leaving the yard.

Finally, he cycled into the pit yard, where, like the rest of the men, he pulled to the side, dismounted and pushed his bike to the shed, shoving it against the others. He tipped his cap at those who pushed in and around him. They called to one another, and to Ralph.

'Howay.'

'Bit of a breeze.'

'See you at t'club.'

He walked through the yard with them, hearing the wind in the winding gear, smelling the last of the Woodbines before they were stubbed out, for they didn't mix with gas. The lamp room was in sight, and at the entrance stood the lampman, and Ralph's marrers, for he was indeed one of a team now, and the thought made him prouder than anything else. His acceptance had come when he and Sid had protected Beth against the trickery of Norris Suffolk. Together they had fought him and his gorillas, and seen them off. It was the turning point between being seen as the boss's son and as a pitman. He wore his blue coal scars with pride. Yes, to him, those were his medals, because he'd earned each and every one.

Ralph forced his way through to join the three lads, who had already collected their lamps.

'What time do you call this, then, lad?' Stan muttered, his cap pulled down, while Sid and Norm's were tilted to one side as usual, Sid's to the right, Norm's to the left.

'Almost late, you are,' Sid grinned, throwing a mock punch.

'Yet I'm not,' Ralph said.

A young lad from Middle Street stopped beside them, staring at the hooks screwed into a massive wooden board, some of which held two tokens, others one. The lad looked bewildered.

'Just take one of two tokens,' Ralph said, his voice low, 'You'll be on the tubs, I expect, taking the coal from the face for the Galloway ponies to haul along to the cages and up to the screens, where I expect you used to work?'

'Aye, I were on the screens before, but me uncle said I must get meself underground, now I'm grown.' The lad looked barely more than a child, or at least just a little older than Ben, Ralph thought.

'So, get a lamp, too, then you'll have one token on the hook and the other on your tub. Then, if you . . . Well, if you get lost—'

'Hurt you mean, Mr Massingham?'

'Sometimes, but . . . but don't think of that. The thing is, just do the job you're paid to do. By the way, I'm Ralph, and remember, if something goes amiss, we'll know and come to find you, not stopping until we do.'

The lad nodded and moved across to an older man, who called, 'Ralph, thanks for that. Our Charlie thinks he knows it all and don't want to ask, just like we all were at fifteen. I'll be watching him, never you fear.'

'I'm sure you will, Tony. Listen to your uncle, lad, he knows all there is to know.'

'Just take a moment to listen to our Ralph,' Stan muttered to Sid and Norm, loud enough for Ralph to hear. 'You'd think he'd been in the pit all his life, handing out advice as though he's an old hand. Soon there'll be no living with him, he'll be such an expert.' He lowered his voice. 'When will the ring be ready, lad?'

They joined the queue for the cages to take them down into the murky depths, or that's how Ralph always thought of the pit at this stage. He shrugged. 'Wrights will telephone or write to let me know.'

Norm jogged him. 'Soon be an old married man, eh? That leaves just Sid and me to sort, though Sid's got Beth by his side. What's more, he'll soon make an honest man of himself and the lass when the bliddy divorce is sorted, that's if she'll have such a toerag.' They shuffled forward when the cage could be heard rattling to the surface. 'Any news on that, our lad?' he asked.

'Nowt,' Sid shrugged. 'The beggar's gone quiet. I'm just afeared he's changed his mind and'll turn up, turn her head and turn her off me.'

Ralph tipped Sid's cap over his eyes. 'Don't be daft, for much as we've gone on about you being a waste of space, the lass takes no notice.'

Sid grabbed Ralph's cap and threw it in the air, only for Eddie Corbitt to catch it and send it on again. Round and round it went until it reached Stan, who stuck it in Ralph's pocket just as the cage arrived. The banksman unhooked the chain across the front, allowing the last of the night shift to slouch out, dragging their feet with tiredness, the whites of their eyes startling against the black coal dust, their smiles weak.

As the men moved forward into the cage, the banksman

called out, 'Get a bliddy wriggle on, anyone'd think you don't want to get to work.'

'And they'd be right,' someone called.

The four men squashed in with the others and Stan gripped Ralph's arm. 'Do you still feel as if your bread and dripping's in your throat?'

Ralph nodded, for he hated the drop. Stan's reply was the same as always. 'Well, for the love of God, don't let it out.'

Around them, men chuckled, and Norm muttered, 'If you do, spout it over our Stan, eh?'

The banksman hooked the chain over and said to Ralph, 'Aye, turn to Stan, that's a boy.'

Ralph's smile was weak, but his shoulders straightened for he was a hewer, and proud of it. He concentrated his mind on the ring: two small diamonds and an emerald. He'd had it redesigned because he hadn't liked his mother, any more than his father had liked his. But that's where it ended, because Sophia was virtually his mother and he adored her. Sophia had made an excuse to compare her middle finger against Viola's, on the pretext that pregnancy had made her fingers swell so much they looked like sausages.

Ralph smiled, for Sophia's hands could never look anything other than full of grace, like the rest of her, though you could hardly call her bump full of anything except the most exciting of events, a baby no less. But as the two women compared their hands, it became clear that Viola's middle finger was the same as Sophia's. It had to be that one, for the lass had had her ring and little finger amputated after the Scottish factory explosion.

'Off you go then, ta-ta, lads,' called the banksman. They all fell silent, though the clamour of those waiting for the next cage continued to reach them until they whooshed down. As always, Ralph thought: it's broken, we're falling, I'll die.

Ralph steadied himself, breathing in the smell of the pit, the coal, the muck. He could hear the whispers around him, see Stan and Sid hard at it, quarrelling about who owed who a pint, and Norm counting in his head because he hated the bliddy cage, and he said as much whenever he got the opportunity. Ralph smiled. He was where he belonged.

To his right, Eddie Corbitt was not talking to anyone, just standing, staring at nothing. Could he really be Tim Swinton's man? Was he the one who had set the charge that had brought Bell Seam roof down and killed Joe Hall and Tom Bedley, Corbitt's own marrers? Tim made sure that no one in his cell knew anything about anyone else, which was the nuisance of it all, for if Ralph had the names of contacts, and particularly the top man, they could close it all down. But no, it was just shadows, and guesswork.

He thought back to the incident in which the roof had fallen. Had Eddie known that Joe and Tom would be there? Surely not, for Ralph hadn't and he thought he had killed them, which was when he had come to his senses and turned against Tim, working instead for counter-espionage, happy to risk his life to make good his former actions.

He eyed Stan, for Joe Hall was his father, and Tom Bedley was Davey's, and though Ralph hadn't killed them, he still hadn't the courage to confess he had been there. It wasn't only that he couldn't face telling the lads or Fran the truth, but because if he did, it was likely that his counter-espionage cover would be blown.

Eddie Corbitt was still staring at nothing. If he was involved, he had to be removed. Ralph shook his head, thinking of Fran and Davey. Had they made up? Was the girl Davey's babe? Who knew – who knew anything? Who was Eddie? Who was the top man? Back to Davey – was he someone who had fathered a child and lied? No, he couldn't believe it. Not Davey. But Fran was worried; Viola had told him.

The cage continued to plummet, but Ralph bent his knees a little for it was slowing and then it slammed to a stop. Charlie bounced. His uncle gripped him tight. Poor beggar, for he'd shove the tubs full of coal until he thought his back would break, and then keep going. Just like they'd all done in their time.

They left the cage and set off down the roadway, which was lit by lamps screwed into the walls. Ralph listened, waiting, and sure enough Stan started the sock banter. 'You see, if you don't wear socks, they don't need dadding at the end of the shift.'

It was Sid who continued, saying, 'Maybe, but we don't get the blisters, the . . .' On the lads went, but someone was walking with them. It was Eddie, his bait tin slapping against his thigh, his flask clanging into it. Ralph glanced at him, surprised.

Eddie nodded. 'How's your da, then, lad?'

They walked on, the wall lamps flickering along the wide roadway, past a deputy, Merryweather, working in his office. Ralph glanced at Eddie again, then remembered he was working in Nugget Seam and would peel off. He relaxed.

'Much as always,' Ralph said, trying to place his feet gently into the coal dust, listening to the socks-or-no-socks discussion.

Now Stan was saying, 'So, you wore those yesterday, our Sid. Dadded 'em on the wall, but they're still full of dust.'

'They'll stink, but still better than blisters,' added Ralph, for that was his cue, but he was wondering all the time what Eddie was doing there, with them, for God's sake.

Corbitt nodded and jogged Ralph. 'Busy man, I 'spect your da's busy, what with the war an' all?'

Ralph felt his mind speed up. Why was Eddie asking, if he was nothing to do with Tim? 'He's always busy, Eddie.'

'Down to London, I reckon, more often than not.'

'Well, hardly, there's Sophia to think of, of course.' Ralph knew he had to be careful.

Eddie pressed on. 'London's where the real war planning is going on, and it must involve coal production. 'Spect he sees that professor a fair bit?'

Ralph called out to Stan, 'You going to go back to university when this lot is over, Stan? I was talking to Smythe about it myself, at Fran's wedding – about both of us returning, maybe.'

Only then did he turn to Eddie. 'The Professor has a post at the university, and included in that is the mentorship of the Massingham scholarship boys, so yes, Father sees him. Sometimes, I suppose, they meet at the club, though I doubt it's often. Father's always in a rush to get home. But back to the scholarship boys. Imagine how tedious it must have been, having that lout slobbing around at Oxford.' He pointed to Stan and, dodging a pretend punch from him, laughed. 'I didn't exactly cover myself in glory, not like Stan,' he added.

Eddie just nodded and they caught up with young Charlie, the putter, and his uncle, Tony Ellis, who was saying, 'Pick yer feet up, for the love of God, lad. You're scuffing up the dust and making a bliddy nuisance of yourself.' He coughed on the last word. 'Don't trip on the rails, neither. You'll be pushing your tub along here soon enough, so treat 'em with respect.'

On and on they walked, the roof lowering, the half-mile of roadway lights long gone, relying on their own lamps. Ralph heard the creaking of the coal, which he now understood was like a living thing. He imagined the great weight of it pressing on the roof planks and squeezing the side props, desperate to fill this empty seam. He looked around at his marrers: he was a hewer like them, with the muscles to prove it, while at home there were the children, his parents, and Viola. His life was good.

He looked ahead to Stan, who still missed Davey – well, they all did, but the decoding had been a godsend, because that last accident when he was buried beneath the coal had damaged Davey's leg too badly for him to work here. Mark you, the lad's limp was hardly noticeable now, except when he was weary, so would he come back to the pit when the war was over? Well, Ralph sighed, Davey'd better get some leave soon, for he needed to be face to face with that wonderful wife of his to get things squared away. But he hadn't even phoned, Stan said, not since Fran had hung up.

'Deep in thought?' It was Eddie again. Why the hell was he still there? He should have peeled off into his own seam.

'Yes, just wondering what the weather would be like today. I often think that, stuck down here. Must be like being in a submarine. Aren't you heading to Nugget Seam today? We passed it a few yards back.'

Eddie shook his head. 'Albright's put me on your team till bait break. Reckons you could do with help to hit your target. Bit awry yesterday.' Eddie lowered his voice. 'Affects war production, it does – targets are targets.'

The lights of main seam didn't extend this far so Ralph kept his eyes on Stan who was walking ahead, his lamp cutting through the darkness, the beam jolting with every step. He longed for Corbitt to shut up. Did he suspect Ralph was one of Tim's men? Did he want confirmation? But why? Secrecy was all in the Fascist book. Ralph said nothing as the roof grew lower and lower and they bent with it. Tony Ellis muttered, 'Bit worried about the lad, I am. Needs to learn the ropes.'

Ralph said, 'We'll take care of him, and keep him busy

too. We had a load of slate yesterday to get through, so we need to catch up today.'

Tony peeled off down Windgate Seam and Ralph said to Charlie, 'Howay, lad, come by me, and best bend your knees, for you'll whack your noddle and see stars in the darkness, not coal.'

Charlie's laugh was false, but it was one, and that was a measure of the lad. Ralph smiled. 'Remember those days, Eddie?' he said. 'I do, though in comparison to you, I'm still the new boy.'

Beside him, Eddie grunted, coughed, then said so quietly Ralph almost missed it, 'Aye, I remember them, it's a lifetime with too much water gone under the bridge, and too much to regret. But that's life, and it's a bliddy beggar if you ask me.'

Eddie walked on, bent low, each footfall raising barely any dust. The depth of the mine meant greater and greater heat, and Corbitt was now calling to Charlie, 'If you're too hot, take off your jacket, but if you do and you leave it here by the side, the blacklocks – you know, them cockroaches – will take it over, or the rats, so give it a right good shake when you pick it up.'

'Aye,' Sid agreed. 'Them blacklocks are right little beggars – fall down your neck soon as look at you, and wriggle about where you'd not like a ferret to be. Best tie your trousers below the knee or the rats'll run up to meet the blacklocks and fight over your crown jewels.'

The men laughed quietly while Ralph wondered what Corbitt had meant. Did he regret bringing the roof down on Joe and Tom? If, indeed, he had. Or perhaps he was just a man with regrets about the loss of his marrers? Ralph gave up. He'd report the conversation to Smythe and he could do with it what he wanted.

Stan led them off to the right, into Ypres Seam. It was

a bugger, and they bent low. An overhang jutted out. 'You'll keep well down, and shove the tub,' Norm called to Charlie.

'Aye,' panted Charlie, sounding exhausted before his day had really begun.

They arrived at the face, streaming with sweat, and tore off their outer clothes, tossing them in a bundle on the ground, leaving them wearing just drawers, socks and boots. But no socks for Stan, Ralph thought with a grin. They got straight to work, poking, prying and hacking at the coal, glad to have got rid of the slate.

Charlie picked up a shovel left by the previous shift and filled the tub, then shoved it along the rails. Hour after hour they worked, and no one bothered with a Jimmy Riddle, for they were so dehydrated. At about eleven, the hewers took a break, sitting in the dust, leaning back against the pit props, eating one half of either a bread-and-dripping round or a jam one, crunching coal dust along with the bread. It was good for your teeth, Ralph told Charlie when he returned with an empty tub and joined them. Slowly, exhausted, the lad opened his bait tin, then looked for somewhere to wipe his hands.

'Wipe 'em down your legs, lad, or on your trousers.' Sid nodded towards the pile of clothes. Charlie stared at it, then at his black-dusted legs, then stuffed a bread-and-dripping round into his mouth and gulped some cold tea. He reached for the jam ones.

'Make 'em last, bonny lad. One round's enough,' Stan muttered. 'You'll get a bellyache because you'll be straight back to work.'

The lad sighed and replaced it in the tin. 'Glad I were on the screens sorting the coal, or me hands would hurt as much as the rest of me, and I'd stamp me foot in a tantrum, setting off the dust, then one of you'd clip me ear, so that would hurt an' all. Someone clip your ear, Ralph, when you started?' The lad winked at them all.

The pitmen stopped chewing, staring at Charlie and then at Ralph. 'Best you put him over your knee, Ralph, eh?'

Then they laughed, and Ralph thought that Charlie and Eva must never meet, for they'd be the tyrants of the world. Corbitt slapped the lad on his back. 'By, you'll fit,' he said.

They were back to work too soon and joining in the banging, cracking and swearing that always rang through Auld Hilda. At the end of their shift, with their quota filled, Ralph muttered to Stan, 'I wonder if that lad should be down in the pit? He'd be better trying for Father's scholarship as you did, and as I hope Ben will.'

Stan just shrugged, and stayed quiet. As they came out into the main seam and made better time, Ralph wondered what the hell was the matter with the man.

'Grand though the scholarship is,' Stan said, looking round to check the lad wasn't close, 'down the pit the lad will be earning, and it's money the family need. So, though the scholarship covers the fees, it doesn't cover living and what he'd contribute. That's why I worked with Professor Smythe, helping on his research into the rise of the Nazis, which so disturbed him at that time. Quite right, an' all.'

Corbitt came up behind them. ' I didn't know you worked with him on such a subject.'

Next to Stan, Ralph almost winced. Was that too much information from an unaware Stan? Would bloody Corbitt put two and two together and arrive at four for Smythe?

Ralph said, 'Smythe's subject is philosophy, politics and economics so he would be interested. Didn't you say, Stan, that he was going to cover Stalin and Communism in more depth, next?'

Stan nodded, and Ralph continued. 'I will talk to Father about the award. It's finding him able to concentrate, what with work, Sophia and her blood pressure, the children and their plans for the Christmas "do" for Melanie, and before that, Viola's birthday party. I'm just waiting for them to turn the "do" into a nativity, now that we have Lisa, and soon a new Massingham babe. I'm pretty sure they'll think two baby Jesuses can't be wasted.'

'Oh, no, the chaos,' Sid spluttered. 'What would be worse is Eva as Mary. Not exactly good casting.'

They were all laughing quietly as Corbitt said to Ralph, again, 'I reckon your father is a really busy man.'

Sid butted in. 'Well, of course he is, Eddie. He's got a few factories now producing for the war, plus Auld Hilda with more men needed after so many got out and into the services, before they closed the gate on that.'

As they passed a ventilator door, Ralph felt the draught and heard the scrabbling of the mice, and somewhere the squealing of fighting rats. Probably squabbling over a piece of bread that someone had dropped.

At last they reached the cage and were hauled, jolting and shuddering, to the surface. As keen as Ralph was to see Viola, he was also anxious to bring Smythe up to date on Corbitt's questions.

But even as he cycled home with the lads, who peeled off in Massingham, he thought of Fran and her mam, busy with a bairn when their lives were already impossibly full. Bloody hell, Davey, he thought, where the hell are you? Best you get in touch or I'll come down and drag you home. Because Fran *is* your home.

Chapter Ten

Fran, Sarah and Beth slept on one another's shoulders as Bert drove towards Massingham. As he passed St Oswald's Church on top of the hill, Fran jerked awake, wondering where she was for a moment, but then she heard Bert mutter, 'If an owl were a cat, it'd be lucky, but as it is, it just shocked the living daylights out of me.'

'Did you hit it, Bert?' Mrs Oborne called.

'Did I hit it? You mean, did it hit me? And no, it just came at me like a bliddy Spitfire, then turned tail.'

'I reckon he got too big a fright seeing your face peering through the windscreen,' said Maisie. 'I 'spect he thought an' all, "These beings shouldn't be out, jerking and bumping their arses on them slats." If we had the sense we were born with, we'd be asleep in our beds.'

Sarah yawned and scratched her arms. 'Or on a chaise longue eating peeled grapes.'

'Brought by a prince,' Beth added, 'and he'd scratch our itches, an' all.'

It was Bert's turn to say, as he swung the bus round the sharp bend that became Main Street, 'Ah well, Sunday tomorrow, which is in five minutes. So a lie-in and a day off, except for those with a bairn to settle, eh, Fran?'

'Aye, Bert, but let's hope she's well asleep,' Fran called.

'Do you feel any better about her now, Fran?' whispered Beth.

'Oh, she's only a bairn, so what can we do but look after her as best we can, but I don't know what I *feel* about her.

All I know is what I feel about Davey, which is how I miss his calls, how I wish I hadn't doubted him, for I can't live without him no matter what's happened in the past. But I reckon nowt did, because he's my Davey. I was just . . . Oh, I don't know. So muddled, so angry . . . confused. I just lost my way and have probably lost him. And I know just what I feel about that, though you know an' all, for I've mithered enough to you both.'

Sarah and Beth looked at one another and sighed, but said nothing, for how could they go down south and drag Davey home, or to the phone, or . . . ?

The bus continued its journey. Outside, owls were hooting, foxes screeching, the wind in the winding gear was whistling, and yes, Fran thought, sulphur would be leadening the air. She stared out into the darkness as they pulled up at Main Street.

'Fore shift come Monday, so bright and early like the little flowers you are,' bellowed Bert. 'You ducked night shift for some reason, which is a blessing, for it means I have an' all.'

'We did two weeks of it a while back, remember,' Maisie called from two rows in front of the girls, straightening her back and rolling her shoulders. 'By, I could do with some shut-eye, so I could.'

The women were scrambling up and making their way off the bus, heading towards their terraces, hardly lifting their feet, they were so tired. Mrs Oborne yawned as she followed Maisie, with Fran leading the other two. As always, Fran felt as though she was following a galleon in full sail. Mrs Oborne stopped at Bert's cab. 'You behave yourself on your day off, you silly old fool. No nonsense, mind.'

'Get on yer way, Tilly, and leave me to fight off the ladies, eh.'

Tilly climbed down the steps to the kerb, calling back, 'In your dreams, you daft old fool—'

Fran was alongside the cab now, but saw that Mrs Oborne had stopped dead. 'You all right, Mrs Oborne?'

'Oh, right as rain, but don't you be sweet-talking Bert, he needs his beauty sleep, so get on down.' Tilly was laughing, and now Maisie was joining in.

Behind Fran, Beth whispered, 'What on earth . . . ?'

'Probably that handsome prince with peeled grapes has been lurking behind the bus shelter for his fair maiden,' said Sarah.

'Thanks, Bert, take it easy tomorrow,' said Fran, heading down the steps and hearing Sarah mutter, 'Don't do anything I wouldn't, Bert.'

Fran saw Stan emerge from the shadows at the side of the shelter. 'Howay, our Sarah,' she called, 'me brother's come for his wife. He must have been scared you'd run off with Bert, so he's here to put a stop to any nonsense. Is that right, our Stan?' She was ready to head on home, but Mrs Oborne blocked her way, with Maisie standing beside her, their arms spread wide.

It was then that Stan came towards Fran, but it wasn't Stan, or Sid, or Norm, it was him, her husband, her Davey, saying, 'By lass, it's long hours you keep.'

She still couldn't *see* him, her Davey, her love, the one who hadn't called, whom she hadn't believed, perhaps still didn't quite believe, but she'd rather have him, and the doubt. His arms were around her now and she was where she belonged, his forehead against hers, his breath on her face as he whispered, 'Oh my darling Franny, my dearest bonny lass, my love. Forgive the mess I've brought to your home.'

She whispered as the bus drew away, 'It's a babe, not a mess, and it's *our* home, but I'll skelp your backside anyway.'

He kissed her then and applause broke out. They jerked

apart, and there, as the moon came from behind the clouds, she saw Stan with Sarah, Sid and Beth, Norm and Ralph with Viola, who pulled Tilly Oborne and Maisie towards them.

'Howay, you lot,' Fran called, 'haven't you homes to go to?'

'Your mam's expecting us all for a late-night cuppa, even though the clock's chimed midnight and our clothes have turned to rags with not a glass slipper in sight,' Davey said, holding her even tighter.

Ralph pulled Viola to him, holding her close. 'Tell them the rest, lad.'

Davey was shaking his head. 'Not here, but over that cuppa, for I've got leave to clear things up, and for us *all* to understand.'

He kissed her again, harder, saying against her mouth, 'Come. You need to see and read.'

He turned, pulling her with him. The others clattered behind, talking quietly, Sid saying to Beth, 'Hush, lovely lass, you'll just have to wait, for it's worth it.'

'What's going on?' whispered Fran. 'Oh, Davey, I miss you, I love you. I've been awful, but it were a shock—'

He pressed his finger to her lips. 'No, you are never awful, it was me behaving like a bliddy fool, or so Daniel and the other two shouted at me. It was a shock, such a—'

Fran's arm was around his waist and she pulled him closer, if that was possible. 'We've made a right pig's ear of it, but it's Daisy at the bottom of it all, and nowt to do with the bairn. Or so . . .' She stopped, for there it was again – the doubt.

'Wait,' he whispered. 'I reckon you'll feel differently in a minute.'

She ran those words through her head. What was the secret?

They turned into the back lane and all were hurrying

now, for Tilly was fretting about her Steve. 'By, he'll think I've run off with Bert and left the old beggar in the lurch.'

'Nope, no need,' said Stan. 'We nipped round and let him know you'd be late, though we did say it were because you'd be out dancing with your fancy man.'

They tried to stifle their laughter, but not well enough, for a dog started barking, a back door slammed and someone coughed on their way to the netty, calling out, 'Bit of a party? What number, eh? I'll get me togs on and come on round.'

'Members only, Geoffrey,' Stan called. 'Get yourself to bed, or it's a pumpkin you'll turn into, for it's gone midnight.' The only answer was the netty door shutting. Finally, they turned into the yard tiptoeing past the hens' coop rather than set off the cockerel.

Ben stood at the door, his finger to his lips. 'Come in quietly. I could hear you clattering and laughing down the bliddy lane from here.'

Fran grinned as her mam growled, 'Language.'

They trooped in, shutting the door as quickly as they could, conscious of the blackout, wondering just why they were here. Annie Hall was pacing, Lisa cradled in her arms. She raised her eyebrows at Fran, but it was Davey who came to her and took the bairn, holding her up to his shoulder. 'You sit down, Mrs Hall, pour the tea. I'll nurse Lisa, while Ben, you show the girls and old Mrs Oborne and young Maisie the letters and photographs.'

'Less of the old,' Mrs Oborne muttered, her eyes on the box in the middle of the table. Stan pulled out a chair for her, and another for Maisie, and all the time Davey watched Fran as he patted Lisa's back and swayed from one leg to the other.

He could tell she was thinking that there they were, da and daughter together.

Pulling out a chair at the end of the table, Ben said, 'Stop looking so gormless, Franny, and thinking Lord knows what. Take a look at these and then we'll all be done with the . . . well, the mithering about.' He pointed to the chair. 'Come on, everyone, get your peepers on them papers so we can all go to blidd—' He stopped, looked sideways at his mam and continued, 'To bed.'

The women all sat as Annie poured the tea. Fran reached for the letters and photographs but Ben forestalled her, picking them up and handing them to her as though they were a precious gift, saying, 'Daniel's da sent these to Davey's workplace. They were left with a friend who promised she'd keep them safe for when Daisy could fetch 'em back.'

Everyone sighed. 'Oh aye, like the bairn, eh?' Tilly Oborne grimaced.

'Hold hard, our Tilly,' whispered Annie Hall, 'for it's not quite what it seems.'

'Look at the photographs when you've read the letters,' said Viola, 'if you can bear it, for it's all so sad.'

Fran put the pile on the table in front of her and leafed through the letters. There were none in Daisy's handwriting, which she knew so well from reading and rereading the note that had come with Lisa. These were well-thumbed letters from a Peter Renfrew, who must have been Daisy's sweetheart. But there was also a notification telegram, and she read this first. Peter *was* dead, as Daisy had told Davey and the lads. She read Peter's letters now, pausing at one in particular: *Dearest Daisy, how lucky I am to have met you. I love you so much, and you are everything to me. Really, truly, you are my family, for I have no other. Together we will create our own little world, when this bloody mess is over.*

She read through the others, with all the news they shared with one another, and then: *We will marry, of course, and have this child, and we will be a family.*

She passed the letters on to Sarah, feeling sadness drag at her because here was the father, and he, as much as Daisy, had wanted a loving family. Looking up at Stan, she asked, 'You've read them?'

Her brother, as dark-eyed and dark-haired as she, nodded. 'Oh, aye, but have a look at this now.' He pointed to the photograph Ben had handed her and which now lay on the oilcloth. She saw such a happy young couple, so in love, Daisy dark, Peter so fair. Because it was black and white, she had no idea of the colour of his eyes, but there was no need. She closed her eyes. Fair, like her daddy who had never seen her but who had so longed for his own little family. Fran passed this on too, and as the others looked, they became still and quiet.

Davey brought Lisa to her. 'Sit on your auntie Franny's lap, eh, lass.' His eyes were focused on Fran. 'Now you see why I had to come. If I lost you, I'd go strange – and Daisy had fear and loneliness to tip her into somewhere that was dark, frightening and mad.'

Fran was cradling Lisa, who was trying to sit, so she sat the babe on her lap and looked at her own mam. 'I'm ashamed.'

Annie nodded. 'I reckon it got on top of us all. We were worried who the father was, for it would be a dreadful betrayal from someone we know so well.'

Across from her, Fran saw Ralph flush and look down, shaking his head slightly. She nodded. 'You're right, Ralph. I let me doubt get the better of me, but that's an end, eh, Davey?'

Tilly Oborne and Maisie were the last to read the letters and study the photographs, and as the clock chimed half-past twelve they stood. Tilly cleared her throat. 'Fair made me want to cry. This tyrant Hitler has a lot to answer for. Aye, the bairn must be protected until her mam comes back. And if she doesn't, then Massingham will do what it does and be her family, and right safe she'll be, and that's that.'

She straightened her mac and turned to Maisie. 'You taken root or are you coming?'

Maisie just nodded at Annie. 'You're doing a good thing, our Annie, and you, Fran.'

Ben piped up from his da's armchair. 'I do me bit too, Maisie.'

Maisie followed Tilly out of the door, then called back, 'Right enough, Ben, how could I not have noticed? You've a right way with a bairn, so I'll get you to babysit, eh?'

Ben didn't answer, looking instead at the range, shaking his head and whispering to his mam, 'Our own's fair enough, but—'

Maisie popped her head back round the door. 'If I pull the other leg, will it have bells on?'

'Oh Maisie,' Ben grumped, 'get on home.'

Maisie shut the door gently behind her.

By one o'clock everyone had left and Davey held Fran in his arms in the comfort of their bed, having taken back the front room. She rested her head on his shoulder. At last it was just the two of them. He said softly, 'I wanted them all to see the facts, for it's been bad for you and I've been as much use as a damp flannel. But it'll make us all feel more kindly about Daisy, and also the bairn.'

Fran touched his face. 'I tried not to feel badly towards her, I really did, but I was frightened – for if she were yours, where was the truth between us—'

'Hush,' said Davey.

She struggled from his arms, up onto her elbow, looking down at him in the darkness. 'No, I have to, for you've never lied, never been unkind, and I let myself doubt.'

He pulled her down. 'I got so angry with you, not able to see why you would think the worst of me, but the lads put me right. You see, I love you so much, and any little wrinkle . . .' he paused, '. . . let alone a great big beggar, makes me scared I'll be without you. So it's the end of it all now. The lads and Tilly and Maisie will spread the word, and our Lisa will be cared for with a clean sheet. We'll have to deal with Daisy if she comes back, you know, make sure she's sorted and able to care for her, for we can't have the bairn unsafe.' He paused, reaching over, stroking Fran's face. 'She's a sweet little thing, and I reckon Peter would have been a grand father, having read the letters.'

Fran relaxed in his arms and they lay together, at peace, until finally they fell asleep.

The next day, the marrers and the girls headed up to Massingham Hall to meet Viola and Ralph, who were putting together a picnic. Davey towed Lisa in the cart, with Fran behind, keeping an eye on her. Lisa was wrapped up tightly, and what's more, had done them the great favour of sleeping through the night, from just after one till eight in the morning. It was Sunday, their day off, Davey was there until Wednesday, which was an unheard-of luxury, and Fran could hardly breathe for happiness and relief.

'It's high time we went to the beck,' Sarah called from behind. 'With the sun out, me brother home and Lisa needing to be introduced to it, today is the day. We always head off in the autumn – it's bracing. Do you remember our das saying that? We'd say get the fire going, and then we'll agree.'

They all cheered, laughed, agreed, for they had all day and could be there for as long or short a time as they wished. They raced along the drive as Lisa giggled.

'It's you making her happy, Davey,' called Beth, 'so you

can't go back, you have to go AWOL and stay here for ever with us and your marrers. We'll hide you in the henhouse and throw in seed, but not too much red millet.'

'Aye, you should,' said Sid. 'Or you could get yourself back down the pit, put your shoulder into it again, for I reckon you're going flabby. I can hear you panting from the back, bonny lad. Last week we had Eddie on the face for a day or two and he's not the man he was, so come back on the team. What do you think, Stan?'

It was Davey who replied. 'I'd rather hide in the Canary Club shed with the birds and Simon's home brew while me wife's working hard.'

The boos were loud, but they still didn't disturb Stan and Sarah, who were chatting and laughing together. At last, they crossed the gravel in front of the porticoed house. Sid repeated the question he had posed to Stan, and this time received an answer.

'Aye, I did notice the lad were flabby, but it could just be he's getting older.'

The group smiled, knowing Davey would get fit again once he was in the pit, but how else could he be, sitting at a desk, exercising his fingers and little else? The crunching noise of the gravel made Lisa laugh louder as Sarah rode alongside, peering down into the cart. 'You all right, bonny lass?'

They swept under the arch and into the yard to see Sandra Young talking to Alfie in the garage. They braked so hard that they skidded.

'Sandra?' shrieked Sarah. 'Put that lad down at once.'

Sandra walked over while Alfie started polishing Reginald's Rolls-Royce as though his life depended on it. 'I'm here,' Sandra said, 'because me and mam've come up with the co-op and she said I were to ask for a job, helping Viola. Seems there might be a need with the new bairn coming.'

'Oh, that's the best news for a long time, except for Davey coming home,' Fran cried.

Just then, Eva came roaring up the steps from the kitchen and across the yard, just ahead of Viola, shouting, 'We're coming to the beck too, 'cos Mr Ralph said yes, even though Viola dithered, but he said, "It'll be all right, for I'll keep an eye on the little devils." Viola said, "You and whose army?" and Mr Ralph—'

'That'll do, thank you, Miss Foghorn,' called Viola as Ralph bounded up the kitchen steps behind her. 'What I actually said was that you could all come if anyone was prepared to put you on their crossbar, or perhaps Alfie could take you in the Rolls. Mark you, if he did, then he'd have to stay at the beck, so of course Sandra would have to come, for she can't be the only pretty young lady remaining here helping Sophia, along with the old women. Wasn't that what you just called the co-op, Miss Eva?'

The gang looked at Eva, who was putting on a magnificent show of being aghast. For a rare moment the child was silent.

'Aye, she did,' came a voice from the top of the kitchen steps, 'just when we said we could teach the bairns the samba, but we can't of course, if we're too old and creaky.'

Eva opened her mouth, then promptly shut it again. Sandra looked at Viola, and their expressions said everything. Davey leaned against Fran. 'These two will work perfectly together.'

Madge was now making her way towards them. Today her eyepatch was royal blue. Eva muttered, 'Madge sent down a dark green eyepatch for Mr Moran. She said it was almost black so the shock of the change wouldn't be too much for a fiddle-de-dee schoolmaster, even if he had a bass voice.'

Ralph sighed. 'Tell me you didn't tell Mr Moran that.'

'Of course I did, Mr Ralph, because we didn't want him doing, you know, *fiddle-de-deeing* all over the place.'

It was Madge's turn to look aghast. She turned on her heel and headed towards Alfie, who had been listening but now resumed his frantic polishing. They heard her say, 'If you don't wipe that smile off your face, young Alfie, I'll do it for you with your very own duster. Now, the beck? You'll drive the horrors? Dr Dunster came this morning and says nothing will be happening with the brood mare – yes, *his* words. So, Reginald is happy for you to take the car and stay a while. If he needs to rush off with Sophia, he has Ralph's roadster.'

'Please,' begged Alfie, 'anything but them bairns, missus. Really, *anything*.'

Fran smothered her smile and turned back to Eva, who was just shaking her head. 'He's so daft,' Eva said. 'He knows we won't eat him, besides, Abe says he's too skinny to be tasty.'

She turned and they all looked after her. Davey whispered, 'She's really very, very scary. Too sharp by half. She could rule the world with one arm tied behind her back, just like the co-op.'

'Ah,' said Sid, as though he'd just discovered the secret of the universe. 'That's it, she's picking it up from them *old* women.'

Madge strode back across the yard, calling out, 'Get yourselves to the beck, or the bairns will be there before you. This isn't a variety show, it's a bliddy madhouse. And I'll see you later, young Sid.'

Ten minutes later, Ralph emerged from the kitchen brandishing a big hessian bag. 'Beer, water, tea and sandwiches, and even half a scone each, made by the bairns with hands well washed, no noses picked, so no bogeys. Blankets are going in the car, along with this.'

Alfie came to take it and placed everything in the boot.

Those on bikes set off back down the drive, and Davey said, 'I had forgotten quite what it was like, and I wish I hadn't remembered, for it will be harder still to leave.'

'As we said, don't go,' Sarah urged her brother.

They all laughed, and Fran, cycling alongside Davey, slowed. Abreast of the cart, she looked down at Lisa, whose hands were waggling about as though she was trying to catch the breeze. 'I'll keep an eye on you, and so will everyone else, because you deserve the best we can do for you. It's for your mam and da's sake as well as your own, little Lisa.'

She caught up with Davey, again, looking at the trees growing around the edge of a ploughed field, remembering how she had said to him not so very long ago that she wanted a bairn, for it would be something of their own. Well, Lisa wasn't theirs, but she would receive the same love as though she was. They passed the freshly turned earth, and now a few late lambs were gambolling in the meadow beneath the weak winter sun, which looked threatened by a racing cloud.

As the cloud's shadow swept along the fields, another thought came to settle on Fran: what must not happen was for her mam to lose her heart to Lisa, for now, having read Peter's letters, she felt Daisy would eventually reclaim the visible evidence of their love. But that was something they would face head-on, just as they did everything else.

Chapter Eleven

As they neared the beck they heard a toot. 'It's the Rolls,' called Sid, bringing up the rear with Beth. They slipped into single file and their crocodile of cycles was overtaken, the children and Sandra waving out of the wound-down windows.

'We beat you,' yelled Abe, 'and'll set up the blankets on the bank.'

Eva must have pulled him down, because he was gone and she appeared. 'Sandra says we'll start the fire too. She's having a bit of a spark with Alfie, too busy to talk—'

Eva disappeared as though she'd also been pulled down. Then Melanie stuck her head out. 'Sandra says she doesn't know what the bairn's talking about and we've to sit down, and what's more we're to behave.'

Behind Fran, Ralph called, 'It all makes me tired. Do they ever run out of steam?'

'Oh, foolish man, that's not worth answering.' Viola groaned, ringing her bell. 'Time out, bonny lad. Relax. We've the day to get through yet. It will only get worse.'

Beth called to Fran, 'Oh, I loved coming with the parents when it was chill and we snuggled up by the fire. I can remember them saying, "Run off some energy, or you'll end up in the beck." You called out, "Is that a promise, Mam?" and your mam threw you in.'

Fran roared with laughter. 'It was as well I could swim. And she rubbed me warm and tucked me in the blanket by the fire, and it was the best feeling ever.'

'Even if you couldn't swim, she'd have saved you,' Davey called over his shoulder. 'She needed someone to hang out the washing.'

Finally, round the long bend was the lane leading down to the beck. The Rolls had been parked hard against the hawthorn hedge. Ralph muttered, 'Better not have scratched the car. Father is good about most things, but damaging his baby is not on the agenda.'

They sniggered as they left their bikes by the hedge just before the lane led onto the path. Davey unhitched Lisa's cart. 'Should you carry her, Fran, or is she happy to be pulled?'

'Giddy up, Dobbin, and let's find out.'

The group walked behind the cart, hearing giggles from Lisa as she was jerked up and over stones and into ruts. It was Davey who was swearing under his breath as Sid sidled up beside him.

'Best not teach the lass bad words, Uncle Davey.'

'Best you keep your words to yourself, lad.'

The going was much easier when they reached the beck path. The sun glinted off the water and on the far bank the rope swing swayed gently in the breeze.

The blankets had been laid out and a fire started by Alfie, who had sent the children on a kindling- and log-finding mission. Beside Sandra was the hessian bag of provisions. Davey slumped onto the blankets, patting the ground next to him, but Fran was looking across the beck, at the bairns.

'Did you really send them over there for kindling?' she asked Alfie, who was blowing at the reluctant flames.

'Where?' he called.

Davey was standing on the bank, shouting across, Stan beside him and Ralph behind. 'Do not swing on that rope. Do not – we haven't tested it. Get the kindling, as Alfie asked. Eva,' he warned, 'do as you are told.'

Alfie was fanning the fire now. 'They can't reach it, so there's no danger.'

Sid and Norm were ferreting around in the hessian bag. 'I've built up a thirst – anyone else?' Norm asked.

Sandra pulled out a flask. 'Tea in here.'

The boys shook their heads, pityingly. 'Oh my, what winter picnics have you been on?' said Norm. 'Alcohol trumps tea, any day.'

Sid drew out a bottle of beer and waved it at the lads. 'Beer, come and get it.' They did, drinking it from enamel mugs while the girls sipped tea, and though it was moving on towards the end of October, the sun was warm, the light was playing on the beck and the birds still sang. Davey sat next to Fran, his arm around her, his kisses gentle on her neck.

'I reckon the beck is heaven on earth,' he murmured. 'So many memories, and it's our place. Not just the two of us, the whole gang's.'

As he said it, Ralph pointed to Marty who was sprawled on the branch that held the rope, swinging it towards the evacuees. 'What the hell? Stop,' Ralph yelled, leaping to his feet, but Eva, Abe and Melanie had jumped and caught it and were swinging out over the water. The rope broke.

'Bloody hell,' yelled Ralph. They were all on their feet as the screams began and the men ran, diving, streaking across the beck, for it was deep so near the bridge. The girls stayed on the bank, hesitating, uncertain, then grabbed blankets while Alfie rushed for towels from the boot.

'We'll rub 'em like Mam rubbed me and . . . well, all of us when we swam in the autumn. The bairns will be fine. A good rub, then wrap them in blankets – the men too,' Fran ordered.

Marty then plummeted from the branch, flailing in the air, all arms and legs, shouting, 'Bliddy hell.' He landed in the water, managing to miss everyone, and his shout was more a gurgle as he sank, only to be yanked back to the surface by Davey who had grabbed his hair.

Davey took hold of his shoulders and dragged him back towards the bank. 'Stop struggling. Do as you're told or you'll be skelped.'

Sandra was building the fire, fanning it with one of the towels Alfie had brought back. Fran told Beth and Viola to get to the other side of the beck. 'Herd the dry bairns back here, they're tizzying.'

The marrers were splashing out of the water, onto the bank, carrying the four bedraggled children. No one said a word, not the men or the bairns, until the men flopped onto the blankets, still holding the children, who were half lying on them, shivering with the cold and shock.

'Will you bliddy well learn to do as you're told,' Viola raged at the bairns, sending the dry ones who had run back to collect kindling and firewood to build up the roaring fire even more. The adults ripped off the bairns' clothes while Sarah held up a blanket to shield them from the wind. The men had headed behind the bushes and emerged wrapped in blankets and still rubbing their hair with the sodden towels.

Sid laughed. 'Bracing, eh?'

'You used a bad word, Viola. You said bliddy,' Eva managed to say, though her teeth were chattering.

'Never mind that, Eva,' Viola snapped. 'Sit down on that blanket nearest the fire. What were you all told? What?'

The children sat down, next to the men, and hung their heads. Marty heaved himself to his feet. 'It were my idea, Viola.'

Everyone looked at him, then at Eva, who was struggling to her feet too, gripping the blanket tightly. 'Marty, don't be daft. It was mine, and it could have been good fun, because it was just hanging there. And I reckon it was, now we're out and by the fire.'

The men were looking at one another over the heads of the children, grinning, and it was only then that Fran remembered the lads doing the same thing and getting a skelping for it, and Stan, too, saying, 'It was just hanging there.' Her da had told her mam that it was her fault for she'd thrown Fran in the year before, so maybe he should throw *her* in. Her mam had laughed fit to burst. They had swum every year since then, but she was blowed if she was going in now she was an adult. So there.

'Do you remember what my da said to Mam . . . ?' she said to Sarah.

'I was just thinking it.' Sarah and Beth both began laughing, and though no one knew why, they all started, even the children.

An hour later, the shivering had stopped, the roaring fire having practically dried the half-drowned rats, as it always did. What's more, the sandwiches had been eaten, the children had sipped warming tea, a couple of bottles of beer had been shared between the marrers, with just desultory talk amongst them all, and Fran realised that the gang had taken their parents' places. It was a strange feeling.

Davey watched as Fran sat Lisa on her lap and played 'This little piggy went to market' with Lisa's toes, and then pretended to nibble them to gurgles of delight. He had heard Fran taking control of the situation as he was busy in the beck, and knew without doubt that she was a replica of her mam – and it made him proud. Sitting next to him as they sipped the remains of their beer, Sid muttered, 'Is it me, or are women scary?'

'No it's not, and yes they are,' Ralph answered, after a

pause, 'and I reckon our Eva has been spending too much time with the co-op, for she's a sergeant major in disguise, and too clever by half.'

'Brave too,' added Norm.

'Well, all the bairns are. There are the orphans just getting on with it, and the others away from their families,' said Stan, adding his twopenn'orth.

They turned to look at the children as Eva stared into the fire, Melanie leaning against her. Their dried hair lifted in the breeze, with the sun warm on their backs. The birds sang and the beck rippled as Eva said, 'I were scared, you know, Mr Davey. I couldn't find the ground, and I thought there were monsters lurking in there. I thought they'd grab me feet, pull me down, chomp away me flesh and spit me out.'

The children stared at her in horror. Enid said, 'Oh no, like a fish when it's been filleted, so there's just the bones.'

Tommy turned to Viola. 'There aren't monsters, are there, Viola? And what's lurking, when it's at home? Our Eva uses these long words—'

'That's because I read, but I can't spell them all and sometimes don't know how they sound. I got dessert and desert wrong, remember, in school. I read out that the raspberry had got lost in the desert. The teacher laughed.'

Abe cut in. 'The bairns didn't, though, and I reckon Mr Moran wouldn't. He said he'd learned a few lessons in the desert, and one was to keep his head down.'

Fran looked at Davey and neither could think of a reply, but they didn't need to, for Eva filled the gap, as she so often did. 'Aye, but if he had kept his head down properly he wouldn't have struck up with our Madge and be given a better eyepatch.'

Out of the mouths of babes and sucklings, thought Davey, wondering not for the first time what engine was working away in Eva's inner depths to make her such a force. But a force for what? Ah, for good, or to be a master criminal? He grinned to himself, only to see Fran looking askance. He merely raised his eyebrows and tipped his head towards Eva, and Fran nodded. No more needed to be said.

Silence had returned and the children looked uncertain again as they examined the water. Perhaps, Davey thought, the shadow of the monster was bearing down and he didn't want any more horrors for them to handle. Thinking long and hard, he finally said, 'How about I make up a story, and you have to help me?'

Abe sighed. 'Will it be a sort of crossword-puzzle thingy, Mr Davey? For I don't feel like thinking too much. But if it would help you . . . ?'

Right, thought Davey, no puzzle, just a straightforward story. For a moment he turned to watch Fran, sitting next to him, spooning some sort of vegetable mix from a jam jar into Lisa's mouth. The bairn looked like a little bird waiting for a worm. So, something about a worm? 'You have to help me if I get stuck, is that all right?'

The children nodded, grinning.

Davey scrabbled desperately to find the first line about a worm, but nothing came. Instead it was the beck and a kind monster that nagged at him. Fran was leaning against him now, her warmth seeping into him, as Lisa slept, her mouth wiped clean. What had been grubby and mucky was now beautiful, and suddenly he was close to an idea and he began.

'Once upon a time, when the day was bright and sunny, a poor lonely monster was swimming about in the beck, holding his breath, diving down amongst the reeds, wishing he could spend more time in the world, but he couldn't, because he had been banished to the bottom of Massingham beck—'

'Why?' interrupted Enid, inching away from Tommy, who was leaning past her to listen. 'Sit up, Tommy, you're blocking the heat.'

Ralph took over. 'Because he was a prince who had . . .'

Ralph petered out, only for Viola to pick up the story. 'Who had trodden on the foot of a bad-tempered fairy called . . .' She looked at the children, her hands outspread. 'Help is needed, you bairns.'

Tommy had been listening avidly. 'Antoinette.'

'Why's that her name?' queried Eva. 'It's too bliddy long.'

'Language,' the adults shouted.

'Because she told people they could eat cake,' Sandra called across to Eva, 'not knowing they couldn't afford it. Mr Reginald talked about her at teatime, don't you remember, Eva?'

'Oh aye, she were French, snobby and proud.' Abe looked round for agreement and got it.

'All right,' Davey said, 'the monster is a prince who has been bad and has been changed into a monster because—'

'Stepping on a grumpy fairy isn't enough,' Alfie interrupted.

Davey had no idea what would be. Alfie continued 'Well, we'll decide that in a minute, but for now let's have him hating being a monster, and, um . . . well, he's not nibbling legs, but instead let's have him try to save some bairns who've fallen in.'

'Well done,' Fran whispered, 'that should sort out any nightmares tonight.'

Melanie got to her knees, looking at Fran. 'He might save them and bring them to the bank, but if he's horrible to look at, we'd still be frightened.'

Eva gripped her blanket. 'Aye, we would, but what if he spoke and it was a kind voice? What if he said—'

' "I'm trying to save you," ' Abe butted in. ' "I want to be

nice, then the cross fairy might let me be a prince again."
You see, he did something more than tread on her foot, like
Alfie said. He did something really bad, then called her a
bad-tempered old witch. Like I sometimes wanted to tell
me teacher in Newcastle.'

The adults laughed, but the children weren't listening.
Instead, they were talking over one another, ideas tum-
bling from their imaginations.

Davey listened, loving every second of these bairns putting together a story that he could never have dreamed of
creating.

On they went, their fears forgotten, he hoped, looking
around at the gang who were all listening, and if they were
anything like him, they were picturing it: the beck, the children, the kind princess up on a swing looking after the
prince so no one hurt him, the bairns the monster had saved
helping him achieve the three or perhaps four kindnesses
the cross fairy had insisted must be performed before he
could return to dry land and live as a prince again.

Now Abe was pacing, his bare feet and legs red from the
heat of the fire, his blanket wrapped round like a toga. Stephen was poking the fire with a charred stick. The sparks
flew up into the air. Finally, as the lad checked the end of
his stick, which was black enough to be charcoal, Stephen
said, 'I reckon it's like being sent outside the classroom
door. You go back in when you can behave. It feels lonely
out there, and must have been right lonely for the prince
being stuck in the beck.'

There was another long silence, until Eva whispered,
'Poor monster. Like Alfie said, a fairy wouldn't be so mean
if he'd just trodden on her foot, even if he were a rude prince
and it was a bad-tempered fairy. And why would a princess be fiddling about on a swing to keep an eye on him,
Abe? It's your idea, so tell us.'

'Got it,' Davey called out then, feeling ridiculously excited as he solved this part of the puzzle. 'When he was a prince, he was trespassing . . . er . . . in a secret garden owned by a nice duke . . . The duke had told the prince it was private, but the prince didn't care. He liked the flowers growing there—'

'Aye,' Norm interrupted. 'So he went in and picked 'em . . . because he'd been spoilt . . .'

Ralph whispered to Davey, 'I reckon that prince isn't a million miles from me.' Davey offered him a Woodbine and they lit up. 'But you've done many kindnesses, lad,' Davey muttered, 'so no one thinks that now.' Suddenly a thought flashed across Davey's mind. 'I know,' he almost shouted, 'the old fairy magicked him into the beck – for ever – for picking the flowers, but there is a princess who loves him.

'Let's see . . . She is the daughter of the duke whose flowers the monster had picked. She tells the old fairy to banish her too, so that she can support the prince . . . until his kindnesses are done.' He looked across at the rope swing.

Ralph, his mind full of Viola, went on. 'The old fairy does that, and the girl has to sit on a swing hanging from a tree over the bank. The old fairy gives her just one wish. The princess chooses a wand which has a teaspoon of magic in it, to help the prince.'

The bairns were nodding. 'The crosspatch fairy magics the princess into a pretty dress as well as giving her the wand,' Eva decided. 'The princess waves her wand a lot, and if it was Christmas she'd sing carols and there'd be a tree growing by the beck, all decorated.'

'Aye,' Melanie muttered. 'But she couldn't just magic him back to being a prince, because it were only a teaspoon of magic, so she needs help to make him keep going till he's done his kindnesses . . .' She petered out.

'That would be us, the bairns,' said Eva. 'And his first kindness would be saving us, then she could do her magic so that part of the monster changed back to a prince, so we would see his posh shirt and so on.'

Abe took over. 'He'd do two or perhaps three more kindnesses, with our help, and suddenly he'd be a complete prince, and free and so would the princess, and if it's Christmas we'd find presents magicked under the tree by the old fairy.' Abe dusted his hands, as though he had saved the world. Davey grinned at him as Abe saluted the adults.

The children were tiring of it all now. Viola tested their clothes, which were completely dry, and so were the men's. She said, into the quiet of a story done and dusted, 'I think that was wonderful, and you're all very clever. I reckon a round of applause, and one for the grown-ups who put in their halfpenn'orth. But let's clap quietly, for Lisa is still asleep.'

They did just that, and over it Eva said, 'I reckon the story could be made into a Christmas play, because with the fairy, the magic—'

'No,' shouted Melanie. 'Not a Christmas *play*, but a Christmas *pantomime*. There's even a Christmas tree with presents – just think of it – for my farewell thing. Oh, yes, let's do that.'

Fran groaned quietly, but Viola whispered to her, 'I refuse to panic. Or think of the set, the costumes, the food or the state of the ballroom, because tomorrow there will be another idea.'

Ralph leaned across. 'Yes, indeed, probably an opera. Perhaps we should accept the idea of the panto.'

'Oh no we won't,' Sid said, raising his mug of beer. Beth laughed, sipped her tea, then sniggered.

'Oh yes we will,' Sandra called, holding up a blanket.

'Come on, bairns, get dressed, then a bit of a run about is a good idea, I think.'

'Oh no it isn't,' yelled Davey.

Fran groaned again as Eva, sharp as a tack, called, 'That's what they said in the pantomime I went to see, and then they yelled, "He's behind you."'

Fran, Sarah, Viola and Beth looked at one another. Beth murmured, 'One, two, three . . .'

Together, the girls yelled, 'Oh no he isn't.'

Fran was cheering up because she'd heard Melanie muttering behind the blanket, 'I reckon a variety show would be easier. We could just sing and dance.'

After the men had chased the bairns over the bridge and then back again, the gang relaxed around the fire while the children played tag along the path. Viola and Ralph sat together, watching the children, loving the whole day.

Ralph examined his scarred hands, flexing his fingers, and as he did so, Viola traced the blue ridges. 'Truly a pitman, bonny lad,' she whispered.

He nodded. 'And you are truly a princess.'

'I think Melanie's farewell is a toss-up between a variety show and a panto,' she said. 'And we really need to sort it out.'

The others agreed. She continued. 'We have just over two months until Christmas, so we'll press the children to make a decision over the next few days. If it's not something they've chosen, I'm not sure they'll put in the effort.'

Again, everyone agreed.

'There'll be scenery if it's a pantomime,' said Stan, 'and a swing for the princess. There'll be music, songs, an audience, the interval drinks. Will the audience be just us, or the parents of those bairns too, those that have them? If it's a variety show, who will do a turn? For either, do we do food?

163

Are there costumes to make? Whatever we do, remember we need to smarten up the ballroom, so Viola is quite right, we have to get a move on.'

Norm was busy with a piece of string he'd knotted because Enid had asked how to do a cat's cradle. 'We'll need the Christmas tree, whatever they decide, and I reckon presents *would* be a good idea, to be opened after whatever we do. Will there be a Father Christmas distributing the presents? Will—'

'Oh, stop,' Sid muttered. 'It's messing with me head.'

At that moment, the children traipsed back along the path and Sandra murmured, 'Batten down the hatches. Get ready to repel boarders.'

As the bairns arrived and squeezed in between everyone, Eva stared out across the beck to the field of cows. 'We saw those and thought we could have a cow in the pantomime. She could be asked if she would keep the monster company while the bairns went home. Maybe the cow could bring him a branch with berries on it, and it could stick out of its gob.'

'Or wild flowers.' It was Enid, sitting with Norm, trying to do the cat's cradle.

'Nah, a prince wouldn't eat flowers, only berries.'

'Who said anything about eating flowers, our Marty? It were just a present to the monster.' Enid's small hands were managing the string, her face a picture of concentration, much like the girls in the Factory, Fran thought.

Abe looked at Ralph. 'We've decided it's to be a panto and I reckon we *should* have a cow in it.'

Enid forgot the cat's cradle and said quietly, 'Me mam and da took me to a pantomime, it were Boxing Day. There were decorations in our houses, a tree, it were like magic, and then it was time for the pantomime and that were magic, and the fairy's dress, the music, the lights. It was right grand, happy, and we sang, and the mams and dads laughed a lot and shouted, "He's behind yer." Aye, it were magic, and then we came out and in the entrance there was Father Christmas, and we had a present each. I had a bar of chocolate. I kept it till the summer because it were so . . . well, magic.'

'Well,' whispered Davey as the bairns stared into the fire, probably remembering past times, 'that's it then. Somehow it'll be sorted, but that'll be everyone else's chore, for I'll be back down south.'

Sid threw a clump of grass, which fell to the ground before it reached him. 'Canny devil.' But the gang knew they had no choice but to agree, and they fell silent too as they remembered their own Christmases growing up together.

'I remember St Oswald's put up a Christmas tree outside the dairy,' Fran said quietly. 'Before the war, people put presents under it for the bairns who queued on Christmas Eve. I got an orange.'

'I had a couple of walnuts,' said Davey. 'Da cracked the shells with a brick.'

Viola was nodding. 'Well, we definitely need to have a tree at the panto then, with gifts. But first we need to see if the ballroom can handle a stage.'

Ralph agreed. 'But let's not leap at it. We have a bit of time and we need to get it right.'

He squeezed Viola's hand, as Fran asked, 'And who is to be the rear end of the cow?'

The laughter was long, with Sandra almost singing, 'Oh, I do so love Christmas, it's so different and happy and away from real life. What's more, it was when Jesus was born and we'll have the *two* bairns by then, so it will be a grand memory for our Melanie to take with her.'

Eva jumped up then and squealed, 'That's right, it'll be right wonderful and magical. There'll be lots of singing and dancing, and grown-ups will laugh at the bad fairy being grumpy, making the spell, and at the cow, and there's a custard tart in someone's face, which is funniest of all. The princess on the swing will have a right pretty dress, and a wand. Listen, listen, we can decorate the ballroom with Christmas paper chains, and I reckon we should have the villagers there to say goodbye to Melanie, and the bairns from school. We could do the pantomime for them as a big thank you for *their* kindnesses. We could feed 'em an' all and we'll end up singing carols. All the bairns will have a present. You never know, Father Christmas might like the idea and come with his reindeer. Oh, it will be the best Christmas pantomime in the whole wide world.'

Marty was on his feet, trying to stop her jumping. 'You're making me feel sick, so stand still.' She did. He continued. 'The co-op could do the clothes—'

Melanie stood up, facing him, hands on hips. 'Costumes, silly.'

Eva was pulling Abe to his feet. As the hullabaloo grew, all the bairns were milling, with Melanie trying out some dance steps and wondering who was going to play the piano, or would Viola play the saxophone?

'Don't be daft,' said Enid. 'She should be the pretty princess on the swing, sweet on the prince, for if Mr Ralph is the prince, it would be real, wouldn't it?'

Ralph hugged Viola, whispering, 'Yes, it will be real, just as it is now, and I think the pantomime is a wonderful Christmas thing, and it'll keep them busy, happy, and we'll have the ballroom pretty organised anyway for your party. Maybe Miss Walters would bang out tunes on the piano? That would be one problem solved.'

'Why not just put a cork in it, Ralph,' Norm muttered, trying to light another cigarette, holding up his muffler as a windbreak.

Sid elbowed him, knocking the match from his hand. 'Don't be a misery. Imagine if Iris Walters was playing the organ, making rude noises. That would be a panto on its own.'

'Oh no it wouldn't,' yelled Beth.

'Oh yes it would,' Stan responded, then lit his Woodbine, throwing his matches to Norm, who had run out.

The marrers were laughing fit to burst, and the bairns had stopped talking and were looking at them as though they were mad. Ralph grinned to himself, because perhaps they were, or drunk on fresh air, sun and yes, beer. But also on the blessing of friendship and a childish excitement about a special Christmas.

Stephen was asking, 'But where will we get the cow?'

'Oh, shut up, Stephen,' Eva said. 'It will have to be a pretend one. A real one would probably poop, and then people would slip in it. The pantomime I saw had a cow, but there were two people in it, me da said. One were its arse, t'other its head.'

The grown-ups sat back and let them talk, and all the while they were getting ideas of their own, even Norm, and suddenly it seemed the best idea in the world because it would bring everyone together, and they'd just have to make it work. But who would write the panto, wondered Viola, just as Dora said, 'We really, really must ask the parents to come – those who have 'em. It is Christmas after all.'

Ralph nudged Viola, who nodded and called, 'We'll talk about all of this over the next few days and get things straight in our heads, but enough lounging around. Let's find some leaves we can press.'

Chapter Twelve

Davey and Fran made their way home at the end of the day, tired and happy from time spent just being together as the beck flowed gently in the background. Lisa was quiet in her cart, and Fran was in her heart.

She smiled at Davey, only to find he was already smiling, at her. They dismounted outside the gate into the yard. She opened it and led the way through, Davey towing Lisa. They parked the bikes and he lifted Lisa out, resting her on his hip, showing her the hens.

'Hello, ladies and gentleman,' Fran murmured, her fingers hooked into the holes of the chicken wire. 'This is Lisa. When she's older she will poke cabbage leaves through the wire, but today I will do it.' She took some from the bowl her mam had left on top of the feed bin, tearing them into strips, showing Lisa, who was chewing her fist. 'See these, little one? We need to feed the hens, and they will give us a drippy egg for your breakfast one day soon.'

She prodded the leaves through. 'I wish you were here every day, Davey,' she said. 'I wish Lisa was our real child, but nevertheless she'll be well loved.'

Davey gripped Lisa tighter and drew Fran to him. 'A lass under each arm, eh? I know, sweet Franny, but it is what it is, I suppose, and you know if I was here, I'd help.'

They stood together and talked about the dreamy, lazy hours they'd spend together over the next few days – once her shift was finished, that was. But those plans came to nothing, for the next day they found themselves up at

Massingham Hall, standing in the disused ballroom amongst the bairns, the co-op, the marrers, Uncle Tom Cobley and all. They had been summoned after their shifts to 'sort out the panto'. When they arrived, Abe repeated this instruction, and even clicked his fingers to show how easy it would be.

The adults raised their eyebrows and looked around the ballroom, which not only looked sad and tired, but smelled it too. The ceiling was the worst, and had a damp stain near the rear corner. Reginald Massingham tilted his head to get the full picture, then nodded. 'A leak, repaired some years ago, though not painted. The room hasn't been used since Ralph's mother died. Somehow, extravagant soirées are not quite to Sophia's and my liking. But I had forgotten that the ballroom is, in itself, an elegant room.'

Enid clasped her hands. 'Oh, I can just imagine an extravagant whatever-you-called-it with people twirling and foxtrotting because it's a ballroom. I reckon their tiaras and diamonds would be glinting, and over there –' she pointed to the corner at the far end '– an orchestra playing.' She swung round to Eva. 'Let's have a dance instead. It would be so pretty. We could wear dresses – ones the co-op would make, wouldn't you, Mrs Hall?'

Annie, who was chatting to Maud and Audrey, didn't hear. Enid called, louder, 'The co-op could make party clothes for the bairns, couldn't you, please?'

Looking a little wild-eyed, Annie nodded, not sure what party, but not about to ask.

Enid nodded. 'Then you don't need to make ragged clothes for the beck bairns, and we'd not have to get in and out of a make-believe beck.'

Please, please, thought Fran, for she, her mam and Davey had been worrying about the massive project of a pantomime, and it seemed they were not the only ones. Moving over to the bairns, she said quietly, 'When you actually think seriously about a pantomime on top of renovating the ballroom, there's just too much to do. The first of which would be to find someone to write it.'

'Aye,' said Marty. 'A party would be good. We could learn to dance, and The Factory Girls could sing.'

Eva, though, was shaking Marty's arm, aghast. 'No, it'll be like a wedding tea and they're just ordinary. Remember Fran's so close to Sarah's? Just the same, they were.'

'Well, pardon me for living,' muttered Sarah.

'Well, if you *were* a monster, Madame Eva,' said Fran, 'you'd have to do ten kindnesses for that – four wouldn't be nearly enough.'

The minute she said it, from the way silence fell on Eva and Melanie and flowed out to the other children, Fran knew she'd made a dreadful mistake.

'Oh, Fran,' Melanie sighed. 'You made me think about the poor old monster, the pretty princess on the swing, the cow, the bairns, the fun. Eva's right – it'll be so much better than a lot of grown-ups twirling and dancing and tripping over us when we're trying to dance too.'

Eva crossed her arms, nodding. 'I reckon, from the one I went to, that there's an interval, so there'd only be time for snacks. If it's a dance, they'll need proper food, which'll be more work for the co-op.'

Marty piped up, 'We could ask some of the villagers to play parts, and it's like we said yesterday, it would be the best way to say goodbye to our Melanie. It'd be all Christmassy, you see. And the tree could go over by the French windows, and maybe Father Christmas would leave presents, because we have been quite good. Oh, Fran's *so* clever to remember the monster and the kindnesses.'

Fran gave up. Had Marty and Eva manipulated her deliberately? Well, she wouldn't put it past them. Finally,

Beth beckoned Fran over, and muttered, pointing to the far end, 'That's where the stage should be.'

A moment later, Sarah asked, 'But how would we hang the curtains? From the ceiling?'

'Oh Lord, heaven knows,' Fran said, realising that the panto was set in stone.

Davey came up behind her. 'I think we have been well and truly backed into a corner, and from this day forth we must watch every word we say to these little rascals. You walked right into this, so think hard about the curtains, little wife, or you'll end up being the one to sort out the problem.'

Fran slapped his arm, but was watching Eva bouncing up and down in front of Reginald.

'So we will have a pantomime, won't we, Mr Reginald?'

Abe was more serious and answered for Reginald, who stood as though dazed. 'Oh, of course we will, but we need to get it right, and the ballroom looking nice.'

Marty was staring up at the ceiling, his hands on his hips. 'The ceiling has to be painted in time for Viola's birthday anyway. A panto would hardly be any more work. We'd just have to learn our lines.'

Fran heard Reginald groan. 'It'll need a bloody miracle, that's what it will need.'

'It seems, if I've just heard correctly,' Viola muttered into Fran's ear, 'that a panto will be no work, for all that has to be done is for the bairns to learn their lines. First, I'll skelp your Davey for starting the storytelling, and then I'll strangle you for reminding them of the kindnesses.'

'Oh,' Enid was saying, 'I heard that, Mr Reginald, but I reckon you're wrong. I don't reckon it needs a bliddy miracle.'

'Language, Enid,' Sandra called.

'Well,' Enid said, 'it were Mr Reginald's bad word, not mine.'

'Language, Mr Reginald,' roared the adults.

Enid looked satisfied. Stephen, still preoccupied, merely said, 'We just need some strong grown-ups, eh, Mr Reginald, to sort out the stage, the scenery and—'

'Perhaps you're right, Stephen,' Reginald said, in retreat, physically and mentally. This time he avoided eye contact with everyone as he backed away to the long windows.

Viola nudged Fran. 'I've an idea.' She raised her voice. 'I'm happy with just a few drinks at the Rising Sun for my birthday, so if *I* am, I'm sure the village would be too, and would pop in for a pint – so no need to rush the ballroom.'

'The Rising Sun? But *we* couldn't be there because pubs are for grown-ups, and we are to have some smarter clothes the co-op is making just for your party,' Marty objected.

'Silly me,' Viola chided herself, mouthing 'Sorry' to Fran.

'Yes, silly you,' Ralph agreed, and got a whack from Viola for his pains. He doubled up in pretend agony, which was ignored by the bairns, who were deciding that the Christmas tree definitely should be by the French windows. At this point Stan started doing a Reginald and inched back towards the door, for there had been a suggestion a while ago that he was the Christmas-tree man, but it was too late, for Enid ran after him.

'You can't go yet, for you haven't heard how high the tree needs to be, and what room we need beneath the lowest branches for some presents, but don't worry, for Mr Reginald can show you where to find the right one.'

Reginald, who was looking out over the garden, turned, bewildered. 'Can I?'

Ralph called, 'Oh, of course, dear Father—'

Reginald fixed him with a 'shut up' stare, but Eva had already cut right across Ralph. 'You know where everything is because it's yours, Mr Reginald. If it were all mine, I'd know, eh?' The children nodded.

Fran heard Abe turn to Stephen to say, 'She's right clever is our Eva. I wouldn't have thought of that.'

Suddenly Fran was shaking with laughter. Davey came alongside, whispering, 'By all that's holy, we are standing watching history repeat itself, for I always thought you were right, and so did you. Bossy little madam, you were.' He received the whack this time.

Now Dora and Tommy, who had been chattering together, turned to Viola and Sandra. 'We can write the programmes,' Dora explained. 'And maybe Mr Moran will let the class help?'

Tommy took over. 'Mr Moran said he would join a sing-song for Melanie's Christmas farewell, so I reckon he'd be in the pantomime instead.'

'But we haven't got a pantomime written yet, have we?' asked Sophia, waddling in.

The children looked at one another. Eva took over yet again. 'Well, we've got a story about a beck monster, so I reckon that can be written as a panto easy-peasy.'

Abe nodded and clicked his fingers again. 'Just like that,' he said.

This brought the bairns to the hook to attach the princess's swing to the ceiling, because the swing should hang on a wire or even two, Stephen said. Marty, who, like Tommy, spoke little but listened a lot, put up his hand.

'Aye, and it should be near the pretend beck, for she's keeping the monster safe. I saw a panto with me mam and da, and the wires that the swing hung from got stuck and the fairy yelled, "Get me down off this bliddy swing before I stick me wand where you don't like it, Andy." Me da said it weren't part of the play, and Andy was the man who did the props, but I don't know what those are.'

It was such a long speech that everyone was amazed, even Eva, and they all took a moment to envision the scene, which was a mistake, because the adults' laughter rolled around the ballroom. Fran heard Marty say, 'All the adults laughed then too, until they closed the curtains and a man came through them and said, "Please to remain in your seats while the issue of the fairy is addressed." Then they laughed again.'

Eva stared at him. 'You remember all the words?'

'Oh aye, because me da went to the pub the next night and came back telling me mam he'd told his marrers, and after that, they kept repeating it all night. Me da were laughing when he told me mam till the tears ran down his face. He's buried in the desert now. I reckon me mam would have liked to come to our panto an awful lot, Sophia. A panto would be right good, wouldn't it, if it makes people laugh?'

Sophia and Reginald exchanged looks just as everyone else was doing, because after that little speech there *had* to be a pantomime, with guests, including the parents or parent of the evacuees, those that had them, and it had better be the best damned panto there'd ever been.

'I agree with Marty that we should ask the parents that are available because it's going to be such fun, and fun should be shared,' Sophia said quietly. 'And for those of you without parents it will be nice to get to know your friends' mams, don't you think?'

The children nodded, but Fran could tell that a cloud had passed over the orphans. Eager to fill the silence, she hunted for the right words to change the subject, but came up empty. Davey, though, uttered quite the wrong words, which achieved the same end.

'If we need a stage, why don't we just have it at the Miners' Club hall, where they have all these things?'

Ralph, Stan, Sid and Norm were all nodding when the wail of outrage from the bairns made them change tack and shake their heads. Stan, back with them, gestured to his marrers to step away, as though Davey was contagious. 'He said it, not us,' muttered Sid to the children.

'You have permission to kill me,' Davey almost whimpered to Fran, 'if I ever speak without permission again. From the safety of the south, I will await with interest the report on the arrangements for I clearly cannot be trusted with any role of importance.' Again he received a whack. This time it hurt. His 'ouch' was loud enough to draw attention. He waved an apology. Silence fell.

'Well,' Davey ventured, eager to make amends, 'everyone here could put together a stage, easy-peasy. It doesn't have to be a big one. There's a lot of old wood in the barn, after all, isn't there, Mr Massingham? Yes, I'm sure Stan could sort that out, and maybe you could just borrow the chairs from the Miners' Club hall?'

Stan's voice was strong. 'In spite of our southern friend, I'm not so sure that Stan could do such a thing, easy-peasy. I'm not very good with me hands.'

Eva had a little notepad and was writing furiously. She looked up, puzzled. 'But you're a pitman, Mr Stan, so of course you can do anything.' She licked her pencil and said as she wrote, so all could hear, 'Mr Stan and his marrers to make the stage.'

Abe clicked his fingers again, beaming, then a thought clearly struck him. He turned to Sophia and Reginald. 'If your other missus used to have that extravagant thing with the foreign name, there must have been some chairs for them ladies and gents to put their bums on?'

Reginald looked at his watch. 'Do you know, I am expecting a telephone call. I'd best be away.'

Fran wondered if she was the only one to hear Sophia breathe, 'Oh, I think you'd best not, Reginald George Massingham.'

He did not, but was visibly wracking his brains, finally saying, 'You know, I think you're right, Abraham. We did, and they must be somewhere. I can't vouch for their comfort, but better than nothing. Leave that with me. That'll be my job, eh? Best away to have a look.'

'That'll be a grand start for you, Mr Reginald.' It was, of course, Eva calling after him. Everyone heard Mr Reginald's groan as he left the ballroom. Finally, Annie put up her hand.

'I can hear Lisa crying outside, so I am going to put the kettle on. Tea in five minutes and home-made biscuits, if anyone's interested.'

There was an unseemly rush to the door and for now, though only for now, Fran knew, the Christmas pantomime was forgotten. In many ways, she was so very glad that it was to happen, but how on earth they were going to pull it off, she had no idea.

Davey's leave drew to a close, by which time he had grown used to carrying Lisa on his hip, and had discovered that a babe was not only heavy, but also needed feeding and changing; they dribbled, too, and often didn't sleep when the grown-ups did. He also discovered he loved it all, and Fran even more than he'd thought he could ever love, and that lying in bed with his arms around her, talking and laughing about the day, was the best of all worlds.

He also discovered that though his marrers had added Ralph to their number, it didn't mean he had been dropped. But above all else, he realised that he, as much as they, were enslaved by, and at the mercy of, eleven nine- and ten-year-olds who had a dream of a farewell Christmas pantomime that *had* to come to life as they smiled, planned and mercilessly exploited all those around them.

These were his thoughts again as he stood on the cold,

windswept platform, breathing in the sulphur, hearing as always the noises of the pithead, seeing the slag heap and the air heavy with coal dust, waiting for the train that would take him back to the war and away from his home, like so many others. Around him stood his marrers, and Fran's, plus his mother-in-law, Annie, jiggling Lisa up and down in her arms, a knitted bonnet tied beneath the babe's chin. Her tooth had broken the surface of her gum yesterday. 'Three now, eh?' he called to the babe. Annie smiled at Lisa, and then him.

They all heard them then, the bairns, clattering through the ticket office, Abe calling, 'Mr Stationmaster, has the London train come yet?'

'No, young man. It's for our Davey you're here, I expect.'

They stormed onto the platform. Eva was waving a pad of lined paper calling, 'Here you are, Mr Davey. We want you to write the pantomime because you're not doing anything else, and we knew you'd want to help because everyone else is, and it's your story, anyway.'

Abe ran alongside her and reached them, the others in their wake, 'It was her idea that you should. She's clever like that.'

Davey heard the smothered laughter from his marrers, but pulled Fran closer to him. She whispered, 'Oh no, I'm not a shield, Davey Bedley. You face 'em.'

Davey took the pad, flipping through the empty pages. 'But I don't know how to write a pan—'

'Well, as Mr Moran says,' Eva interrupted, raising her voice as the train seemed to roar around the bend, screeching and whistling, 'you'll just have to find a way. Sir's clever like that, isn't he, Abe.' It wasn't a question.

Now Sandra ran onto the platform, Alfie behind her, waving and yelling, 'We managed to park, but let Davey say goodbye to Fran now. You've given him the pad?'

The children nodded, Davey too, grimacing. Melanie stopped in front of him as the train eased along the platform. 'Your face'll stay like that, Mr Davey, if the wind changes.'

Davey felt Stan's hand grip his shoulder. 'Get on the train, man. It's the only escape.'

'Aye,' Sid called. 'Or throw yourself under the bliddy thing.'

Sandra and Alfie were shooing the bairns off the platform as they waved to Davey. Eva yelled, 'We've decided we really do need it by the end of the first week of November, Mr Davey, so we can start practising.'

'Rehearsing, not practising, she means,' yelled Abe. They were still arguing as they disappeared into the ticket hall.

Train doors were opening, people were disgorging. Everyone said goodbye and followed the evacuees until there was only Fran left, and they just held one another until the guard yelled, 'If you don't get on, we'll go without you.'

Fran leaned back in Davey's arms. 'Go, write, make it good, or heaven knows what the penalty will be. Ask Daniel and the other smarty-pants to help you. It should be easy-peasy'.

Chapter Thirteen

It was 2 November and Davey was traipsing up the drive with Daniel and the other two to start their shift at Bletchley Park, heads down, talking nineteen to the dozen. Behind them, one of the Wrens called, 'Get a move on.' They speeded up, waving an acknowledgement, but instead of mithering about the weather or the food or wondering whether the Allies would maintain their momentum in North Africa, the boys were busy arguing about what Bernie the Beck Monster's third kindness should be.

Davey smiled as he listened, for what seemed like a day long ago at the beck had created a monster all of its own, one that first had to be written and completed, and now the smile faded, to be replaced by a sigh, then a groan.

Daniel turned to him. 'What's up?'

'We're only halfway through and still have the third and fourth kindnesses, and on the telephone last night Fran passed on a message from the bairns.' He stopped.

'Go on, what's the message?' asked Colin.

Closing the gap between them, Maureen, one of the Wrens, called, 'Don't keep us in suspense.'

They passed beneath the magnolia branches, which would look magnificent in the spring, but were skeletal now. Davey muttered, 'They said "Chop-chop, remember we need it by November the sixth because . . . " ' He stopped again, then said in a rush, ' "It's easy-peasy for you." '

While Fran said, 'But not for us, for we have the costumes

to make, the cast to organise and at this rate we'll need a bliddy miracle to be ready.'

'No, don't laugh,' he shouted, feeling harassed. 'We've got to finish it within the next two days, to get it in the post to arrive by Friday. I reckon they think we're sitting about while being waited on hand, foot and finger.'

Colin's novel was under his arm, as usual, his pipe clenched between his teeth, just as Martin's was. Was pipe smoking catching? Davey wondered, but then Colin removed his.

'Calm down. You did a lot on the train and with us chipping in we've got the first and second kindnesses written into scenes, and the top half of Bernie's monster costume has by now changed into a prince's doublet. The third kindness should reveal the hose, the fourth the head. Good that the princess narrates when necessary, in partnership with the old fairy. Ralph's still to be the prince, didn't you say?'

Davey nodded. 'Aye, and Eva thinks the princess should be Viola, because, as the little madam told Fran, they are "still in love".'

'So come on, what's the third?' Colin's gesticulations were so wild, he dropped his book and the bookmark six-year-old Dawn Siddely had made out of wallpaper fell out. He cursed. 'If I'd turned down the corners, this wouldn't happen.'

Daniel mimicked Dawn. ' "Well, Mr Colin, that's vandalism, my mum says, so shame on you." '

Colin sighed and rushed after the bookmark, which was fluttering across the path in front of the Wrens, who'd dropped behind them. 'Stop,' he bellowed. 'Right there.'

They did, watching but not helping as he bent to pick it up from the ground in front of Maureen. 'Come now,' she said, 'no need to bow.'

Colin settled his fedora, which was his latest affectation.

By the time they neared the huts, Maureen was alongside them once more. 'You'll have to have a think and meet over lunch, but you'd better do what you can in the common room and at Mrs Siddely's, and best you stop dithering about – it's serious. It's for the lass's last Christmas with her pals.'

'There's always one whose role in life is bossing us poor men about,' muttered Colin. 'Maureen deserves the name of Eva.'

They turned off for their hut, while the girls continued on their way, and Colin looked after Maureen, murmuring, 'She's really rather wonderful.'

Norah was at her desk, her cardigan hanging almost to the floor as always, her pockets stuffed with the usual collection of bits of paper with scribbled messages, rubber bands, paper clips and handkerchiefs. She noted that the lads were early.

'Get into that common room because I hear you're fiddling about with the third kindness. The second is the monster teaching them to swim? That'll be fun – lots of shrieks and splashing about, though there's no water, just blue paper, so you could cut up bits of paper and throw them around as splashes. Who's directing?'

'No idea, and there's nothing to direct yet.' Davey broke into a sweat because Fran had sounded a bit desperate on the phone.

Norah shook her head. 'Well, I've been thinking. What if a bullying bairn turns up while the others are having a picnic? The bully torments them, wanting some of their lunch. Bernie comes out of the water with a fish, and with his doublet showing. He listens and shouts, "Enough." The bully leaps back, but notices the others aren't scared.'

The four of them were listening intently and Davey was imagining it, just as Norah must have been, because she was waving her arms and acting tough. 'The fish could be flipping about in Bernie's hands. It was for him, but now it's for the bully. "Take it home, eat it for your tea. You look hungry." The bully blusters, falls quiet as he looks at the fish, then says he can't eat it because he's looked into its scared eyes and it's like he feels a lot of the time with his da gone to war.' She paused.

'Go on,' said Colin. 'Don't leave us there.'

'The other bairns look into the lad's eyes now and see that, yes, he is scared too,' Norah went on. 'They start whispering amongst themselves, not wanting to be nice to the bully. The monster notices, so he puts the fish back into the water, swims across the beck and returns with berries. He suggests they all share their bait with the bully, and have these berries as pudding. They agree and become friends with the bully. They turn around, the fairy waves her wand and the prince's hose goes. The bully is amazed. But they still don't know what Bernie really looks like. The bully becomes the bairns' marrer, and helps look after the monster.'

Davey reached over her desk, took hold of her waving hands and kissed them. She blushed, then snatched them away. 'Go on with you, get into the back room and get to work writing it up. They'll need it in Massingham so they can sort the cast, costumes, sets, props . . . Lord, it'll be a miracle if they pull it off. There's so much to do.'

The men walked past the night-shift cryptologists, who were heads down, working, yawning, stretching. They had eight minutes before the change of shift.

In the common room the rest of the fore shift were scribbling letters, or so Davey thought. But when Sam, the newest member of the hut, from Oxford University, saw them, he waved his sheet of paper, snatching others as they were held out. 'We've been writing up Norah's third kindness and we've come up with a fourth idea too. We reckon that should do it. The panto can't go on for hours.'

The others on their shift leaned forward as Davey, Daniel, Colin and Martin listened.

'Here we go. It's not written up perfectly yet, so you can edit. A heron – I reckon a costume would be easy – lands badly, hurts his leg and Bernie picks him up, brings him to the bank. The heron could be Eva? By the way, Norah has a white and silver doublet – she was a bit of an amateur-dramatics queen in days gone by. She might have the hose too. She saved a fair number of costumes when her group shut down with the war.'

Davey grinned and passed the script along to the others after quickly scanning the pages. It was all there. He sat back. 'You're all bliddy marvellous. Over lunch I'll tidy it up and include the custard tart and the cow, then read it out. How about that? When we feel like a walk to the pub, the beers are on me.'

Sam put his pen back in his breast pocket. 'It would be fun to see it performed – maybe we can pass a copy on to the drama group here, what with Christmas coming . . . ?'

Davey agreed. 'You're on. You wrote a fair bit of it anyway.'

'Time's up,' shouted Norah, and they rose, because the day had begun and there was still the trivial matter of the enemy's messages to decode.

Viola stood in the ballroom with Fran, Sarah, Beth and Cyn Ellington. They were all relieved that the fore shift had been forced to end early, when the electricity had failed. It couldn't have happened on a better day, given the time pressure. So here they were, wearing paint-splattered aprons as they watched the lads climb on the scaffolding they'd cobbled together using long ladders and planks borrowed from the pithead. These had been transported on a coal lorry as far as the Miners' Club. From there they'd been picked up by Farmer Thompkins, precariously lodged on the trailer and festooned with bunting to alert any other travellers to the length of his load as he rumbled up to the Hall with it.

It was Thursday 5 November, and the co-op were in the kitchen with Lisa and the bairns, and for once they were all quiet, reading through the script that had been sent to Massingham Hall by Davey a day earlier than he had thought. Most of Davey's hut had contributed to the script which had saved time and some had even drawn Bernie the Beck Monster on the front page.

Sophia had been sent to bed for a few days to reduce her blood pressure, but Sandra and Alfie were on hand to help, along with the co-op. Ralph slapped his brush back and forth, working at one end of the scaffolding while Norm, Sid and Simon Parrot worked in the middle and Stan at the other end. It seemed there was as much emulsion on them, Viola thought, as there was on the ceiling, but at least they had thought to cover the woodblock floor with dust sheets.

Viola felt panic rising and she wished everyone wasn't so intent on celebrating her birthday on 14 November, because without that there would be more time to get everything in place for 19 December, now ringed in red on the calendar. 'Oh Lord, but it all has to happen and that is that,' she murmured aloud.

'Talking to yourself, bonny lass?' asked Fran.

Viola smiled. 'I seem to have done that for quite a while,' she said. 'I'm either mad or a genius.'

'A genius, then,' called Sarah, looking up just as Stan called, 'Oops.'

'Steady on, Stan, you'll be off that plank in a minute.'

Stan steadied himself and brushed on. They switched

their attention to Ralph, who had reached the area of white gloss that had been painted over the water stain. It had been Mr Oborne's idea, because emulsion alone wouldn't cover a dollop of spit, he'd said. They'd all wished he hadn't, as it put them off enjoying their scones.

Several tins of white emulsion was all Alfie could find in the garage, but it would brighten things up. Alfie and Reginald had unearthed some delicate chairs stacked up behind the stables in the storage unit. The children had wiped them clean.

Ralph called down to Alfie, who was standing below, his head upturned. 'Anything showing through?'

Alfie shook his head, but then called, 'Nowt, but it wouldn't yet. Your emulsion has to dry, Mr Oborne said.'

'Make sure the doors are open so we get a draught,' Ralph called to the girls.

'Aye aye, Captain,' called his father, who had just entered. Ralph laughed. Reginald made his way towards the group, waving the script.

'I feel nervous,' muttered Fran. 'What if they've not got it right, what if they've—'

Reginald reached them. 'Your Davey and his pals have done a first-class job, and look at these drawings on the front.'

He pointed out the various efforts decorating the front cover, then lifted the top sheet. There was a cast list, in Davey's handwriting. Ralph was the monster, the princess was Viola and the old fairy was Stevie from the Rising Sun, who had volunteered for a part. The bairns were the bairns. The cow was Bert and Mrs Oborne. Daniel had written: *Make sure she's the bum.* The marrers were the trees, the three Factory Girls the washerwomen and Reginald was the bossy female owner of the laundry. He was to receive the custard tart, a note beside his name stated.

The heron was not a child but Sid, because he was skinny,

Davey had noted on the side. The bully was Mr Swinton; the lady with some flowers was Beatrice Adams, the love of Swinton's life. There were even some songs. Fran could have wept, it was so complete.

'It made me laugh, and the bully made me cry, well, almost,' Reginald said. 'It's the costumes that pose a bit of a problem, there are so many needed, but apparently someone called Norah has a doublet and hose and various others, and is packing them up to send right away, so we must hope they fit. The co-op have also read the script and are now busy talking about the costumes too. Apparently, the tart must be yellow paper.'

Reginald then checked the ceiling, murmuring, 'By Jove, I think the gloss will work. How very clever. You know, of course, that before Steve Oborne would come up with the solution he said it was on the condition that Tilly was to be the rear end of the cow.'

The girls roared with laughter. 'When Mrs Oborne saw Davey's cast list, what did she say about her role?' asked Beth.

Reginald grimaced. 'It can be distilled into the one word: "No." ' While they sniggered away, he saw Sandra standing in the door.

'Half an hour until footie. Will that fit in, lads? The light will be going if we wait longer than that, and the bairns are so thrilled now the script is actually here, I think they'll burst if we don't run off some of that excitement.'

'We'll finish this run,' Stan called down, 'and then see how it looks tomorrow. Hopefully, the stain is covered, and the ceiling and walls only need one coat, but if it's awful we'll have to think again. What does everyone say?'

'Good idea,' said Reginald. 'Let's run off some of their energy, for Viola, Sandra and I will be left holding the bairns this evening.'

*

Ralph led the gang to the field half an hour later, picking the emulsion off his hands while Sandra chivvied the bairns, confiscating the football because Tommy was dribbling it along the uneven ground, missing it and then going back for it.

Once they were there they split into teams, Ralph, Viola, Alfie and Sid on one team with half the bairns, and the rest all together. Annie Hall was the referee, though she knew nothing about it and only blew the whistle when it seemed the play was getting a bit rough, and that usually meant the grown-ups.

Finally, Viola, of all people, scored a goal, and Ralph rushed to pick her up and ran right up the field, holding her high while she squealed to be let down and the others laughed. Watching, Fran thought how the snobbish lad had gone and a proper man was in his place. Her da would have liked this adult Ralph.

They returned to find that the rest of the co-op had left a note for Annie saying they would meet her back there the next day, and Lisa was with Sandra while she cleared up Eva and Melanie's bedroom. They had left milk and sandwiches for the children, and beer and sandwiches for the grown-ups, and gone on their way. There was tea to make for their men and their own bairns. They had left designs for scenery and costumes, and a suggestion to go hunting in the attic for material. Christmas decorations in the form of paper chains, they said, were to be finished by the middle of December.

Later, a Pied Piper moment occurred when Viola led the way upstairs to find the trunks. The adults and bairns searched through them and on shelves that Annie had marked with chalk. They chose the material, which amounted to heaps of curtains and curtain net, and placed it all in a pile beneath the skylight to be collected as needed.

As they left the attic, their job done, Eva sidled up to Viola and said, 'This has been one of the best days of me life, Viola. I felt really happy, really, *really* happy, and safe, here with everyone, and with you.'

Later that night, when his father had retired to bed, Ralph sat in the drawing-room armchair by the fading fire, just for a moment, pondering the day and his happiness, and realised for the first time ever, really, that he was excited at the thought of Christmas and living his life amongst the Massingham people and his family.

The telephone rang. It was nine o'clock. Tim Swinton, his handler? Thank heavens Viola had gone to bed early. He made his way to the phone in the hall.

'Massingham Res—'

'Hello, Ralphy. Long time no see, not that I *see* you, but I do have news of you, so rest assured, you are not alone.'

Ralph wasn't scared, but who was giving Tim the news? He said nothing, just let Tim Swinton speak.

'Listen, I have it on good authority that Miss Cartwright and her big mouth are returning to the Factory, just when they thought they had got rid of her. I'd love to see Bolton's face tomorr—' Tim coughed.

'Now, my lad, you've been mightily quiet, and it will not do. I need information. We need to interrupt production. Things are not good. America is fighting hard, Montgomery has done well in North Africa and our leader, the Fuhrer, is fighting a war on two fronts, with a Russian winter approaching so his advance will be stalled. Therefore we Fascists must damage Britain, cut the munitions and coal flow, and our section isn't doing its bit. For God's sake, man, it's not hard to gather information we can act upon.'

Ralph cleared his throat. 'There really is none.'

'Well, when Amelia gets back, take her to the Pig and

Whistle, eh? Have a nice evening, and go soon. Be a good boy, for you don't want me to tell the world who you are – a traitor, in their eyes at least. I need something, anything.'

Then he was gone. Ralph replaced the telephone. Tim really was getting careless – or desperate. None of the girls had mentioned Amelia returning, and why would she be reinstated? But what, and how, did Tim know?

Ralph waited, his mind racing. The telephone rang again. It was Yeland, Professor Smythe's colleague.

'Evening, Ralph. That was interesting. Quite an error by Tim, eh? I happen to know that our man Gaines who wrote the investigative report would have heard from Bolton if Amelia Cartwright was returning, and he would have reported the news to us. So, how did Tim know? From the head of the cell? But again, as always, who is that? Someone at Head Office, we are sure, but who?'

'That's the problem.'

'Indeed, Ralph. But on to other things. We have eyes on Eddie Corbitt, as you know. We are almost certain now, by ways devious and thanks to your input, that he was involved in the act of sabotage in Bell Seam. Thanks to you, we know Corbitt is also interested in the comings and goings of your father. With what we have obtained recently, it puts him on the wrong side of doubt. We are ninety-eight per cent sure he is the local eyes and ears. Though perhaps there are others, so we will leave him in play. Enjoy Viola's birthday party, which your father has mentioned to the Professor. Sounds fun. But a lot rests on your shoulders, lad. Don't relax for a moment.'

Chapter Fourteen

In the changing room the next morning, Miss Ellington checked Fran, Beth and Sarah for metal, silk and nylon. She was so quiet that Beth asked, 'Has the cat got your tongue, Cyn? Fore shift getting to you?' There was no reply, not even a smile.

'What's amiss, lass?' Mrs Oborne asked. 'It's not your Simon, is it? You're still getting wed, for we're expecting you to celebrate at the pantomime. December the nineteenth, it's been decided.' There was no answer as Cyn Ellington and Mrs Raydon moved on to other people.

As she was being checked for contraband, Valerie asked Mrs Raydon if everything was all right with the electricity, or was it still a problem? When she received no answer, she looked at the others, puzzled. All that happened was that Mrs Raydon moved on to Susan and proceeded to examine her hair, finally saying, 'We security officers heard all about the panto. The costumes'll be tricky. Bernie, indeed. He's a clever lad is Davey.'

'What do you think, Cyn?' called Beth.

The shift waited for a reply, but there was no answer and the two security officers just worked on. Mrs Oborne raised her eyebrows at Fran, who nodded and said into the silence, 'What are you thinking of for Bernie's costume, Mrs Oborne?'

Before she could answer, Maisie chipped in. 'Well, why don't we collect up some of the fallen leaves before they get too wet and spoiled? We can pin 'em to some netting—'

'Or use dark green cotton and tack on the leaves,' called Beth, 'and then tack on the sleeves, which Ralph can rip off in the beck after he's been kind. Revealing the hose will need a bigger yank. Finally, for the fourth kindness, he'll lose the head, so he can just tip that off in the beck, perhaps. The men'll have to build up a sort of bank behind which he can hide, then splash about in the ripped paper, whipping off each bit as needed.'

'Or for his costume, just use the green material and whack on great splodges of brown paint?' suggested Miss Ellington.

There was a pause.

'Ah, you're back with us,' said Fran.

Miss Ellington merely nodded, but she still looked, well, different as she continued to check the shift.

Fran continued watching Miss Ellington and Mrs Raydon, who were stolidly working their way around.

'Where is Mr Swinton?' asked Valerie suddenly, of no one in particular. 'It's quarter to six.'

The security officers straightened, looked at one another, then Miss Ellington nodded and turned to the women. Just as she was clearing her throat, Mr Swinton swept in and glanced at the clock, nodding curtly. 'We have to go through the rules.' His hands were bunched in his pockets as they used to be, before he became human.

The security officers finished and stood either side of him as he began: 'You must concentrate at all times. You must not talk in the detonator workshop, you must not talk of internal matters with anyone, inside or out ...' He stopped, sighed and then, as though rallying himself, rushed through the rest. He finished at about three minutes to six, looked round at Miss Ellington and raised an eyebrow. She shook her head. He sighed again.

'Right,' he said. 'Pellets for Fran, Beth, Sarah, Mrs Oborne and Maisie, for you'll be needing to think and maybe exchange a word or two about the pantomime.' He put up a hand. 'Talk of the pantomime will be a bright spark in an otherwise bliddy awful morning.'

The women gasped, for Mr Swinton never swore. He said no more, but gestured to the door, and said the pit-man's prayer as they began to move towards it: 'Be safe.'

The women had almost reached the door when Mr Bolton entered, his face white and expressionless, his voice too, as he said, 'I have to tell you that Amelia Cartwright is back in administration. Head Office have decided that in this time of war every experienced worker must be utilised. She is under supervision, let me assure you, and understands that "teasing", as Head Office described it, will not be allowed. Do not let it trouble you. Do not let it distract you. We have the matter in hand.' His hands were also bunched in his pockets.

'Aye,' Mrs Oborne ground out through clenched teeth. 'In your fists, more like.'

They eased past him and walked down the corridor, and as they did so, Fran, Sarah and Beth tried to process the news that the girl whose pleasure in life was lording it over everyone, and cutting them to the quick, had returned. How?

As they turned to discuss it, Mr Bolton called after them, 'Don't you worry, all eyes will be on her. Relax, work, be safe. If anyone hears her speaking out of turn in or outside the Factory, I want you to inform me immediately. She can have this one chance, but that is all.' They jumped as he bellowed those last words before storming back to his office.

Before they entered the workshop, Fran muttered, 'I'll have her guts for garters if she causes trouble, but perhaps she has learned her lesson and will guard her tongue.'

Mrs Oborne called from behind, 'I reckon her mam and

da wouldn't have liked her being sacked. Probably had a word with the high-ups. Her da's a solicitor, isn't he, or some such thing, so bound to know someone in London.'

Beth was tapping each of the war posters as they passed, something she had stopped doing when it was no longer any business of hers if Bob was in peril on the sea. They entered the pellet section. The tannoy was playing Glenn Miller quietly as they headed for the workbenches to relieve those on the night shift.

Veronica from Minton was wrapping the last of her batch of inch-long fuse pellets. These would charge detonators and send bullets on their way. She stepped back, her turban covering her hair, her hands sticky with the paste. 'All yours, bonny lass,' she said to Beth, who nodded.

'You get yourself home and to sleep, Veronica.'

As Veronica turned to go, Beth went on, 'Amelia is back. We've just heard.'

'Oh, what?' Veronica pulled a face. 'We'll need to watch our backs with her around.'

Beth slipped up to the workbench. 'But she's one, and we're many.'

Sarah raised her eyebrows and whispered, 'By, you been reading a book of quotes, or are you just brainy?'

'Not brainy, a genius,' Beth said quietly as they all began pasting the fluted paper around the pellets, trying to ignore the chemical mixture coating their fingertips, knowing that by the end of the shift their fingers would be stained a deep yellow and that it would feel as though the chemical was seeping through their skin. It was all the usual procedure, just as the rashes were. This was part of their lives now.

They pasted another, and another, blessing the mams' sphagnum-moss dressings that soothed and prevented any scratched rashes from becoming septic. 'I'll have to help meself to some of the moss, or maybe the lavender grease, tonight. Smells better and helps me sleep,' Fran muttered, tired out, for Lisa had not slept well. But then she pictured the bairn, drowsy, just needing reassurance, and at last, heavy in her arms, snuffling as she finally dozed. And smiled.

'I can almost feel the rash getting worse,' grumbled Valerie from further along the bench.

They worked on until the meal break, hour after sticky hour. They headed into the washroom, washing again and again, then to the canteen, joining the queue for whatever it was. It was only when they had finished that they sat back, sighed and looked at one another. Mrs Oborne was about to speak when they heard *that* voice, Amelia's voice, and saw her approaching.

She waved. 'I'm back.'

'Really,' said Mrs Oborne, 'I thought it were a nightmare.'

'Yes, we heard,' said Fran.

'I have friends in high places. They thought an injustice had occurred and that Mr Gaines was misguided to insist on a warning in the first place. It wasn't loose talk at all, and it was Beth's fault for saying in the Rising Sun that it was.'

They all sat quite still, but said nothing, because this girl really must have friends in high places and they needed to keep their jobs.

Amelia wasn't finished. 'Then, to pick me up for a bit of badinage with you, Fran. How is the dear little soul, anyway? Still with you?'

'Yes,' Fran said, hearing the ice in her voice. Without a word, Sarah began stacking the plates.

Fran felt Amelia's breath on her neck. She stood, knowing Amelia would have to step back. 'I need to get on, Amelia, there's a war to win.' Everyone else rose, with Mrs Oborne nodding towards the corridor just as Miss Ellington appeared in the canteen, making her way over to them.

Miss Ellington stood at the head of the table. 'Should you be here, Amelia? It's not the administrative office's meal break yet, and certainly the electrical fault hasn't changed *today's* timetable though yesterday was a different kettle of fish.'

Her voice was similarly icy. By, thought Fran, the lass should be frozen to the core. For a moment she felt pity for the girl, who was walking towards the door, looking crestfallen. Amelia stopped and turned, tentatively putting a hand out towards the women's table.

'I want to be friends. Things became, well, a bit strained—'

'Well, I wonder why that was,' snapped Valerie.

Amelia turned to her. 'I think because we were all rather weary. I'm sorry your mother is out of pocket now I've gone, Valerie, but I'm back if the room is still available. I bunked up with Rosie last night. You know, one of my singing trio.'

Valerie merely shook her head. 'We have my nan living with us now.'

Amelia scowled, then her brow cleared. 'I don't mind sharing with you, but of course the rent would have to be reduced.'

Fran watched Miss Ellington close her eyes and sigh.

Valerie shook her head. 'No, I need my privacy. I'm sure the administrative office will have a list of suitable boarding houses. But we have to go – things to do, people to see, other monsters to deal with.'

Amelia looked confused. Miss Ellington took her by the arm and led her from the canteen. 'Let's see what your boss, Mr Andrews, can find for you. There'll obviously be a list . . .'

They were at the door before Amelia knew what was happening, then into the corridor. Everyone sat down and Mrs Oborne just shook her head, and went on shaking it.

'You'll feel sick in a minute, shaking your head around

like that. Or we will. Keep it still, lass,' Beth said. 'It's worse than Bob'd be feeling in a storm.'

They laughed. What else could they do in the face of Amelia being reinstated? How much trouble did one person have to cause before action was taken? Fran told herself to shut up, think of something useful. She fixed her mind on the ballroom, where they were to work on their return from the Factory. The marrers would be there, doing just the same, because there wasn't a moment to waste.

Across the table, Susan leaned on an elbow and looked hard at Beth. 'Have you heard anything more from Bob?'

Beth just shrugged. 'No, he'll know better than to write. I told him the next letter needed to be from the solicitor, but so far nowt's come. It's strange, because it seems an age ago, or rather, he does. That bairn of his and Heather's must be a few months old by now. Not as old as our Lisa, but . . .'

Mrs Oborne nudged her. 'You're still sending them your allotment money, though, which in anyone's book makes you a saint.'

The women were being beckoned back to work by Miss Ellington, who waited by the double doors. Beth laughed as they pushed back their chairs. 'I'm no saint, I'm just glad to see the back of him.'

'Helps having Sid, who loves you to bits, too,' Fran murmured.

A flush rose on Beth's cheeks. She whispered back, 'It's as well he does, for I love him to bits an' all, but hush. We need to keep quiet about it in the Factory and village, for I'm still married, Fran. What were I doing with Bob? Were I mad? I should have looked for someone I've known for years.'

She and Fran followed the others and found themselves walking alongside Mrs Oborne, who said quietly, 'I hope you're not forgetting about Viola's party. The lass deserves a bit of a do after the time she's had, and her injuries and all what. You see, all the talk seems to be about the panto-mime. Be a shame to . . .' She petered out.

Beth looked round at her and saw the worry on Tilly's face, and they knew she was right.

At four, the three girls cycled up to Massingham Hall. The cold hadn't lifted all day and the leaves they collected along the way and put into Annie Hall's hessian sack were damp. It was no problem because Beth knew the co-op would dry them off, as they'd done the others, so that they could be tacked onto netting, if they could obtain any.

She watched the leaves falling in the wind. Soon the trees would be bare and the real winter would be upon them. She gave thought then, following Tilly's prompt, to Viola's birthday party. What were they to sing? What food would the co-op organise? What gift were they to buy Viola, their friend, their marrer? Would the ballroom be ready, even? What if it wasn't?

Feeling frantic all of a sudden, Beth caught up with Fran. 'Look around. Winter's not far, but Tilly's right, we're nowhere near ready for Viola's "do". It's important she has a good time after all she's been through.'

Fran stopped humming 'Cheek to Cheek' and spun round. 'Oh Lord, it had faded from me mind again. I don't know, what with everything else, I keep forgetting. Well, not forgetting, but not concentrating on it.'

Sarah had heard and cycled up alongside Beth. 'I was just thinking that the ballroom ceiling needs another coat, and they haven't started on the walls, though we've washed 'em down, and the stage, which isn't started . . . And some-how we need to squeeze in the panto rehearsals, the scenery, the props, and finish these cardigans and knit up tree decorations . . . And a song list.'

Even as she listened, Beth could feel a flutter in her chest and knew they needed thirty-six hours in every day.

On they cycled and eventually swooped into the garage yard, dumped their bikes and tore into the house, along the corridor and into the ballroom. The smell of emulsion greeted them, and there were the lads, up on the scaffold, as it seemed they always were.

They started to take off their macs, but Sid, wiping his paintbrush clean, called, 'No, Beth, not you. We need a pianist for the panto, it seems. Some sort of silent-film sound effects, like thundering when the monster comes out of the beck, and as accompaniment for the songs, or that's what Sophia's decided. So she's fixed it for us to go along to Miss Walters now.'

Beth shook her head. 'And you allowed me to cycle up here, just to go down again?'

Sid descended the ladder, jumping the last few rungs before wiping his hands on a rag, while above, Stan sang 'Blue Moon'. 'Sorry, lass – didn't have a carrier pigeon.'

'The thing is, Sid, I've just said to the girls we're spending too much time concentrating on the panto when we have the party too. Or actually, it was Tilly who said it.' Beth felt the panic stirring again, because how could any of it happen in time?

Sarah was picking up some sandpaper from a pile Alfie had left, about to rub down the washerwomen's table made by Old Ted, as promised. 'Where is Viola anyway?' she asked.

'Ah,' Stan yelled down, 'with the co-op and the bairns, rug-making, as they have orders to fill.'

'Point taken about the party, Beth,' called Ralph, 'but you girls aren't in this alone, remember. We promise the decorating will be done, the soirée chairs are here and, hopefully, the stage will be ready for the gramophone to be set up and the Factory Girls to entertain us. If not, there will be a platform of some sort. Trust us, for my sweet girl will have the best party ever.'

'But to get back to the bairns,' added Stan. 'They're checking through Davey's cast list to try and come up with descriptions of the costumes.'

Sid came to Beth, who lifted her face for his kiss. His smile was warm, his russet hair dappled with white paint, and his face too. He whispered against her mouth, 'I love you so much, bonny lass, and Ralph *does* have it under control. Just come up with a song list and . . .'

She looked into Sid's eyes and her panic subsided. It was all right; they were all in it together.

Beth and Sid cycled alongside one another, heading for the Rectory, which was in a hamlet of a few houses near St Oswald's, chatting and sometimes breaking into song, until Sid shook his head.

'That "Blue Moon" song gets in your head, mithers away and comes again. What's a blue moon anyway?'

'Me da always said it's the second moon in a month, so it doesn't happen often, but the song's nice, quite easy to sing. Should that be one for Viola's party? Ben and William are coming to handle the record player. Best check what they're playing so we don't replicate it. Then we need to think of her present, though I haven't a clue what. Presents are so difficult now it's wartime.'

They were passing a derelict barn. Sid jerked his head towards it. 'Bet we could get some more wood for the stage out of that. But curtains? How're we going to get curtains long enough? Those in the attic are short by a foot.'

Beth groaned. 'Answer me about the present first.'

Sid nodded. 'You're right. We lads were talking about what she'd like, though she's getting something from Ralph which might put everything else out of her head.'

Beth braked. 'What? Not a ring?'

'I can't say,' shrugged Sid, 'and neither must you. But I'd love to give you one too, sweet Beth.'

Beth pedalled on. It was the first time Sid had actually said something like that. She could tell he was watching her. Finally, she murmured, 'I'd like to wear it, but we must be careful, for it's not decent to be obvious except with our friends. I'm still married.'

'I know how you feel,' said Sid, 'I really do. I just wish the beggar would get on and get that divorce through so we can be open.'

The Rectory was in sight, its holly trees overhanging the verge, their berries scarlet against the green, or at least what remained of them after the birds had feasted. They hurried because it would be a right pain to cycle back with just the slit of bicycle light allowed. They leaned their bikes against the drystone wall, then pushed open the wicket gate that hung on a single hinge. Sid squatted. 'It just needs a screw in the bottom one. Hang on.' He felt around, but it was Beth who found it. Sid screwed it on with his penknife.

'You still have our penknife?' Beth asked, reaching out to stroke his hair, but remembered where they were and let her hand drop.

Sid knelt on the crazy-paving path. 'Oh aye, you girls and the lads gave it to me when me da died. I remember being so surprised, so pleased. It helped.' He dropped his voice. 'So of course I kept it, sweet lass.'

He sprang upright and tested the gate as Miss Walters called, 'My word, how kind. That definitely deserves a cuppa. Come in, Mrs Jones, and I don't believe I've met . . . ?'

While Beth was absorbing the misery of being called Mrs Jones, Sid stepped forward. 'Sid Barratt, but Sid will do. Beth and I have come—'

Miss Walters waved dismissively. 'Never mind why, it's

just good to see some young people, and I must think of other little jobs for your penknife, young man.'

She ushered them in, but winked at Beth. 'Wouldn't dream of it really, but one must have a little tease or one would go stark staring mad, wouldn't one?'

Was it really a question? wondered Beth, still trying to push the sound of 'Jones' into some dark corner, for she was Smith to herself and her friends.

They followed Miss Walters along the hall and into the kitchen, where a range was gurgling and gaslights spluttered on the wall.

'Sit. I have tea ready. Dear Sophia telephoned, for of course the Vicar must have a telephone. Don't like the things myself, you never know who it is, and I dread the very few ghastly old bores that all villages have.'

Beth sat on the chair Sid pulled out. Should a vicar's sister be saying such things? she wondered. Sid, though, was grinning as he sat at Miss Walters' command. On the table was a brown teapot with a knitted tea cosy that was stained beneath the chipped spout. The cups, though, were bone china. Miss Walters sat down at the end of the table.

'Shall I be mother?' Without waiting for an answer, Miss Walters poured, then pointed to the milk in the white jug. 'Do help yourselves. No sugar, but that shouldn't worry you two – sweet enough, I dare say. Sugar is a luxury for now, but after the war I dare say we will come to think it is not.'

Beth poured milk into Sid's cup and then her own. He winked at her. She wondered if winking was catching. Around Sid's nails the white emulsion had dried and she could tell he longed to scratch it off. There was a white streak along the back of his right hand. It contrasted with his dark scars. She often liked to reach out and run her finger along them, but she was still Mrs Jones and they were in a public place.

She became aware of the silence and looked up. Miss Walters, her head cocked to one side, was watching As Beth's gaze met hers, the older woman nodded, as though to herself, and frowned slightly. Beth looked away. She knows about me and Sid, she thought. She knows, too, that there is still a Mr Jones.

Sid's fingers were too big for the delicate cup handle and so he used both hands, leaning his elbows on the table. Miss Walters grinned, and suddenly her face was transformed. 'How sensible. I like a man who knows his own mind. I feared for one dreadful moment you might cock your little finger. My brother and I are sticklers for drinking tea from bone-china cups. This set was our mother's and she was right about one thing, at least: tea needs bone china.'

'"At least"?' queried Beth, only realising as the other two stared at her that she had spoken her thoughts. She put her own cup down. 'Oh, I'm sorry. I . . . Well, I . . .'

Miss Walters stroked her greying hair, pulled back from her face in a bun. 'Oh, well spotted, that lass. She was a good soul, but ruled by decorum. But enough of that – why are you here? Sophia muttered something about a favour. Such a dear girl, but one worries – a babe at her age.'

Beth laughed. 'Oh, don't let her hear you say that, for it's what several said when she discovered she was having a bairn and her response was on the edge of violent.'

Miss Walters roared with laughter. 'All I meant was that her first labour and birth are likely to be tough going. She's made of strong stuff, though, is our Sophia, but let's not divert ourselves. What favour can I grant, or not?'

Beth nodded at Sid. He explained about the pantomime being a farewell to Melanie, and about the script written by Davey and his friends, the food and costumes made by the co-op, the ballroom decorated by the marrers and the girls, the stage about to be built, the evacuees organising the cast list, the songs—

Miss Walters was trying to keep up and raised her hand. 'No,' she said, cutting across Sid. 'I will absolutely not be the back end of any cow.'

Beth and Sid looked at one another and laughed, more in surprise than anything else. Sid finished his tea and replaced the cup carefully in the saucer. 'Perhaps the front end?'

Miss Walters chuckled. 'Now you're teasing, young sir. You need a pianist?'

'You guessed?'

'Sophia asked, but I said I wanted to talk to you both, so she arranged for this little meeting. Needing someone to plonk the keys was as good a ploy as any.'

Sid, who sat opposite Beth, touched her foot with his, his face suddenly looking strained. Beth half rose, because she didn't need a lecture, didn't need a vicar's sister discussing the merits of decorum, didn't need – well, anything from anyone.

Miss Walters waved her down. 'Do sit and listen.' Beth subsided. The Vicar's sister reached for her hand, holding it tightly. 'I have observed you two since Mr Jones departed and, well, something else began. It makes me remember so much.'

Beth looked at Sid, not at this woman who had no business to observe, or comment. There was no way Beth would give up this man, and surely he wouldn't listen and walk away? For a moment, doubt swirled around her, but Sid turned to her, and the love in his eyes made her strong.

'Best say no more, Miss Walters, though I know you mean well,' Beth said quietly, pulling her hand away and biting down her fury. She sipped the remainder of her tea, which was cold. When it was finished they would leave. It was only then that she noted the fulsome flavour.

Miss Walters felt the teapot. 'Still warm. Let's finish it. Fresh leaves are too good to dry for a later day. What say you?'

Sid watched her pour. 'A treat before the lecture you're about to give, eh?'

Beth poured in milk, her hand trembling slightly. After she'd set down the small white jug, Sid reached across and held her hand, giving it a squeeze. 'Off you go, then, Miss Walters. But first things first: will you play the piano for the panto songs?'

The Vicar's sister smiled. 'Naturally, it will be an unmitigated relief not to be whacking something out on the organ only for it to produce wheezes, belches and sundry unmentionables.'

They laughed, how could they not, though they were still annoyed. Miss Walters rose and walked to the dresser. She brought back a photograph. It was a sepia image of an old army ambulance, on what could be a First War front line, probably in Belgium or France, judging by the churned earth and stunted trees in the distance. Behind it and to the left was a heavy artillery gun partly covered in camouflage. Two nurses stood in long macs and hats near the rear of the ambulance. By the driver's door stood a Tommy with a Red Cross armband and a woman dressed as the other two were.

Miss Walters pointed to the man and then to the woman next to him, before gently placing the photo between Sid and Beth, as though it was fragile beyond measure – or precious? Beth looked from it to Miss Walters.

'Not sure who took this,' Miss Walters said quietly, then pressed her lips together. She said nothing more for a moment, then looking straight ahead, she continued. 'No, I don't know that, but a friend sent it to me when I lost Freddie.' She stretched across, pointing to the Tommy. 'My

Freddie.' She then pointed to the woman by the driver's door. 'Me. We were both drivers – oh, and medics. We fell in love.'

Her voice was as distant as the tree stumps as she touched the image of Freddie. 'My Freddie died on March the twenty-second, 1917, at three minutes past three.' She pressed her lips together again, so tightly that they disappeared, just for a moment, though, until Miss Walters swallowed, still looking at the image – the *precious* image, Beth thought. Just as she would look at one of Sid. She squeezed his hand at the same time that he squeezed hers. From the look in his eyes, he was thinking the same.

'We had driven under shellfire to a dressing station to collect some poor wounded souls. Before we reached it, a German artillery shell fell, one of many that day.' Miss Walters placed her hands on her lap, looking up at Beth, then Sid. Beth held her breath, not wanting to hear more.

'Yes, it fell just to the left of the ambulance. I was driving – that gearbox was always a bugger. We were laughing as I fudged the wretched thing, though we couldn't hear the crunch of the cogs, of course, in the mayhem of the barrage. We laughed a lot when shells were falling, because it kept us sane. Freddie nodded to me and at that moment we suddenly couldn't hear anything at all. Another shell had exploded near the passenger side, you see, much nearer.' She was looking, really wanting them to see what she could envisage. Sid gripped Beth's hand tighter now, his face pale and still. Beth knew it mirrored hers.

'It blew us off course, one might say. An explosion is strange, it makes everything silent, sort of sucks the sight and sound and then the air out of you. It blew in the side; Freddie's side. The door became rather like your penknife, Mr Barratt, blades of steel digging deep. Perhaps if I hadn't fudged the gears we would not have been just . . . there.'

The silence in the kitchen was broken only by the ticking of the clock. Sid released Beth's hand as Miss Walters touched the photograph again. It was Miss Walters' hand he held now as she said, with absolute control, straightening up but holding on to Sid's hand so that her knuckles showed white, 'But I did fudge them, and that was that. I held him, kissed his forehead and bent close to his poor face, and there was still some light in his eyes, and love, but also a depth of pain that I could, sadly, imagine. I said, "You can go now, my love. Rest easy. I will drive the ambulance, and I will get it right, never fear." I think he heard me, for the sounds were returning. So, yes, I do think he heard me.'

Beth listened to her words and they seemed to echo in the hush that had fallen in the kitchen. 'When the detonator workshop had an explosion as we were passing, Miss Walters, the sound came and went, and we were aware, all the time, and yes, finally, we heard one another.'

Miss Walters relinquished Sid's hand, patting it and smiling at them both as though she realised she was actually in the vicarage kitchen and not where shells pounded and the world was full of horrors. She placed her hands flat on the table, and looked again at the photograph. 'Yes, yes, I do believe he did. But what I wanted to say to you, Mrs Jones, and to you, Mr Barratt, is that my mother was a devil for decorum. She never realised that in war there is the need for something . . . other.'

Miss Walters picked up the photograph. 'I loved my Freddie. He was married, but separated. We didn't wait, we lived and loved, and quite frankly, we thought: bugger decorum. There was a bloody war on. Life was cheap. I have had our time together and that memory to hold to me through the rest of my life. I know your Bob has gone, Beth, so I feel that you are no longer Mrs Jones, but Beth Smith. You shouldn't waste a minute. Be brave. Live. I'm sure you'll find our dear Massingham is its usual kindly self, so trust it. Become public.'

At that moment, the Reverend Walters came in from the back garden, carrying leeks with clumps of earth clinging to them. He kicked off his wellingtons and padded across to the drainer in the scullery, calling back, 'A pianist is what you came seeking, I believe, and have you found one?'

Beth and Sid stood, seeing that the gloom outside was now the darkness of night. 'Yes,' said Sid. 'And a nice cuppa, and a chat.'

Reverend Walters tiptoed across to look at the photograph, then at his sister. 'Bit of a pep talk too. Iris and I did talk about it.' His hand was on his sister's shoulder. 'But on other matters, Sophia has enlightened us to the fact that costume-making is about to commence.'

Beth nodded. The Vicar pointed to the heavy gun in the photograph, standing huge behind the ambulance, barely visible beneath its camouflage. 'See this? Well, camouflage netting might be right for Bernie's costume, don't you think?'

'Aye, I think that's being sort—' Sid began.

Reverend Walters interrupted. 'Good, but it's the stage on which all this is being performed that I also had some thoughts about. In fact, it floated into my mind when I should have been writing my sermon. Shows how dilatory I am. But my thought was, why not dismiss all idea of building a stage? The Miners' Club stage is in sections. Ask to rent that instead. I suspect this is probably not a new idea to you eager beavers, for time is the enemy here. One cannot have building materials in the ballroom for Viola's party, and thereafter it is only five weeks to the Christmas panto.'

His sister came to stand beside him. 'Dear Edward, chop-chop, these young people need to get back to Massingham Hall.'

Reverend Walters grinned, then saluted. 'Indeed, but I rather feel a section at a time would fit into Farmer Thompkins' trailer. It might be worth having a word. Eddie Corbitt's on the committee, and as you work alongside him sometimes, Sid, he could probably help you.'

With that thought, Miss Walters picked up a cardboard box from the second shelf of the dresser. 'I so wonder if dear Viola would care for this, as a gift you girls and boys might like to give her? You see, we have two bone-china tea sets, or perhaps I should say, one complete set and these two cups and saucers left from another. Presents are so hard to acquire these days. You young people have so much to do, so perhaps this will make your list just a little shorter.'

She waved away their thanks. 'Oh, it's nothing to us, but I think you'll agree, it does make a cuppa rather special. Sophia felt that it would not be impertinent for me to make such an offer.'

Sid took it as Beth struggled to find the words, but Iris Walters was already shooing them from the kitchen. Beth thanked her from her heart as Miss Walters opened the front door, and Sid added, 'Thank you for telling us about, well, about Freddie, and that we should trust in Massingham. You see, Beth feels the shame of divorce keenly.'

Beth felt the heat of her blush. Miss Walters leaned forward and kissed her on the cheek, saying, 'Life is too short to feel shame about something you have received, not done. So, off you go, but before you do, let me tell you that I have some camouflage in the attic, although the present-day sort would be better. I'm sure minds all over the village are puzzling over food, costumes and all sorts, but if all else fails . . .'

They started down the path, her voice reaching them. 'Drop in the music, and perhaps we should have some rehearsals in the ballroom when the panto is further along, eh? Should I also play at Viola's party, tinkering in the background to give Ben and William a rest? Just let me know. It will be a chance to get some sparkly togs on.'

That was it. The door closed. Beth and Sid collected their bikes, placing the china cups carefully in Beth's basket, and cycled off, following the beam of their slit lights. St Oswald's seemed to peer down at them, dark against the star-rich sky. 'I reckon Miss Walters talks sense, for we do need to move on, our Beth. What if she and Freddie hadn't? Fair tore me heart out, it did. Let's take it steady, for what I feel for you is nothing to be ashamed of, and I reckon we should hold hands in public and see if the sky falls in. At least as a start.'

Beth's heart was singing, because Miss Walters and Sid were right – she couldn't bear to die and not have acknowledged her love for this man. As she cycled on, though, she knew that if Sid died, she, like Miss Walters, would still be alone at fifty, for there could be no one else, ever.

Sid looked at her as the moon joined the stars, his face deadly serious. 'You know, Beth . . .' She waited, wanting to say, no, we can't live together, not yet. '. . . I reckon Reginald could get us some camouflage for Bernie's outfit if anyone can. Otherwise, we have Iris's offer, not to mention the gift. We're so lucky in the people we know.'

Beth grinned, loving him more than life itself, for he was a Massingham lad, and she knew him inside out, and he her. She said, 'I reckon you're right, bonny lad.'

Chapter Fifteen

Wednesday, 11 November

'This time in three days it'll be party time, we'll be thinking of putting on some slap the minute we get home, then roaring up to Massingham Hall. The co-op will already be sorting the food, and Stevie from the Rising Sun will be supplementing Reginald's wine from the cellar—'

Susan interrupted Beth, shouting from two seats in front as Bert roared along, 'Wonder how Reginald's plonk will stand up against Stevie's elderberry. Reginald's is French and I reckon it'll be running for the hills, waving a white flag, the minute it sees the sharp end of the corkscrew.'

The whole bus erupted with laughter just as Bert drew up at the Massingham stop, and the three girls gathered up their knitting from the back seat. They had let it drift once the backs and sleeves were finished, but they'd made a start on the fronts today because last night they had wiped down every piece of the ballroom chandeliers and watched them being hoisted up to the ceiling and screwed in tightly.

Fran muttered, 'Once these cardigans are in the nursery drawer, Mam has patterns for the robin, the manger and the shepherds for the Christmas tree.'

They sighed.

'Last one off's a cissy,' bawled Bert.

'I don't mind being a cissy now you've made us happy girls, Bert,' Fran yelled back.

'Aye, well, you might be, but I don't reckon I am. I just

lost me mind for a moment, saying I'd be the front of the ruddy cow. And you listen to me, our Tilly Oborne. I'll not have you pinching me bum while you're tucked away in the cow's arse. Tempting it'll be, but behave yourself, you hear.'

Mrs Oborne clambered down the steps, grumbling, 'I don't know why I said yes, I really don't.'

Beth tucked her arm through Tilly's and waltzed her down the street to the sound of Bert's *toot toot, tooty toot*. 'It's because you felt like being a star, Mrs Oborne.'

From the other side of Beth, Fran crowed, 'Oh yes you did. And you will be, for at the end you'll reveal yourself with a flourish and bring down the house.'

Tilly's answer was indistinct, but they all knew the sort of thing she was saying as she peeled off down her back lane. She was clearer when she called, 'Viola's party arrangements *are* more or less in place? I have brown and red wool for the Christmas-tree robin decorations when we think of the pantomime evening.'

'Oh aye,' replied Sarah. 'I thought someone would say they had. But on to other things: the food is sorted for Viola's party, and Ralph says the drinks are. Seems the babe is on course for delivery soon too, as Sophia's getting more and more uncomfortable, but the co-op have told her it can't be born till Sunday at the earliest. But if she gets cracking after dancing the Highland fling, the Hall is big enough for a whole load of midwives to descend and not disturb the party.'

'But it's going to be a big 'un,' Maisie called before heading towards her mam's corner shop. 'Fair bit of pushing and shoving'll be needed, so we best make sure she's on her back more than her feet at the party, and get her straight back to resting once it's over.'

She stood for a moment. 'I have to start cutting out the

urchins' costumes for the sewing workshop. Bolton and Swinton are happy for the ladies to use their breaks, and the new workshop supervisor, Cathy, is equally happy to check 'em. Mark you,' Maisie turned to shout this, 'Amelia started sounding off because she hadn't been offered the part of the girl on the swing, saying that sewing shouldn't be diverted from the war effort. They took no notice because Briddlestone's had sent the sewing thread, zips and some camouflage so it was costing the factory nothing.

The girls carried on and Fran was eager to get home and see Lisa, who grew bonnier by the day.

'I reckon Bolton is keeping a beady eye on Amelia,' Sarah said, 'so that he can have a cast-iron reason for forcing that Plomer buffoon to back down and take her away. The talk is she does little work in administration, just crosses her legs and pulls up her skirt while she takes shorthand in the boss's office. But Mr Andrews takes no notice, being in cahoots with Bolton to get grounds to shift her out.'

'Mam's making the fairy costume, or cutting it out to be sewn by the workshop,' puffed Beth, catching them up after easing a stone from her boot. 'By, you'd never think it was a short panto. Imagine the work if it were a proper one.'

The other two nodded. 'I don't know how to stop me head from spinning,' muttered Sarah. 'What with the party *and* the panto, and the Christmas presents we have to find for under the tree. Oh Lord, I almost forgot. I have to pick up the cut-outs of Reginald's bossy washerwoman from your mam, so I'll walk with you.'

Beth linked arms with her. 'I'm taking some of the other characters to me mam an' all, to share amongst the Massingham women.'

They turned down the back lane, with Fran thinking of the co-op's rugs for Briddlestone's, which were now finished, as were the ones made by the bairns, which would give them some Christmas shopping money.

As they neared the rear of number 14, Fran had moved on and was telling the girls that she and her mam would have to devise a playpen as soon as possible to contain Lisa, or there'd be little done from dawn to dusk . 'Mam wishes she'd kept the one Da bought for little Betty from the second-hand shop in Newcastle, but at the time she didn't want to be remind—'

A shriek tore through the lane, and then a call. 'No, no.' It was Annie Hall.

'Mam? Mam.' They rushed down the lane just as Annie burst through the back gate with Lisa in her arms, pulling the blanket over the babe's head as she tore towards them – but no, she passed them. The girls followed, catching up, Fran shouting, 'What, Mam? What?'

Annie focused, tears streaming down her face. 'I picked her up, having walked her round the block. She jerked, almost fell from me arms. She – she caught her head on the cart. I should have thought, I should . . .'

Fran pulled the blanket down. There was a bluish bruise already appearing near her temple, but apart from grizzling, Lisa seemed fine. Sarah and Beth also examined Lisa, who merely smiled and reached for them.

'Oh, she's as tough as the rest of us,' Beth grinned. 'She'll have a right shiner, though.'

Annie Hall stepped back, still carrying the child. 'Never mind that, I have to get her checked by Dr Dunster.' She pushed on, rushing towards Main Street. 'There now, bitty lass. There now. Let's make sure, eh? Can't have nowt happening to you – what would your mam say, eh?'

Sarah pulled at Fran. 'Come on, she's in a fret because Lisa isn't hers. Let's go with her, bless her.' With Beth alongside, they caught up at Main Street and made Annie slow to a walk, telling her of their progress with the knitting as they passed a black canvas-sided truck with someone working under the bonnet. Instead of rollicking them about the fact they hadn't even finished one of the fronts, Annie only said, repeatedly, almost wailing, 'I feel so guilty. Oh, how could I do it? Look, she's gone quiet.'

Fran just smiled. 'Oh Mam, she's asleep. Look.' She touched Lisa's hand. The babe moved, sighed, opened, then closed her eyes.

'Howay,' Beth pointed, 'we're nearly there.'

As they turned into Dr Dunster's street, the truck roared past, waking Lisa. Beth and Sarah turned. 'Damn, what a racket,' Sarah said, but Beth was staring after the truck, shaking her head, frowning.

'I saw that yesterday, whistling through, it was.'

Fran was watching it as well. She turned to Beth. 'Not our business. Probably delivering goods.'

Sarah shrugged. 'But what goods? one wonders. Black truck for the black market?'

The other two laughed, and even Annie said, her voice low and hushed as she rocked Lisa back to sleep, 'By, you're getting too sharp, lass. Black for black market, eh?' They smiled as they approached the doctor's house.

Annie hushed them as they chatted about their prospective joy at seeing Sid in his heron costume and laughed again. 'Lasses, keep the noise down.' She rapped on the door.

Mrs Dunster opened up. 'Annie?'

'It's Lisa – I bumped her head.'

They were ushered in, with Mrs Dunster muttering, 'She looks fine to me, but let the master have a dekko, eh?'

It was five o'clock before they cycled into Massingham Hall's garage yard. Fran braked, unclipped Lisa's cart, smiling down at the child, who had been given a clean bill of health by Dr Dunster. Her mam's relief was all the thanks he needed, he'd said, waving away her money. 'And stop worrying. It if had been Fran, you'd have seen it for what it was. Relax.'

Her mam had promised.

Looking around, Fran saw Alfie standing by the Rolls, his arms stretched wide. The others were parking their bikes as Beth called, 'I'll regret it, lad, but I have to ask why you're standing there doing nothing, like a scarecrow that's lost its post.'

'No, you don't, you really don't have to ask, our Beth, just take yourself off to your man, eh. They're in the ballroom and I'm supposed to be servicing Ralph's roadster.'

Sandra came out from behind the Rolls, chewing a pencil. 'But first I have to measure you for your doublet and legging things.'

The girls gaped, puzzled. 'But Ralph's the prince?'

'Aye, but I'm to be his servant – that's as well as a tree with waving branches, sorry, I mean me arms. It's a tree that wears cardboard and camouflage, with branches stuck in me, and as my legs are even skinnier than Sid's, I am now also the heron.' Alfie's face was a picture as Sandra measured his legs and wrote in her book.

'Don't be daft, lad, no one wants to know about your legs, and the branches aren't stuck *in* you.'

'Well, they'd better not be either.'

Sandra skelped his legs. 'Stop fussing and stand still, you're a right fidget.' She looked across at the girls. 'Have I got it right that Davey's Norah has some costumes she's sending? Thing is, our Alfie's such a skinny rabbit—'

Alfie dropped his arms. 'That does it, I'm not playing any more, for I'm sick of hearing about me skinny this and that.' But he was grinning as he said it.

'You'll do as you're told, lad,' Madge called from the top of the kitchen steps. 'As the poster says, England Needs You, so you'll stand there to be measured, but we've just decided you're only to be the heron and a tree, for there's no need for a servant.' She was making her way to Lisa's cart. 'We can't have too many handsome young men in leggings, you know. We women will get too out of control.'

Beth and Sarah sniggered and joined Fran at the cart. Madge was pulling the blankets up around the sleeping child. 'She's such a pet. Not heard from Daisy, I suppose? When your mam arrived she told us what had happened today. Bless her, she must have pedalled like a mad thing to get here before you, all because she was so worried about letting the co-op down. She's tired, Fran. Needs to change the pace a bit. Don't disturb the babe. Alfie can keep an eye.'

Sarah also leaned over Lisa. 'Look, see, Madge, it's just a bruise. Dr Dunster told Mrs Hall to stop worrying after he'd checked her. Said babies bounce and she should know that, so relax.'

From the bottom of the steps, Mr Moran called, 'We're needed in the ballroom. Stan wants to make sure we're all involved in the decision about the position of the stage when the sections arrive. They should be here in time for the party. Right, now I'm to tune the piano. Sophia says we can't have that sounding strange or people'll begin to think it's Miss Walters, not the instruments she plays.'

Fran stroked Lisa's hair, very gently. 'You sleep, sweet babe. Our mam'll be out to check on you.'

The girls pushed Fran towards the steps, Beth nagging, 'Leave her, Fran, she just wants to sleep.'

'I've me arms down now,' Alfie yelled, 'I'll watch her. Get on and keep the lads happy, eh?'

They passed Mr Moran lingering at the top of the steps

and muttering, 'Get your mam into bed tonight, so she sleeps, eh? You and Ben get up for Lisa, leave her undisturbed. Although I know you and she share the shifts, a whole night off never goes amiss.'

Fran smiled. 'Have a word with the woman herself, Mr Moran. Ben and I say it every night, but it's because she feels Lisa is only loaned, so she's more nervous and won't leave her to grizzle as she would her own. Use your best schoolteacher voice, and she'll maybe listen.'

Madge followed, and the girls heard her say, 'There you go, find a schoolmaster's voice, lad, for it's all down to you now.'

Beth looked round and was sure she saw his eyepatch shrink under the pressure of his instructions.

They left their boots in the boot hall and tiptoed across the kitchen flagstones, waving at the co-op while Mr Moran followed them. Madge held him back. 'Oh no,' she hissed. 'First the schoolmaster voice, and only then may you follow us.'

Madge tagged on behind the girls and chatted about the costumes as they headed to the ballroom. 'I've sorted out the costumes for you three girls. You'll look a picture in the extra camouflage Monty Moran's found tucked away in the school cupboard. There wasn't enough in the Briddlestone's parcel.'

'What?' shrieked Beth, spinning round.

Madge was grinning. 'Can't you take a joke? You are to be spirits of the beck and have floaty green outfits, made of the gauze Sophia found tucked away in the attic. Then it'll be a quick change into the washerwomen outfits. Sophia says we can use what we like, as long as she has pride of place in the audience. She doesn't want to miss a moment.'

The girls had stopped. 'Sophia? She's been up in the attic? For the love of—'

'She'll not be doing that any more, let me tell you.' They set off again and Madge asked how it had gone with Amelia today.

Fran shrugged. 'We barely see the girl, but she can't resist a dig when she passes us at mealtimes in her clickety-click high heels and her silk stockings. A present from Daddy, I heard her tell Rosie. She offered to sing at Viola's party, which was met with a big no. I reckon it'd finish Viola off, what with Ralph's old friends from Newcastle coming.'

Sarah was shaking her head. 'Viola's in a right tizzy, scared they'll think she's not good enough for Ralph, but Reginald met their fathers at some meeting and found himself inviting them before asking Ralph. It seems the lads are on leave.'

They kept going and Mr Moran caught them up in the corridor. 'Job done. Mark you, I had the battalion of the co-op behind me. Your mother promised she'd stay in bed tonight, and also that she'd stop fussing.'

Beth noticed that he and Madge were wearing matching eyepatches and nudged Fran, whispering, 'I reckon that's sending a message to the rest of us.'

Fran nodded, whispering back, 'Aye, a bit like you and Sid. There must be something in the air.'

They reached the ballroom and through the open double doors saw that the wooden floor had not only been cleaned, but polished.

'Well, what do you think?' Ralph asked, holding hands with Viola and stepping forward.

The girls grinned. Beth raised her eyebrows at Sid, who was waiting with the others. 'By, I'd say it was perfect if I didn't think it'd go to your heads.'

The lads looked at one another. Sid grinned. 'We put cloths on our feet, stroked on the polish, then sort of skated over the floor to polish it.'

Fran crossed her arms. 'Then what're you doing in the pit? You could be floor polishers when the war is over.'

They just laughed and came over to stand with them.

'So,' asked Ralph, 'where should the stage go – that end, or the top end?'

The girls all pointed to the far end. Mr Moran agreed. Fran took over, pointing around, 'Then the seats can be here, with an aisle down the centre. But we don't have to even think of that now. We have time, just, after the party. Best we sort out where to put the party food – this side, or in front of the windows?'

The girls looked around the room, but Mr Moran butted in. 'The piano should be up there too, so that Miss Walters can bash out some tunes when William and Ben want a rest and your voices need a break.'

He pointed towards the piano, which was waiting in the corner. Madge pursued him. He ran, she followed, until he was backed against the piano, begging for mercy.

At that, the laughter began again.

They set off for home, after they had brought in the trestle tables and worked out where they would place the chairs. It was dark, but their slit lights lit the way well enough. The co-op rode with them, and Fran towed Lisa, who was now fed and watered, thanks to Mr Moran giving her a bottle after her cereal.

As they entered Massingham, the rest of the co-op peeled off, eager to get home, while the girls continued, talking about the song list for the party and wondering if Viola should really play her saxophone.

'I reckon she should have a night off,' Annie Hall called from behind.

'It's her party after all,' Beth said as they cycled down Fran's back lane, 'and Ralph is planning something special, or so Sid thinks.' They were cycling slowly, because although Lisa enjoyed being rattled and rolled, they were conscious she had a bruised head.

'Aye,' Sarah said, 'Stan is sure he'll propose too. He's sorted a ring. It was his mother's and he had it altered, I think.'

Fran laughed quietly. 'There you go, there *is* something in the air.'

'There's what in the air?' her mam called.

'Good things.'

'You're probably right. That ballroom looked a right picture, the rugs are done, the costume-making has begun and our Lisa is fine and dandy.'

Ralph and Viola sat together in the sitting room. Reginald had joined Sophia, ready for an early night. Sandra was in bed, the children were settled and there was still a glow to the fire. 'I don't think I've ever been so happy,' Ralph murmured, pulling Viola even closer, if that was possible.

She laid her head on his shoulder. 'There's something wonderful about thinking of Christmas, Ralph, and making plans, bringing them to life, and it's even better when a person is sitting with someone they love.' For a moment Viola paused. Had she been too forward? Why couldn't she shift these waves of doubt that still swept her from time to time? But, as she looked around, she knew it was because she couldn't really believe she was sitting here, in this grand room, which she could only have dreamed of at home in her family's backstreet terrace in Newcastle. What's more, she was sitting with this man, the son and heir, whom she loved with all her heart. It was all too perfect. Aye, too perfect – so, would it crash?

She felt Ralph kiss her hair and he said, 'Wonderful isn't a big enough word. Amazing, spectacular, heart-stopping is more like it, because I can't believe you love me, though let me tell you, Miss Viola Ross, it can't be as much as I love you. I just don't deserve you, because I've been such a toe-rag one way and another, and to have you beside me is perfection.'

They kissed; she stroked his cheek. There was a new cut above his eye. That would become a scar. She drew away. 'The pitman's brand,' she murmured.

'Something to be proud of.' He kissed her fingertips. They sat back, quietly, with just the tick of the clock and the warmth of the fire. She wondered what he was thinking, but when he spoke, she nearly laughed. 'We should have a Christmas tree in here, as well as in the ballroom. After all, the children will roar down to see if Santa has been – again – on Christmas morning.'

Viola raised an eyebrow. 'Put it on Stan's list, though it could be the straw that breaks the camel's back.'

'Never, his back is broad and strong, or so I shall tell him when he moans. But I'll brief Father. He'll pick a few out, or Old Ted will, and we can all help. We have decorations in the attic, though we might have to take some off the tree in the ballroom too, after Bernie the Monster has done his stuff.'

They fell silent again. Midnight drew close, but neither wanted to move. Would they marry? Would they have children who would gather round the tree with Sophia's bairn, who would be an aunt or uncle to them? Would the evacuees accept all these babies without feeling threatened? She knew they would. She shook her head free of her dreams. It was enough to be here, with him, her beautiful boy, her Ralph.

Chapter Sixteen

The shift in the stemming workshop was its usual messy, foul self, and the girls knew the sheets tonight would be stained with the yellow chemicals they sweated out of themselves. 'We'll look like daffodils standing on that stage, warbling,' Sarah grizzled on the bus back to Massingham.

'Aye,' Beth muttered, trying to scratch her back and failing. She leaned forward. 'Give it a scratch, one of you.' Both Fran and Beth did, but then, as they left Sledgeford, they expected the same from her. Finally, they sat back as Bert rounded the bend, whistling.

'When we reach Massingham,' Mrs Oborne yelled, 'I'll take your measurements, though we know your head'll be bigger than anyone else's. It's the only bit of the costume we haven't cut out.'

They all grinned, waiting for the reply, as Bert put his foot down and they were pressed back against the wooden slats of the seats.

'We need something to balance your great arse, our Tilly.'

'You should have seen your face, Mrs Oborne,' yelled Valerie, 'when Amelia offered her services as the fairy on the swing because she wasn't yellow.'

Mrs Oborne crossed her arms, a sure signal she was still angry. 'It were a bliddy cheek as Viola won't be yellow, anyhow.'

'Which you surely told her,' Susan said as Bert slipped into third to press on up the hill. Fran was looking out of the window at the slag heaps of Minton and Sledgeford, shaking her head at Amelia's cheek.

Miss Ellington was on the bus with them, travelling to see Simon at the Canary Club on the allotment, and added, 'I just had to smother my laugh when she stared at you all at the table and said, "Well, that's your last chance." Honestly, it was as though you had turned down the biggest star in the universe and you'd regret it when you saw her name in lights. She's reverted to type so quickly, but there's nothing Bolton can really get a hold of. When there is, he's going to track down Gaines and they'll put together a demand that Plomer transfers her. Reckon you've all heard knocking from Bolton's office most days? Well, that's his head against the desk.'

The laughter was weak because everyone was just so angry that on top of their wretched jobs, Amelia was her usual self, smug in the knowledge that a higher being was covering her back. Fran just shook her head and made herself drag out the pieces of Sophia's babe's cardigan in order to start sewing the sleeve seams together. 'Come on, the mams want to get these washed, for they reckon the babe must be coming any minute.'

Beth was already sewing hers, and Sarah rummaged in her bag and got to work, calling, 'Steady round the bends, Bert, careful work going on here.'

He merely hooted in reply, before yelling, 'About time, and what's to do if baby comes at the party? Bit of a conversation stopper, eh?'

Mrs Oborne nodded. 'But we've thought it'll be here every day for the last two weeks, so best just get on as normal.'

'Poor woman, 'spect she looks like a barrage balloon,' bellowed Bert.

The gasp around the bus was loud, and this time it was

Cyn Ellington who called, 'I'll be telling her that. Just the thing to set up an expectant mam.'

'You tell her, Cyn, and you'll not get another lift on me bus.' Bert sounded preoccupied. 'Anyway, it's given me a bit of time to sand down me teething ring. Oak, it is. A hard wood, so shouldn't get many teeth marks. And I'm finishing one an' all for our Lisa, so that'll be in her little hands any day now. And while I've been given a moment to talk, how are the scripts getting on? Finished, are they?'

'Oh aye, copied out by the schoolchildren in Mr Moran's handwriting class. Some are better than others and one little lad's has drawings all over it. Monty says he should go to art school. He's going to try and raise some money, but there's time yet. He thought if the village raised some, he could then ask Mr Massingham for a grant. Best to show we've done something, Monty said, before holding out the begging bowl, which is a poor lesson for the bairns.'

The bus carried on, the girls sewed and Fran thought about the yellow, as they called the powder that shot out of the machine when they pulled the handles, whooshing into the rubber thingummybob containers, the powder drenching their masks, which clagged up with the moisture from their mouths. The powder sank through their turbans, upping the streaks in their hair, the awful colour seeping from their bodies into their sheets. What the hell was it doing to their bodies?

While she let her mind roam, she heard Mrs Oborne worrying about Sophia and only really came back to the present when Valerie turned to the girls on the back seat as they passed St Oswald's. 'Poor Davey, not seeing his "baby" performed on stage.'

Fran looked up. 'Aye, sad for his marrers too.'

The shaft of longing for Davey overwhelmed her, as it so often did, but that was all. There was no distrust, just love.

Fran slid a look at Beth, for quite suddenly, she too was openly happy. She and Sid held hands or linked arms, and he had kissed her in public when he had seen her off on the bus that morning. But it was Sarah who said to Beth now, 'At last you're showing you're a couple. Massingham was waiting for you to start being joyful. What brought this about?'

'Oh, there's a war on. Who knows what's to happen and time was a-wasting. If some people think I shouldn't because I'm Mrs Jones, then they can sort things out in their own heads, not on my time.'

Fran grinned, and squeezed Beth's hand. Beth squealed. 'Careful, nearly stabbed meself with the sewing needle.'

'Seems to me the tide is turning here, and in the war, and our party is on Saturday, and the panto near Christmas. We finished the babe's cardigan fronts on the bus this morning. Hip hip . . .' She waited.

Everyone shouted, 'Hooray.'

The bus was, for that moment anyway, full of relief, hope and joy.

The bus arrived in Massingham, and there, waiting, were Stan, Sid and Norm, along with Simon Parrot. 'Oy, oy,' called Mrs Oborne as she set off down the aisle. 'On your feet, our Bert, and onto the pavement. Let's measure you, eh?'

Bert shook his head. 'I'll not stand out there with the world watching.'

'Oh aye, you will,' said Fran as Mrs Oborne hoisted him up by the collar. The lads hung back when they saw Bert stepping down from the bus to the pavement.

'I'll not be fiddled with, mind,' Bert said, standing with his arms outstretched.

Mrs Oborne slapped them down. 'Don't be daft, Bert, your arms won't be doing anything, or they'd better not be.' She whipped out her tape measure, and there and then measured from his shoulders to his crown and, finally, the circumference of his head.

Sid grinned. 'Howay, smile, Bert, we've all had that. If we're not trees, we're shabby old workers—'

As Bert climbed back onto the bus, he yelled back, 'Well, you'll not need a costume for that.'

He started the bus, still grumbling, while Sid put his arm around Beth, kissing her forehead. 'Good day, bonny lass.'

Cyn Ellington was holding hands with Simon, leading the way along Main Street and answering his question. 'They behaved, though I couldn't say the same for that Amelia Cartwright,' she said. 'I thought she were going to throw a hissy fit when she were rejected for the star part.'

'She'll try and get her own back. You watch your backs, girls,' Stan said.

Simon and Cyn left and headed for the allotment. 'See you later at the Canary Club?' Simon called without turning.

'Aye, after tea.'

As they continued along, the lads nodded when Stan said, 'Right glad to get time off from beavering up at the ballroom, but I reckon after the party it'll be non-stop. At least we can test our lines while we eat our bait.'

'The rats and blacklocks'll want an encore.'

They were turning into Fran's back lane, clattering on the cobbles. 'Haven't you got your own homes to go to?' Fran asked, desperately needing a bath, but knowing if they came back with her it would mean making a cuppa for everyone.

'But we thought we'd see Lisa, take her out and about. Give our mam a break, eh? She's getting weary, and we've been saying that we need to do more,' Stan said.

Fran looked at the three pitmen, their coal-grained faces, the weariness more marked than hers, and could have shaken herself. 'You lads're the best people on this planet, you kn—'

They stopped dead at her mam's voice. 'No, no . . .'

Stan took off, running down the lane, the rest of them racing after him and Fran thinking, surely she hasn't bonked Lisa's head again?

They heard the stern voice of Mr Smithson. 'I'm sorry, Mrs Hall, but we have had a complaint, and there's a witness.'

They reached the back gate. Stan slammed it back on its hinges, and they saw Smithson entering the kitchen, with Annie pulling on his jacket, the cart empty. 'Talk to Dr Dunster – he said she was all right.'

Stan headed through the kitchen, following them down the hall, trying to get past his mam. The front door was open and the man stormed out onto the street, Lisa in his arms. Lisa was crying as Mr Smithson handed her to a woman who rushed her into the back of the waiting car. The driver had the engine running, the exhaust fumes huffing out into the crisp air.

Annie Hall was wringing her hands. 'But it was an accident. She isn't hurt.'

The man turned, and Fran squeezed past her friends to stand next to Stan. Mr Smithson put up his hand as Annie reached out, but dropped it when Stan bellowed, 'Don't you dare touch my mam, you hear, and don't think you're taking Lisa any bliddy where till we hear what's happening.'

During the commotion, Norm had taken it upon himself to stand in front of the Austin, his hands on the bonnet, while Sid stood between Smithson and the car. Beth joined him. Sarah was beside Norm. Fran was frantic. *What complaint?* Dunster had checked Lisa and all had been well. 'You must stop fussing, Annie,' the doctor had told her over and over.

Fran saw all the neighbours were watching from their doorsteps, including Mrs Pritchard at number 18, and couldn't bear any of this. She saw the woman in the back seat as Lisa struggled in her arms. Lisa, bonny Lisa, who they'd finally managed to settle and who was content. The driver had a peaked cap, and was looking left and right.

Just then, Ben burst out of the house, onto the pavement, and was shoving his way through everyone. 'Mam? Stan? Franny? What . . . ?'

Smithson stepped back, into Sid, who pushed him forwards. Smithson flinched, then gathered himself together. 'This is most unfortunate, and our business shouldn't be conducted in public.'

Annie stepped even closer. 'It hasn't been conducted at all. You turned up, barged in, yacking about a complaint, a complaint about me hurting the bairn deliberately and saying I was seen, someone had spoken up. Who? That's what I want to know. Who? For it didn't happen. Ask Dr Dunster.'

Mr Smithson waved both hands up and down as though calming the seas. Fran wanted to rip his starched collar off him and throw it into the wind, which was whipping up now. 'My dear woman, we did indeed ask Dr Dunster. To assist, he showed us his notes. It explained the "accident", the bruise. He had not seen what happened, he could only parrot what you had said.'

'"Parrot"?' Mrs Pritchard asked, and it was then that Fran realised the whole of Leadenhall Terrace had converged around the car and they were listening, and waiting, arms crossed, fury evident on their faces. 'That's not the language or attitude suitable for a man in your position. Let me tell you that Mrs Hall, our Annie, would not have laid a hand on this child.'

Mr Smithson tried soothing again. It didn't work. 'And

yet, dear lady, there is evidence of a bruise, there is the statement of a complainant who heard an altercation in this backyard, there is a witness statement which supports her compl—'

Fran cut across him. '*Her*?'

She looked at Mrs Pritchard, who shook her head. 'Not me, I've not heard a wail or cross voice. Never from our Annie, she's a good woman.'

Mr Smithson's voice softened. 'Ah, but worn out, as I can see, perhaps a bit too old to be caring for a babe, eh? People snap when tired. The problem is, as I have said, we have a verified complaint. First the report, then your confession of guilt, Mrs Hall – overheard.'

The girls were holding Stan back and Sarah was soothing her husband. 'Don't touch him, my love. We can sort it.'

Annie was whispering, 'How could it have been heard? It didn't happen, not like that. She jerked as I was lifting her from her cart, that's all. She jerked – I felt bad, guilty, and I said as much, but . . .'

Fran was looking at the neighbours; was it one of them? Even if it wasn't, did they believe Smithson? Just then there was a toot. The group stepped out of the road as Dr Dunster drew up, climbing out of his car, his Gladstone bag in his hand. The women parted before him. Fran watched, remembering Sunday School and the parting of the Red Sea. She wanted to be there, in the vestry of St Oswald's. There, with the hymn books so many hands had held, and so many generations had read.

She came to with a start, looking from Dr Dunster to her mam to Smithson, who was intent on taking Lisa away to some orphanage. 'Because of a complaint by someone absolutely wicked, and an overheard confession, because of a load of bliddy lies. But by who? And why?'

Smithson and Dr Dunster turned and stared at her.

'Someone wicked is right enough,' said Dr Dunster, rattling on, his bag in his hand and his stethoscope round his neck. Did he wear it in bed? *Shut up, shut up.* Why wouldn't her mind stop traipsing about the place?

Dr Dunster was very close to Mr Smithson now, his chin jutting out. 'I thought you'd bustle on round when you left me, so here I am, and I see you're taking Lisa from her perfectly good cot, in a *loving* home, and rushing to get your busy arse out of Leadenhall Terrace.' Dunster looked around. 'But we can't stop him, everyone. He has the authority. He *is* the bloody authority. But you listen to me, Smithson.' He was jabbing the man with his forefinger. 'We *will* expect to see you again very soon, well before Christmas, and we *will* expect an apology, to be given on your hands and knees when the truth comes out.'

Smithson stared at nothing, said nothing, but had visibly paled. Dunster continued. 'Norm and Sarah, stand aside. Stan, open the passenger door. Time for you to go, Smithson. I can't call you mister, for you are a fool of the highest order, one who is capable only of listening to hearsay—'

'Facts, not hearsay. Two independent—' stuttered Smithson, stopping when Dunster closed in on him. He scrambled into the passenger seat.

Stan slammed the door behind him, shouting, 'Daisy left her in Mam's care. And, Smithson, you are quick enough to listen to hearsay from a complainant, but not to a doctor.'

At that, Smithson wound down his window. 'Facts. Your mother was heard declaring her guilt as she carried the child to the doctor. I have it written down.' He scrabbled for his notebook. ' "I feel so guilty. Oh, how could I do it?" '

'Who heard this?' Stan roared. 'They don't know me mam, that's clear.'

Mr Smithson shook his head. 'Your mother has just

confirmed that she did indeed use words such as these when she took the child to the doctor. And apparently the witness does know of your mother and said he had heard damaging rumours before.'

Staring at him, Fran remembered the lorry, and the man working on the engine, and . . .

She looked round, and knew that Beth and Sarah had remembered as well. 'That was panic, a damaged sense of responsibility, nothing more.' She was aware the neighbours were nodding, approaching again, talking amongst themselves, their colour up and faces grim.

'I am sorry,' Smithson called out, 'but the child's wellbeing must come first. There is a bruise, there is the original complainant, the witness and, of course, Dr Dunster's records. We have to get this sorted. Carry on driver.'

Smithson wound up the window as the car roared off.

Fran leaned forward in her da's armchair, with Ben perched on the arm. Her mam sat opposite as the darkness of the evening closed in on them. There was a tap on the back door and Fran rose. It would be the co-op, who'd been round earlier and said they'd be back. So had the lads, but there was nothing anyone could do, so best if they stayed away and let her mam rest. But how could she do that? Fran watched her darting eyes, her trembling hands, which could barely hold her knitting needles.

The tapping came again. Ben hurried past Fran to reach the door first, pulling it open. It was Mrs Pritchard, in her slippers, a shawl around her shoulders, who slipped into the light. Ben shut the door quickly. 'Don't want the ARP yelling "Put out that light," ' he said.

Mrs Pritchard smiled, brandishing half a bottle of brandy. 'It could be Madge on duty tonight.'

Annie called from the chair, her voice so strained that it

broke Fran's heart, 'Sit yourself down, Daphne, and aye, I think it is Madge's turn. She's even roped in Mr Moran. They've two good eyes between them, she says, so no one can escape.'

Mrs Pritchard took the empty armchair. 'I'm not waggling this bottle about for the good of me health, I'll have you know, our Fran. It's best in a glass, well, four glasses, for though Ben's not of an age, he's been through a bit today.'

Fran had never seen Ben move so fast as he headed to the dresser in the alcove to the rear of her da's chair. Her mam looked at Fran, and winked. It was a good sign.

Ben poured the brandy. 'An inch only, our Ben,' Annie warned.

He and Fran turned two kitchen chairs around and then sipped. Ben coughed, his eyes watering.

'You need to sniff it,' said Mrs Pritchard. 'Gets up your nose, into your sinuses, clears 'em, or so my old man used to say. My Cathy left it when she went back home. I had to take her to task, for she was buying it from some toerag here, just after the war began, when she were trying to get over the babe. What were his name now?'

They sat there, watching the range firebox and sniffing the brandy. Fran held hers up to the light. It had a warm colour and for the first time she realised how some people could turn to drink, for with the second mouthful she felt the warmth of it.

'That's it, Norris was his name, Norris . . . now what was the rest?' Mrs Pritchard shook her head. 'No, it's gone, but he was a beggar, didn't want to let her go, bit like . . .' She looked down at her glass, flushing.

'Maud,' Annie finished for her. 'And that's not talking out of turn, Daphne. We all know the truth of it.'

'Aye, Beth did a good job there, and I'm right pleased to see her happy. She didn't deserve that Bob. Or the likes of me, speaking out at that wedding. Taught me something, or Iris Walters did, telling me to shut me gob until I had something interesting to say. She knew me before Cathy's troubles, you see, and me old beggar walking out.'

Fran knew this, of course, but hadn't really thought about it, only about Mrs Pritchard's sharp tongue. She told herself she needed to look behind the obvious, like her mam had, for she had been more tolerant of Mrs Pritchard than most of them, except when her tomcat trespassed.

Mrs Pritchard swirled her brandy. 'By, it hits the spot.'

Fran and Ben smiled, Annie too. Mrs Pritchard also. 'There you are,' she said. 'A smile and a drop of brandy, but only a drop – or two.' She winked at Ben. 'Once our Iris brought me up short, I realised I felt the better for me old man going, and Mr Reginald let me stay on at the house, but you'll know that. I reckon we can all have another little inch, eh, Ben? What do you think, our Annie? It's up to you to say.'

Ben's face was flushed. Annie said, 'A half-inch for the lad, I reckon, but I'll have a full one, eh.'

So that was what they drank, and it was after Fran had finally clambered into the double bed, longing for Davey to be with her and thankful that she had been able to talk to him this evening, that Mrs Pritchard's words came back to her. Norris? That lorry while her mam said what she'd said? Could it be him? She closed her eyes, thinking back, picturing it, but no, she hadn't seen the driver, though what was the number plate . . . ? Yes, D . . . something and then an 84 something as she had told Davey, but she still couldn't picture the final two letters and the number.

Who could she tell? Then she thought of Lisa, in a strange cot, in a room with lots of other cots, strange babes in them, people she didn't know clipping up and down. But it was too painful. She turned on her side and took herself back to the 'her' who had made the complaint: 'her', the woman. Who on earth? But no. Nothing came. She moved away from her pillow, now damp with her tears, and pressed her fist hard against her mouth.

Ralph sat in his father's study, staring at nothing. Who was the female complainant? Was Norris really the witness, as Davey had wondered when they'd spoken about it on the telephone earlier? Poor Davey, who was in a hellish state after Fran had telephoned him, and he wondered if it was Norris Suffolk? Why would even a bastard like Norris make a witness statement? How would he even know a complaint had been made? Perhaps someone knew him and had gone to him to ask for his support. Ralph rubbed his eyes, because he was just going round in circles and all the time he could picture Lisa in a dormitory, and Annie, Fran and Ben at Leadenhall Terrace.

Would someone like Norris come forward, though, and draw attention to himself? What reason would he have to hate the Halls that much? Any beef was with Ralph and Sid, after their row about selling booze to Beth outside the Miners' Club during the wedding tea. The fight he and Stan had had with Norris over Maud's drinking supplies was too long ago, surely? And besides, Lisa wasn't even a Hall child.

Could it be Daisy? But why, when she had left Lisa with the Halls in the first place? It didn't seem to be Mrs Pritchard. Or was it? No, it must be the act of an insane woman, or someone twisted and evil, or . . . or . . . out for revenge, but what could the Halls possibly have done to warrant such a thing? Was it someone who wanted to get at Daisy? Or someone who had lost a child? Hadn't Mrs Pritchard's daughter? But she was not living near here.

Ralph paced back and forth, too agitated to think of

sleep, desperate to clear his mind enough to present the case to Smythe and bloody beg for his help if he had to. After all, the Prof knew Smithson, or of him. That was how the path to Annie's guardianship had been smoothed in the first place.

He sat again, picking up his pen, staring at the blank notebook page before writing: *Background: Complainant – who? Witness – truck driver? Registration D–– 84.* The telephone rang. Ralph jumped, checked the clock. Eleven. Yes, it would be Tim Swinton.

He picked up the receiver. 'Yes, Massingham Res—'

'It's me, Ralphy.'

'Good evening, Tim.'

'I've had no calls from you to any of the call-box numbers at the correct time, laddie. Tut tut.'

Oh God, thought Ralph. Laddie? The idiot was turning into a Scotsman.

'Ah, that's because there's no news, Tim.'

Tim's voice was icy. 'Really? I thought there might be – after all, that loose-mouth Amelia is back. I believe I said I needed information, and she's one of the most likely to cast it like pearls before swine, surely. Didn't I mention the Pig and Whistle would be suitable for a drink if she ever did return?'

Ralph's jaw hardened. So, he was a swine now? What the hell was the matter with Tim? If he wanted information, why insult him? But then he didn't know that Ralph was not under his control, but in fact working to bring him down, so he must be careful and not bite back.

'Oh, yes, Fran or one of the other girls might have mentioned it. We've been a bit busy—'

'Yes, I heard. A party. Well, best you invite Amelia, there's still a day or so before the excitement. You can have a dance, a bit of a chat. You know you won't get anything from the Hall and Bedley girls. Yes, do that. Now, any other news?'

Ralph was just shaking his head, when he thought of Lisa. What if he said nothing and Tim knew? 'Just a little domestic nonsense. Some cock-and-bull—'

'Now, now, Ralphy. Cock and bull can mean many things, but cruelty to a child is never to be taken lightly. Any complaint must be upheld.'

Ralph looked up, staring at the wall. Tim knew. What the hell . . .

There was silence for a moment. Finally, Tim said, 'One of my informants, who is far better than you at keeping his ear to the ground, shares what he hears. I decide what it is I need, Ralphy. You do not, though admittedly your task is specifically the Factory floor, and the pit. It's the Hall girl and the other two who are actually where we need someone to be all ears. So, listen to anything they might let drop, and to Amelia Cartwright, who knows other things. Glean from her what you can about deliveries, rotas, and do not waste the party. Fran Hall could be vulnerable, not thinking, perhaps drinking. We need a success, laddie.'

He hung up.

Smythe would have got that, either by recording it or actually listening in.

The telephone rang again. It was Smythe. Ralph told him everything, about Lisa, the car registration, Amelia's return. The unknown woman who had made the complaint.

Yeland had clearly taken the telephone from Smythe. 'Sorry, old chum, it's me. We did listen, hence the phone call. So let's deal with that first. Our Tim is getting in a state. He's being pushed. Somehow, Amelia is back in the office, in a helpful place. He's thinks, or so I believe, that Fran might drink and be careless with information now. Valuable information, since she is in the main workshops.

More fool him. She's too tough for that nonsense. Is Norris Suffolk part of the cell? If you recall he was so on hand to supply Beth's alcohol, as was proved at either Sarah, or was it Fran's wedding tea when you intervened, I forget which particular bride, but no matter. Or is it all quite coincidental. But I'm a hopeless cynic and don't believe in such a thing. Which brings me to the lorry. Was it Norris working to some sort of desperate plan of Tim's?—'

Ralph interrupted. 'This mulling is all very well, but we need to get Lisa sorted. This is the number plate: D something, and then 84 something.'

There was a pause, some muffled conversation. Smythe came back on the line. 'Smithson's actions are official, so we can do little. So you are right, tracing the registration number would be a start.'

'But how the hell do we do that?' shouted Ralph.

It was Yeland again. 'You ask nicely, laddie.'

'Oh don't you start,' muttered Ralph. 'Anything but laddie.' He drew a deep breath. 'Please, please, on my knees, kissing your feet, please trace the number plate.'

Yeland chuckled. 'Already made a note. I will phone any results through. But off to beddy-byes now, Ralph. You have a party on Saturday, then the next stop is Christmas. Such a lovely time, magical, even cynical old me finds it so. And a pantomime? Sounds altogether rather fun. Keep alert to Eddie Corbitt. Don't fret. Lisa will be back, and I believe it will help us catch the traitors, too. Got to go.'

There was a click. Ralph replaced the receiver, his head whirling. Smythe had warned him at the beginning that you never knew what was going on. You just did what you could and hoped it was enough.

He sighed and did as he was told, climbing the stairs, looking down the corridor to Viola's and the children's rooms, turning left past Sophia and Reginald's. His father was still reading *Tom Sawyer* to her, he expected, as the light was showing beneath the door. Ralph smiled slightly, hoping that Sophia liked the story as much as his father did. But he expected she found the mere sound of her husband's voice soothing. He knew he would find Viola's so.

He also knew that Annie's distress had upset them both, sorely. Annie, the best woman they knew, they had said many times. Tomorrow they would have to tell the children. Ralph found his way to his room, wondering how on earth they could convince the orphans and the others that they were quite safe as evacuees, and that guardianship was definitely agreed, as his father had confirmed, having had a worried discussion this evening with his solicitor. But of course, for the orphans their parents had already been taken, so why not the Massinghams.

He flopped down onto the bed, staring at the ceiling, wishing someone would read to him, because he couldn't stop thinking of Lisa lying in a cot, lonely and without love, though probably people were kind. Probably. But would they remember her name? What if it had been Eva? Or one of the others? Or all of them? He rolled onto his side, his shoes and clothes still on. He should undress. He couldn't. All of this was unbearable, and grown men shouldn't bloody cry.

The next day in the pit, as they chewed on their bait, all beyond words or discussion of Lisa, they talked instead of the lorry's registration number. 'I asked a friend. He's chasing it down,' Ralph said, throwing a stone at a rat, one too impatient to wait for the crumbs. 'Well, a friend of my father's, actually.' He slurped cold tea.

They merely nodded. Sid and Norm collected their picks and returned to the face while Ralph asked Stan, against the noise of Charlie's shovelling, to ask Fran to deliver a party invitation to Amelia. He dragged it out of the pocket of his trousers, which were folded on the ground. It was wrapped in a paper bag to keep it clean. A blacklock fell from a roof cross beam. Stan swung round, his lamp lighting the pitch-darkness for a moment. Ralph said, 'I forgot to give it to you above ground.'

'But why give it at all? The girls hate her. Hang on, do you suspect she's the complainant? Are you going to grill her?'

Ralph had been ready for reluctance, but not this. It hadn't entered his head; it was ridiculous. 'No, Amelia's nothing to do with it. I just thought it was a good way of perhaps bringing everyone together outside work, you know, to make her feel involved, a final hand of friendship, if you like, to get her off their backs. Some of my school friends will be there – she'll be in her element, showing off. You know what she's like. But forget about her. We need to find the driver, make him talk, and then work back to the one who made the complaint. I mean, in order to support a complaint, he must know who made it.'

He hesitated for a minute. He could see that Stan was standing quite still, then he lifted his lamp to stare into Ralph's face. They both shook their heads at the same time. Stan sighed. 'I start imagining things, everyone is guilty, everyone . . .'

Ralph gripped his shoulder. 'One thing at a time. We must find the driver, and go on from there.' They set off for the face. Stan leading, Ralph just behind.

Chapter Seventeen

Viola smoothed her hair, tying it back in a ponytail. It was Saturday, 14 November. She was twenty and loved by Ralph Massingham, and today there were no doubts, because this was a party for little Viola Ross. She looked in the mirror and could see the light in her eyes, which had grown brighter after the girls had given her two bone-china cups and saucers yesterday, so she and Ralph could use them for their morning tea. They had explained that Iris Walters had wanted Beth and the girls to give them as a gift, from the three of them.

Viola could have wept because she had never had bone china of her own. Fran had whispered, 'We feel Iris gave it to us, for you, because you are special and deserve something and someone fine. Ralph is that someone.'

Again, she checked her hair in the mirror. Now she was out of the Factory, she was finally able to grow it, and there were no streaks caused by the chemicals. Before the party tonight she would put it into a French pleat, leaving her left ear for all to see, even Ralph's friends, who she so wished weren't coming. She frowned and stepped back, tying her apron, hearing the children getting up. But there was one other who was invited, and it was kind of Ralph, but . . . surely Amelia wouldn't actually turn up?

She looked in the mirror one last time and had second thoughts. Perhaps she *would* keep it down, but then she could hear Ralph calling her ear a war wound, cut off in its prime, like his in the car crash, and what did it matter, with

Lisa gone? She suddenly felt weary. They shouldn't be having a party, but as Sophia had said, life must go on, if not for them, for the bairns, who hadn't yet been told and wouldn't be until Annie gave permission. So, she *would* put her hair up, and as Ralph joked, they would look like two bookends – made to be together.

'I love you so terribly much,' he'd whispered as they'd left the ballroom close to midnight after doing a final check of the stage. 'I will give you my present tomorrow, sweetest angel.'

The bairns were scratching at her door. Checking the clock, she realised they were right, it was time to get up and at it, as Reginald had taken to saying. She hurried out into the corridor, her finger to her lips. They clustered round, and as she had done for several days now, Eva murmured, 'Is it born yet?'

She looked at the faces lifted to hers, but had to disappoint them again. 'A quiet night,' she whispered, herding them along, 'Quick, quick, down the stairs and let's sort out a rushed breakfast and a cuppa for Sophia – perhaps toast? Then it's back to work, sorting the refreshments table.'

The bairns were quiet whilst crossing the hall, but grew louder as they pounded into the kitchen. They sat around the table while she and Sandra made the porridge and a pot of tea. Viola poured a cup for Sophia, placing it on a tray with a slice of toast, which was all the poor woman said she had room for. Reginald would be down any minute, and once Sophia had all she needed he would return and be ready to do her and the co-op's bidding.

Melanie looked at the tray, and the single piece of toast. 'I reckon there are two bairns in Sophia's belly, it's so huge.'

Alfie, who had just arrived, gasped, 'What?' Sandra and Viola were struck dumb, though Viola saw Reginald's face as he entered.

'Oh dear heavens, really?' Reginald whispered, turning pale. He had broken out into a sweat.

'Morning, Captain,' called Abe. He had told Reginald he resembled the captain of a ship a few days before. Reginald's reply had been: 'One that is totally rudderless right this minute, dear boy.'

'So, it was a good night?' Viola asked.

Reginald nodded. 'Yes, thankfully. She'll be up and at it this evening. We'll just have to stop her doing the American jive, eh?' He tweaked Abe's ear before picking up the tray, his colour returning to normal.

'She best not do that Highland thing, either, Captain,' Eva said, her expression solemn as she rested her elbows on the table. 'She's so fat she'd flatten anyone she banged into.'

Reginald exchanged glances with Viola and Sandra. They bit their lips. He just shook his head, even more harassed. 'I'll be back in a moment.' He left.

Melanie was saying to Tommy, 'What was it you said, you bet sixpence that it's only the one? Well, I'll say sixpence it's two.' She spat on her palm, and Tommy did the same to his before slapping her hand.

The conversation moved on to the odds of two babies versus one, while Viola drank her tea and Sandra poured a cup for Alfie. Were they wondering, as she was, if this was the first time the bairns had indulged in gambling, or was it an established ring? Viola sighed, knowing that such a thing was more than possible, but she was not about to tackle it today. And where had they conjured up this ridiculous notion that it could be two?

She slipped out of the back door, lighting a Woodbine and leaning against the wall, even though the chill made her shiver. She stared up to the sky. Did these bairns really have to be informed about Lisa? Couldn't they just be fibbed to and told she was on holiday or something for as long as it took to get her back?

This was the question that she, Sandra, Sophia and the co-op had agonised over yesterday when the bairns were at school. Reginald had come in with Alfie for a tea break while cleaning the ballroom windows inside and out, and it was he who had felt the truth must always be told, because that's what the bairns had been promised.

As she leaned against the cold bricks, now, she was listening and waiting and hoping for Annie Hall's arrival, even though it was only six in the morning. Ralph had insisted, and quite rightly, when he returned from the fore shift yesterday that actually it was absolutely Annie's decision.

After he'd said it, Madge had snatched a Player's from him, lighting up, pacing the kitchen. 'Annie won't be up today, as you will have guessed. She will be in bed, or cleaning the house, or collecting the last of the runner beans at the allotment, or any damn thing she can think of to get herself together, because by tomorrow, she will be back with us, ready to get on with the last minute party preparations. She will also, you mark my words, have decided what the bairns should be told.'

Eva's voice interrupted Viola now. 'You know Mrs Hall weren't here yesterday, when we needed her? Well, why not? She's not having a bairn like Sophia, so is she having a problem? Isn't Lisa sleeping or something?'

She came to stand beside Viola, holding a half-finished slice of bread and dripping. 'Something's up, Viola, we can feel it, which is why I'm going to give this to the birds. You see, there's too much not being said, and me stomach's rolling about because Mrs Hall, our Annie, is the leader of the co-op, and will she come today? And if she doesn't, I don't feel like having fun at the party, so there.'

The child went up the steps and stood on the cobbles

beneath the empty washing line, tearing and scattering the bread, but then there came the sound of voices and bicycles entering the yard. At last, thought Viola, and she was up the steps in a shot, waiting at the top to see . . . Oh please be here, Annie. Eva came to stand with her. It was indeed the co-op, and yes, there she was, talking and laughing with the rest, looking tired, a bit drawn; Viola put her arm around Eva's shoulder. They pressed close together.

The co-op dismounted and waved. Annie called to Eva, her voice almost as usual, 'Come on, labourers needed, there's food we've baked and packed up in the cart, and sandwiches we've cut for the party. They must be taken, carefully, to the kitchen, quick, quick.'

Eva ran at Annie and hugged her. 'You didn't come yesterday. We wondered why, but you'll tell us. Aye, you will.' She was looking up as Annie stroked her hair.

'I have something to say,' Annie said gently, 'but you *know* you are safe. You are all safe, and you have to remember that, and trust the Massinghams with all your heart.'

Annie repeated this to the other bairns, too, who had come outside and collected in a group around her.

The food was brought from the carts and unloaded onto the kitchen table. Maud Bedley flapped a tea towel at Enid and raised an eyebrow at the rest of them. 'I see you've not plaited your hair, or rather, Eva hasn't done it for you yet.'

It was so normal, and Annie blessed her, for the darkness of the hours since Lisa had gone was lifting, because it had to, and that was that. More to the point, Stan and Fran had said there was the number plate to trace, and Ralph had promised it would be done.

They would discover what had happened by tracking the connections, then take the truth to Mr Smithson and clear up this mess they had said. Now they had a plan, she must face the awfulness of Lisa in an orphanage and remain strong, for there would be damage to be healed on Lisa's return. What's more, in the meantime there was a party, a Christmas panto to prepare for, and these bairns to reassure, and she had decided that it must be with the truth.

Reginald entered the kitchen with the tray; the toast was gone. Yes, he mouthed at Eva, who turned to Annie. 'You see, Mrs Hall, she squeezed some in, but we reckon there could be two in that bump for she's as big as a tent. Has Fran finished the cardigan? What about your Sarah, Mrs Bedley, and your Beth, Mrs Smith? I reckon we might need two of everything, not that I've laid me bet yet. And what's wrong with you, Mrs Hall, for something is?'

The co-op were blinking. 'A bet?' whispered Madge, almost speechless for once.

The children were not deflected. Instead they waited. Alfie came back from taking tablecloths to the ballroom and Enid muttered, 'Your hair's like a bird's nest, for you haven't brushed it, I reckon. But no need to speak, Alfie, for we're waiting to hear what's wrong, and if people talk, Mrs Hall can't.'

Alfie leaned back against the door, running his fingers through his hair.

Annie took a bag of broken biscuits from Beatrice. 'We'll need these when we stop for a cuppa to boost our energy – for there's much to do. But the first is to explain what has indeed happened.'

'It's to do with Lisa,' called Marty, 'for you didn't bring her, and we're not daft as brushes.'

Stephen pulled at his arm. 'Well, she wouldn't fit in her cart, would she? It were full of food, and so was the proggy-rug one.'

Abe shouted then. 'Hush, let Mrs Hall talk.'

'But she's Annie. Why're we calling her Mrs Hall? Why're we calling any of them Mrs?' Marty asked.

'Because we don't know what's going on and we might not like it. So we might not like them.' Melanie had her arms crossed and was tapping her foot.

Reginald was sweating so much it had begun to run down his face. Was it only Annie who heard his whispered, 'Oh dear heavens.'

She stepped forward, her hand up. 'This stops right now.' Looking round, she continued. 'Yes, and Mr Reginald is coming to stand with me, Viola too, because we have something to tell you, but we wanted to be absolutely clear on the truth, and our plan to sort it all out. We have this, now.'

She handed over to Reginald, who was wiping his face with his handkerchief. 'Well, the first thing I have to say, is that I am placing a bet that it's one baby. Do you hear? It'll be a big one, but it's *only* one.'

Everyone was looking at him as though he'd lost his mind. Madge shoved him in the back. 'Do get on, we've so much to do.'

'Aye,' Eva said, 'we haven't all day. It's Viola's birthday party, and Fran, Sarah and Beth'll be here at four to rehearse—'

Again, Annie held up her hand. 'Enough. Do you want to hear the problem and the solution or not?'

Silence fell immediately. Viola watched her charges carefully as Annie and Reginald explained the past situation and the present. It looked as though clouds and then sun, and then clouds again, were passing over the children's faces. 'So, you can see,' Reginald finished, 'Mrs Hall, our Annie, had been given temporary guardianship. Some appalling toerags have accused her of hurting Lisa. We can't tell you what is happening to find these people because it must be a secret. But let me tell you, all of us –' he pointed round the room '– all of us are working to a plan.'

Eva stepped forward. 'With Mr Ralph helping to lead everyone, along with Annie?'

Viola hid a smile, and stepped forward in her turn. 'Oh yes, he and the pitmen, the girls, the co-op, even Professor Smythe. And of course Sophia.'

'Alfie too?' queried Abe.

Alfie stepped forward, saluting. 'Aye aye, Captain. Present and correct.'

'Anything else you need to know?' Reginald asked.

Melanie raised her hand. 'How much will you bet on just one?'

Reginald whispered, 'The whole world.' The women laughed.

Melanie seemed to be thinking. 'Aye, well,' she turned to the others, 'we'll say a bob, eh?'

Work began, but a close eye was kept on the children, because the news would rumble and trundle around their heads, and questions, not to mention fears, would surface.

Madge had control of the kitchen, alongside the cook, Lily Phillips, who had just arrived. Alfie had dug out cardboard boxes from the garage, and these were filled as instructed, one plate on top of another: 'Not too heavy, not too light.'

The bairns were sent up the stairs from the kitchen and along to the ballroom, where Annie, Viola and the others laid out the tables. By ten o'clock Farmer Thompkins had arrived with a trailer containing a barrel of beer, some bottles of wine, although there were already bottles from the wine cellar on the table. He also gave Viola a gift, wrapped in brown paper with a few splodges of paint to cheer it up.

It was a quotation in cross-stich by Mrs Thompkins, framed by Mr Thompkins: *If music be the food of love, play on.* There was even a saxophone in the corner.

Viola kissed him, almost speechless. 'I will write to thank her. I have hardly any words getting past the lump in my throat. It's so kind.'

'Tell her this evening,' he replied.

Mrs Phillips made cheese sandwiches and pastries, and then she and Maud carried them on huge trays to the ball-room while the others continued plating up and delivering more food. Then it was time for a break for broken biscuits and a cuppa. The bairns sat with nothing to do, faces strained and worried. Abe looked up from his sandwich. 'We have Mr Reginald and Sophia as guardians, so some-one can take us away too.'

Reginald was leaning on the back of the armchair in which Sophia now sat, her fingers and feet swollen. He said, 'Ah, but rest assured we have been given *permanent* guardianship by the authorities for you three orphans and besides, as all eleven of you are evacuees we have already been approved as carers – for you all. We have some more information especially for you, Abe, Eva and Marty. We have applied to adopt you, to keep you in our family for ever. We have people finding out if you have relations any-where who would lay claim to you.'

Abe said, 'My family is all in Hungary, like the other Jews in their village. My dad left when I was little. My grandda is dead. I don't really know them.' The other two bairns weren't as sure.

Reginald continued. 'Don't worry about a thing, because even if some are found, we will be talking to them and per-haps adoption can still continue, or at least we will do our best to work out a way to keep you here.'

Melanie was holding Eva's hand. 'You see, Eva, like me

you will have a mum and da, and two brothers as well and Mr Ralph makes three, then there are the two babies.'

Reginald grimaced and patted the sweat from his face again. 'One,' he said firmly.

Viola sneaked up to him. 'Never fear, Sandra and I will be here. We can look after one each.'

'Oh, dear heavens,' Reginald groaned, while Sophia laughed.

'Don't be silly, darling, they're teasing you,' she said. 'Dr Dunster would have heard two heartbeats.'

Lily Phillips came out of the scullery with a huge pot of tea. She placed it down in the middle of the table and returned for cups. 'That's right most of the time, but my cousin pushed out two when only one were expected, for one of the little tinkers were hiding behind the other.'

Reginald clung to the back of the armchair. 'How kind, Lily, just what I wanted to hear.'

Melanie and Tommy were deep in discussion.

'Is there a problem?' Viola asked.

'Tommy doesn't know if he should change his bet now we've heard Mrs Phillips' cousin. Were she like a barrage balloon like Sophia, Mrs Phillips?'

Sophia's smile collapsed. Viola's mind went blank, but just then Mr Moran entered and smiled at Madge. 'I hope I didn't hear anything about pupils of mine betting? I'd better have not.'

There was no answer, just a crossing of arms and scowls. Annie grinned at Viola. 'This won't be over until the barrage balloon gives birth, you realise that.'

As Sophia roared with laughter, Viola noticed that Abe's gaze was distant again. 'That person who made the complaint needs to be found, you know,' he said. 'Because she might make one about us. That's the trouble, the real trouble, for when do bad people stop, is what me da said.

But that were about Hitler. Mind, he thought Stalin were a bully an' all, and Mr Wilson's boy who lived on the corner.'

'Tell us that later,' Eva ordered. 'For the problem is now – what if whoever it is, tells fibs about Sophia, or Reginald?'

The bairns were all agreeing. Reginald nodded to Viola, who replied carefully, 'They *could* try to cause trouble, of course, but they wouldn't succeed with the Massinghams, and as for Lisa, remember, we have a plan and we must all trust that plan to work. The lorry driver will be found.'

'Is that a promise?' asked Abe.

'We will try our utmost, and we trust it will work.'

Yet again, for the moment, the bairns all trusted too, and the best thing was to make sure it all worked out. Viola looked round at the co-op, Sandra and Alfie, the Massinghams, all of whom were nodding. After all, Ralph had promised her he would find the man in the lorry, and she had put her trust in her beautiful boy and, in Annie Hall's words, that was that.

She clapped her hands. 'Right, now we need to check the chairs are in the right place, eh? Finish your milk and biscuits, then off we go.'

Chapter Eighteen

The bairns were as subdued as everyone else when they gathered in the ballroom at eight o'clock that evening. Ben and William were on the stage and Ben's tie hung loose and his sleeves were rolled up.

'Don't think I can't see you and your tie, lad,' called Annie. 'But just this once you can get away with it – and you can wipe that grin off your face. Why not play one of the Glenn Millers, eh? We feel a bit gormless standing about, waiting for the charge to begin.'

Sophia was strolling slowly around the ballroom, Reginald half supporting her, while Ralph and Viola waited, hand in hand, to greet the first of the partygoers entering from the corridor. Scanning the room, Viola saw Eva make her way to Sophia, her attention on the bump. Surely the bairn wouldn't produce a hidden tape measure to check its size, or, heaven forbid, ask for a feel to see how many feet were kicking? Should she go over? But then Eva nodded, seemingly satisfied, and made to walk alongside her guardians, as she had called them when they'd finished putting out the chairs. 'There,' she had said. 'Are the guardians happy?'

Solemnly, Reginald had nodded. It had seemed to seal something in Eva.

The guests were to enter by the front door and traipse along the corridor, because it was too dark to find their way round to the back of the house in the blackout and enter via the double doors to the right of the orangery.

Besides, there were tables in front of the windows with the drinks on.

Ralph hugged her. 'Is there anything you haven't thought of?'

'Of course not,' Sophia called, drawing near. 'Because this young woman is more than capable of handling this, and us.' She lowered her voice. 'Not forgetting the eleven bairns she has somehow reassured about their continued security here. She also suggested that any attempt to induce the guests to bet on the number of babies I produce would deserve banishment to bed.' She and Reginald moved on, walking round the ballroom again because Sophia said that sitting all day had given her a backache, so best to walk it off.

Viola looked about her now, mentally ticking off the arrangements, hoping and praying she had remembered everything. She drew in a deep breath and made herself relax, because the co-op were here, and their preparations had been beyond perfection. But this was her debut as Ralph Massingham's sweetheart, and Sophia's right-hand lass. What's more, his smart friends would be bound to be judging.

Ralph's grip tightened around her as he murmured, 'I like your hair like that. Mother said it was a French pleat?' He kissed her temple as she ran through his words again, because he'd called his stepmother 'Mother' for the first time. She glanced across at the two Massinghams, who had moved nearer again, ready to welcome the guests. They must have heard, because Reginald was beaming and Sophia's eyes were full of tears.

Viola nodded, leaning into Ralph, full of love for this son of theirs. He whispered, against her hair, 'I said "Mother", didn't I?'

'You did indeed.'

'Well, she is, and not just to me.' He looked around. 'There are all these terrifying brats too. How can my parents have hearts big enough?' He waved to the children milling around.

'It's like yours, I suppose,' said Viola, 'because if anyone attempted to hurt these terrors you'd tear them limb from limb.'

They laughed together, and viewed the bairns in their smart new clothes made by the co-op. Viola grinned at the women who were giving the chairs a final push and shove, making sure that everyone had sight of the dance floor, telling Fran, Sarah and Beth to get up on the stage and practise their steps.

Would Ralph's friends be rude about her ear, her hand, her Geordie accent? What would she do if they were? She went back to her list in order to calm down. Ralph's friends would come by car, no doubt, and Alfie was out there, muffler on against the chill, and would direct them to park opposite the front of the house. The villagers would come by Farmer Thompkins' trailer, or on bikes. Coats and macs should go on the trestle table Reginald and Norm had erected in the hall. Hats to go on the small table, next to it. Oh . . . She put her hand to her mouth. 'Norm,' she called. He turned, but so did Stan, Beth, Sarah and Fran. 'Did you put a cloth on each of the tables in the hall?'

'No,' he said. 'I used them to polish the car.' Viola laughed.

Fran came to her, linking her arm through her friend's. 'Relax, you've sorted everything. I think she should be running the world, shouldn't she, Ralph?'

'She's already running mine,' he said, patting his pocket.

Mrs Oborne came across at that moment, leaving her son, Colin, and husband, Steve, eyeing the bottles of beer and ignoring the fancy French wines. 'Maybe I should be on duty at the front door, eh, get 'em to scamper on through, chop chop.'

Viola thought she heard Reginald saying, 'Oh dear heavens.'

'Ah, but we need you in charge of the alcohol. You'll be firm.' Viola's voice was grave.

Steve called, 'She will that. I reckon she'll turn into a ration thug.'

'Turn?' called a voice. Bert, of course. There he was, coming into the ballroom, removing his cap and shoving it in his pocket. 'Didn't like to leave it on the table, someone might pinch it, and it's been me pal for more years than I care to remember. Snowing out there,' he muttered. 'Glad I weren't driving the bus, so you get behind that counter, our Tilly, and I'll be first in the queue to wet me whistle.'

He set off across the floor, while Steve called, 'Oh no you won't, you old beggar. You'll be third.'

Viola grinned and gestured to Sandra to take up position in the hall to welcome the guests. At about nine, the girls would sing, while she accompanied them on the saxophone. The piano was set up for Iris Walters, who'd tickle the ivories if needed, as she'd put it. Viola nodded to herself. Yes, that was about it. And at midnight, oh, at midnight, everyone would leave and she could relax. But what if they didn't go, just lingered and lingered? How did one get rid of people in a house like this? Her da would have just said, 'On yer way, lads.'

For a moment she panicked, but then Ralph muttered, 'Don't worry about getting rid of them. Father is good at that. Suddenly they'll all just drift away. It's a skill I haven't learned, but I will, because we'll have more of these. It's good to get people together.'

'Please no more of these,' muttered Viola, 'not until the panto's over anyway. But I still wonder if I should have asked you lads to put up the Christmas tree your da's marked out for the panto?'

'No, save it for Bernie and Christmas.'

The Factory Girls could be heard practising their steps on the stage which had been brought up in sections by Farmer Thomkins from the Miners' Club. She smiled up at Ralph, who was easing his neck, fingering his collar. 'Leave it,' Viola insisted.

Ralph grimaced. 'It's too tight.'

'Poking about won't help.'

Stan, standing next to Bert, a tankard in hand, called, 'Oy, oy, under the thumb, eh?'

'And a nice place it is, Stan Hall,' murmured Ralph, about to fiddle again.

Sid came over to him, hand in hand with Beth. 'Leave it, lad. Be proud, for the pit thickens the neck, gives you muscles where you didn't know you had places.'

Reginald called, 'A lot of truth in that, Ralph.'

'Stop your fussing and fidgeting, lad, you're not a bairn.' It was Annie Hall, and she sounded *almost* her usual cheery self.

Abe came to stand in front of Annie. 'You're not all right, we know that, it's still in your voice. But you mustn't worry, and we mustn't either, because a promise has been made that everyone will do their best. For if you don't believe a promise, you're not helping it to work.'

The ballroom fell quiet. Sophia made as though to rush to Annie – or was it to Abe? – but Reginald held her back. Everyone was waiting and now Annie looked at Abe, then stroked his dark hair. 'Aye, lad, you're right. Tell me again what the promise is?'

Melanie and Eva led the other evacuees to stand with Abe. Marty said, 'Why, that your Stan, Ralph and the lads, and the girls, the co-op and Massingham, each and every one will do their very best to sort it. If they do, then Lisa will be home, for the lies will be shredded.' He turned, looking doubtful. 'Shredded what's you said to me, on the quiet, wasn't it, Mr Reginald?'

Reginald nodded.

'Stan said the lads have ways of getting at the truth,' added Eva, 'and we reckon they'll slap that witness around a bit when they find him . . . My da whacked me arse when I lied. I didn't do it again. Stops you, a sore arse does.'

Viola saw Sophia slap Reginald's arm, and just knew he'd said, 'Oh dear heavens.' Suddenly, she laughed, and couldn't stop, until they all were, and the bairns were looking at the grown-ups as though they were mad, which they seemed to think rather often. Ben put on another Glenn Miller record, turning up the volume. Like moths to a flame, the guests began to arrive, with Cyn Ellington and Simon Parrot hurrying in, shaking the snow from their hair.

Sophia was already on her way to the windows, peering through the curtains. 'It is still snowing heavily.' She turned to the room, smiling gently. 'Perhaps those from afar will think twice. One worries for their safety.'

Viola heard the hope in her voice. Ah, so she wasn't the only one who didn't want to have to meet strangers.

Sophia beckoned to her. When Viola eased away from Ralph's grasp and reached her, Sophia muttered, 'Somehow, my dear, I just feel I want to be surrounded by our friends, safe in our nest, as it were. Poor Ralph feels the same, I can tell – the war has changed so many things.'

Reginald was shifting from one foot to the other and butted in. 'Yes, I know, my dearest, and also that it was my fault, one of those ridiculous things. The moment I gave the invitation to the councillors' sons, I regretted it. But it is a truth that once upon a time the lads were friends, and perhaps still are.'

Ralph was on his way to join them.

'But then to invite Amelia?' his father grumped. 'It's like one of those weddings where the list gets longer and longer and those one "should" invite are added . . .' He shook his head. 'Enough, it's done, and if they're snooty, or Amelia is difficult, we'll ignore them, eh? And as you say, they might not come in such inclement weather.'

Sandra came hurrying up to Ralph. 'Sorry to butt in, but there's a Professor Smythe on the telephone. He said he wanted to give you a message to pass on to Viola. Happy birthday, I expect. Quick, follow me, for it's a trunk call.'

Ralph followed, calling back, 'It's as well I know my place, which is to obey.'

Stan lifted his tankard to Ralph. 'Oh, well done that pit-man. He's got the idea right enough.'

Ralph entered the hallway, which was filling with guests, mostly from the pit and the Factory. 'Be back in a moment, splendid to see you,' he said to those he passed. 'Sandra will point you towards the ballroom.'

Then he saw Amelia Cartwright picking up the receiver from the hall table. He hurried over and took it from her. 'Nice to see you, Amelia. Sandra's in charge.'

Sandra reached him. 'I'll replace it in thirty seconds, Ralph. Off you go.'

He headed for his father's desk, and the telephone, checking the time as he lifted the receiver, listening for the click of the receiver bang on thirty seconds. 'Good evening, Professor. Sorry, I had to arrange to have the hall phone guarded, as someone had hold of it.'

'Who?' Smythe asked, and Ralph told him. 'Oh yes, how interesting . . . But no matter. Let's move on to the owner of the vehicle, a name that is not a surprise.'

Ralph could hear someone in the background. Smythe

came back to him. 'Thomas Suffolk, who, it transpires from our investigation, is the father of Norris. Need I say more?'

'No.'

Smythe was off again. 'Well, I will, because it would seem that Norris really does want to bring down the Halls and Bedleys . . . But why? It has to be personal, but there is no such connection between the families and Norris. No, the connection lies, we now understand in the dynamic between Tim, Stan and Davey. It was the latter two who drew for the Massingham scholarship and pipped our Tim at the post, snatching university from his grasp. It transpires that all through their schooling, it was the Hall and Bedley boys that trumped him. It can rankle, in the mind of a weak and brainwashed character, one already full of admiration for a tyrannical cause, such as Fascism.

'It is this personal obsession, we believe, that is Tim's Achilles heel. As you can see we have been busy since we spoke. Norris is undoubtedly Tim's tool, don't ask how we know. Norris fed Davey's mother's drink problem – and later, Beth's – for Tim's personal revenge . . . It must have been then that Tim realised an addiction such as Mrs Bedley's could be further used to help the cause. Through a sodden Beth, he hoped to receive information on deliveries, production, et cetera, in return for booze. Don't ask how we know. That's our business. We need grounds for scooping Norris up and into our custody without alerting Tim unduly. *Thomas* Suffolk lives in Lower Thetford, which is not a million miles from you. It is where we understand Norris also resides.' Smythe paused, coughing.

'Are you all right?' Ralph asked.

There was a final cough. 'Of course. Now, fancy a bit of a bike ride tomorrow to investigate? Bicycles are quiet. Take the Halls, and the marrers. Hunt Norris down, get out of him what you can regarding Lisa, then contact us. We'll take it from there for our ends, as it were. All that will be publicised is that he gave a false statement. Lisa will be returned, but by the end of *our* questioning , we'll no doubt have our foot in the door of Tim's Fascist group. Incidentally, Tim's father is whiter than white. Beyond reproach. He will need support, but I rather feel Beatrice will give it to him, if it ever comes out.' Smythe read out the address. 'Back to the party now, and wish that amazing young woman a very happy birthday.'

As he replaced the receiver, Ralph wanted to punch the air, because now he, or they, could do something for Annie; after all, she was always doing things for everyone else. He hurried out of the study, but waited as Mr Swinton approached.

'How nice to see you, Ralph.'

Ralph walked a little of the way with him, telling him that Beatrice Adams had already arrived with Maisie, and was probably eager for a dance.

Mr Swinton laughed. 'Now, what could you mean by that?'

Letting him go ahead, Ralph called after him, 'Ah, I remember the samba at Fran's wedding tea.' Then he stood quite still, running his conversation with Smythe through his head again, deciding to wait to tell the lads about the bike ride until after the party. What he didn't want was for them to roar off straight away, leaving everyone mystified and offended. Nor could he afford to be left here while they dug Norris out, for the situation was bigger than they could imagine.

In the ballroom twenty minutes later Viola relaxed, because Ralph's friends had bent over her hand, almost kissing it, expressing their delight, and were now recapping their schooldays. Peter, a trainee solicitor in Newcastle, was talking about their history teacher, who had assumed everyone loved the subject as much as he did.

'Yes,' replied Ralph, 'but I begin to see what he meant, for how can we understand what's happening in the present if we don't understand the past? I have to say, I've recently read quite a few books on—'

Peter cut across him. 'My word, I never knew you could read books down in the dark with a pick in your hand. I mean, who can you discuss such things with around here?'

Infuriated, Viola searched frantically for Stan, gesturing him over. Ralph smiled, understanding immediately, and introduced Stan, and then Sid and Norm as they joined them. 'Stan,' he said, 'Peter who has just started as a trainee in his father's legal practice was at Oxford too. He read PPE, like you.'

'Oh aye,' Stan smiled. 'You know Professor Smythe then?'

Peter and the others recovered from their surprise, and Peter nodded. 'Oh, that old duffer. I have no idea how he manages to wear matching socks.'

There was a silence for a moment, before Stan said, 'I might go back one day, to finish, but we were needed in the pit, just like me sister's needed in the Factory.'

The men exchanged a look that bordered on a sneer. Stan continued. 'It's one of them places that make pots and pans. The sorts of pots and pans that took our Viola's hand and ear, so she matches our Ralph. Bliddy hero, she is, and your lad, too, crashing the car rather than hitting the Factory bus.'

By this time the three young men were shifting awkwardly. Sid said to Peter, 'What is it you do again, man?'

'I'm becoming a solicitor.'

There was a longer pause. 'Ah, I see, and you lads?' Norm asked.

It transpired they were both civil servants, not servicemen, as Reginald had assumed. 'Service of a sort, nice and clean, eh?' Sid said, his voice carefully neutral, but somehow a wealth of meaning in those few words.

'Well, of course, there needs to be a certain rationality and brainpower behind politicians and their decisions.'

'Oh aye? But away from the sharp end, then?'

In the cold pause that followed the girls were called up to the stage. Viola raised her eyebrows at Ralph, who kissed her. 'Break a leg, darling girl.'

Once the girls were on the stage the guests stopped dancing and prepared to listen as Viola strapped on her saxophone. The only movement was Amelia as she threaded her way through the crowd to Ralph. Viola grinned as he grimaced in return, then introduced the girl to his old friends. As Ralph explained that Peter was to be a solicitor in Newcastle she became totally animated, turning her back on the others.

The pitmen took the opportunity to melt away towards the drinks table, leaving Ralph marooned with his pals.

The Factory Girls launched into 'Yes Sir, That's My Baby', with the saxophone soaring as the girls stepped forwards, sideways and back. Near the window, Amelia and Peter began to dance. He was jigging about, she was giggling. He swung her round, and she almost fell. The giggling continued.

Other dancers took to the floor and Viola saw Ralph making conversation with his friends, then intercepting Sophia, who was leaving with Reginald, probably off to bed. She'd done well. Viola raised her saxophone, playing a riff as Ralph walked with them to the door. The girls were on to 'The Man I Love', but now they were disturbed by Ralph's friends' raucous laughter, which grew louder by the second. A loud guffaw put the girls off their stride.

They missed a beat, but then found the rhythm. Viola raised the saxophone as she played her solo.

They worked through 'Putting on the Ritz', and then 'Making Whoopee', playing on against the rising noise from the corner. They sang louder. The guffaws competed. Viola and Beth began to sing 'Ten Cents a Dance'. Viola heard Amelia's shrill laugh. The audience were looking around, exchanging glances, and as the laughter grew ever louder, Stan, Sid and Norm headed towards Ralph's friends, weaving carefully through the guests. And all the time, the girls kept going.

But it was the evacuees who reached the group first, with Eva and Abe pulling at Amelia's dress, making her turn.

'You're rude,' Eva shouted above the song. Silence fell. 'You all think you're so clever, so posh, but you have no manners. Your mams should skelp your arses.'

'Aye, they should an' all,' agreed Abe, now joined by Marty.

Hands on hips, Eva glared at them, one by one. The silence continued. Ralph's friends looked around as Peter blustered, 'I say, that's a bit rich from you little tykes. I thought it was a party, and supposed to be fun.'

Stan and the other two had almost reached them, but Sid held them back, pointing to Eva, who was wagging her finger at Peter. 'It's not fun with people like *you*. We don't like show-offs. You and the lady should be sent to your rooms and given no tea, because you're behaving like the smallest of bairns, and I expect you pick your nose, too, and wipe it on your sleeve.'

Peter looked down at her. 'You're a child, and should be seen and not heard.'

Abe stood his ground. 'No, it's you who should not be heard. We have famous singers here who have been on the wireless.'

'Well, I was too,' said Amelia.

'Only because you pushed your beak into the *Workers' Playtime* programme, like a playground bully,' said Marty, 'and you can't even hold a note, so there.'

Amelia flushed. 'Ridiculous child.'

Marty stepped close to Amelia. 'Don't you be rude to children. That *is* what a bully does.' He looked round at the evacuees. They nodded their agreement.

Ralph had re-entered the ballroom and reached Stan, who filled him in. He swept towards his friends. 'It's still snowing, lads. Time you were off, you've a long way to go.'

He saw the empty wine bottles on the floor behind them. 'Down in the pit we know there's a war on, which is why we hack at the coal, cut ourselves open, dig our marrers out from beneath roof falls. Here in Massingham, it's share the pain, share the food, share the effort. Looking at these bottles, it seems to me you've taken far more than your measure, and not a bloody scar on you.' His face was grim as he took Peter's glass from him. Stan took the other glasses, whilst Sid and Norm gripped elbows and herded all three out.

Amelia stepped away, watching them. 'I'll be in touch, Peter,' she called.

The girls began singing again, very quietly, 'All or Nothing at All' and Annie Hall called out to the guests, 'We've all had a bit too much to drink at one time or another, and felt badly for it. But let's forget about what's happened. This is our Viola's party to enjoy, though seems to me she's done the most to make it lovely.'

The singing became powerful, the dancing began again and Amelia turned to Ralph. 'We didn't mean anything by it, but let's face it, we've heard these girls so many times it gets a bit boring.'

Ralph knew he should be nice for the sake of his position

as Tim's eyes and ears, but it was a lost cause. 'Those riff-raff from Newcastle hadn't heard them, and besides, even if they had, that behaviour was a display of arrogance and bad manners I would not expect from any friends of mine.'

She tossed her hair, which had once been mousy, but was now almost blonde. So she had managed to find some sort of hair dye while the girls' hair was being ruined by munitions chemicals? 'You'll have Peter's address, I suppose?' she asked hopefully.

Peter reappeared in the doorway, holding up a business card. She ran to him, he kissed her hand with a flourish, then waved to Ralph, mouthing, 'Sorry, old chap. It was the others.'

Oh, Ralph thought. That was the Peter he was beginning to remember from school, always sliding out of trouble, always saying sorry, sir, it was someone else's fault, which was the last thing his pitmen marrers or anyone here would do. He looked around, finding Stan, Sid and Norm watching The Factory Girls, and then shifted his gaze to the girls themselves. He searched further and there were the ladies of the co-op, especially Annie, mingling, smiling and offering titbits from the plate she held, even though she clearly hadn't slept much since Lisa had been taken. Lastly, he turned back to Viola as she played on and on with her injured hand.

It was this wonderful girl he stared at, adoring her, and only then did he swing round, but Peter had gone. Instead, Amelia was turning away from the doorway, bracing her shoulders, plastering on a smile for the benefit of those watching. There was a certain courage in that, Ralph thought, but it was in no way enough to redeem her.

She tilted her head as she always did when she was about to flirt. He sighed, and knew it was an opportunity to say to Tim that he had talked to her, but . . . Oh glory be, Peter had reappeared yet again, beckoning to her, imitating driving. She hurried to meet him and Ralph watched them leave, relieved beyond measure.

At the end of the singing, Mrs Oborne boomed over the clapping, 'Cake for anyone who wants it. Queue to the left of the table. And you, Ben, time to do your bit on the gramophone, and William too.'

Ben pulled a face and Iris Walters called out, 'A tune or two instead, from an old bag, Ben? Might replenish your energy and be a bit of music to accompany the cake. Lots of honey in the cake. The bees will be glad they could help.'

His smile was her answer.

The girls headed for their men. Ralph helped Viola remove the saxophone, lifting it over her head. As Stan and Sarah approached, Ralph handed the saxophone to Stan. 'Come with me, Viola. Come outside while everyone is busy. Come on, just for a moment.'

She stared at him. 'Have you gone stark staring mad, Ralph? It's freezing.'

Nevertheless, he dragged her towards one of the windows and pulled the curtains for a quick peek. 'Oh, bugger.' Looking around, he saw everyone was eating, laughing, drinking and chatting to one another. 'Well,' he said, 'here is as good a place as any.'

He dropped to one knee.

'What in the world are you doing, Mr Ralph?' Eva called, heading away from the queue, towards him.

Ralph despaired because it was all going wrong, and then he saw that everyone in the room, alerted by Eva's cry, was watching, the cake forgotten. His marrers at the bar had swung round and were grinning at him with tankards in their hands, raising their eyebrows and shaking their heads. Their looks saying 'Here? Really? Of all places?'

Ralph didn't know what to do. It was like a Roman amphitheatre, and he was the lion, not the gladiator. The evacuees were closing in. The marrers galvanised themselves and Stan caught Tommy, but missed Eva. Sid shouted, 'Get on with it, or I'll give her the bliddy ring, man.'

Ralph eased his knee, trying to find the words, but then his father called from the doorway, 'Get the doctor, Ralph, and stop messing about. I think labour has begun. It wasn't an ordinary backache.'

Everyone turned towards Reginald now, and then back to Ralph, who was shaking his head. Labour? His father took another look. 'What *are* you doing down there?'

As Eva came to his side, peering down at him, Ralph shouted in desperation, 'Dunster will have to wait, just for a bloody minute, Father. Viola, I love you, I have to marry you, be with you for ever, you are perfect, and I am not, and this collar is choking me, and my old friends aren't my friends, but everyone here is, and my knee hurts, and now Mother's in labour, and I have to call the doctor. The ring is made for your middle finger, because you haven't got a ring finger. Oh God, I didn't mean to say that.'

Viola said, 'Yes, of course I will.'

But Ralph didn't hear, because Eva was asking, 'Does it mean the bairn's here?'

Abe had reached Eva and asked, 'What's he got for her middle finger?'

His father was still in the doorway, and his mother needed a doctor. Did every woman having a baby need a doctor? Or was something wrong . . . ?

'Yes, I said,' Viola shouted again, 'so go and call the doctor.'

Stan and Sid were hurrying to him, pulling him to his feet. Stan laughed. 'She said yes, man. Give the lass the ring, for pity's sake. We'll call Dunster.'

Annie had already reached the doorway and was shooing Reginald back to Sophia before turning to the room. 'No need Stan, bit of a panic's got hold of our Reginald. It's the midwife who's needed, but probably not yet. We'll go and decide what's what. You carry on.' She beckoned to the co-op. 'But not you Madge. You dance with Mr Moran. Tilly, maybe you'd better stay and guard the drinks, keep everything under control, and Bea, you're in charge of the cake, not to mention our Mr Swinton. Why not bang out a samba, Iris?'

Everyone laughed, and relaxed. Still, Annie hadn't finished. 'We are having a pantomime here on 19 December. We need you to come to say goodbye to Melanie, and I know lots of you will be sewing the costumes, but we would like helpers for scenery and suchlike. So you'll not be allowed to leave till you've decided what it is you want to do. Franny and the girls will explain what's needed.'

'We will an' all,' called Eva.

Annie looked at her. 'There wasn't one second when I thought you wouldn't, Eva. One more thing: Cyn and Simon, perhaps you would help Viola and Sandra keep an eye on the bairns who're partial to a bit of the elderberry wine. That includes our Ben and William. Co-op, upstairs, if you please.' She was gone.

Viola came into Ralph's arms. He just stared at her, not moving. 'You said yes? It really is yes? I couldn't bear it not to be because—'

She kissed him, saying, 'Oh, I said yes, because it's what I've wanted more than anything for a very long time.'

Iris was playing a waltz and Ralph held her close as they danced, and as they moved as one, their eyes were locked, and the love they each saw in the other was the same as the love they were feeling. They kissed again, then Viola pulled back, just a little. 'I don't know what to do with myself, for

I want to tell the world, and Mam and Dad, and me brother. But I will in bed tonight.'

They danced on, unaware that the guests had given them space to be alone and were trying not to watch, but couldn't stop doing so, because this was love in a difficult world. This was happiness and joy, and must be soaked up and remembered.

On and on Ralph and Viola danced, as Iris played, saying how much they loved one another. In time the guests began to drift onto the dance floor, or to the trestle table for cake, and Ralph whispered, 'Would your family approve, would they perhaps like me?'

Against his lips she murmured, 'They would love you, for you are a good man, Ralph. Good to the core.'

Chapter Nineteen

At midnight, Annie laid aside the seventh Christmas-tree robin she had knitted and stretched, easing her back as she sat beside Sophia, who was propped against pillows, resting between 'bouts', as Tilly had just called them. She'd come to check on the 'brood mare' and Sophia replied, 'Just this once I will smile, but if anyone says that again, I'll draw blood, is that clear?'

Outside the door, Bert laughed, then bellowed, 'You get yourself out of there, our Tilly, or the missus'll do us all a good turn and finish you off.'

'I reckon I should tick you off for that, Bert,' Steve Oborne said, also from the other side of the door, slurring and sounding a bit wobbly. 'But there's no way I'm going to, for she'll do a better job when she next sees you. But you take care our Sophia, there's a good lass. We're off now.'

Tilly touched Sophia's hair, which was damp with sweat. 'Aye, never fear, my lass. 'Twill be over with the dawn when they're in your arms, which is when the hard work begins. But we're here. It's that rabble outside the door who are going but wanted to say goodbye.'

'*They're*? You said *they're*?' Sophia gripped Tilly's hand in panic. 'Two? Twins? You tell my husband I'll kill him if he ever comes near me again.'

Tilly laughed. 'I meant all of ours, each and every babe.' She looked round at Annie, then Audrey and Maud. 'Don't say Eva's right?' she whispered, her eyes wide.

Annie grimaced, her eyes showing her uncertainty, but

269

her words were too quiet for Sophia to hear. 'Course not. Get the men on their way home, and no, they're not to check on the bairns to get the latest odds, for they're sleeping.' The two women smiled at one another.

Leaning over Sophia, Tilly said, 'As the day wakes, you'll be part of the gang, right and proper, sweet Sophia.'

As another pain came, Sophia held her hand tightly and Tilly just waited, her fingers whitening. All the women were counting, and then as the wave eased they checked the clock. They would call the midwife again when the pains were down to ten minutes apart. They were seventeen. Sophia opened her eyes, and looked up into Tilly's. 'Mum called me sweet Sophia too.'

Tilly eased her hand away, 'Aye, lass, that's because you are. She'd be right proud.'

There was a weak smile in return from Sophia, who muttered, 'There'll only be the one.'

'We all say that,' smiled Annie. They fell quiet, listening to the men murmuring on the landing, then Sophia looked wild-eyed as she tensed. Surely it wasn't seventeen minutes since the last one?

Audrey was watching the clock while she wiped the sweat from Sophia's forehead. 'Fourteen minutes,' she mouthed to Annie and Maud.

'It will pass,' Annie soothed as Audrey replenished the enamel bowl of water from the jug on the side table, dabbing Sophia's forehead. The women knew it could swing back to seventeen minutes, so Annie returned to her knitting as the men clumped away.

Down in the kitchen, Viola and Sandra kept water simmering as Tilly had instructed, though they still didn't know why, beyond that sterile water would be needed. Viola whispered to Sandra, 'I don't really want to know why, do you?'

Sandra's look of horror was enough. Reginald and Ralph helped the Factory Girls clear up and now Viola left the pan simmering, and told Reginald, as he arrived, carrying a tray of empty plates and glasses, that Eva had pulled her down onto the bed and asked how the betting was going.

Reginald just laughed, and said, 'I don't mind just so long as Sophia is all right, and so is our child.'

It was two in the morning before the party was cleared away. The co-op sat around the table in shifts, drinking tea until three, which was when Annie came down to snatch a drink. 'May I go and sit with her?' Reginald asked.

'Of course, but best to say nowt of sore feet and tiredness, eh. Not sure it went down well last time,' Annie suggested.

Everyone looked down at their tea, or busied themselves with something, but the sniggering couldn't be contained. Ralph looked confused. Annie scowled at them all, which made it worse.

'Lord, they're all punch-drunk,' she said. 'So, up you go when you're ready. Remember what I said last time. She'll likely be snappy, because she'll blame you. She might even be rude. When it gets messy, we'll turf you out.' She looked around the table, her hands cradling her cup. 'I reckon it were a grand party. Did you enjoy it, Viola?'

Viola waved her ring hand. 'Oh aye, best evening of me life.'

Reginald came round and kissed her cheek, looking relieved that this was something he could do that wouldn't get him into trouble. 'And one of ours, to have you accept our oaf as your husband, and us as your family. Sophia was delighted when I told her, but then she . . . Well, she was busy, so hasn't had a chance to tell you.'

He looked pale again.

Stan patted his shoulder. 'Brace up, lad, can't have you wilting on us. So up those stairs, but quietly. Don't wake the bairns, stamping about.'

Reginald looked into his cup. 'May I finish my tea first?'

Ralph's slap on his back was too hearty, and the tea slopped. Reginald looked around, blinking. 'Perhaps I'll go, promising not to stamp around, not to talk about my very, *very* sore feet, and what's more, I'll take my tea with me.'

Stan grinned, then stood up. 'Let's be getting home, lads. I could do with a bit of shut-eye. You coming, girls?'

Fran looked towards Annie, who nodded. 'Oh aye, this isn't the first time nor will it be the last we've seen the dawn in and a new babe at the same time. Just make sure our Ben's asleep in the attic room. William should be in the box room. If they're awake and smoking together, tan their behinds. Remember, there's a meeting here at three, for we have to get on with the pantomime planning.'

They straggled up the steps to the yard, with Ralph bringing up the rear. 'I'll see you off the premises, can't have riff-raff lingering about.'

When they reached their bikes, Ralph pulled at Stan's arm. 'Wait, please, all of you.' Only then did he tell them what Smythe had passed on to him, and which Ralph had whispered to the co-op already. Stan drew deeply on his cigarette, his face grim. 'I should have known. I'll bliddy kill the beggar.'

Sarah shook her head. 'No, you won't, not before he's told Smithson that he took the words of a worried mother and turned them into summat else. He'd better tell us who the damned woman is too, because she started it and needs to come clean.'

Stan dropped his cigarette stub, grinding it to dust beneath his boot and nodding. 'You're right. We need a plan.' The snow hadn't settled, though the wind was still bitter. They huddled together, thinking.

At last Ralph muttered, 'How about this? We leave Massingham at eight, cycling to catch him early, because he'll do most of his work at night and'll be laying in his pit. If he's not there, but on his 'rounds' we'll find out from Thomas Suffolk where he is.'

Alfie, having come out to look for Ralph, had listened in, and said, 'You're not going without me.'

The marrers all turned. 'Oh yes we are. You might be needed to take Sophia to hospital. Sorry, lad.'

At that, they all fell quiet. Sophia? Hospital? Lisa? The home? Suddenly they all felt exhausted. 'By,' murmured Stan, 'how do our mams do what they do, the hours they work, the worry about so many things?'

'That's why we've got to do something to sort out this mess and get our Lisa back, so that's one problem solved,' said Sid.

The girls were dragging their bikes from the garage.

Stan tipped his cap at Ralph. 'We'll be waiting at your turn-off and head to Lower Thetford. He'll not hear us getting close. Not till we knock down his door, anyway.'

'We girls might have to be backup here,' Fran said, 'for there are the bairns to look after and keep out of the way of the new babe.'

Ralph waved, then pointed to Alfie's quarters above the garage. 'Best get some sleep, just in case you're called.' He tried not to sound worried, but it didn't work.

Alfie merely shook his head and gripped Ralph's shoulder. 'That's not going to happen. You're staying up, I reckon, with Sandra and Viola, so I'll be there, too.'

Ralph sighed with relief. 'I hoped you'd say that, or I'd be stuck with two bossy women.'

The marrers, including the girls, were laughing quietly

as they cycled away, but in every one of them anxiety still lodged down deep, and not just for Lisa.

At four in the morning, Annie called Laura, the midwife, from the telephone in Reginald's dressing room. She reported: 'Labour pains moved to nine minutes, all of a rush.'

'Right you are,' Laura said, calm as always. 'Best if Alfie swoops down for me. Quicker than pedalling up the hill on me bike.'

That was all, but the message was clear: quick, quick.

Annie got rid of Reginald by sending him off in search of Alfie with the message. He tore off, Annie hurrying after him and calling from the top of the stairs, 'You stay down there. It's not your role to clutter up the place when there's real work to be done.'

She distinctly heard, 'Oh dear heavens, I'm too old for this.'

As Annie hurried back to the bedroom, Audrey met her at the door. 'I'm worried. I reckon we need Dunster an' all, for what if it is twins, as well as a rush? I just have a feeling.'

Annie made the call. Mrs Dunster said he was on his way back from an emergency at old Mr Trouter's, but the minute he came in, he'd set off again.

As dawn was hinting it would break, a perfect little girl was placed in Sophia's arms, and all tiredness was forgotten. 'She's a tiddler,' declared Laura, after weighing her on portable scales. 'Just six pounds.'

Reginald stared in awe as he stood by his wife. He reached forward, touching her cleaned-up hair. 'I'd forgotten how small they are. Just to think, Ralph was . . .' he hesitated, turning to his son standing in the bedroom doorway '. . . about this size.'

Dunster shook his head. 'No, he wasn't – a ten-pounder, he was – but the next one might be similar.'

Sophia shook her head just as Reginald smiled at her. They both said, 'There won't be a next one.'

Dunster raised his eyebrows. 'Actually, dear old things, there will be, and very soon. There is another heartbeat.' While Reginald blanched, and Sophia gaped, the doctor saw Ralph checking his watch. 'Holding you up, are we, Ralph?'

'Oh sorry, miles away and a bit shocked. Can't quite juggle my thoughts. Two? Wonderful. I can't quite . . . I want to stay, but I must meet the others at eight, and it's seven thirty. I'll tell them that a sister has arrived for wonderful me. Don't worry, we'll be back for the panto meeting at three. Oh Lord, I don't want to leave until number two is here, but I simply must.' He looked at Annie, who knew where he was going and nodded her thanks, but added, 'Phone in to find out all is well. Oh, and everyone, Melanie has won her bet, of course.'

Annie flapped him away, he nodded, and disappeared. Dunster had a word with Laura, both checking their watches, then he examined Sophia. Finally, looking up at the new parents, Dunster said, 'It's almost upon us. Little rascal was hiding behind the other. I should have put money on with Melanie, but we had no idea, had we, Laura? I'm afraid young Eva is going to clean up on this after making side bets with Tommy and others.'

Audrey Smith swooped down and snatched the baby from Sophia's arms as pain gripped once more. Annie thought Reginald was going to faint. She dragged him from the room and into the corridor, where she was amazed to see the bairns were all sitting cross-legged. They leapt up. 'Can we see her, please, please?' Melanie asked.

Annie shook her head. 'Sit. Not yet. Mr Reginald has

come over queer.' Viola came out of Eva's bedroom, took one look at Reginald and helped to lead him to the spare room while Annie whispered the news.

'Oh no,' whispered Viola. 'I've lost me bet.'

Reginald was looking from one to the other. 'I've lost a bob.'

'Never you mind, Father-in-law,' soothed Viola. 'All will be well.' Though her voice was calm, her eyes asked a question. But Annie didn't know any more than that Dunster seemed perky enough.

Half an hour later, Sophia, still too shocked to speak, was holding both babies: two girls, identical. Reginald, however, was holding a goblet of brandy, sipping it, when Sophia, finding a thready voice, asked Maud to hold one of her babies, leaving her a free hand to snatch the goblet out of Reginald's hand and take a gulp. She looked round at them all. 'Oh, shut up. It's good for shock.'

Dr Dunster stepped out into the corridor to see Viola and Sandra busy shooing the children into Eva and Melanie's room. He stepped back in. 'One of you, please, to the drawing room, where there are goblets for us all, but what use are they without the decanter?'

Maud slipped away as Sophia said, 'So, will you four co-op members be godmothers? Please. Two for each of our girls. Maud, Audrey, Madge and Annie. With Tilly everyone's auntie. You take your pick.'

Reginald rubbed his hands together. 'Oh, that's a wonderful idea, and please thank the girls for their lemon cardigans. They certainly have their mothers' talents.'

Annie smiled. 'Do please tell them that, if you will, Reginald, but we have to be there when you do.' The three women laughed, and poor Reginald simply looked even more confused, especially when Maud brought him the baby she had been holding.

'Open your arms, lad.' His panic was writ large as she placed one of his daughters in his arms. 'Be a man, Reginald,' she whispered, 'for they'll run you ragged, but today they'll adore you. You need yet another nanny, you know.'

As he enjoyed the brandy that Maud had brought up, Dr Dunster asked, 'But what will you call them?'

Chapter Twenty

Beth puffed up the hill alongside Sid. 'I feel scared, you know,' she panted. 'He's a rough, cruel man, what if his sidekicks are there? What if they hurt any of us? What if he sees me and yells that he sold me black-market drink when Bob left? What if the police—'

Sid sighed. 'Oh, don't be daft, bonny lass. Ralph and I have seen him and his gorillas off once. Stan's had a go too. And remember, you had the strength to stop the drink before it really got a hold. He'll not be hurting anyone today. The seven of us are more'n a match for him and his goons.'

In front of them, Fran turned round. 'I can't get over two bairns. *Two wee girls*? Thank the Lord, Ralph telephoned from that call box we passed. I don't think I'll ever forget his face, thrilled to bits with it all, but dazed. But I bet it weren't a patch on Reginald's.'

Ralph was leading with Stan and as they approached the hill to Sledgeford, he shouted back, standing on the pedals, as they all were, 'I still can't believe it. Both six pounds, so no wonder poor Sophia was huge. Poor, poor woman. She must be exhausted. She'll need more help. I mean, that's thirteen bairns, for goodness' sake. It's more like a home for the disorderly. I wonder who made the most money? I lost mine.'

Fran's and Beth's jaws dropped open. 'You didn't have a bet?'

'Eva thought I should.'

'Oh well, if Eva thought . . .'

They tore through Sledgeford, heads down as the biting wind was getting up. Beth hoped there wouldn't be another bout of snow for it might lie, but her mind was only fiddling about with trivialities. The babies had made her long for the divorce so that she and Sid could have their own family. If she didn't send through the allotment every month to the address in Grimsby, would he get on with the divorce? she wondered. Should she threaten to withhold it?

As though reading her mind, Sid asked, 'No news from Bob?'

'You know the answer.'

As they passed St James's Church on the outskirts of Sledgeford, flakes of snow began to fall, but only a few.

Norm, riding beside Fran, yelled, 'Oh, snow's the icing on the cake, eh? Imagine slogging home through that.'

Sarah replied, 'It'll pass. Look at the sky. There's not a lot up there.'

They all felt as tired as Ralph looked, because sleep had eluded them; their minds had been too full of Sophia's labour, and Lisa, and how to get the truth out of Norris, should they find him.

They cycled on in silence, but Sarah dropped back to be with Fran and Beth while the men pedalled harder to catch up with Ralph and Stan, their hands cold despite the gloves.

Fran's muffler was tightening around her neck as the wind caught the ends, and the snow was making it moist. She hated that, but hated Norris more. It was true her mam had said she felt guilty, but how had the woman who made such a lying complaint come together with Norris? How the hell had he known to go to Smithson? Who hated their family so much? None of it made sense, and at the heart of it was a bairn.

'Stop it, Fran,' insisted Sarah. 'I know you're mithering and it does no good. Just concentrate on getting something out of Norris. He's just got to be there. Come on, the lads are getting ahead of us.'

From Sledgeford they headed west until they reached the outskirts of Lower Thetford, heading for the main street. To the left they could see the local pithead and smell the sulphur, but when couldn't they? The slag heap was smouldering in the wind. 'Straight ahead, then a few of us will take the back lane, the others down the front street.' Stan pointed ahead to where the front of Morton Terrace lay. 'Fran, Beth, Norm and Sid, you knock at the front. Sarah, you come with Ralph and me. I know none of you girls will sit on the sidelines.'

Nods were his answer.

'We'll head on, leave the bikes against that far wall. Sarah and Ralph, we'll find the yard of number nine and stop the beggar if he makes a break for it.'

Ralph was looking at his watch. 'We'll be in place in . . . what? . . . two minutes from now.'

Sid checked the watch he had inherited from his grandda. 'Come on, then.'

They dismounted, leaving their bikes at the end of the terrace. Fran and Norm agreed to hold hands, ready to walk along the terrace as though they were out for a Sunday stroll, Sid and Beth lined up behind them, then they were off.

The others made their way almost silently down the back lane, where the black lorry was parked, half blocking the lane. Ralph tried the sneck to the yard. It was locked. 'He must be here.' He scanned the wall. 'Too noisy to scale it. We'll have to wait. What do you reckon, Stan?'

Stan nodded, looking both ways. 'Aye, he's probably got his booze stacked in a shed in there, he wouldn't leave it in the truck – and that gives me an idea. If he comes through the gate, we'll grab him and take him back into the yard. Threaten his booze, which might save bruised knuckles.'

His face was as grim as his voice.

Fran and Norm stopped just before the Suffolks' front door with twenty seconds to go. Norm stooped to fiddle with his laces.

'I've counted twenty in me head,' muttered Beth.

Norm twisted his wrist, checking his watch. 'Get knocking, Fran.'

She did. They waited. In the front room, a curtain lifted, then dropped. At last the door opened. An old man stood there, wearing just a vest and pyjama bottoms, a roll-up hanging from the corner of his mouth. Inexplicably, he wore a cap, but his white hair bunched out from beneath it. 'Aye, what yer after?'

Before Fran could speak, Norm said, 'Is Norris Suffolk here? We're after some booze.'

The old man shook his head, hoisting up his pyjamas. 'No, don't know the name.'

Sid called over Norm's shoulder, 'Oh, I reckon you do.' They heard the slam of the back door. 'Best let us through, Mr Thomas Suffolk.'

At the mention of his full name, the man paled and stepped aside. The four of them entered. Beth waved him in front of her. He stank of stale booze.

They urged him into the kitchen, where cardboard boxes were stacked against the wall, 'Beer', 'Tea', 'Sugar' written on them in a scrawled hand. The back door was open and they could see that Ralph and Stan were in the yard, pinioning Norris's arms behind him while Sarah shut the gate, drawing across the bolt.

Beth looked from them to Thomas Suffolk. 'Men are

dying in merchant ships for your slimy, disgusting trade. Shame on you.'

'Sit down,' ordered Sid.

Instead, Suffolk flicked his cigarette at Beth. She dodged it, stepped on it, grinding it to dust on the torn linoleum. Sid shoved him down onto the chair.

'Mind me shoulders, it's me rheumatics,' Thomas whined.

'My heart's breaking, man,' Sid muttered, looking with distaste at the table, which was cluttered with unwashed plates and cups. The range was burning brightly, a kettle was simmering. Noises were coming from the yard, and then Norris stumbled into the kitchen, his arm held up behind his back by Ralph, who forced him into the chair at the head of the table.

Norris wore a vest too, and his eyes were bleary.

Fran stepped forward. 'You know why we're here. You somehow joined forces with a woman to get a small bairn taken from us. You lied to the authorities and now Lisa sleeps in a cot, one of many, in an orphanage. A bairn who has already lost her mam, a bairn who was given sanctuary with us, the Halls. The Halls, whose mother has already lost a bairn through death. You and this woman are completely responsible for taking this child from a safe home.'

Norris merely shrugged. 'Business is business, pet.'

Thomas Suffolk swung round and looked at his son. 'You bliddy fool. So, that's where the money came from? A bairn? We don't deal in bairns. And now look, we've no bliddy business left, for you'll go down for this.'

Fran turned to look at the elderly man. 'So, it's only because it's ruined the business, is it? Not that he could have destroyed a child's life?'

Thomas merely shook his head, not looking at her. He murmured, 'We don't hurt bairns. I want no part of that.'

'Oh, shut it, Da.'

Fran dug her hands into her mac pockets because it was the only way she'd not grab Norris by the ears and shake him until his single brain cell rattled.

She turned to the boys. 'He's all yours. Do as you must, until you find out the whole truth.'

At that, the old man half rose, then sat back down as Sid grabbed him again. Fran waited as Ralph, Norm and Stan removed their jackets. While Stan rolled up his sleeves as the others were doing, he said, 'Keep the old man sitting, Sid.'

Norris was looking at the muscled, blue-scarred forearms, then at the faces, and could not have seen anything other than merciless rage.

'Tell him, son,' his father said, 'use your nous, do a deal.'

The girls moved nearer to the range, and waited. Ralph nodded. 'Oh yes, a deal. Well, what do you think might make us roll down our sleeves?'

Norris started to shrug, then thought better of it as the three marrers took a step closer to the table. 'Information, and then you shower of idiots scarper,' he grunted.

Ralph couldn't believe it was to be so easy, and clearly neither could Stan, for he bunched his fists, ready to spring. Ralph held him back. Sid pressed down on the old man's shoulders, as he had tensed. Was he about to leap to his feet?

'Depends on what you tell us,' said Stan, 'then we will consider our options. It's that or we take those bottles, throw them against the yard wall, then work our way through the house doing the same with all the other stuff.'

'Don't forget the shed. Bet there's a load in there too,' Sid muttered.

Ralph grinned. 'Of course, well said, Sid. You remember our friend Suffolk, don't you, from the smacking we gave him outside the Miners' Club at the wedding tea?'

'Oh aye, and that were when the gorillas were there an' all. And today they're not. You bolted the back gate shut again, Sarah?'

'Oh yes, tight as a bug in a rug we are, for as long as we need.'

Mr Suffolk roared, 'Tell them, Norris, get on with it. I'm too old for this, you stupid beggar.' But instead of waiting for his son to begin, Thomas Suffolk galloped on. 'This bloke rang through to the bar at the Pig and Whistle, knew Norris'd been under the bonnet in Main Street when Mrs Hall and you girls had gone past with the bairn – must have eyes everywhere. He told him to report to this bloke called Smithson, even gave him the number an' all.'

'Report what?' Fran shouted.

'That he'd heard Mrs Hall telling you all that she'd done to hurt the bairn deliberately, for this bloke knew you'd gone to the doctor. But it weren't wrong, because Norris did hear her say she felt guilty. So Norris did nowt wrong, not really.'

Stan's voice was worryingly quiet. 'Oh, but he did. He lied and said he knew it had happened before. So why did Norris do what this bloke said, and what's more, make it worse than it was? Did he know him or something?'

'Tell him, Norris.'

Norris eyed his father, his brows drawn together in rage. 'You daft brick. You don't know what you've done. You told him without getting the deal on the table.'

Mr Suffolk merely shrugged. 'I told you, I want no part in a bairn. He did it because this bloke said someone would give him money if he got himself to Sledgeford, but I reckon our Norris had worked for him before, but doing what I don't know. But I tell you what, my daft son spoke as though it weren't the fir—'

'Shut the hell up, Da,' Norris roared.

Thomas shrugged again. 'A woman would leave the

money behind the milestone near the telephone box, the bloke said.' Now it was Mr Suffolk's turn to glower at Norris.

'How much money?' asked Ralph.

'Twenty quid,' muttered Norris, shifting in his chair.

His father kept his glower in place, though it deepened. 'You devious beggar. You said it were fifteen.'

Fran moved nearer. 'The name of the woman?'

'I don't know, why would I?' Norris muttered. 'I don't ask questions, I just do as I'm told—' He stopped, realising what he'd said.

Beth asked, 'So, your da is right, it's not the first time, then? Did this bloke give you a time to pick up the money?'

'Course he did. You wouldn't just leave money for anyone to find.'

Sid took over. 'I bet you got there early so you could see her come, see her go, find out where she came from? That would give you something over her, or that's what I reckon. So tell us more about what you actually did, and who planted the money?'

Norris was beginning to look really scared. 'All right. Aye, I got there early. I parked up along the street a bit, let her drop the money, then followed, at a distance, in the truck. She turned off down Pond Close. I kept me eye on her, saw her going into a house with a privet hedge, then I kept going, came back around, picked up the money.'

'So what did she look like?'

'Sort of blonde hair, high heels. She waved to someone on the way back. I had me window open. She were posh, from down south.'

Ralph sat down. 'So, she waved to someone, called to them? They called back?'

As they watched Norris they could almost see and hear the cogs struggling to turn behind his blank dark eyes.

Thomas Suffolk leaned forward. 'Tell 'em.'

'Be quiet,' hissed Sid.

Norm moved closer to Norris, just as Ralph closed in too. Norris looked up at Ralph, and then Stan. 'All right. Like I said, she were posh, and were called summat like Ann, but . . . No, not quite Ann, a fussy name, it were. Emma? No, Amelia. Aye, that's right, Amelia.'

Ralph expelled a breath, nodding. Stan said, quietly, 'Who's a good boy then? Now, the Pig and Whistle is in this village – that's right, isn't it? Pond Close is in Sledgeford, though?'

Norris nodded.

Stan asked, his voice cold as ice. 'Anything else you want to tell us, like who this "bloke" on the phone is?'

Norris paled, shaking his head. 'Never heard from him before. My da's daft. Don't listen to him.'

Sid gripped tighter. 'What about you, Mr Suffolk?'

Thomas Suffolk opened his mouth. His son shook his head. 'Da, don't.'

Ralph shook his head at Sid, knowing that there was no need, for Smythe had plenty to go on, and if there was more, which there clearly was, he would find it. For now, they had all they needed as regards Lisa: it was that little cow Amelia, and if the caller was Tim, then they had a connection.

'Right, we've all we need to get Lisa back but now I've a phone call of my own to make,' Ralph said. 'We passed a call box on the way in. Guard our unsavoury pair while I'm gone.'

Norris swung round, his arm crooked over the back of his chair as Ralph hurried to the front door. 'Who's he phoning? Not the bliddy cops? I mean, we had a deal.'

It was Stan who said, 'You should know that deals go wrong, people lie, bad people get put away, and not just for black-marketeering, but for helping to change the life of a bairn. You see, someone who does that deserves no better. But maybe you'll not get as long if you tell the police even more, with names. Maybe.'

Stan enjoyed the panic on both men's faces.

Ralph ran, his legs and arms pumping, feeling for change in his pocket. He prayed there was no one in the box. There wasn't. He then prayed that either Smythe or Yeland was in the office. Yeland was, and Ralph could hear Smythe in the background. Ralph, panting, blurted out all that the Suffolks had told them.

'Ah, at last,' muttered Yeland, 'we have a bird in the hand, ready to be plucked. What do you need right away?'

'What we need is to get Lisa back. But Amelia? How could she? Is she really one of Tim's? Is Norris?'

Ralph could hear Smythe say, 'Let me.' It was he who answered, 'We'll recheck every tiny little thing we know about her and Norris. Even if she's not involved, Tim might well have kept a weather eye on her, after Oxford. We're pretty sure someone tipped her the wink about vacancies at the factory, and to see her so recently reinstated ... Oh, Tim lad, so much vindictive obsession is so very foolish when you are in your game. As for Norris and Tim, further information indicates there is a link.'

Yeland spoke in the background. Smythe said, 'Yes, you've a point, Yeland.' He sounded as though he was thinking aloud.

Ralph dived into the pause. 'I'm sorry, Professor, but what we need from you is for Smithson to be told *and* to be presented with Amelia's and Norris's statements.' He drew in a breath; his tiredness was making him feel sick. 'We need the bairn back,' he shouted, hearing his voice cracking. 'That family have been through enough. God almighty, it could have been our evacuees taken.' He paused. 'And I need to know what to do with Norris, and his father, now, this minute.'

There was silence. Then Smythe said, 'Sophia? Any news?'

'Oh, twins. I have sisters, identical.'

'How wonderful, and Sophia?'

Ralph nodded, then realised the man couldn't see, so almost yelled, 'Quite safe, but we need this sorted.'

'Of course, dear boy. We need the police to attend number nine immediately so they can arrest the Suffolks for black-marketeering, then we can take over the questioning once they have a statement on that and Norris's part in Lisa's shambles, including names. I will arrange that immediately. So, all you have to do is babysit the unsavoury pair for twenty minutes or so until the police arrive. Once things are sorted on the Lisa front, I will contact Smithson. This should not alert Tim. It is a straightforward arrest for black-marketeering, on the basis of information received. No mention of anything else.'

Again, Yeland was talking in the background. Smythe said, 'Just a minute, Yeland.' He fell silent again, but not for long. 'Yes, all right. It won't do any harm to pick her up, get her statement, purely on the basis of Norris Suffolk's evidence. Worry not, Ralph, pop back, dear boy, and inform everyone that the police are on their way. Later, on the ride back, you can of course mention that Lisa will be home by the end of Monday I would imagine. If not, then Tuesday.'

Ralph leaned heavily against the side of the booth. Lisa was coming home. What was more, it was the beginning of the end of the Fascist cell.

'Ralph,' warned Smythe, 'you *must* understand we have to leave Tim in play – we haven't located the cell's top man.

I suspect we'll find he resides in Head Office, but who knows what Norris will tell us—' Ralph could hear more voices in the background. Smythe went on, 'So, well done, all of you. Trust us.'

Then he was gone. Ralph ran back to the house.

Chapter Twenty-One

On Monday morning the girls were yet again on the fore shift, and as they travelled past St Oswald's, Fran glanced out at the moonlit countryside. The sky was clear and the stars seemed to glow, which was more than she was after yesterday's ride out to the Suffolks' and then the panto-mime meeting in the ballroom, but at least Lisa would be home probably today? It was a question, because until she was, no one even dared to think of her. Instead, Fran came back to the present and wriggled. 'By, these slats seem to get harder every week.'

'Grand party for Viola's birthday. How are the new bairns? Such a surprise, a lovely one.' Maisie's voice was still heavy with sleep.

'Aye,' Mrs Oborne yawned. 'And I reckon those bigger bairns are looking right pleased with themselves. Turns out more people than we thought were in on the betting, and the little 'uns have shared the profits. Sometimes I wonder quite what the Massinghams have created – seems to be like a Fagin's kitchen that'll go on to keep 'em in their old age. Either that, or the rascals'll end up in clink. Who got the biggest pot of gold?'

'Seems like it were Alfie, when we thought it would be Eva. He's quiet but deadly,' said Sarah.

The women summoned the energy to laugh.

'I don't know about this daft cow's head?' called Bert. 'I mean, how heavy is papier mâché? I don't want a heavy lump around me head, and don't forget I've got to breathe. You listening, our Tilly?'

They were heading over a drovers' bridge, and they always taxed Bert's patience, and the usual performance began as they neared it. 'Don't you bliddy take me mirrors, you hear me? You bliddy behave yourselves.'

The passengers sniggered, as always. Fran said, 'I suppose we could have Bernie the Beck Monster snatching mirrors too?'

Beth and Sarah groaned. 'No, then we'd have to build a bridge,' said Sarah. 'Don't even think it, let alone suggest it. It would do Old Ted's head a mischief, and the lads' as they sort the set and props. But as Stan said, at least he and the marrers are the trees who have to stop Ralph escaping, so they don't have words to learn, just have to make noises and do a bit of arm waving.'

Ten minutes later they approached Sledgeford and the engine laboured up the hill, Bert eventually changing down through the gears. He hated to do it, and hardly ever went into first because then there wasn't another gear left. As they reached the top of the incline, the bus seemed to sigh with relief as it coasted down through the village, stopping at the bus shelter. The girls clambered on, Valerie in the lead.

She headed for the back and sat with Maisie. ' 'Ow do?' Fran called, but then fell silent. For Sledgeford was where Amelia lodged. What had happened? Had Amelia been taken in for questioning by the police?

'How could she do such a bliddy thing?' she whispered, though it was more like a venomous hiss.

'Because she's Amelia,' Sarah whispered back, careful not to be overheard, because they'd decided to keep it all quiet, just in case Lisa didn't . . . But no.

Fran yawned again, exhausted, because she hadn't slept much last night. Neither had the others. How could they, with so many loose ends? She stared out of the window, wanting Davey back, wanting Lisa home, and wanting her mam to relax and be happy.

They had both risen at two o'clock that morning, unable to sleep because it was Monday, and Lisa might be back. They had made tea with fresh leaves. Fran had taken her da's chair, her mam the other, then the door had opened and in had come Ben, his hair tousled. He'd poured himself a cup, and sat on the arm of Fran's chair. All three of them had stared at the fire until Ben said, 'I wish you'd taken me, I'd have told that Norris a thing or two.'

'Oh, I know, but you had homework, and then the panto-mime meeting,' Fran said. 'I just wish Davey could see how the bairns looked as they almost ate their scripts, then lived and breathed the story as they rehearsed.'

'But will Lisa really come home?'

They couldn't answer, but he knew that. Annie Hall said softly, 'It's part of growing up, knowing much, but the more you know, the more loose ends there are and the more patience we need. Being a wee bairn is easier, as you don't know things.'

Ben had looked at her. He said, 'I remember thinking when I was about five and didn't want to go to school, how I wanted to be back in your tummy. I reckon I feel a bit like that now. I want to be a bairn again. But then look at Lisa, Eva, Melanie. Things can happen even when you're a bairn. At least adults can try and change things, but bairns are helpless. It's a strange world.'

They all sat quietly, and time passed until Fran had to prepare for work and Annie said she'd sort her bait. Ben had just looked at Fran. 'You be safe,' he'd said.

She grinned. 'I always do my best.'

Before she left for the bus, Ben said to their mam, 'I reckon that's it, isn't it, Mam? We just do our best, and keep on breathing.'

Fran had laughed. 'Oh Ben, and we laugh – don't forget that.'

Bert drew into the Factory car park. They clambered off the bus. Barry Evans checked Fran, Beth and Sarah's bags, and their passes. 'Still no news of how Lisa is getting on?' he asked, shivering in the cold.

'Oh, we hope she's all right,' Fran said, which was the answer the three of them had arrived at, because, of course, it was completely true, and because they didn't dare believe the police would get anywhere with that slippery customer Norris, let alone with Amelia, knowing from the boys that she had been the woman involved.

Today they were assigned to the detonator workshop. 'Good,' whispered Beth as they walked along. 'Something to concentrate on.'

Cyn Ellington came along behind them, slipping her good arm through Sarah's. 'Just to say, our wedding is being moved forwards. We decided we couldn't reduce the spotlight that should be shining on the pantomime. I will tell you the date when it's sorted. The wedding tea is in the Canary Club allotment shed.'

The girls roared with laughter. 'Small and cosy then,' muttered Beth.

'Oh aye, with only the club members, and there'll be good behaviour, if you please.' Cyn's frown was as false as her tone. 'Can't have you running amuck amongst the leeks.'

Once in, they headed to the workbenches as the night shift rose, groaning and stretching, their turbans looking tired. The fore shift took their places at the Perspex screens and within minutes Mr Swinton came to stand behind them. 'Any news?' he whispered.

Fran spun round. 'We are always hopeful.'

He smiled, his eyes soft, and put his finger to his lips. 'Indeed.'

They worked on, and eventually the clock showed the meal break would soon be with them, and everything had been as usual, but they wanted something that wasn't. What if nothing changed? that if the police believed Norris's denials, for he wouldn't confess easily? What if Lisa stayed sleeping and weeping in a row of cots?

Mr Swinton walked along behind their workbench. 'Meal break, off you go,' he murmured to each of the women in turn.

As they walked along the corridor, Beth patted the posters three times for luck. Tonight, as most nights, the girls would itch. Their mams would smooth on sphagnum-moss mixture for open scratch marks, lavender grease for closed.

They washed, then dawdled into the canteen, queuing for their meal of something indescribable but warm. Cyn Ellington entered and hurried across to them as they stood with their plates. 'Amelia has been escorted from the premises by men in suits,' she whispered. 'I watched from the door, then Mr Swinton escorted me to the main pathway. We saw the police waiting in their cars. The barrier was raised by Barry Evans. They waved Amelia and the men in suits through, but Amelia stopped and wailed, "I didn't mean anything by it, I'm tired, I get confused."

'One of the men then said something. Amelia backed away, horror on her face. They took her by the arms, one on either side of her. She was made to walk towards a black car and they eased her into the rear seat. One of the men climbed in next to her. The other went round and took his place on her other side.' Cyn hardly paused for breath. 'A police car led the black one away and another police car followed. The bar was lowered again. Then Barry Evans dusted his hands, and Mr Swinton and I came back. We'll find out what is going on and report. But for now we wait.'

'We seem to do that a lot lately,' Fran said quietly.

Cyn squeezed her arm. 'Mr Swinton has been called to see Mr Bolton. Now eat your meal, though it will be cold, and say nowt about owt, eh? You will probably be called to the manager's office very soon. But remember to concentrate on those detonator caps. There's been more than enough drama for one day.'

The call to Mr Bolton's office came at one fifteen. It was for all three girls and Mr Swinton escorted them from the workshop.

Again, Beth tapped the posters. Again, Fran watched. The whole matter was surreal. There was a band around her chest that grew tighter as they followed Mr Swinton in his green overalls. 'I can hardly breathe,' gasped Sarah. As they reached Mr Bolton's office, Sarah and Beth gripped Fran's hands.

Mr Swinton turned, smiling. 'It'll be all right, lasses, for you at least, and the bairn. Bear up now, almost at the end of this dreadful journey.'

He opened the door. Cyn was sitting opposite Mr Bolton, who rose from his chair and waved at the chairs in front of his desk. 'Well now,' he smiled. They sat. Fran was glad to feel the hardness of the chair. It was something solid.

'Well now,' Mr Bolton repeated. 'I have to report that Miss Amelia Cartwright has left us today. She became unwell, the result of a high temperature which caused a sort of hysteria, which appears to have been something that first appeared some days ago, and caused her to say things that were inaccurate. The infection and temperature reoccurred just this morning. For her own safety she has been taken to a hospital where she can be cared for. Never fear, we were able to remove her before any infection could spread.'

Fran ran the words through her mind. Mr Bolton was looking embarrassed. Mr Swinton stared at the ceiling. So, had Amelia been arrested, or was she just ill? She closed and opened her eyes. Inaccurate statements, eh? She and the girls knew all about that. Did this mean Lisa was coming home? Would Bolton know? But why would he, he just thought she was ill? Or did he? The other two girls were leaning towards him as though they were going to pounce. Well, she *had* to ask or burst.

'I don't want to know about that girl's health,' Fran almost shouted. 'I want to know if Lisa is coming back.'

Mr Bolton stiffened.

'So Amelia'll be back here soon, if it's an infection. But what is it?' snapped Sarah.

Mr Bolton stared at Mr Swinton, panic writ large. Mr Swinton cleared his throat. 'As to returning, it depends, lass, on whether she makes a full recovery, or so Mr Bolton were told. We were also told that you should let your friends know about her . . . Well, let's call it a bout of influenza, occurring today, no need to go into details about anything else. Or perhaps add the high temperature if you must. So there you are. And tell those in Massingham the same if asked, of course. There is no harm in that.'

'Harm?' Fran queried. 'She should be locked—'

'To answer your question regarding Lisa,' Mr Bolton interrupted. 'It has been established that undoubtedly Lisa is to be returned – today in all likelihood so let's leave Amelia well and truly out of this, as the police have decreed. Morale is important.' He sat back, flushed and uncomfortable.

Fran felt limp with relief. One particular word broke

through her whirling thoughts. *Undoubtedly*. She ran it through again, hardly daring to believe it: u-n-d-o-u-b-t-e-d-l-y. Thank you, thank you, policemen, she wanted to shout out loud, not caring if they had to leave that ruddy girl out of it, even though she had caused it all, out of spite, and not because she was unwell.

'That's the best news ever,' whispered Sarah. 'Aye, it is.'

'Just the best. One back, one gone,' Beth added.

There was a long silence, during which many questions whirled around their minds, though they knew there would not be any answers. And what about Norris? He wasn't poorly. No one spoke, except Fran, who from time to time whispered, 'The bairn is coming home.'

Then, 'Thank you, thank you.'

Then, 'Mam's heart will mend now.'

Finally, Mr Swinton and Cyn coughed and looked at Mr Bolton, who nodded. 'Well, that's it, girls. So if you would spread the word that Amelia will not be back, possibly until after Christmas, if ever, that would save me a job. I wouldn't normally broadcast sick leave, but Amelia was a particularly noticeable employee, and in the void of her absence, questions will be posed. So let's cut them off at the pass, shall we.' It wasn't a question.

There was another moment of quiet. 'The main thing,' Mr Swinton finally said, 'is that Lisa will be on her way home any minute now. Nothing else matters.'

'No it doesn't,' muttered Fran.

'Oh yes it does,' burst out Beth, laughing.

'Oh, but it doesn't, and he's behind you,' Cyn said, and the three girls began laughing, but it was really with relief and joy, as Cyn explained to Mr Bolton that once she and Simon said those lines, Reginald Massingham would receive a custard pie in his face. Mr Bolton looked confused, but Mr Swinton waved the girls away.

'Off you go, lasses, the detonators await.' He turned back to Mr Bolton. 'There's to be a pantomime at Massingham Hall,' he said. 'Aye, we might even find you a ticket, if you'd like.'

As Fran was about to close the door, Mr Bolton said, 'I rather think my son would enjoy that. Three tickets would be most welcome. Let me know how much.'

Fran smiled, closed the door gently, then stared at Bolton's nameplate, trying to absorb what had happened and make it rock solid in her head. Lisa, Amelia, her false accusation, Norris. What did it all mean? The other two were looking at her, and Sarah whispered, 'I reckon there's much more to all this, but we'll never know because it would raise so many questions about the Factory, wouldn't it? It's a secret place, so of course that's the line – say nothing. I can see the sense of that. Tell you one thing, though, I don't reckon she'll *ever* be back.'

'Yes, so we say Lisa is coming home, Amelia is off sick, and that's that, all right?' Fran looked at Beth and Sarah.

'Lisa's coming home, so what else matters?' said Beth.

Cyn escorted them to the detonator workshop. Fran whispered the news of Lisa's return to Mrs Oborne, and then told her about Amelia's illness.

Mrs Oborne sighed with relief. Behind them, Cyn touched Mrs Oborne's shoulder. 'Be careful, the shift is not quite over yet. Think of Lisa afterwards.'

At last they were on the bus. Bert muttered as Beth passed, 'A good day, I hear.'

Beth grinned.

'Ah,' said Bert, his smile gentle. 'Well, I'm right pleased. But while I think of it, since there'll be the twins in the kitchen at Massingham Hall now, not to mention Lisa too when Annie is at the Hall, Sophia will need another pair of hands. Me niece were a nanny. She came home to look after her mam who's gone on now. Reckon I'll give our Ralph a call. What do you think?'

'And the man only thinks about it now?' Tilly boomed from the steps. 'Honestly, you could wring the beggar out, he's so wet.'

Bert laughed. 'No, it's Ralph that'll be wet – he's the monster, isn't he?'

There were groans throughout the bus. 'That is so bad, Bert.'

The girls continued to their seats, and suddenly it was all over. Lisa was on her way home. Amelia was gone. For now. The whole busload sang as they pulled away, and kept going until they arrived at Massingham. Then Fran laughed. She needed to sleep, but of course she wouldn't and neither would anyone else at 14 Leadenhall Terrace, for the bairn would need settling all over again.

In his office, Mr Bolton sat musing over the telephone call. First, he had been reminded of the Official Secrets Act by a Mr Yeland of MI5, then he had been told that certain personnel would be appearing on the dot of 11.20. He was to call Miss Amelia Cartwright into his office at eleven and dictate some letters to her. Yeland's own men would collect Miss Cartwright from his office at the aforementioned time. Once she was removed, Mr Andrews in administration was to be informed that she had, quite suddenly, descended into a serious hysterical state as her temperature had soared and medical personnel had escorted her from the premises. Bolton was forbidden to contact Head Office with this news, but if asked by them, or anyone, he was to say she was on sick leave, with influenza. He was to encourage the three girls to spread that news, and he also had permission to inform Fran that Lisa was to be returned.

Though, Yeland had said that any connection between the two events was purely coincidental. Bolton did not believe in coincidence, though this he did not say.

He had been scribbling it all down, out of habit. 'Got that?' barked the man's voice. He'd confirmed that he had. 'If you've been making notes, burn them.' Yeland had hung up. Bolton had burned them over the office waste-paper bin.

'What the hell?' pondered Bolton out loud, but knew he would never know any more, though what gave him pause for thought was that he could say nothing to Head Office.

As the bus arrived in Massingham, Fran decided that Ben and she would take shifts that night, and she couldn't stop smiling because Lisa would be back and she couldn't wait to tell Davey when he phoned tonight.

There was no one to meet them off the bus, but they knew there wouldn't be, for the lads were up at the Hall, starting to build up a bank for the beck, while Alfie and Old Ted put together the table for the silly custard-pie scene set in a kitchen. Beth grinned at the thought, and hoped that the co-op could come up with a good idea for making the pie.

They walked through the village, arm in arm, Fran trying not to hurry, but failing. As their pace quickened, Beth said, 'The backcloth for the custard-pie scene could be a picture of a range and a wash . . . No, that won't work, for the wash tub needs to be on the table.'

Sarah started laughing. 'What on earth did we think about before this really got going?'

'We thought about whether Daisy was coming back, and then if Lisa was going to be coming home,' Fran almost shouted, 'and she probably is already.' They ran, all three of them, until the breath caught in their throats, their boots clattered on the cobbles and the running made their skin itch more and more, but it didn't matter. Now, at last, they were at the back gate.

Sarah and Beth disengaged. 'You go in alone – it's your family's happiness,' said Beth.

Fran grabbed their hands. 'But I am you, and you are me, both of you. Come on.'

She opened the gate, quietly, closing it behind them just as quietly because there was Annie Hall, crooning to Lisa as together they watched the hens. Lisa reached for the chicken wire, grabbing at it with her chubby little fingers and trying to shake it while the hens clucked and fluffed. Fran's da had done this with Ben, and had told her he'd done it with her too. She looked skywards and smiled, murmuring, 'There, Da, she's home. We'll keep her safe from now on. There'll be no one who can take her from us again, not till her mam comes for her.'

They stood either side of Annie, and Fran thought of her da, Joe Hall, while Sarah looked skywards, probably thinking of Tom Bedley, for he and Joe had been killed together in the roof fall in Bell Seam. Tubby Smith, Beth's da, had succumbed to black lung, so the men were all together now. Finally, Fran slipped her arm around her mam, who rested her head against her daughter's. 'Mr Smithson brought her back a bit after midday. He explained that there had been a misunderstanding, but his eyes said there was more to it. The man apologised, our Franny. Said he might even manage to come to the pantomime, because he'd give his right arm to see Reginald Massingham receive a custard pie.'

Fran looked up to her da, telling him that Ralph had not only saved everyone on the bus by steering his car towards the tree, but had also fought Norris Suffolk side by side with Sid when he'd barely recovered from the accident, and now he had used his contacts to find out who owned the lorry. So, Da, she told him, that toffee-nosed pitman really has come good, though what on earth is really going on, we'll never know.

Sarah and Beth slipped away, leaving the Halls to their peace. The girls' steps were lighter than they had been for days. They talked a little of Amelia, thinking that the truth must wait, or remain buried. Nothing mattered now the bairn was home, for Smithson would not dare remove her again. Only poor Daisy had the right to do that.

'Where *is* Daisy, do you think?' Sarah mused.

Beth shook her head, then just before she left Sarah on Main Street, she said, 'She'll just turn up, or not. What we all have to do is keep her alive in Lisa's head, but make the bairn feel she is in a family too. Somehow we'll make it work. See you in an hour. I'll wait at the top with me bike, then we can head to the Hall for a rehearsal. I don't know if Fran will come, but what I was thinking is that we have no tickets to give or sell, so maybe Viola can get the Massingham bairns to make some. What'll we put the money towards?'

She headed down the back lane as Sarah called, 'There's this art scholarship thing that Monty Moran was talking about for one of his boys, but anyway, I bet Eva's got an idea.'

Beth burst into laughter, and called over her shoulder, 'Don't say "bet", or she'll ask for sixpence, spit on her hand and expect you to shake on it.'

Chapter Twenty-Two

Beth swung into her backyard, dodging the washing flapping on the line. It was so wonderful that Lisa was home. So ... very ... wonderful ... She didn't touch the clean clothes, not even to test if they were dry. She wouldn't until she'd scrubbed the chemicals off. All along the back lane she could see other clothes flapping on lines, held up by clothes props. She nodded to herself, for it would be an idea to drape some specially made bloomers on washing lines for Reginald's scene. They'd have to get some false bosoms for him to wear, and for Stevie's bad-tempered old fairy.

Grinning at the thought, she almost danced into the kitchen. 'Amelia's gone off sick.' Then she stopped. 'Well, that's the first bit of good news. And the best is that Lisa is home. Smithson made a mistake, he says.'

Her mam wasn't really listening, she was just standing, her back to the range, holding an envelope, her face strained. She said quietly, 'I know about Lisa.'

For a minute Beth didn't understand, but when her mam held the envelope up, she saw the address was written in royal blue ink. Beth felt for the kitchen chair, her happiness gone as she sat down with a thump. She closed her eyes. Bob. Bob had written, but she had said she would only open a solicitor's letter.

She could remember the canary shed, her da's old plot on the allotment, the feel of the spade as she had tipped soil onto the torn-up strips of his final letter all those months ago, strips of paper she had not read. The girls and she had then planted runner beans in the freshly turned earth, beneath which the letter had disintegrated. They had eaten the beans as August loomed. It had felt to her as though she was putting his wretched words, whatever they were, to good use. Well, that's what she would do with this one.

Her mam, as always, could read her mind. 'I reckon you should read it this time, before you bury it. Then you can answer him properly and really be done with it, one way or another. Perhaps he wants you back?'

Beth nodded, but instead of sitting and reading it, she washed quickly, then grabbed it and cycled full pelt up to Massingham Hall. The exercise drained her of her rage, but not her uncertainty. What had he said? What more could he take from her? All she wanted now was a divorce, then marriage to Sid, and a family.

She pushed hard and flew across the gravel, under the arch, and rested her bike against the wall. There was no sign of Alfie, just Ralph's roadster alongside the Rolls. He would be in the ballroom busy with the other marrers, including her Sid. *Hers.* Beth knocked softly on the back door. Sophia was in the kitchen, a muslin nappy over her shoulder, one babe in her arms, Sandra holding the other, and they were standing, swaying from side to side, talking quietly together. They waved her in.

Beatrice Adams sat with the evacuees at the table. They were writing out more scripts, because Davey had sent an additional washerwomen scene after Eva had said that the custard pie couldn't happen just because the bossy washerwoman was in a flounce.

'So now,' Beatrice said, 'Reginald, as bossy washerwoman, has the temerity to tell the three younger washerwomen, how to wash clothes. It makes a more sensible scene, what with the fun with the wet washing, and then the criticism and the pie in the face.'

In spite of herself, Beth smiled at the thought. But who would deliver the pie?

'Well, Eva had decided the girls would toss for the pleasure, so that's what they will do,' Beatrice said, copying yet another page, one for each cast member, so everyone knew what was happening.

'I'm only here for a moment,' Beth explained. 'I just need a word with Sid.'

The bairns took no notice, but Sophia frowned slightly. 'Is everything all—'

Before she could finish, Beth had fled up the stairs, across the hall and into the corridor. As she neared the ballroom she could hear the banging, and also the singing. It was the song the Bletchley lads had written about kindness creating miracles.

> You just have to believe,
> As the trees shed their leaves,
> That magic exists.
> If the kindnesses reach high,
> Almost up to the sky,
> Magic exists . . .

She heard Viola's voice as well as the lads singing, and stopped just outside the door to listen. Then, as Ralph had once told her, she made herself feel the ground beneath her feet and took a deep breath, and then another, counting to four as Joe Hall had once told them. So much good advice from so many people.

Beth muttered, 'Once two is two, two times two is four,' as Sarah had told them to do to calm the mind. She rested her forehead against the cool of the door, realising now that it wasn't fear that was overcoming her, it was rage. How dare Bob trespass into her world, which contained Sid, the gang, the co-op, Massingham, everything she loved, but nothing of Bob.

She gripped the doorknob and entered, clapping. 'Bravo, that sounded right pretty. I can imagine you, Viola, with your wand, sitting on the swing above the bank—'

'Aye, well,' Viola laughed, 'Old Ted and Mr Johnson the butcher are just deciding where the swing should hang from, and reckon they can build a frame that looks like saplings, because they don't want to damage the ceiling. It's too high, anyway.'

Sid left Stan, Ralph and Norm sizing up the bank and jumped from the stage, coming towards Beth, a smile on his face, the bright winter sun catching his hair, making it more russet than usual. He kissed her softly. 'Howay, lass, weren't expecting to see you yet awhile. Have you seen Lisa?'

Viola called, 'Smithson phoned Reginald, knowing Annie would be here, Beth. She tore home on her bike, while I went to meet the bairns from school, and we piled into Farmer Thompkins' trailer. He parked in Main Street, they jumped down from the trailer and literally ran down the back lane, with Farmer Thompkins and me trying to catch up. Annie had said to bring them, you see, to show them the plan had worked. They promised to be quiet, and they were. Do you know, they actually tiptoed across Fran's backyard and peered in the kitchen at Lisa. It really has settled them. Eva whispered to me, "You all tried and here she is, home. Till her mam comes, anyway, then she'll still have all of us as her marrers, for we'll never forget her."'

Beth and Sid smiled. Sid stroked back a strand of hair that had fallen across Beth's face. He said over his shoulder, 'They seemed rested, somehow, when I came up.'

Viola turned her attention back to the lads. 'Where are the trees to go if you've finished with the bank?'

Norm and Stan chalked the stage. 'What about around here?'

'Seems fine to me, and how high is the bank?'

It was Sid's turn now. 'At least a foot, if not more, to hide Ralph when he is supposed to be submerged.'

While the others discussed exactly where the beck was to run, Old Ted and Mr Johnson the butcher made notes, staring up at the ceiling, and Iris Walters tinkered on the piano, running through the music she had composed, guided by Davey's script, Mr Moran sitting alongside, turning the pages, as he was the only one able to read music. Sid slipped his arm around Beth and pulled her to him, saying, 'Now, pet, what's to do, for something is?'

Beth drew the letter from her mac pocket. He released her and took it, turning it over and over. 'Royal blue ink? So . . . Bob.' It wasn't a question. 'What are you going to do with it?'

That was one of the many things she loved about Sid. He asked her, he didn't tell her. 'Oh, I'll open it, read it, then bury it. But before that, I might reply. It depends on what he says.'

So, she did read it out to Sid, because there were no secrets between them.

Dear Beth

I have been a fool. I know you are sad, but I want you back. Heather isn't for me, and I'll tell her that. I need to stay in Grimsby, and you can join me. We can rent another house, then I can see the child from time to time. We could even have our own. Let me know when you can come.

From your husband, Bob Jones

Sid's face was a picture, and then it was as though the floor was collapsing beneath him, because he reached for the wall, steadying himself, but just for a moment. Then he took control, stood straight, staring at the stage. He turned back to her. 'Oh Beth, it's your decision. I wouldn't stop you, you know that. I just want your happi—'

Beth kissed him, silencing him. The kiss went on and on and his arms came round her, lifting her off her feet. He pulled back, smiling. 'Why don't we live together, after the panto and Christmas? What does it matter if we're not married? Nobody minds. Iris is right, life's too difficult not to find happiness where we can.'

At that there was a clatter of applause, and they looked around, and there were the marrers, Iris, Mr Moran and the evacuees, watching.

'Can you breathe when you kiss like that?' Abe asked coming to them, with Eva beside him.

Eva nodded. 'Aye, we came just in time. We've been having milk and biscuits. So, can you breathe?'

Sid pulled her pigtails. 'You've all got milk moustaches.'

Melanie just shook her head. 'He's changing the subject, but he's alive, so I reckon you *can* breathe when it's a long kiss.'

The clapping had long ago changed to laughter. Beth held his face and drew Sid closer. 'I'll write back, asking, no, *insisting* on the divorce. Time the lad grew up and stopped being such an arrogant beggar.'

Behind her, Eva was saying, 'I did bet sixpence they'd marry.'

'But Sid said live together. It's not the same,' Melanie insisted.

'It is, if there's sixpence in it.'

They continued to argue, but for Beth, the toing and froing was over and done with.

At nine on the dot, the telephone rang and Ralph answered. He knew it would be Tim Swinton. It was one of his call times and he'd probably heard that Amelia had been taken from the Factory, but not who had taken her. It was the medics as far as anyone was to know, though perhaps Smythe's men could have worn white coats, because Yeland had mentioned they had arrived in suits.

'Ralphy, what's new?'

Ralph shrugged, determined to sound casual. 'The pantomime is coming along, and . . . er . . . Oh, Amelia has gone off sick. I gather she had a high temperature from flu, or so the girls say, so there won't be much chance for me to pick what brains she has over a drink at the Pig and Whistle.' As he said this, he thought back, and realised – of course – it had been Tim's suggestion to take her to the Pig and Whistle, which was the pub where Norris had received his message Why the hell hadn't he put two and two together before? He smiled to himself, suspecting that Smythe had.

'You still there?' asked Tim.

'Of course. I was just thinking that I hope she'll get better. Then I can pick up with her when she returns.'

'Who were the men who came for her and where is she now?'

Ralph affected surprise. 'Not sure where she is. The girls said she was taken by medics of some sort.' It seemed the best answer.

'Oh, for God's sake—'

'Oh, hang on, yes, I remember now. The girls said she had to be taken to a hospital for her own sake. Yes, that's right – a really high fever made her terribly unwell. Let's hope no one else gets it.'

There was a long pause. 'All right,' Tim said, his voice taut. 'Well, an influenza epidemic could slow production, like the First War. Millions died, you know, worldwide, especially in the second wave. Daft buffoons came out of quarantine in spite of all that to dance in the bliddy streets at war's end, making it worse. Well, keep an eye on that. If we could spread it ... The child's back, though, I hear. Why?'

'Stan said that Smithson told them there had been numerous counter-claims from people such as the Vicar, Mr Massingham, Sister Newsome and her doctor husband both working at the Newcastle Royal Victoria Infirmary which, together with Dr Dunster's guarantee of close monitoring, made it feasible for the child to be returned.' Stan knew, of course, that Yeland's hand was in all of this.

Again there was silence. Finally, sounding weary now, Tim muttered, 'Don't forget the pit. We need to show endeavour. I'll get back to you.'

Click. Then an empty line. Ralph replaced the receiver, leaning back in his father's chair, the blotter carrying inky mirror images of many words. He waited, longing to go and look at his twin sisters yet again, because they were like two peas in a pod and he found them fascinating and amazing. They were so small, so sweet, and Sophia, his mother, was so pleased and his father proud, and scared, beyond measure.

The telephone rang again. As expected it was Smythe. 'Interesting. He didn't pursue why Norris had been arrested, and he's clearly being pressurised to achieve something. We're talking to Norris, and to Amelia, but so far little to report, but we'll get to the ins and outs in time. These two idiots are small fry, but it's a huge, clumsy mistake by Tim to phone through a message to the Pig and Whistle. I'll keep you in the picture.'

'If you would, and just for your information, and not sure if I mentioned it at the time, but Tim suggested I should take Amelia to the Pig and Whistle, and it was in the Pig and Whistle that Norris received a phone ca—'

'Oh, indeed yes, that is something with which to press Norris, as we continue with the questioning. And Tim fell for the influenza . . . Excellent. As these conversations with him are being recorded, we have, by now, quite enough to haul him in with his thoughts on a flu epidemic stopping work, but we do so need the rest of the buggers.' Smythe sighed. 'Keep a close eye on Corbitt. With the Axis running for the hills in North Africa, together with Russia putting up a good fight things are looking much better. So, we expect sabotage attempts to go up a notch, as a symbolic and actual national threat, damaging British morale as well as production. We are already on high alert. Goodnight.'

The next few weeks seemed to fly by, what with work at the Factory, rehearsals and the delivery of the material from the attic to the village as most of the women had volunteered to set about sewing the various costumes, while the girls and the lads did a bit of everything else: painting the backcloth, the scenery. The girls were on the aft shift, so they had time to work on the pantomime in the mornings, but that was perfect, and what's more, Lisa came to Massingham with Annie, so they saw her for at least a few hours.

Fran realised that the bairn was growing up in her own little gang, just as they all had. Lisa, and the evacuees. Would they all go to the beck? Swim, picnic – in winter too – as they had done as bairns? Well, it was up to her, Davey and the others to make sure they did.

Petronella, Bert's niece, had started at Massingham Hall to help with the twins, which made life for Viola, Sandra, Annie and Sophia easier, though, as expected, everyone pitched in and helped with everything, and that included the evacuees.

By Sunday, 13 December, Beth had still not had a reply

from Bob and she realised that afternoon, as she walked to the Canary Club with her marrers and the lads, that she had barely thought of him. Why should she? She was in love with Sid, and that was that. Sid's arm around her was strong, and so was her heart, because though marriage would be perfect, the alternative would be too.

The back lanes were gloomy but not dark, though even if they were they could find their way blindfold to the allotment, so it was no problem. If necessary, on their return, they could always use the slag heap as their compass when they recited their lines, as they were doing now, acting out their parts as they walked between the terraces and down the narrow lane.

Stan opened the allotment gate, moving on to the songs as they walked single file between the plots. They were on their way to celebrate the marriage of Cyn and Simon, Mr and Mrs Parrot, which had taken place yesterday. Sid laughed. 'What's so funny?' asked Beth.

'Oh, I'm just happy for them, for Lisa, who seems so untouched by her "stay" in the orphanage, and for us. And the pantomime is just good fun, though I'm bliddy glad I'm a tree and haven't any lines.'

They laughed together. Ahead, they saw Stan move a wheelbarrow blocking the path, allowing the others to pass. 'We could have jumped it, of course,' he said. 'Makes me wonder if Simon carried Cyn over the threshold?'

Norm laughed. 'What, at the Canary Club shed?'

Over the laughter, Ralph said, 'No room, really. But I wish we could have been there, instead of them nipping off. I know they didn't want to stop our labours in the ballroom, but ... Anyway, I hope they had a couple of nice witnesses. I gather they pulled them in off the street.'

'We should try and get a decent present with the money collected at the Factory and pit.' It was Norm again.

'They said they preferred the money, so let's leave it at that, eh?' Sarah insisted. 'You've got it safe, have you, Stan?'

They were just passing an allotment that had been cleared except for the cabbages, and Beth realised they should have taken down the remains of the runner beans on theirs.

'Oh aye.' Their breath puffed into the cold crisp air. Stan asked, 'You girls got the robins and all the other ornaments knitted up for the tree, and mittens for presents? We've knocked together some wooden toys, and the paper shop found us some pens.'

Fran nodded as they neared Simon's plot, and Ralph pulled Viola close, saying loud enough for everyone to hear, 'Father is so enchanted with his world at every level this precise moment, I fear he will insist on a panto every year.'

'And a new set of twins too?' Sid shouted. The groans of horror just made them laugh.

'Wait until he gets the custard pie in his face, Ralph,' said Beth, 'for the co-op are threatening a real one, but it's a secret. That'll settle his fancies.'

'I told Davey that might happen,' Fran laughed. 'It makes him and the boys more determined to twist Norah's arm to give them a day off. As he said, they're the scriptwriters, after all, and want their round of applause. They've worked it all out and will get an overnight train north, spend a day with us, and then the midnight train back. It'd be grand if they—'

'Are you expecting anyone, Beth?' Ralph was looking ahead to Beth's allotment.

Before she turned to follow his gaze, she knew who would be standing there. They all fell silent as they too saw Bob.

Fran came to stand beside her friend. 'Let's all the girls go together, or you must take Sid.'

Beth merely shook her head, her eyes on Bob, who looked weather-beaten and tired, but that did not affect her one little bit. 'I'll talk to him and see him off.'

She walked away from her marrers, feeling almost strong, and almost certain. The wind was bitter, perhaps there would be more snow? If so, Sid and the elderberry wine would warm her. Once two is two, two twos are four . . .

Bob was watching her. She was not looking at him; instead, she checked the sprouts and the leeks, because the trembling had begun. She made herself look at the leeks again. They would pull a few before they went home. Finally, she concentrated on the dead runner beans, still wound around the bean sticks. Beneath these were the remains of his letter. She stopped near Bob, who stood in the lee of the shed.

'Hello, Bob. You look tired.'

'I am.' He reached out a hand. 'I'm so sorry, Beth, I didn't mean to be such a fool. Come home with me, as me wife again, please. Let's start again. I need you. There's a war to fight, I get tired, I get stupid. Please, I'll make us a nice home . . .'

'But, Bob, I am home. And your home is with your bairn. I read and replied to your letter, it's buried under there.' She pointed to the beans. 'That was the end of us, and I say again, you must go home to your bairn, and to Heather.' The trembling had stopped; she was really strong, really certain. 'It's time to grow up, Bob. Be a man, a *good* man, for you're not there yet, lad.'

She turned and lifted a hand towards Sid who stood with the others, clustered in front of the door to the club, knowing they were there to keep her safe. 'See over there? That's a good man, *my* man.'

Bob gaped, then looked at the group who used to be his friends. Sid stepped forward. Bob's face fell. 'Sid Barratt?'

'I want to be Mrs Sid Barratt, so you are to go home, for it's Christmas soon, and home is the place to be. You are going to sort the divorce, and then we can both rebuild our lives.'

Bob stepped closer, held out his hands. She took them. He started to say, 'But—'

She said, her eyes meeting his, 'You take care, Bob, of yourself and of your family. Buy the bairn a gift, or make one, but go.'

They stood for what seemed like hours but was only a few minutes and all the time she smelled the sulphur, heard the clatter of boots on cobbles, the winding gear, the call of a bairn, the laughter of women. She would give him this much of her time but no more, ever again.

Finally, he released her hands, nodded, smiled even. 'I will. I'll get on with the divorce, never fear. Got to go and make it right with Heather now, if you're sure?'

She matched his smile, wondering what she'd ever seen in this man.

'Best go, then,' he said.

She merely nodded. He walked away, waving limply to her marrers. She moved over to the runner beans, tearing them down. Sid came to her side. 'Shall I help?'

'Right you are,' she replied. It was then that they shared a look; he laughed, she smiled. 'I do rightly love you, Sid Barratt.'

'Course you do, for I'm irresistible.'

Cyn was calling from inside the Canary Club. 'Come on, get a move on, we've my wedding to toast and it's freezing out there.'

Sid replied, shouting, 'You hearing your missus, Si? You realise you've married a shrew? Nag, nag.'

Beth clipped his ear. They laughed together, and leaving the runner beans in a neat pile, they walked back to the warmth of the Canary Club and took their places on the barrels while they waited for Simon to pour the wine. Aye, thought Beth. Just as usual and as it will always be.

That were easier than I expected, thought Sid, and I've never been happier in me life.

Chapter Twenty-Three

On Wednesday, 16 December, with the pantomime only three days away, the lads saw off the girls at the bus stop in the dark of the bitter midwinter morning. Beth called to Sid before she disappeared further inside the bus, 'Don't forget, we have to put up the tree in the ballroom when we get back. Farmer Thompkins is bringing it on his trailer.'

'We'll have the help of the bairns, remember,' Fran laughed as she followed Beth. 'And may the Lord help us.'

Sid heard Beth shout something from deep inside the bus. 'What'd she say?' he called.

'And we'll all have smiling faces, or you'll have your leg skelped.' Fran disappeared too as Stan, who was standing next to Sid, roared with laughter.

Behind them, Norm, who was using Sid as a windbreak in order to light his Woodbine, took the time to poke him. 'So it begins. The wife knows best.'

Bert started the engine. 'Just so long as you don't try putting our Tilly on top as the fairy, for you'll need a hoist and what's more, she'll squash the poor blessed tree flat.'

The passengers' replies were lost as he roared away, leaving the lads waving at the slitted rear lights and billowing exhaust fumes before they headed for the pithead and the fore shift with the other workers. Their bait tins clanged, their boots clattered, just the same as always, thought Sid, or the 'always' he had now. He and Beth as tight as a drum, filled with love and the promise of a colliery house of their own in the New Year, from Reginald Massingham, whether the divorce was through or not.

'These things take time,' Reginald had said, as he fiddled with the Christmas-tree lights they'd bought from Briddlestone's before the war. 'But you two have plenty of that, whereas I have less, and if I don't find this wretched loose bulb so the damned things work when you bring up the tree, I will feel even more like ninety.'

Of course, Eva chose that moment to come alongside him. 'That'll be a penny for the swear jar, Mr Reginald,' she called. 'Abe,' she commanded. Abe had, of course, come running, waving the half-full jam jar that was Eva's idea, ever since hammers had hit many thumbs as the scenery flats were made and erected and props created.

Sid grinned to himself at the memory of Reginald's face as he had looked at the jar, opened his mouth, then closed it again, shaking his head and laughing before handing over the penny. Sid shook *his* head now as they entered the pit yard. Eva and Abe reminded him of Fran and Davey, almost joined at the hip since they first became aware of one another, and each knowing their place: the bloke always second.

He walked across the pit yard, sniggering to himself, then realising that this was, in fact, the fate of all men if they knew what was good for them. He wondered as he dodged round a pitman if Davey would be able to get home for the pantomime? And what about Norah who wanted to come too, and why not? She had sent up the doublet, after all, and tree costumes, not to mention the washerwoman's bosom.

Ralph was playing with the thought of his own monster costume and trying to divest himself of it at the appropriate moment, and how the young washerwomen, in the shapes of Fran, Sarah and Beth, would break off from washing clothes in the beck to throw the fish back in the water, and then wash him with the broom after his third kindness. Everyone should fall back in amazement, even the bully, as Ralph's costume came away to reveal the hose as well as the doublet, but would they? Then they'd sing with all the children. It was later that poor Reginald would get the pie, and the backcloth looked really good, with the glowing range, and the shelves at the side.

He collected his lamp and tokens and joined the gaggle as they waited for the cage, with the song reluctant to leave him.

> You just have to believe,
> As the trees shed their leaves,
> That magic exists.
> If the fairy swings high,
> Almost up to the sky . . .

The marrers joined in with *'Magic exists . . . '*, though it wasn't just the marrers now, it was all those waiting for the cage, for they had heard them sing it enough times.

As the laughter rang around him, he fretted, because it was the dance he kept forgetting.

'You just have to believe . . .' He stepped forward.

'As the trees shed their leaves . . .' He stepped right.

Stan interrupted, stepping right too. 'Oh damn. We haven't fixed a way to get the leaves to come down every time.'

'That magic exists.' Ralph stepped back.

'If the fairy swings high,' Steve Oborne called. He stepped forward with everyone. 'Well, throw the leaves – get a few backstage people behind the side flats to bung 'em at you.'

His son Colin said, *'Almost up to the sky.'* Everyone stepped back as Colin added, 'I could toss the leaves, because I have

319

to keep tugging Viola on her swing anyway, but it'll be tricky.'

The cage rattled up as the pitmen in front and behind added their twopenn'orth on the problem of the beck ripples, which wasn't yet sorted. Finally, Eddie Corbitt, hidden by the queue, called from the front, 'By, I've been thinking about it for days, it's been driving me bliddy mad, and the song is in me head. But it came to me last night, in me bed. Why not just dye a sheet and have someone in the flats and someone behind the backcloth lifting and dropping the ends, so it looks like ripples and low waves? Save all this bliddy cutting up of paper, except for when you really need it.'

Next to Ralph, Norm yelled, 'That's an idea, Eddie. Mark you, they'll have to be standing low down.'

'Aye, I thought of that an' all.' He said no more because the cage had clattered and banged to a stop. The banksman unhooked the chain, yelling, 'Let the beggars off first. Don't be so eager. Don't forget to put your lamps and tokens back, lads.'

The men coming off shift shook their heads, their faces black with coal dust, drawn with tiredness. As they went past, Eddie called to one, 'Been surveying?'

'Oh aye, me and Rob. I reckon some props need to be replaced and then some of you'll be working Franton Seam.'

The song left Ralph's head, the steps forgotten. Why had Eddie asked that? Was he going to blow the roof as he'd done before? He half turned to tell Albright, the shift manager, but then stopped. What if Eddie was pulled over, asked about it, and then he told Tim? It might scare Swinton and end any chance of getting to the head of the cell. He'd have to let it play out, but not without doing *something*.

As the queue eased forward, Ralph called across to Rob, the surveyor, who was replacing his lamp. 'So, will the props go in this week, or next?' No one would be surprised at the son of the owner asking, even though Auld Hilda was under the management of the Government for the duration of the war.

'Oh aye, we'll sort the props next week. Let the blacklocks have their peace for a while longer, and the rats. Then you can break the cobwebs we missed and get to work.'

The men laughed, and squashed into the cage. Ralph relaxed. If the roof came down, at least that would be proof of Eddie's involvement, for many must have overheard his question, or so Smythe might think. Silence fell, the chain was hitched across, they rattled down, and as always his stomach came up into his mouth, his legs felt like water and the cage just seemed to fall and fall into the darkness. Would this be the day it kept on falling?

He started to sing the song from where he'd left off: '. . . *That magic exists. If the fairy swings high, Almost up to the sky* . . .' He realised everyone was joining in and ended with, '*Magic exists.*' They started at the beginning again, and sang it through. As they reached the last line, the cage arrived. They herded out, heading along the main seam either side of the tub 'train' pulled by Donald the Galloway.

Charlie, their tub lad, stopped to stroke Donald, then the lad seemed to get a bit of energy and hurried ahead of them, but without kicking up any coal dust. Ralph watched, thinking how quickly Charlie had learned the ropes, but he was distracted by Eddie calling as he walked ahead of them, 'By, I can't get the song out of me head. It'll be a grand night – you should do it every year. Good for Massingham to have something other than the war.'

Stan stared after Eddie. 'He's got a lot to say for himself?'

'Chatty, which is strange, but a good idea about the sheet,' Norm muttered. 'We could get Steve Oborne to stand in the flats, and Colin is behind the backcloth anyway.' He paused.

'We could manage the bliddy war, you know, with all the thinking we've had to do for this.'

They coughed, laughing, and walked on, Ralph, as always, conscious of the rock and earth above and around them. They were nothing but a pack of moles, burrowing. Pitmen were turning off down their seams, but Ralph, Stan, Norm and Sid continued on past Franton Seam on the left, then took the next turning into Outen Seam, where they were working now. 'Reckon Charlie might be there already. He were out of the blocks pretty damn quick after he'd given Donald a stroke,' Norm said.

'A bit like Bert's niece turning up to help with the twins,' Sid joked. 'But that was a bit of good luck. Though Petronella's a strange name.'

'Nowt strange about it, nowt strange about anything to do with her, she's right grand,' said Norm. 'She says her mam took on a flight of fancy when she were born. No one knows how it came into her head, least of all her. Anyway, everyone calls her Nell. Everyone close to her, that is.'

'Oh aye,' said Stan. 'You call her Petronella, then, I 'spect, for she'd not want to be close to you, lad.' He winked at Sid.

Norm laughed. 'Ah, well, that's where you're wrong, our Stan, like you often are, about so much, but I reckon your Sarah lets you know that regular like.'

They made their way along Outen, lighting their path with their lamps, and had to crouch down as the roof became lower, eating their own dust, then ducking down even further. Stan caught his back. 'Bliddy hell.'

'That's another sixpence for Eva's jar,' Ralph muttered.

Stan just laughed, and they carried on to the face, where Charlie waited, stripped off. They got to work, for there were tubs to fill, enough to keep Charlie busy. They heaved at the coal and dug with their picks, and Ralph was damn glad it wasn't so low that they had to lie on their sides, working their picks from there. They broke for some bait, hunkering down, their lamps casting a dull light, eating bread, dripping and dust, slurping cold tea. Then they were back at it again, and though they worked relentlessly, they practised their lines as well.

As the shift drew close to the end, Stan eased his back, his face completely black. 'It's these dance steps I can't get right. I mean, those tree costumes are stiff and I can't get me legs forward. Or back.'

Norm agreed, and muttered, 'We could cut the bottom off and use gravy browning for our legs.'

Ralph wondered aloud if there was some brown material in the attic. 'I'll look, because if we did cut off the bottoms and fixed the material to the trunk, we could return them to Norah for the drama club she's got going in her village.'

Sid rested on his pick. 'Aye, that'd do it.' He stretched. 'I reckon I'm getting old.'

'No, you're just lazy,' Norm laughed.

They stopped suddenly, because there it was, the sound and the judder that Ralph had half been waiting for after Eddie's questions about Franton Seam. Was it a natural roof fall, or the result of a charge? It was nearby, that was certain. They all looked at Stan, Charlie too, his shovel held in mid-air.

'Franton, d'you reckon? It were close enough?' Sid asked.

'Maybe the roof's come down. They said it needed props,' Norm said.

Stan shook his head. 'I reckon I heard a charge . . . And aye, in Franton, but there shouldn't be anyone there.' He was off, powering along, although he was bent over under the low ceiling of the passage.

The others followed, Norm protesting, 'You're hearing things.'

'Oh aye, and what about Bell Seam supposed to be

empty, but me da and Davey's were under it. Get a bliddy move on.'

They did, desperate to reach the main seam, turning into it, running along to Franton and into it, fighting against the rolling, billowing coal dust and the cobwebs too thick to brush aside easily. Stan was ahead, Ralph behind him, then the rest. They reached the fall; the tumbled coal and rock, lit by their lamps, were blocking the seam. 'Anyone there?' called Stan.

Ralph held up his lamp, letting the light play on the ground and the sides, squinting and coughing in the dust. No answer, nothing to be seen. But what was that? 'There, over by the side,' he called. And there it was – a pick. So, someone was there? He heard the roof creaking, but it always did. It didn't mean it would fall again.

Norm made his way over. 'There's a lamp and token here, with the pick, laid out neat as a pin,' he said.

'And bait tin?' Ralph called, heading over to stand with Norm as the dust swirled. Stan continued to call.

In the light from his lamp, Norm said, 'Neat and tidy, aye, well we know what that means, and it's Eddie Corbitt's name scratched on the tin.' It was what Ralph had already suspected, and yes, he could smell the charge, and if he could so could the others, but no one said anything about it.

Charlie had finally caught them up, and was panting heavily. 'But why's he laid them all out?'

Sid spun round, looking at Ralph. Ralph held his gaze and told Charlie, 'Probably doing a Jimmy Riddle.'

'But why's he in *here*?' Charlie argued.

'Probably got caught short, and this was as good a place in a crowded coal face, lad.'

Stan's shout drew them over. 'Off you go, Charlie, get the overman, and be quick but quiet about it, you hear? Say nothing about anything – leave it to us. We'll need a stretcher and the rescue team to clear and prop the roof, but that's all you tell him. Except that we're here.'

'You're about to learn how to be a pitman,' Sid told Charlie. 'Go. Remember, say nowt more to anyone until you get to Merryweather.' He turned to Stan. 'He's the overman today, isn't he?' Stan nodded. Sid went on. 'Then tell him Stan says it needs to stay quiet. Got it?'

Charlie tugged his cap down, not understanding, but took off.

Over at the coal fall, they searched carefully, gently, and beneath a pile of coal and slate they could see Eddie's legs. They were moving, just a little.

'Right,' Stan ordered. 'We get the coal from over him. It's only a yard deep here, where it's scrabbled outwards.'

They began moving the coal, and Sid said quietly, 'There are other ways to end it all, you know. Never seen this, but heard of it. What the hell has got the beggar down this much?'

Ralph said nothing, because he suspected Eddie had killed his two marrers, Joe Hall and Tom Bedley. Just as Ralph thought he himself had done when he'd set a charge at Tim's instructions. Ralph had lived with the guilt, hating himself, wanting death, until Smythe and Yeland took the weight of the past off him explaining it was someone else who had laid the real charge, his was merely a charade, to give Tim power over him. That was when he had started working with Smythe against Tim.

They dug carefully, so carefully, and all the while Eddie's movements slowed, until only one leg was twitching.

Albright arrived then, not Merryweather, with the rescue team. Together they all worked until finally, Corbitt was free. Earlier, Stan had stamped on the bait tin, crushing it, and the other lads had crushed Eddie's lamp, filling it with coal dust. They had thrown these items and his pick to one side, as though they'd dug them out.

Everyone would accept that Eddie had wanted to do his business in peace. Questions might be thought, but nothing would be said. Albright merely looked at them all, and nodded. 'Charlie seemed to know nothing much when he talked to me,' he said. 'Nasty accident, eh?'

'Aye,' muttered Stan.

They eased Eddie's body onto the stretcher and started towards the main seam, but as they drew abreast of Ralph, Eddie croaked, 'Put me down, just for a minute. I have to say something to the boss's son.'

Ralph knelt beside the stretcher as the work went on behind, clearing the fall while some others began shoring up the seam. Eddie reached up and tugged Ralph's arm, his lips moving. Ralph couldn't hear and leaned close. Stan knelt at the head of the stretcher and lifted it a little by the handles, bringing Eddie up, just enough.

Eddie's grip tightened. He seemed to be gathering his strength. 'You didn't kill Joe and Tom. I did, I set the charge, yours was deliberately useless . . . Neither of us knew . . . anyone was there.' He was gasping between every word. Shut up, Ralph wanted to say, because Stan could surely hear.

'Get out of it. Shut him . . . down. My wife. He said he would . . . kill her. She was ill and died . . . anyway. This . . . my way out. The guilt . . . Not you. Me. Not any more. Too much . . .'

Ralph could sense Stan looking at him, his face expressionless, continuing to hold the stretcher up. 'My house . . . Floorboards . . . Bedroom . . . Papers . . . Tim suspects I have evidence . . . Quick.' His hand loosened on Ralph's arm. Ralph turned, nodded to the rescue team.

Albright said, 'Leave it to us now. It was the end of the shift half an hour ago. Get yourself to the cage, eh.'

Ralph turned and headed off, knowing he had to be quick, for word could pass swiftly, as Eddie had hinted. But who would let Tim know? Or had someone already done so?

Ralph almost ran down Franton Seam, his lamp's juddering beam picking out swirling coal dust, but showing the way, then back down Outen. He dressed, then finally ran out into the main seam, going against the tide of the aft-shift stragglers. He hadn't told his marrers; he just had to get out, get to Eddie's, find the evidence, and put Tim down, once and for all, for Ralph's rage against Tim knew no bounds. To threaten a man's dying wife? Had Stan heard that his charge was useless, that Eddie's was not? Had he heard that there should have been no one there? Oh God . . . But not now, he had to get the papers.

The cage seemed so slow, but finally he headed to the lamphouse, then dashed to the bike shed. The pit yard was quiet, as one shift had gone home and the other was bedded in.

He tore out of gates and down into the town, steering round chatting pitmen and women with prams crossing the street, along past Dr Dunster's towards the outskirts of Massingham, tears streaming down his face: to threaten a dying wife . . . He skidded to a stop outside Eddie's house. As he flung his bike down behind the hedge which divided the front garden from the pavement to keep it out of sight, he looked at the closed door. 'Oh, God.' He didn't have a key. He ran round to the back, wondering if he should have telephoned Smythe. But there was no time. Eddie thought Tim could come, or someone else, to look, find, destroy.

He tried the back door, but it was locked. He tried to think, looked under the flowerpot. Nothing. He ran round to the front again, and there stood Stan. He held up a key on a piece of string, swinging it. 'Looking for this?' His voice was cold, his face set in a mask of fury.

Ralph grabbed for the key. Stan closed his hand over it. 'So, talk to me. The quicker you do, the sooner we'll get to the floorboard, though he could have bliddy said which one.'

Ralph drew in a breath. Behind them the slag heap was smouldering and the smell of sulphur was thick in the air. Drawing himself up, Ralph told this man, who wouldn't remain his marrer, or even his friend, everything. Quickly.

Stan merely nodded. 'I reckoned as much from what the beggar said.'

'I'm so sorry.'

Stan tossed the key to Ralph, nodding towards the door. 'It were hanging inside the letter box. Get on with it. I've hidden me bike next to yours, just in case there's a third visitor.'

Ralph's hands were shaking too much as he tried to get the key in the lock. Stan elbowed him to one side. 'By, you're a daft beggar. Get yourself into all sorts of trouble, and can't even find the hole.' Stan got the key in the lock, and opened the door. They headed for the stairs. Stan took the lead and reached the landing. He pointed to the front bedroom. 'Yours.' They didn't look at one another, but for a moment both stood still, listening, because was that a creak?

Had Tim come? Was he already here? Had he found what he needed? Why the hell didn't the pitman get the paper to someone . . . Well, who? Who could anyone trust? Ralph looked back. Their black fingerprints were on the banister. But who would even care?

Ralph entered the front bedroom. There was a photograph of Eddie and his wife on the bedside table; she looked too thin. He lifted the rug, checking the floorboards, but what for? They all looked the same. He shoved the double bed aside. He peered at the floorboards. Nothing.

'Ralph, get in here.'

He dashed to the back bedroom, where Stan had pushed the single bed to one side. He was pointing at a floorboard with shiny new screws. Stan flicked him a penknife. 'Best get working.'

Down on his knees, Ralph frantically unwound the screws. He dug the blade into the gap between the boards and prised it up. He peered in, Stan standing at his side. Ralph reached for the rolled-up papers. But Stan gripped his shoulder. 'Shh.'

They heard the creak of the stairs. Ralph overbalanced, falling to one side. There was a rush of feet. They both froze, then Stan went after the intruder whilst Ralph scrabbled upright, clutching the roll of paper in his hands. He stuffed it in his pocket; it would be smudged with coal dust, but . . . Stan was leaping down the stairs. Ralph followed. They heard a man rushing along the road. Ralph grabbed Stan as he made to follow, hissing, 'Leave him, I don't want them seeing us.' They heard a car roaring off, and finally fading into the distance.

'Aye, as I said, you're a daft beggar, sprawling all over the bliddy floor.'

'Oh shut up and get back in the house, quick,' Ralph muttered. The pair of them sat on the bottom step of the stairs, their legs outstretched. Ralph waved the papers. 'This is what I need, we don't have to catch whoever it was, not yet, for someone else will.'

'Who? What are you going to do with the papers?' Stan asked.

'Someone I'm working for will want them but I want a look first.'

They read it together. It was the record of a meeting

between Tim Swinton, Mr Plomer from the munitions factories' Head Office and one other gentleman Eddie didn't know. He was on lookout with Norris Suffolk when the meeting took place at the Pig and Whistle. There was a list of other meetings, other people, with dates and places.

'Well, well, Merryweather's on the list, eh?' said Stan. 'What have you been up to? Is that why our Charlie couldn't find you? It's all such a bliddy mess, eh?'

He stood up. 'Best get you home, Ralph. I'll cycle with you, for we're due at the Hall. Best phone whoever you have to from there, for it'll be a long one. Let's not rush from here, I would think we need to keep things normal for those we pass. We'd better wash up first or it'll look odd. Was "Tim" that loud mouthed Fascist you used to go to the meetings with?'

Ralph shrugged, 'Yes, that Tim. But I don't know if it was him who came here, and even if it was, he won't necessarily recognise our bikes.'

'But they might be watching in order to take the papers. Come on. Quick.'

Ralph held him back. 'I saw a back gate. Let's go through there.'

'Aye, and then take the back roads to my house, stopping at the phone box for a quick call to ask Alfie to pick you up. Better that way. They can kill you after you've passed it on and it won't matter a jot to anyone but Viola.'

Was he joking, or would Stan like that outcome? Well, why not? They tore back to Stan's house, via the call box, all the while looking and listening but seeing nothing. They flung open the Bedleys' back gate and left the bikes in the yard. 'Mam-in-law will be up at the Hall, or on ARP duty, I forget which. I'll give meself a quick scrub. You can read the newspaper.' Stan took down the tin bath from the hook near the chicken coop. There was a pan simmering on the range.

As Stan grabbed a couple of cloths, lifted the pan up by its handles and poured the water into the bath, Ralph said, 'I'm sorry about what I did. I can't tell you how much. I just—'

Stan replaced the pan, and turned. 'I'd have smashed your face in and then killed you, and I mean that, but for the fact I reckon you've changed. But, Ralph, if you hadn't risked your daft life, saving me sister and me wife by crashing your car, I'm not sure I'd believe you. I knew you were up to something, because you and Smythe were too damned friendly. I just didn't know what came before. I know him, and I know you, and he hadn't much time for you at Oxford which is why it was weird you seemed so close up here.'

He shoved his hands in his pockets, standing silently for a while, then said slowly, 'As I said, you're a daft beggar, but you've become one of us. Eddie did the deed, but given enough of the charge you'd have brought the roof down. The thing is, neither of you meant to kill anyone. I told myself that, riding here. And I believe it. You had the decency to change and Eddie had the decency to suffer. Best say nowt to anyone else.'

Stan held out his hand. They shook. Coal dust from their hands and sleeves fell to the floor. As they watched it, they realised they still had their boots on. Stan groaned. 'Sarah'll kill me.'

Ralph smiled. 'Well, how about I clean it up while you get in the bath, eh?'

Before Ralph had finished talking, Stan was removing his boots and handing them to him. 'Put 'em on the newspaper, my good man.'

Ralph bowed, then took his own off and tiptoed with both pairs to the newspaper. Behind Stan the bath was steaming, the range firebox was glowing and the clock was ticking. Was it really only three thirty? It seemed like midnight, Ralph thought, as Stan tipped in some cold from the jug Maud or Sarah had left on the range shelf. All the while, Stan was talking.

'I reckon Reginald will have filled the bairns' swear jar by the time he found that dud bulb. Then there are the paper chains they've cut, coloured and stuck—'

'For him to hang around the room.'

Stan was stripping off and handed his clothes to Ralph. 'Give 'em a dadding, then leave them in the scullery on the back of the chair. They'll come when I whistle in the morning.'

They both laughed, but for a moment Stan couldn't meet his eyes. Ralph didn't blame him. As the lad eased himself into the bath, Ralph stepped out into the December cold, standing in his socks, dadding the clothes against the back wall, and with each whack the love and loyalty to his friends, family and country was embedded more deeply. There was still guilt, however, and sorrow for Joe and Tom, and that would never go. It was his punishment, and deservedly so.

He took the clothes to the scullery. Stan was drying himself, and pointed to the bath. 'Best get in as you're a pitman, a marrer. But you get it second, not first.'

This time, Stan met his eyes. 'It'll take me a bit of time, deep down, lad. But it's ours to know. Ours to handle, and I will. Because you're ours. And because when you're a daft pillock, things happen.'

Chapter Twenty-Four

Ralph accepted Stan's dirty water. It was what happened only between marrers and in families and it was an honour. Stan found him a pair of his trousers and an old shirt of his father's to wear, took out the rolled-up papers from Ralph's trouser pocket and dadded his clothes. There was a hoot. Alfie was at the front door. They went together, chucking Ralph's clothes in the boot, checking up and down the road. There was no one around. They looked behind them as Alfie drove, but again, no one followed them.

As they pulled in to the Massingham yard and then the garage, they saw that Reginald was waiting for them, standing next to Ralph's roadster. He was making the paper chains, which had curled into a long sausage and lay across the roadster bonnet. Alfie hurried into the house, but before he went, he muttered, 'Sorry about Eddie.'

Reginald called after him, 'We'll be in when I've finished the last of these. I just want to catch up on exactly what happened in my pit.'

'Aye aye, Captain of the washerwomen.'

'Oh dear heavens,' muttered Reginald. 'I'll be having a word with Davey and his chums when, or if, they get here. Now tell me, although Albright has reported the gist. But I want chapter and verse, especially as I expect Stan has been filled in by you, Ralph, on the inglorious past and rather better present. I dare say he wants to kill you, or give you a good hiding. One can hardly blame him, but I do hope,

Stan, that you can see my son's regret, and sorrow, and the urge he has to do good and make restitution?'

The glue pot stood on newspaper on the bonnet. As they brought Reginald up to date, he merely nodded, then, working on the last of the slips of paper, he sighed. 'Done. But is it done for you, Stan, really? One could understand if it were not.'

There was a long silence, and neither Ralph nor his father seemed able to breathe. Finally, Stan said, 'It was a bit of a facer. As I said to Ralph, it'll take a bit more time to get my head around it, but he's such a daft bliddy bugger, it's not surprising he gets himself into scrapes. I reckon he's out of short trousers now and one of us, so I'll rip his head off if he does any more that riles me. But don't concern yourself. I'm at ease, mostly. The thing is, I've just been having a bit of a think about me da, and I reckon he'd understand it weren't intended to hurt, and for Ralph it'll always be a mite heavy to live with, even with any good he does. That's enough, don't you think? Perhaps now we can have a cup of tea?'

Reginald smiled, understanding that the subject was closed. He gathered up the slippery bundle of chains. 'One of you take the glue, eh?'

Ralph reached for it, feeling the stickiness. 'I need to make a phone call.'

'Yes, indeed. I have made a call of my own to prepare the ground, although there are Auberon's men in the area, never fear.' Reginald nodded towards Stan, then raised his eyebrows at Ralph, who shook his head.

'I don't want him involved. Best he has his cuppa.'

'Up to me to make up me own mind,' Stan said. 'I've come this far. Best you're not in this alone, canny lad. Who knows what a pig's ear you'll make.'

'Come with me, then.'

Stan followed along after Reginald, he and Ralph catching the chains as they slithered sideways and backwards and hearing the mumbling beneath Reginald's breath as the paper chains fought back, he murmured, 'Language, Mr Reginald, or Lord knows how many more jars Eva will fill.'

They were laughing as they made their way into the kitchen, where Annie Hall was working on gathering some brown material that would expand for the tree dance. Stan stared. 'We were talking about that earlier, Mam.'

'Aye, well,' she smiled, 'it were noted when you were fiddling about with your feet at the rehearsal, doing what you called a dance. So bad you were, it was funny.' She paused to check on Lisa, who was in the playpen by the dresser, and on the twins, Bridy and Tilly, who were sleeping together in a crib the lads had made. The names had been chosen by the bairns, and so that was that. Tilly Oborne had been extraordinarily pleased, because Eva had had the sense to say the little one was named after her. Whether she actually had been, the bairns never said.

Ralph looked down at them, and smiled. Then straightened. 'Just have to make a call. You coming, Stan?'

'Of course.'

'Well, at least Eddie will be sitting up on the cloud with his marrers,' Annie said, her smile fading.

It was those words that resonated with the two men as they headed up the stairs, across the tiled hall and into Reginald's study. Once they shut the door, Stan murmured, 'Now there's a thought, all of them together. Remember, this kettle of fish is between the two of us, eh?'

Ralph was asking the telephonist for the number, gesturing Stan to come over. Smythe picked up instantly. 'Your father said a little. Did he see you? Did you see him? Was it Tim?'

'We're not sure who it was, and think whoever it was didn't see us.'

'We?'

Ralph explained everything then. 'Put Stan on,' Smythe snapped.

Stan spoke to the professor, whom he'd helped with research during his Oxford term breaks. Ralph stood beside him. He couldn't hear, but watched Stan nodding several times. Finally, Stan said, 'He's me marrer. We stand together, no matter the past.'

More was said, and then Stan returned the receiver, his hand over the mouthpiece. 'I have to sign some paper or something like that, which'll make me keep me mouth shut, but he wants you to read him the stuff we found, and they'll take it from there. He said they check the line for taps all the time, so it's safe.'

Ralph sat down in his father's chair, dragging out the sheets of paper and reading them aloud.

'Excellent. I will send someone for it this evening,' Smythe rattled off. 'In the meantime, I will be dealing with the contents, or Yeland will, or is, actually doing so, even as we speak. Tim might have got away, but we'll hunt him down. It was the best end for Corbitt. Neat and tidy too, and it was kindly done to muddle up his belongings. Better for any relatives and friends, and stops any questions regarding suicide. Though I suppose the grief of a widower would suffice if it were raised. So, get on with the panto-mime preparations and decorating the tree. I will see you on the evening. Oh yes I will.'

'Oh no you won't,' Ralph replied.

'He's behind you,' Yeland said, having taken over the receiver. 'But Tim won't be, he'll be on the run I've ascertained, so too Merryweather. I wonder if they knew someone would look for the papers. Perhaps Merryweather was tasked – Oh well, ours to sort. But know that we have eyes on you both, just in case. Now, Ralph, you have fulfilled all we asked of you, so you are at liberty to walk away and forget we ever existed. The slate is wiped clean. We're setting you free.'

Ralph stared down at his father's blotter. *Free*? He didn't see the blotted ink marks, he saw Viola, the love of his life, and soon to be his wife. He saw his new sisters, Tilly and Bridy, and the evacuees, Eva, Abe and Marty especially, the co-op, his marrers, the girls too. There was still a war on; the Massingham people needed the efforts of them all.

'Thanks, but no thanks, Yeland. I'm in this for the duration.' He saw Stan nodding. 'Perhaps Stan is too. But you need to talk to him about that.'

'No need,' Stan called across Ralph. 'He's such a daft bugger, Yeland, he's not fit to be out on his own. It'll be the two of us.'

There was no pause. 'Why am I not surprised?' Yeland said. 'We'll sort it. Maybe I'll be with you for your finest hour at the pantomime, too.'

'You'll have to pay for a ticket, or Eva will have your guts for garters and refuse entry.'

Ralph heard Yeland chuckle. 'That child is terrifying.' There was a click.

Ralph replaced the receiver, and they made their way down the hall towards the ballroom. The doors were open, and Sid was saying, 'No, Reginald, listen to me, it's tilting to the left. The fairy's about to plummet to the floor. The tree needs to be moved to the right. The right, I said.'

They entered just in time to catch Eva telling Abe to fetch the swear jar, and Reginald stretching across from the top of the stepladder, finally tipping the tree upright, but too far. 'Oh dear heavens,' came the cry.

'That's tuppence you owe now, Mr Reginald,' Eva called.

Stan and Ralph laughed, and Stan put his arm around Ralph's shoulders and shook him. 'Nothing changes, bonny lad, but everything changes.'

Ralph nodded, for Stan was right, but now Viola was coming to him, her face alight with love. He would tell her everything, but she would stay the course, he just knew.

Everyone had been up at the Hall since the crack of dawn on the nineteenth, erecting the flat scenery, dropping down the backcloth. They had tried out the beck sheet one final time, with Steve and Colin Oborne at either end. The bank the lads had made ended up being a foot and a half high – to hide Ralph's arse, so they said – which meant that Colin and Steve had to raise the waves for when Ralph emerged in a flurry. Tilly was watching from the front row, calling, 'Get some gusto into it, for heaven's sake, Steve.'

Eva called, 'You said "arse" Mr Oborne. Abe, the jar.' The Obornes groaned and dug in their pockets.

Bert appeared in his cow legs, the top hanging down, holding Buttercup's head under his arm. 'How you live with this harridan, I don't know, our Steve.'

'You'd best think carefully what you say, our Bert,' Tilly called as she swung round, 'for I'm going to be in prime position to give your arse a right good pinching tonight, and there'll be nowt you can do about it.'

Bert stomped off, with Abe close behind listening for more pennies, maybe even a sixpence, but most were mindful of the jar by now. Eva got tuppence out of Tilly for 'arse', though.

Iris Walters arrived to play through the music, though she didn't need to. Madge adjusted the princess's costume, and Ralph struggled into the doublet and the hose. The marrers whistled and pinched his bum while he complained of being too hot. Viola was left to explain to him the error of his ways over Lisa's wails, because Melanie had stopped pushing the babe backwards and forwards in her cart near the double doors.

The lads tried on the tree costumes with the new skirts, as Fran called them. Stan just shook his head. 'We'll steal the show, you just wait and see, bonny lass.'

Iris Walters clapped her hands, standing at the piano, which was set up on the floor at the side of the stage. 'My own orchestra pit,' she had crowed when she saw it. 'Right, let's have a run-through of all the songs.'

It started with the bairns at the beck, having a picnic. With Daniel's words, to the tune of 'Teddy Bears' Picnic'. Then the thunderous crashing of the keys as Eva, of course, fell into the water. Fran whispered to Beth and Sarah, 'Only because she wanted to be rescued by her hero, Mr Ralph.'

But the song was interrupted by Annie hurrying in, clapping and waving them to a hush. 'Reginald, the telephone. It's urgent.'

Reginald was still in the 'wardrobe', which had been set up behind the stage, and came out in his bossy head washerwoman costume, which wasn't zipped up and had one shoulder slipping. Fran zipped him up over his enormous bosoms, then let him go.

Annie was picking up Lisa, who reached out to Fran, Bert's teething ring in her hand, but Annie said, 'Not now, precious, we must get back to the kitchen.' To Fran, she said, 'Nell and Sophia are dealing with the twins, and Sandra and Alfie are making sandwiches for a snack. Half an hour, everyone, then we'll bring food up here, with a pot of tea.'

Bert could be heard grumbling, 'I reckon I need more'n tea.'

'Well, you'll get it, any minute now, Bert,' yelled Tilly, 'across the back of your legs.' She spun round to the bairns. 'And there was no swearing or arse, so—'

Eva pounced. ' "Arse", Abe, the jar.'

Fran had to sit down, she was laughing so much, which was when Beth asked what time Melanie's aunt was arriving, and the other mams.

Annie turned on her heel and left them to it, passing Reginald as he returned to the ballroom. Fran watched as he put his hand up to Annie and said something, his face serious. Annie nodded and handed Lisa to Reginald, and hurried from the ballroom. Reginald looked helplessly at the bairn as she started crying. Fran made her way over, taking her from him. 'Is something wrong?'

He shook his head. 'Quite the opposite. Something very right. Smithson has been on the telephone. You might remember I had to appear before him and others with regard to the adoption of the orphans. Well, permission has been granted. But I need Sophia here when I tell them so Annie has gone scouting for her.'

Beth and Sarah waited with Fran, a little behind Reginald, until Sophia arrived with Annie, Nell and the babies. 'Fran, would you be so kind as to rally the bairns and herd them over here.'

But there was no need, for Eva was leading them across, worry writ large across her brow. 'What's amiss? Why are the twins here? They need their sleep, and as their parents you should know that.'

Reginald sighed, and Fran could see the words *Oh dear heavens* wanting to burst forth, but then he looked at Abe's jar, and pressed his lips together. By this time, everyone had stopped; even Iris was no longer playing the tree dance.

Reginald gave up all pretence of a quiet moment with the bairns and moved to the centre of the ballroom. 'Sophia and I have just heard,' he waved the bairns and Sophia to him, 'that our request for the adoption of the children who are so sadly without either parent has been approved. We are now the proud parents of Eva, Abe and Marty.'

'Oh, Mr Reginald, that's so lovely, I'm so pleased.' Eva turned to Abe. 'But I'm sorry, Abe, you can't marry me, for we'll be brother and sister, which is better, because husbands and wives bicker.'

Abe, as always, nodded at the higher wisdom. But then it truly sank in with all three of them and they clung to Sophia and Reginald, who hugged them until they could scarcely breathe, and everyone cheered, even Melanie, who for a moment had looked sad and regretful.

At seven that evening, the ballroom was filling up, and Eva, Abe, Enid and Marty sold tickets, insisting that even Mr Smithson bought his. 'We know you helped us,' said Eva, 'you know, to have parents. Still, though, Mr Smithson, there is the piper to be paid.'

Mr Smithson's jaw dropped, but he paid up, and as Annie stood keeping an eye on proceedings she heard him mutter to his wife, 'I do hope the Massinghams know what they're doing. I find that child alarming.'

'Wrong word. She's frightening,' his wife said, 'but utterly enchanting. Yes, the Massinghams will have their hands full and they will love every minute. You've done the right thing, darling.'

Annie showed them to their seats, which had been reserved close to the front. 'There you are, sit next to Professor Smythe and Colonel Yeland.'

The Smithsons settled and then Smithson introduced himself. 'I was just saying how alarming young Eva is.'

'Frightening, I think you mean.' Yeland leaned across Smythe.

Smythe smiled. 'One day she will rule the world.'

Sister Newsome who had cared for Ralph, and the

marrers, Fran, Sarah and Viola in the Infirmary after their munitions accident sat behind them, and leaned forward. 'I fear she is already ruling the Massinghams' world,' she said. 'God bless the child. She will be a matron one day, and a right tartar, you mark my words.' They all laughed quietly.

Behind the scenes, costumes were being fastened and a bit of slap put on by Viola, though Ralph was already shrouded in leaf-covered netting over his doublet and hose. Deep lines were painted on Mr Swinton's face, suitable for an elderly cowherd who led Buttercup whenever she appeared. His part had changed with every rehearsal.

'I'm so hot,' Ralph complained.

Bert, about to put on his papier mâché head, tutted. 'Try being a bliddy cow, lad. That's when you have a problem. Just a bliddy minute, I need to go to the lav.'

'Careful, she'll hear you, then it's another penny,' Ralph said, forgetting how hot he was for a moment. He felt for a chair, because the thought of needing a tiddle hadn't occurred to him. He shut his eyes in panic.

Bert was still set on Eva. 'Well, I've no pockets so she'll get nowt more from me.'

Melanie piped up now, as Viola fastened up her ragamuffin clothes. 'She'll take IOUs. Keeps them in the same jar, she does.'

Ralph felt quite exhausted at the sheer drive of these children and wandered away, passing Colin Oborne, who was still waving the sheet. 'You watch it. Don't want you lying on the sheet again, Ralph,' he called.

Ralph sat on the one chair, feeling odd, thinking he was going to pass out. He muttered, 'I can't do it. There's too much to remember – the kindnesses, which arm I tear off first behind the bank, the words, the dance. I can't do it, can't go on.'

Viola came to him, beautiful in her princess costume,

her crown painted silver. She slipped her arm around his shoulders. 'Stage fright, bonny lad. It's good luck. You'll be a star, but then you always are to me.' She lifted and kissed his green-painted hand.

'I'm going to be sick,' he gasped.

Viola pushed his head down between his knees as Stan called, 'What's up with the daft beggar?'

Those words penetrated the mist that was enveloping Ralph. He breathed deeply, several times, because he was a marrer, he had had his turn in the mucky tin bath even though he had killed . . . His head suddenly wasn't whirling any more. He straightened. Daft beggar? He looked at Stan, who nodded, and smiled. Yes, Ralph knew that awful, awful time was over and that this not nearly as awful time would also be over within the hour and what's more, he was in it with Stan, his friends, his family, and Viola, whom he loved more than life itself. She was patting his shoulder. He gripped her hand. 'I love you to distraction,' he whispered. 'Please tell me you love me too?'

She smiled, and bent to kiss his green face. 'Of course I love you, and am proud of you, you are the world to me, and sweet boy, you have never looked more handsome.'

They laughed together, and he knew they always would because he had told her his truth earlier, and she had stood with him, and always would, she had sworn.

The four bairns had filled all the seats in front of the stage except for five reserved ones, which were sacred, or so Eva had told everyone as she sat at the ticket desk. As a few more people entered she was head down, checking for any free seats. There were none. 'Standing room only, I'm afraid,' she said, her hand out ready to accept the money. Only then did she look up. 'Davey, oh, Davey.' Her shout silenced the room at the same time as Melanie was saying

343

to her auntie, as they stood to the right of the doorway selling programmes with Dora, 'I really don't want to go to Wales, but thank you for wanting me to. You see I want to stay here with me marrers.'

People turned to look, first at Davey, then at Melanie, to whom Auntie Diana was saying, 'Did you think I didn't know that? Mr and Mrs Massingham think the best idea is that you stay here, and come to me if and when you want. How's that for a deal?'

Melanie spat on her hand, and held it palm up to her aunt. Reginald, watching from a crack in the curtains, muttered, 'Oh dear heavens, what'll the woman think we run here?'

'Don't be silly, darling. She knows it's a thieves' kitchen. Why? Because she'd been here two hours and had to pay into the swear jar, for saying her meat in the pub was bloody.'

Fran came to have a squint through the curtains. There he was, her Davey, and with Daniel too. Two others stood with them, watching to see if Melanie's aunt would spit in her hand. She did, and shook hands with her niece, then hugged her tightly. Davey and his pals clearly felt completely satisfied that they had come all this way, even if only for that.

Fran tore along the side aisle, into Davey's arms. 'You're here, you brilliant man. You are so clever. We should go into the theatre after the war, and bring Eva into the theatrical firm.'

He kissed her mouth, saying, 'Shut up. I am not worthy of Eva.'

They were laughing as she was introduced to Colin and Martin and kissed Daniel, and thanked them for the script from the bottom of her heart. They pointed to Norah, who was buying a programme. But just then Iris bashed a roll of thunder on the piano, and started to play 'God Save the King'. The panto was about to start.

Everyone stood and thought of the King and Queen, staying in London with their two girls, and of Winston Churchill leading the land, and felt in safe hands. As the national anthem died, Eva took the writers to their reserved seats in the first row. 'We've pushed the rows back a bit so you don't have to crane your necks to see *everything*. But now I have to go and introduce the pantomime. Do you like my ragged clothes?'

Norah arrived, and beat the men to it. 'I love them. I can't wait to see the show.'

Eva had been about to go, but she swung back. 'You're the lady who is a tough nut, Davey says, but with a kind heart.'

With that she left and took Norah's heart with her, or so Davey and Daniel decided in a whisper.

Iris was playing the introduction now as Eva slipped through the curtains and Davey and his friends took their places. Eva walked to the front of the stage, swiftly followed by the evacuees in their rags. To their left the lights on the tree sparkled. All around, the paper chains hung on the walls.

The bairns shuffled into a row either side of Eva, checking they were in a straight line. They stood there until Iris finished. Then, Eva started speaking, her voice as clear as a bell and reaching the furthest corners of the ballroom. All the cast stood on the stage, behind the curtain, hardly daring to listen, for she hadn't shared what it was she was going to say.

Iris did another sort of roll of thunders on the piano. Eva nodded, conducted her to a stop with a scything motion and began.

'I asked Miss Walters to do that in case you weren't paying attention, because I have things to say.'

'Oh yes we are paying attention,' called Smythe.

'Oh no we're not,' called Mr Smithson.

Even Eva laughed, then she clasped her hands in front of her as she thought stars should do, for this much she had shared with Ralph when he'd nipped in to kiss her goodnight one evening. Ralph stepped down, and crept round the side of the stage to watch, and could already see shoulders shaking in the audience.

'My *family* and I, for you see, we orphans have been adopted, though we can keep our surnames if we want, or be Massinghams.' There was a rustle of interest, of appreciation. 'The rest of us'll be looked after till the mams take them back after the bombs have stopped falling and the war is over. We all,' she waved behind the scenes, 'wanted to put on the pantomime because Melanie was going to live in Wales and we wanted to do something to thank all of you in Massingham for being so kind to us. And to say goodbye to Melanie. Even though she says she's not going now, we still want to say thank you to you all for welcoming us and helping us.

'It's a big panto. There are presents under the tree. The Factory girls have knitted the robins hanging from the branches, the marrers have made toys, and people have given us things. But only one present for each child. Best you remember that. We copied out the scripts and programmes in Mr Moran's class. He's a tree, so you won't see that his eyepatch matches Madge's. Madge is in the co-op. They're in love, we reckon, which is why they wear matching eyepatches.' She stopped and looked at the others. 'We thought they would like one another, didn't we? We've got bets on them being wed, and can take more in the interval.'

Reginald's call of 'Oh dear God' was audible throughout the ballroom. The laughter was soon drowned out by Eva telling Abe, 'Don't forget to get tuppence from Mr Reginald, because God's worse than "heavens". Do it after the panto.'

Now lips were being bitten, laughter stifled. 'The actors are just about ready,' Eva informed everyone, but sailed on nonetheless. 'And Davey, Daniel, Colin and Martin are here to see how their words come alive, and Norah, who likes to look grumpy but isn't, wants to see how Mr Ralph looks in his leggings, or *hose*, as they're really called, but I 'spect she doesn't know that.'

Ralph watched Davey peering round Daniel and winking at Norah, who was gazing at the child much as someone would witnessing the Second Coming.

'But now I want to say what me mam always said her da taught her. Well, she said it before we were buried under the bricks. When I were pulled out, the man with the tin hat called, "Who claims this child?" No one did, for me mam and da were dead in the bricks, but I were able to say goodbye before they went to their cloud, so I'm lucky, I reckon.'

She stopped talking, and Ralph saw the whiteness of her knuckles as she gripped her hands so tight, and he couldn't just stand there. Instead, he hurried up the steps, in his monster costume, and stood beside her. He whispered, 'I'm here, I will always be here.'

She pressed against him, just for a moment, but then, clear as a bell, said, 'You have to forget you've seen the monster, everyone. You can go now, Mr Ralph.'

He went, but not far, just to the bottom of the steps. This extraordinary child's voice was steady as she continued, and he listened to every single syllable, because his love for her, and the others, knew no end.

'But, you see,' she said, 'it's Christmas, and we have all been claimed now, by our new family and by Massingham.

So I will tell you what Mam's da used to say. Oh, but before I do – I meant to say specially thank you to Farmer Thompkins, for he helped save our Mr Ralph in the car crash, and we so love Mr Ralph. Farmer Thompkins takes us to school in the trailer, and that's how he brought the tree up. It's so pretty, isn't it?'

The evacuees turned, looked and smiled, as did the audience. 'Mr Reginald put the fairy on top, and we got a lot of pennies for the swear jar from that.' Eva pointed again to the tree, with its baubles galore and lights, then, as though struck by an urgent thought, she looked at Abe. 'You did collect *all* the money when he came down the stepladder?'

'Of course I did, but we'll be here all bliddy night unless you get on, our Eva,' Abe said. 'And no, I won't put in a penny, for I am the one doing the collecting, and it's hard work.'

Eva merely nodded. Now hands were up at mouths, and the Vicar was rocking in his chair.

'Anyway,' Eva said. 'The money from the swear jar is going to them that is bombed out, as well as Mr Moran's art fund, and the Vicar will see to it. But we have counted it, Vicar, so nowt to go into the collection, mind.'

The Vicar managed to nod, looking as though he'd burst. But Eva continued: 'This, ladies and gentlemen, is what we want to say to *you*, and to our new family, and all them acting tonight. It's from Jeremiah, and I don't know what verse, or who he is, but he says nice things, so he's probably a nice man. What he says is: "For I *know* the thoughts that I think towards you."' She paused and looked around the ballroom. 'And we do know our thoughts towards you, and they are that we are thankful to be here, where you have claimed us and are kind, and we love you, and Massingham, and the beck, with all our hearts. And a very Happy Christmas to you all, and we bairns never thought we'd be happy again. But you have all made us so.'

She led the children back through the curtain, and now it wasn't laughter but silence, and handkerchiefs. Davey, beyond speech, handed his to Norah, thinking what everyone else was probably thinking, that these orphans had thanked the village, and everyone, and declared their love, when it was the bairns who had given so very much in so many ways. The applause now burst forth and went on, and on, until the curtains were drawn back, and there was the beck.

Iris played the opening bars of 'You Just Have to Believe', and behind the backcloth, the cast began to sing as the ragged urchins emerged onto the stage from both sides. They were playing marbles and hopscotch, talking and elbowing and bouncing a ball on the lower bank, singing as one edged close to the beck, closer, closer, while the waters billowed and the trees waved their arms in the wind.

The slag heap painted on the backcloth seemed to smoulder because Viola had propped a table lamp on a high stool just behind the backcloth. The pithead, engine house and winding gear seemed alive as Viola, sitting above the bank, swinging to and fro as Old Ted, instead of Colin, pulled and released the rope because Colin had sworn and stamped a couple of days ago, and said, 'I can't create waves and pull the bliddy swing at the same time, so that's bliddy that.' It had cost him sixpence.

As the children played, and Eva seemed to teeter on the high bank, Melanie shrieked, 'Come away, Eva.' Too late, with a dramatic cry, and much almost falling Eva held the audience as she prolonged the battle to save herself from a dip in the beck.

'Milking it,' Daniel whispered, caught up in laughter once more.

349

Colin muttered, 'What else, it's what a diva does.'

The singing ceased, the piano thundered, and finally, in Eva went, and then, as the sheet billowed hectically, Bernie the Beck Monster clambered up and out with her in his arms. Eva said, 'No, you're supposed to spring, Mr Ralph?'

The whole audience said, to save him or Reginald the bother, 'Oh dear heavens.' The pantomime had begun, and Davey, Daniel, Colin, Martin and Norah, all those who had been privy to the costumes, the food, the sets, sang along, clapped, roared and then shrieked in horror as they were meant to.

'Aye, we're away,' Davey muttered. He was home. He was where he belonged, and where he would return one day, and would never leave. He looked across at the Christmas tree, knowing it would see a pantomime every year from now on, whatever might come, and their Christmases would always be merry and bright.

Welcome to

Penny Street

where your favourite authors and stories live.

Meet casts of characters you'll never forget,
create memories you'll treasure for ever,
and discover places that will stay with
you long after the last page.

Turn the page to step into the home of

ANNIE CLARKE

and discover more about

The Factory Girls . . .

Hello all my lovely friends,

I have a ridiculously childish sense of humour, and adore pantomimes. Not just because of the interaction between audience and cast: he's behind you, oh no he isn't, oh yes he is. Shall I throw this custard tart? Nooo. Yesss. And the chance to boo the bad fairy . . . Heaven.

But it's more than that. A panto at the professional theatre is one thing, but the local village panto . . . Quite something else. Such a community effort, even today. And community, so embedded in the 30s, 40s and later, must, I believe be encouraged, which is why I incorporated the Massingham pantomime into *Christmas on the Home Front*.

It also gave me a chance to remember one of my finest moments which took place in the west country village near Yeovil where we lived for a while. There was a drama group, so at Christmas there was a pantomime: some villagers sorted out the lighting, some the sets, the props, and then, *and then*, the casting . . .

At last I was given a part – I was to be one of the maids. Well, all right, if we're getting picky, I was part of the chorus line. But the fun of it all, the chat, the help we gave one another: make up, costumes, learning lines, and then – action was so wonderful . . . We performed choreographed moves I'll have you know, one step forward, one to the side, one back . . . People from other villages came to watch, we overacted, we sang too loudly, and everyone loved it. There were 'turns'. I remember how one of the men did his usual piece about a kamikaze pilot on his seventh mission. Dinkie, from Australia was with us. I thought she would die laughing as he explained why he kept on returning. Glorious.

Then, oh then and I can never ever pretend again that I am an unselfish, kind, generous woman because . . . The manager of the local professional theatre was leaving. He

had been quite marvellous to the Yeovil Community Arts Association, of which I was Patron when we lost our funding and premises. He had allowed me to move the YCAA into the theatre at no cost. With Jim, another pal, I set up the Yeovil Literary Prize to bring in dosh, and then the Stage Play Prize, which the wonderfully kind Julian Fellowes judged and even better – attended the first night of the winning entry, *The Gareth Jones Memorial Theatre* by Dick Curran, produced by the fabulous Bruce James Productions Ltd.

Anyway, our Grant was leaving – boo, hiss. What better way to give him a send-off than to do a panto? It had to be something, 'Wot I wrote' so there were no royalty issues, it had to last five minutes because it would be part of a farewell party. But of course, the most important part – so, wait for it, w-a-i-t – for the first and last time in my life I had the starring role, the Beansprout Fairy. (Yes, all right, I did cast it, but then, I did write it.)

It was to be kept secret from Grant, so the lovely Kate

Wigmore let the cast of four raid the wardrobe department. Finally, the big night came. Annie Clarke, aka Margaret Graham, and the cast: Celia a wicked witch, Steve a baron, and Penny a maid, burst into the party held in the rehearsal room. It goes without saying that lovely Grant was surprised. Although perhaps that is an understatement (I wonder if, in fact, he was secretly horrified) as a fairy of a certain age approached, waggling her wand, followed by the startling, fabulous cast. It was heaven: fun, interactive, and a memory for Grant that he would not be able to shift easily. We like to think that is a positive thing.

As for me, I remember every second of the fun, every single person who joined in as we came together, a *community* of theatregoers and users, bound by a fun time that everyone had helped to make possible. So what could be better than the creation and performance of Bernie the Beck Monster to show Massingham's care and love for everyone within its boundaries, including the Factory Girls.

Annie x

Read more from

ANNIE CLARKE

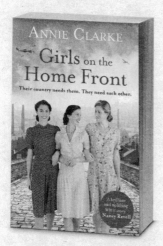

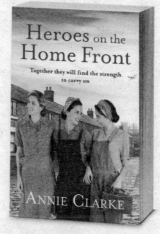

Love the Factory Girls?

Why not try another series . . .

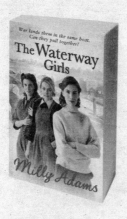

October 1943, West London

Nineteen-year-old Polly Holmes is leaving poor bombed London behind to join the war effort on Britain's canals.

Stepping aboard the Marigold amid pouring rain, there's lots for Polly to get to grips with. Not least her fellow crew: strong and impetuous Verity, whose bark is worse than her bite, and seasoned skipper Bet.

With her sweetheart away fighting in the RAF and her beloved brother killed in action, there's plenty of heartache to be healed on the waterway. And as Polly rolls up her sleeves and gets stuck into life on board the narrowboat – making the gruelling journey London up to Birmingham – she will soon discover that a world of new beginnings awaits amid the anguish of the war.

Available Now

arrow books

Hear more from

Annie Clarke